PRAISE FOR
BESTSELLING AUTHOR LYNSAY SANDS!

"Ms. Sands gives romance readers what they want. [*What She Wants*] is charming, funny, and has very human characters."
—*The Romance Reader*

"Lynsay Sands is a skilled writer. *The Reluctant Reformer* [is] a charming, entertaining read."
—*All About Romance*

"Lynsay Sands has just the right touch of humor and the perfect amount of mystery to hold you in her grasp. . . . *Lady Pirate* is a delicious treat."
—*Romantic Times*

"Intrigue and humor . . . that will make you laugh and turn up the air-conditioning. 4 1/2 stars."
—*Romantic Times* on *Always*

"*The Key* is a happy surprise . . . a whimsical tale that never sacrifices smarts for silliness."
—*The Romance Reader*

"Lynsay Sands's strength lies in creating very light entertainment with elements of comedy."
—*All About Romance*

"Readers are swept up in a delicious, merry and often breath-catching roller-coaster ride that will keep them on the edge of their seats and laughing out loud. A true delight!"
—*Romantic Times* on *The Deed*

DRESSED TO KILL

Jane relaxed until her grandmother picked up the lipstick. Her eyes widened in horror. "That's Lipschitz's knockout lipstick!"

"Good," her grandmother said. "It's the perfect color."

The older woman waited until Jane had reluctantly applied it, then set to work on Jane's eyes, applying a light layer of eye shadow and eyeliner that Jane recognized with relief as her own. Gran picked up a silver bottle of perfume next, however, and Jane drew back. "That's my truth-serum perfume!"

"Yes, I know. It may come in handy tonight. Don't you think?"

Jane nodded. "I suppose. If he gets close enough to inhale it."

"You'll just have to *make sure* he gets close enough." Her grandmother poured the scent onto a cotton ball and dabbed liberal amounts of it around Jane's ears, neck and wrists. Jane grimaced as it was dabbed in the hollow between her breasts.

Her grandmother smiled. "Try to get him close enough to inhale the perfume, but don't let him kiss you. We may have trouble explaining how a kiss could knock him out."

LYNSAY SANDS

THE LOVING DAYLIGHTS

LOVE SPELL NEW YORK CITY

LOVE SPELL®

April 2003

Published by

Dorchester Publishing Co., Inc.
276 Fifth Avenue
New York, NY 10001

ISBN 0-505-52527-5

The name "Love Spell" and its logo are trademarks of Dorchester Publishing Co., Inc.

Printed in the United States of America.

Visit us on the web at www.dorchesterpub.com.

*For Aunt Leigh, a woman who has amazing taste and style
and is as beautiful inside as she is out.
And for my dear friend, Melanie Jackson.
Thanks for sharing Sonora with me.*

THE LOVING DAYLIGHTS

Chapter One

"D and C meeting in twenty minutes, Jane."

"Yep." Jane Spyrus straightened from her work-table and smiled at the tall blonde standing in the doorway of her office. "I'll be ready. Thanks for reminding me though, Lizzy."

"No problem. Want me to stop and grab you on my way? Just in case you get too involved in what you're doing?"

Jane didn't take offense at the offer. She was famous for getting involved in projects and being late for meetings. "No, that's okay. I just have a couple more adjustments to make; then I'll head right over."

Lizzy Hubert nodded then moved slowly into the room. "What *are* you working on?"

1

Jane immediately shifted to block her worktable, aware that her face was flushing with embarrassment. "Nuh-uh. You'll see soon enough."

"Can't blame a girl for trying." The blonde laughed and gave a shrug. "See you in twenty minutes. I'll save you a seat."

Jane waited until the door closed behind the other woman before relaxing, then she turned to peer down at the items on her worktable. She shook her head.

It was silly to be embarrassed about this latest project. It was a brilliant idea. At least, *she* thought so. And she wasn't embarrassed by the BT Trackers she was also going to reveal today. Well, not as much. Yet, somehow, these mini-missile launchers made her blush and want to squirm every time she thought of presenting them. Of course, this was one aspect of her job that she truly disliked anyway. Jane loved creating new weapons and spy technology for B.L.I.S.S. but loathed presenting them at the monthly Development and Creation meetings. She was a very poor public speaker. Stammering and stumbling over her words, she knew she often sounded like a fool. It was amazing to her that Y approved any of her inventions for production.

Jane made a face at the thought of the head of B.L.I.S.S. Y was a hard-as-nails ex-agent who came across as all-knowing and all-seeing. She was the most intimidating woman Jane had ever encountered. Jane supposed it was the woman's lack of expression, which left one uncertain as to what she was thinking. That was also probably part of the reason it was so hard to gauge Y's age. Her face was remarkably unlined, yet she'd been at B.L.I.S.S. forever—or so said Jane's gran.

Gran would know, too. All of Jane's family was involved in the intelligence industry in one way or another, most of them field operatives. Gran herself was an ex-agent and a contemporary of Y's and Jane's own parents, James and Elizabeth Spyrus, had both been working for B.L.I.S.S. when they died. Her mother had been a top agent with the highest clearance. Her father had been a scientist, working in D & C. They had been killed when their car exploded on the way to a company party when Jane was just five. It was later learned that another agent had changed sides and sold the names of her coworkers to a consortium that had been out to put an end to B.L.I.S.S. James and Elizabeth had been two of six employees killed before the agency sorted out the matter.

After her parents' deaths, Jane had found herself living with her grandmother. Maggie Spyrus, James's mother, had seen to it that Jane took all the lessons necessary to grow into a good agent: languages, martial arts, sharp shooting. But in the end, Jane had decided to follow her father's path instead and joined D & C. She just didn't see herself as the risk-taking type. She preferred dusty old books and tinkering with technology to the adrenaline-pumping, life-threatening, derring-do of being an operative. She liked to think that her job developing innovative new weapons and gizmos was just as important though.

Picking up a tiny Phillips screwdriver, Jane made the last of several necessary adjustments to one of the prototypes of the BMML. It only took a couple of seconds; then she straightened, removed her glasses, and stared down at her creation with a pleased sigh. To the unknowing observer, this BMML—B.L.I.S.S. Mini-Missile Launcher—looked like nothing more threatening than a neon-pink vibrator. Which was the idea, of course. That was its

3

"cover." No one would ever dare to investigate, either.

Grinning, Jane began to pack everything away into her briefcase, then reached across the table to turn on the radio. She kept it tuned to an '80s hits station, and "Whip It" by Devo filled the room. The opening beats made her pause and bob her head. There was just something about the song: Jane didn't particularly care for it, but darned if every time it played she didn't find herself stopping what she was doing, cranking up the volume, and moving to the beat. As she did now. With the vibrator-like BMML still in hand, Jane began bebopping around her office. When the chorus started—the only words she knew—she began singing into her creation.

"Am I interrupting something?"

Jane froze, with the neon-pink BMML still raised to her open mouth. Staring down, she wished the floor would split open and swallow her whole. It *would* have to be none other than Richard Hedde, standing in the door to her workroom. His smirk was so wide that Jane's own face ached in sympathy. She would never, *ever* hear the end of this.

Trying to pretend her face had not just gone as red as a tomato, Jane lowered her makeshift microphone, turned off the radio with feigned calm, and faced the one person in D & C that she absolutely loathed. "Not at all, I was just t-testing my latest invention."

It was possibly the stupidest thing Jane had said in her life, and something Dick did not have the grace to let pass. "Truly, Jane, I've always known you were socially backward, but if you don't even know the proper way to test that thing, you're more hopeless than I thought."

Jane hadn't considered it possible, but she actually flushed deeper. Mouth tightening, she put the BMML into her briefcase along with one she'd adjusted earlier. "Is there something you wanted, Dick?"

"Just to remind you that the D and C meeting is in"—he checked his wristwatch—"five minutes. We wouldn't want you to be late. Again."

Jane's teeth ground together in irritation, but she merely closed her briefcase, picked it up, and crossed the room, walking with all the dignity she could muster. "I was just heading that way."

"Sure you were. After you finished testing your invention, right?" He laughed as she grabbed her jacket off the hook by the door and stepped into the hall. Following her out of the room, Dick pulled the door closed behind them. "By the way, Jane. I hate to burst another bubble, but your little prototype there was invented by someone else years ago. It even has a name. I believe they call it a vibrator."

"Ha, ha." Jane picked up speed in an effort to escape her coworker. "Thank you for the newsbreak."

"Any time," he called after her. Though she couldn't see his face and refused to turn and look, she could tell he was enjoying this immensely. Dick seemed to enjoy nothing better than humiliating her. "Always happy to be of help."

Muttering some unpleasant descriptive words under her breath, Jane continued along the hall to the conference room. She was relieved to find it almost full. That meant Dick would shut up. Temporarily at least.

"Jane!" Lizzy was seated halfway up the left side of the table. Jane moved in her friend's direction.

Other than Dick, Lizzy was the only member of

the D & C department who was near Jane's age. All the rest of the members were older and had been recruited when B.L.I.S.S. was first put into operation. A job in D & C at B.L.I.S.S. was a lifetime job; the secrets were too big for anything else. Anyone who was thinking about signing on there had that explained quite plainly before they did. No one joined D & C at B.L.I.S.S., then quit. Jane didn't know what would happen if anyone tried such a thing, but she suspected it wouldn't be good. As far as she knew, it hadn't come up. No one had been foolish enough to try or even wanted to. This was a great place to work, with unlimited funds and almost unlimited freedom.

"I can't believe you made it on time for a change," Lizzy teased gently as Jane hung her jacket over the back of the saved chair.

Jane gave a somewhat forced smile and sat down, very aware that Dick had followed her. Much to her relief, he didn't comment, just kept on walking, taking one of the two seats at the far end of the table so that he sat with his back to the windows.

"Y will be impressed to find you here and not stumbling in after she starts the meeting," Lizzy continued.

Jane grunted. Y never seemed upset by her tardiness, instead was almost expectant of it. Jane half suspected that leniency was part of the reason Richard was so obnoxious to her. Where Y seemed to like her and was very patient with her lateness, Dick didn't get the same treatment. He wasn't particularly well liked by anyone.

As if summoned by her thoughts, the door suddenly opened to admit Y and Jane's supervisor. Y was the head of B.L.I.S.S., but Ira Manetrue was the head of D & C. The gentleman, an old flame of her grandmother's, had taken Jane under his wing the moment she'd started here, and he considered himself something of a mentor to her. All of which made Dick all the more furious. Jane almost understood that part of his unhappiness, but Richard brought his troubles on himself. If he were just respectful and less of a greasy brownnoser he'd get further, but he made himself so unpleasant she couldn't bring herself to tell him so. For the most part, she ignored him like everyone else. Or tried to.

"Good day, everyone," Mr. Manetrue greeted the room as he and Y took their seats at the far end of the table. Settling in with notepad and pen at the ready he asked, "Who's going to start the presentations today?"

His gaze zeroed in on Jane, but she glanced down at the pen she was twiddling. She would have to make her presentation eventually, but she didn't have the courage to actually *volunteer* to do it . . . or be first. Fortunately, the others weren't so shy and several raised their hands. Jane felt relief seep through her as Mr. Manetrue gestured for one of them to start.

Time passed swiftly as the others' prototypes were presented and displayed, but Jane had a terrible time paying attention. She was all too aware that as each person finished his presentation, she herself grew that much closer to giving her own. She started trying to remember what she would say. She always memorized a sort of speech for these meetings . . . and always forgot every word the moment she stood up. This time, the words appeared to have fled sooner than usual. Her mind was a complete blank.

"Jane?" Mr. Manetrue's voice pierced her panicked thoughts. She glanced up to find all eyes turned expectantly on her, and immediately she felt her heart sink. It was her turn.

Swallowing nervously, Jane picked up her briefcase, set it on the table, then stood and opened it. She started to retrieve items, noting with a sort of detached interest that her hands were shaking. Wishing once again that she weren't such a poor speaker, Jane closed the case and held up two small silver boxes.

"I . . . um . . ." She stopped and cleared her throat, then tried again. "Last month we lost one of our agents when she was forced to remove all her clothes and jewelry—including the wristwatch tracker, which is standard issue to all field operatives. She was later found dead." Jane paused and took a nervous drink of water. Forcing a sickly smile, she continued, "That incident got me thinking about a t-tracker that would never be discovered."

"And you came up with a cigarette case?" Richard asked, snickering.

"It isn't a cigarette case." Jane rotated it so that he could see the box's thickness. "Besides, it isn't the case itself that is the tracker." She opened the object so that everyone could see the long white items inside. "I came up with BTTs—B.L.I.S.S. Tampon Trackers."

Taking in the expressions around her, Jane felt her stomach roll over. It was Y who finally asked, "Am I to understand that those are actual tampons?"

Jane bit her lip. While Y didn't sound upset, she also didn't sound overly impressed. "Well, yes. They can function as actual tampons as well. But they also hold tracking devices that have a range of—"

"But what if the agent isn't menstruating?" Y

asked calmly. Richard was staring in horror, but B.L.I.S.S.'s leader seemed unrattled by the invention. Her matter-of-fact attitude had a settling effect on Jane.

"Oh, well, I thought of that. There are lubricated and unlubricated." She held up a second case and opened it. Inside were several more tampons, distinguishable from the others only in that they were an off-white. "The lubricated are easily inserted and easily removed and only serve the purpose of tracking, while the nonlubricated are absorbent and—"

"The tracking device is waterproof, I presume?" Y interrupted again.

"Yes. It's at the very center of the tampon and tightly sealed. The circuitry has an estimated life of two years."

Y nodded, then sat back without comment. Everyone was silent. Most of the older members of D & C were eyeing the BTTs speculatively and nodding. Lizzy was grinning encouragingly. Dick—well, he was sneering nastily, obviously just waiting for an opportunity to tear at her.

Deciding not to give him that chance, and that she'd said enough on this subject for now, Jane replaced the two silver cases in her briefcase. Taking a deep breath, she then removed two more items. One was a four-inch-square flat piece of wood with a spike sticking out of it; the other was a banana. She set the wood, spike up, on the tabletop, then impaled the banana peel and all. Next, she retrieved several foil packets from her briefcase, wondering all the while what on earth she had been thinking. These next inventions had seemed brilliant in an evil gleeful sort of way when she'd come up with them, but now—with all these eyes trained on her—they seemed the most foolish things she'd ever designed. What had she been thinking?

She hadn't been: That was obvious, Jane decided. She tossed the little packets back into her briefcase.

As she reached to retrieve the banana and it's spiked holder, Y asked sharply, "What are you doing?"

Jane paused and flushed. "I decided to skip this item. It's rather silly, and I thought I should just move on to—"

"No skipping," Y said firmly.

Mr. Manetrue nodded. "Even if an idea doesn't work out, Jane, it may spark another from someone else here, or even yourself. That's what these meetings are about, remember?"

Jane exhaled unhappily, then replaced the banana and the spike on the table cloth. She retrieved the small foil packets from her briefcase. "This idea . . . Well, my gran was telling me once about an agent friend of hers who was raped while on assignment. So, well . . . I thought—" Her face was flaming and she knew it, but she had no choice but to continue. Straightening her shoulders Jane blurted, "I c-came up with the B.L.I.S.S. Shrink-Wrap Condom."

Richard was not the only one to laugh this time, although most of the other laughs were embarrassed titters. Jane did her best to ignore them. She walked over to hand a packet to both Y and Mr. Manetrue, then she returned to her spot and opened the condom she'd kept for herself.

"As you can see, the label suggests this condom contains a Viagra-like substance to increase longevity, sensitivity and pleasure." She mumbled, wishing she'd never created the stupid prophylactics. "This is to make it appear more attractive to anyone who might use it, to entice a perhaps otherwise unwilling subject."

She removed the latex circle inside the packet and doggedly slipped it onto the banana, ignoring Dick's loud, uncontrolled mirth. "Once it's fully stretched out and applied, it reacts to human body oils and begins to constrict. Earlier I applied a special cream to the banana meant to emulate those oils, and as you can see the condom reacts quite swiftly."

The room had gone quiet again. Even Dick had stopped laughing. The condom shrank around the banana, forcing it to shrink too. When the peel actually burst, squirting pulpy mash out the bottom of the rubber, he along with most men in the room crossed his legs and grimaced.

"As you can imagine," Jane suggested, "this would significantly discourage any sexual interest or the possibility of rape."

Much to her amazement, Y burst out laughing. The woman eyed the banana mash leaking out all over the table from the now pencil-thin prophylactic. "Diabolical," she crowed. "Although it would probably have more use as a torture device to get information out of double agents or such. I doubt many men intent on rape would take the time to don a condom," she pointed out mildly. "Is there a way to stop it once it's activated?"

"Yes." Jane produced a small jar of cream from her case. "This will make the latex relax at once."

She opened the jar, scooped out some cream, then began smoothing it over the straining condom. As she'd predicted, the rubber immediately loosened around the shriveled banana peel.

Y nodded in satisfaction. "Anything else, Ms. Spyrus?"

Relieved, Jane smiled. She removed the shrink-wrapped banana, wiped up the mess left behind by her experiment, and put it all away. Then she peered at her last two items: The BMMLs.

Dismay again claimed Jane. Looking at the neon-pink vibrator-missile launchers, she suddenly realized that every single item she'd brought today was sexual in nature. Even the Tracking Tampons had to do with reproductive organs! She had to wonder if that meant something. Was she desperate? Lonely? True, most of her time was spent alone in her workroom. As for a social life, she really had none of which to speak. She had the occasional coffee or pizza with her neighbor Edie, or the infrequent lunch with Lizzy, but she hadn't had a boyfriend in quite some time. There just hadn't seemed to be the opportunity since graduating from the university. Was her repression releasing itself now through her inventions?

Jane had taken this job at B.L.I.S.S. right after she got her doctorate. For the past two years she'd worked long hours trying to prove herself. Much of that time had been spent alone in her D & C workroom,—there or on nights and weekends, in the workroom she'd created in her apartment, which eliminated the need for a night nurse for Gran while still allowing Jane to tinker. Yet she still was working long hours, even now. It was no longer out of a need to impress anyone, but simply because she enjoyed it. Jane had a passion for her work. She hadn't really felt a need for a social life—especially not one that included the emotional messiness of male-female relationships.

Not consciously she hadn't felt it, anyway. But now, standing here looking down at the contents of her briefcase, Jane began to suspect that subconsciously it was a different story. Perhaps she was inwardly yearning for something. And that something was possibly emotional, but most definitely sexual.

"Jane?" Ira Manetrue prompted, making her realize she'd stood silent an awfully long time contemplating the possibility that she needed . . . well . . . basically that she needed to get laid.

Sighing, she shoved her concerns aside and grimly lifted one of the BMMLs out of her briefcase. The restless shuffling and soft murmurs that had begun to fill the room came to an immediate halt. Jane ignored the sudden silence and carried her invention down to the end of the table. There she handed it over to Y.

"Oh, my." The woman turned the object over in her hand. "I hesitate to even ask what this is."

"A microphone," Dick spoke up with a laugh. As Jane returned to her seat and picked up the second BMML he added, "At least, that's what she appeared to be using it as when I stopped in to remind her about today's meeting so she wouldn't be late *again*."

Jane ground her teeth and began to twist the vibrator in her hands.

"Mind you," Dick continued, "she *said* she was *testing* it—but she may have had it at her mouth for another reason entirely." He waggled his eyebrows suggestively.

"This is the B.L.I.S.S. Mini-Missile Launcher," Jane announced to shut him up. She forced a calmer tone as she continued. "As you can see, it appears to be nothing more than your common everyday vibrator."

"So they're commonly neon pink, Jane?" Dick asked slyly. "And that big?"

Jane's fingers tightened on her invention, unintentionally flicking its switch. The cylinder began to vibrate. Jane gave a start and dropped it. Fortunately, she caught it before it hit the desk, but she flushed even further as Dick burst into gales of laughter. Jane tried to shut it off. Unfortunately, in her agitation, she pushed down on the switch instead of flicking it off. Much to her horror, the BMML bucked in her hands.

The missile launched.

Chapter Two

It sailed right over Dick's head, the draft from its passing parting his hair dead-center. There was a tinkle as the missile crashed through the window behind him, but that was almost unnoticeable next to the loud percussion that followed. Jane stood completely still, not even breathing. Mr. Manetrue got to his feet and moved calmly to the window to peer out. Jane envisioned dead bodies strewn everywhere behind the building.

"Nice shot, Jane. You hit the explosion test-pit dead-on," Manetrue announced. When he turned, his expression was curious. "That obviously isn't a microphone, and it has an excellent targeting system."

Relief poured over Jane. Her heart began to pump again, sending blood gushing through her veins. She even started breathing once more.

She hadn't hurt anyone. Thank God!

"No. Not a microphone," Y agreed dryly.

Jane glanced toward the head of B.L.I.S.S. who was now holding the other neon-pink BMML as if expecting it to explode at any moment. Grimacing, Jane hurried to retrieve it.

Y handed it back without comment; then Jane returned quietly to her chair, appreciating the sympathetic look Lizzy offered. This just wasn't her day, she supposed. Although, if she looked at it from a different perspective, perhaps it *was* her day. No one had gotten hurt by the malfunctioning BMML. And it *had* malfunctioned. She'd installed a fail-safe that should have prevented it from going off in such circumstances.

Jane's gaze slid along the table to Dick. He was no longer smirking or laughing; he'd gone silent and pale.

Everything had its upside.

"Go ahead, Jane. Explain your invention," Mr. Manetrue suggested. He moved back to take his seat. He didn't appear the least upset that she'd very nearly beheaded one of her coworkers, blown a hole through the room's window, and launched a missile that might have killed them all. In fact, he appeared to be restraining a smile.

"Uh . . . yes, sir." Clearing her throat, she held up the unused missile launcher. "The . . . er . . . B.L.I.S.S. Mini-Missile Launcher is highly nonthreatening in appearance and easily-carried in luggage into foreign countries. Made mostly of polymers, it will not set off airport alarms. Should it be discovered during a hand-search of luggage, it is unlikely to raise concern. In fact, most people would be too embarrassed to look at it closely. Even if they did, however, they will find a functioning vibrator."

She'd remembered and fallen into the speech she'd prepared, and now she moved to flick the BMML's switch to on. Movement out of the corner of her eye made her hesitate.

Dick had finally snapped out of his stunned state, and he was moving to duck under the table, out of the way of the missile she'd unthinkingly turned in his direction. Jane bit her lip. Part of her wanted to smile at the obnoxious twit being sent to his knees that way. The bigger, better part of her felt slightly guilty.

"Er . . . I guess you don't need to see that part of it again," she remarked quietly. Then she glanced toward Mr. Manetrue and Y. "I did add a safety feature, though. It isn't supposed to fire unless you twist the base and tip in opposite directions first, and then you push the button. The safety must have failed."

"You were twisting the base and tip while you were talking," Y mentioned gently. "But this indicates that a more complicated safety mechanism should be thought out. Otherwise, I think it's brilliant."

"Yes, yes." Ira Manetrue looked thrilled. "It will help avoid customs problems without having to reveal our agents to those countries who refuse to help us."

Y nodded. "I'll expect several new safety ideas for your BMML at the next meeting, Jane, and I want to be consulted as to the final design. Now, if that's all, I guess we can adjourn."

After a brief pause to be sure no one had anything to say, Y stood and left the room. Mr. Manetrue followed. The moment the door closed behind them, the room burst into activity. Everyone began to move at once, packing their things and preparing to leave.

Jane blew out a heavy breath, shaking her head at surviving, mostly, yet another monthly presentation. Then she opened her briefcase and set her BMMLs—spent and unspent—inside.

"Well," Lizzy said bracingly as she got to her feet, "that went well, I think."

"Ha, ha," Jane muttered. Her friend grinned. "No. Seriously. You had a little hiccup there with the . . . er, BM-whatever."

"BMML," Jane prompted, shrugging into her jacket. "And nearly blowing off the head of a co-worker is hardly a hiccup."

"It is when it's Dick."

Lizzy and Jane had often agreed the man's parents had been prophetic, if cruel, in naming him. Richard—better known as Dick—Hedde. Jane's gaze moved along the table to the empty spot where Dick had been seated. "Did he leave already?" she asked hopefully. Jane rather supposed she owed him an apology, but she wouldn't be sorry to miss the opportunity if he'd left.

"I think he's still under the table. In a fetal position and sucking his thumb."

Mouth dropping open, Jane bent swiftly to peer under the table. Dick wasn't there.

"Janie, honey, you are so gullible!" Lizzy laughed good-naturedly.

Jane straightened, making a face and closing her briefcase with a snap. "It's part of my charm."

"Yes, it is." Lizzy grinned. "Want to stop for a drink and maybe a pizza on the way home?" They headed for the door.

"Can't. Jill has to leave early to pick up her daughter from the train station. She's skipping Friday's classes to come home from the university for the weekend. I have to get straight back." Jill was the woman who watched Jane's gran, and she was gold as far as Jane was concerned. She was a hard worker, was always on time, was never sick, and most importantly got on with Jane's gran. Which was no small thing. Maggie Spyrus could be a cantankerous mule.

Jane glanced at her wristwatch and frowned. "Actually, I'd better hurry about it too. Her daughter's train gets in at five-thirty. It's already five." She made a face. "This meeting *would* run late on a day I have to be home early."

"Hmm." Lizzy nodded. "That's the way it usually works. It would have gone faster if Lipschitz hadn't rambled on for an hour about his knockout lipstick."

"Knockout lipstick?" Jane asked. They started up the hall. She hadn't paid attention to Lipschitz's presentation. Or anyone else's for that matter. She really had to see someone about this fear-of-public-speaking thing.

"Yes." Lizzy pulled a small tube from her pocket and handed it over. "This is the prototype. He passed a couple around. We were supposed to give it back, but I forgot when he sat down and you opened your briefcase. I couldn't believe it when I saw those vibrators." She shook her head and laughed.

Jane smiled slightly and took the sample, managing to uncap it one-handed. The color was a hot red. Every man's dream, she supposed. "How does it work?"

"There's a clear stick in the other end. You put that on first like a base coat, then put the color over top. Kiss a guy, and poof!" She snapped her thumb and finger together. "He's out cold and you're fine, according to Lipschitz."

Jane pursed her lips. "I wonder if he tested it himself. . . . And if he did, whether he was the kisser or the kissee."

"Good Lord, I hope he was the kissee! Lipschitz in lipstick is just not something I want to imagine."

Jane laughed. Closing the colored end of the lipstick, she turned it over to open the other and stared with interest at the clear glistening tube beneath. "Is the base coat an antidote, or does it just prevent the drug from touching the wearer's skin?"

"I'm not sure. I missed that part of his very long explanation. I kind of zoned out after the first fifteen minutes." Shrugging, Lizzy changed the subject. "So if Jill's daughter is home, who's watching your grandmother tomorrow?"

"I am," Jane managed to say without grimacing. "I took tomorrow off."

"Off?" Lizzy smiled. "As if! You mean you'll work at home. As usual."

"Yeah, well—"

"Lizzy!" At the call, both Jane and her friend paused and looked back. Joan Higate, one of the three secretaries everyone in D & C shared, started down the hall after them. "You have a phone call. A Mark Armstrong."

"Damn. I have to take that," Lizzy muttered. "Well, I'll give you a call this weekend." She turned and broke into a jog back toward the phones.

"Oh, wait! The lipstick." Jane took a step after her friend, but paused when Lizzy waved back at her not to worry.

Shrugging, Jane turned back toward the exit. Recapping the lipstick, she slipped it into her pocket. She'd give it back on Monday; she really had to get home now. The last thing Jane wanted was to piss off Jill. Who else could take care of her gran?

Maggie Spyrus had been an active, sharp-minded agent right up until six years ago. Then, after forty-five years in the business, one year before she would have retired, an assignment had gone awry. She had been training a rookie who'd made a terrible error—one that had cost the girl's life and landed Maggie in a wheelchair. She'd not taken the change well. She missed the action and adventure of her old job. She missed using her brain and body. And she got into all sorts of trouble—or had until Jane hired Jill.

Jill was the sixth nurse Maggie Spyrus had in the year after the incident, but she was also the last. The woman had once told Jane that the secret to her success with Gran: She hid whatever sympathy she felt. When the old girl misbehaved, Jill berated her for acting like a child, accused her of being a nasty old witch feeling sorry for herself. Which was apparently what Gran needed. The last thing Maggie could handle was being pitied or treated like a senile old cripple, so Jill's attitude was perfect. Gran responded well to expectations, and Jill had a lot of them. She expected Gran to do what she could and to behave well. And for Jill, Gran did.

Jane paused at the door at the end of the hall, punched a code into the keypad, stuck her thumb on another pad so it could read her print, then pressed her eye to the retina scanner. A buzz sounded and the door unlocked. Jane immediately pushed it open and stepped out into a small lobby painted a soothing blue. It was very small, perhaps twenty feet wide. The wall facing her had three elevators. A small counter stood at either end of the room, a man in a security guard's uniform behind each.

Jane gave a smile and waved in response to their greetings. As she crossed the short distance to the first of the three elevators, the doors slid apart almost at once, opened by one of the guards.

Jane stepped inside. This elevator was saved for D & C use only. The other two traveled up, carrying people to the higher floors and departments in the B.L.I.S.S. building, but this one was reserved for her department alone. It opened out into the main lobby or traveled down to the first and second basements, where all of the more interesting and dangerous experiments took place. Thus the security for it was very tight.

The doors at Jane's back clicked shut, enclosing her in the mirrored elevator. A moment passed during which she knew she was being x-rayed and what she carried was being recorded. Then the doors in front of her slid open.

Jane stepped out and crossed the large main lobby filled with B.L.I.S.S. workers coming and going. She pushed through the main revolving doors to the outside. Hurrying along the concrete sidewalk, she passed the large sign that read TOTS TOY DEVELOPMENT and had a laugh. It was a dummy sign. Camouflage. There was very little having to do with tots inside that building, unless you counted weapons against terrorists or counteragents or threats to the world order as nifty children's games.

The sight of her little white Miata sports car made her smile. Jane unlocked its door, tossed her briefcase inside, then slid behind its wheel.

Catching a glimpse of herself in the rearview mirror, she grimaced. The light dusting of face powder and rose lipstick she'd applied that morning were long gone. Large naked green eyes peered back at her. Between that and the long auburn hair pulled back into its usual ponytail, she looked about ten years younger than the twenty-eight she was. Someday she'd look her age, she was sure, but by then she probably wouldn't want to.

Jane glanced up at the soft top of her car and considered putting it down. It was November but unseasonably nice, and she loved to drive fast with no roof. She was running late, however, and the latch tended to give her trouble; so she merely undid her window, buckled up, and started the engine. Imagining herself a race-car driver, she shifted the stick shift into gear and roared out of the parking lot.

It was only a twenty-minute drive from the B.L.I.S.S. building to the apartment she shared with her grandmother. Today she made it in sixteen. Grabbing her briefcase, Jane scrambled out of the car and hurried inside. The apartment building had been designed in a squarish C, with the entry way and lobby in the front opening into a long corridor that diverged both right and left for a good thirty feet before turning sharply into the wings. Jane and her gran lived on the first floor in the hallway on the right. Their apartment overlooked the street, so she wasn't surprised when she rounded the corner and found Jill waiting in the open door with her coat on.

"I'm sorry," Jane apologized as she rushed forward. "I meant to get here earlier, but my meeting ran longer than usual."

"That's okay. I saw you pull up and got ready," the slender, fiftyish brunette said. She held the apartment door so Jane wouldn't have to use her key. "I'll get there just in time."

Jane breathed a sigh of relief. "Good. Thanks, Jill. See you Monday." She raised her hand to hold the door herself, then watched Jill hurry off up the hall. When the woman was gone, Jane stepped inside and pushed the door closed. She dropped her brief-case so that she could lock the door, and removed her jacket.

"Janie?"

"Yes, Gran, it's me. Be right there." Hanging her coat on the rack by the door, she picked up her case and moved into the living room.

Maggie Spyrus, seventy years old but still lovely, smiled at her as she entered. "How did the meeting go, dear?"

"Other than firing my BMML and nearly taking off Dick's head, I think it went pretty well."

Gran's eyebrows flew up. "Firing the . . . What did Y say?"

"Nothing about nearly killing Dick, but she did say she thought the BMML was brilliant."

"Brilliant? My!" Gran marveled. "That is high praise from her."

"Yes, and she thought the shrink-wrap condoms were 'diabolical' but would be more useful for tor-turing enemy spies than anything else. She didn't say much about the tampon trackers . . . but she did ask a lot of questions about them."

"She likes them then," Gran said with satisfaction. She absently petted the small white Yorkie in her lap.

Jane merely shrugged, weariness coming over her now that she was home. The stress was over. She wanted nothing more than to have a light din-ner with Gran and maybe watch a movie. Tomor-row she'd start thinking up new fail-safes for the BMML. "How was your day?"

24

"Oh, well . . . I didn't die. But we can always hope for tomorrow."

"Yes," Jane agreed pleasantly. "I'm going to go change into something more comfortable, then see about dinner." The best way to fight Gran's depressive moments was to ignore them.

"Jill made a nice lasagna and salad. She said she put them in the fridge, and that the lasagna just has to be cooked for fifteen minutes or so at 325 degrees to warm it up."

"Jill is a jewel," Jane breathed. "Be right back."

She left Gran watching *Judge Judy* and walked down the hall to the bathroom. Stepping inside and closing the door, Jane realized she still carried her briefcase. She rolled her eyes at herself. Setting the case on the bathroom counter beside the sink, she began to dig things out of the pockets of her business jacket: a small screwdriver, a pencil stub, a pen, Kleenex, a wad of plastic wrap from her lunch. Lipschitz's lipstick was the last thing she found. Frowning at the plain silver tube, she snapped her briefcase open and dropped the lipstick inside. She had to remember to take it back to the office on Monday.

Done emptying her pockets, Jane quickly stripped out of the rest of her clothes, tugged the elastic band out of her hair, then went to turn on the shower. She adjusted the water and stepped under the spray with a sigh. Simply standing under the pulsing stream, Jane enjoyed its pounding on her skin for several moments. At last she grabbed the shampoo and soap.

Ten minutes later, she was turning the water off and grabbing a couple of towels from the rack. Jane wrapped the first around her long hair, turban-style, then quickly dried off with the second. It was when she stepped out onto the floor mat that she realized she hadn't grabbed anything to change into.

Wrapping the towel she'd used to dry off with around herself, Jane snatched up her dirty clothes and turned toward the door. Unfortunately, her jacket caught the edge of the open briefcase and sent it crashing to the floor. Its contents scattered across the bathroom's marble tiles.

Jane stared in dismay at the mess she'd made as one of her trackers rolled to a halt at her feet. The silver case that had held them had snapped open on impact. There were only two left in the case, the others were strewn across the floor.

Jane bent to begin picking them up, but a moment later decided against it. She was naked, cold, and hungry. The mess could wait.

Leaving the steamy bathroom, she hurried to her room and dropped her towel. She dug a pair of clean joggers and a sweatshirt out of the drawer, then pulled on the pants.

"Jane?"

"Coming, Gran!" Jane called. She dragged the sweatshirt over her head, pulling it into place and hurrying along the hall to the living room. "Is something wrong?"

"Tinkle needs to go out, dear."

Jane's eyes dropped to the dog with resignation. The animal was whimpering and circling in Gran's lap: a sure signal she had to relieve herself.

"I don't know what is the matter with the silly animal," Gran fretted. "Jill took her out to do her business just an hour ago. I hope she hasn't got a bladder infection."

"I'm sure she's fine, Gran," Jane said. She sighed. To be honest, she suspected the little dog really didn't have to go out at all. The little beast just wanted to annoy her. Tinkle seemed to have the uncanny knack of "having to go out" whenever Jane was in the shower or busy doing something important. The beast might look adorable with its long white hair and pink bow, but Jane was positive that cute exterior hid an evil soul.

She couldn't say anything to Gran, of course. The woman adored "her little Tinkle." The dog was an angel in her eyes. Of course, it did behave well around her for the most part. Tinkle saved misbehaving for when she was out with Jill or Jane.

"Poor baby," Gran crooned as the dog's whimpers increased in volume. She turned apologetic eyes to Jane. "Could you, dear?"

"Of course, Gran. I'll just get the leash."

"Thank you."

Jane detoured through the kitchen to turn the oven on, then grabbed Tinkle's leash from the hall. She took it out to her gran, who put it on the small dog. Jane then scooped Tinkle up, making sure her hands were nowhere near the animal's mouth where she was likely to get bit. Carrying the beast into the kitchen, she set it on the floor and hooked the leash to the doorknob. Going to the fridge, she retrieved the lasagna Jill had made.

"What are you doing, dear?" Gran called when Tinkle's whining grew in protest at the delay.

"Just popping the lasagna in, Gran. That way it'll be ready when we get back." Removing the plastic wrap Jill had covered the pasta with, Jane matched action to words: she slid the dish into the oven.

"There. All done. We'll be right back," she announced, then stuck her tongue out at the dog. Unhooking the leash from the doorknob, she followed the little monster to the apartment door. As she pulled it open, however, Jane found her neighbor

Edie Andretti standing on the threshold, hand up-raised to knock.

"Oh, Jane! I have a big date tonight and I was just coming over to see if I could borrow—"

"Is that Edie?" Gran's voice interrupted from the living room.

"Yes, Gran," Jane called, scowling at Tinkle. The dog had begun running around in circles, binding Jane up in its leash.

"Come on in, Edie dear, Jane will be back in a minute." Gran called. "You can keep me company."

"Oh, I can't stay long, Mrs. S.," Edie replied. She stepped past Jane into the apartment. "I have a date. In fact, he's picking me up in ten minutes. I was just going to borrow a couple of things from Jane."

"Oh, my!" Maggie Spyrus called. "A hot date is it, Edie dear? And on a Thursday night? You must come tell me all about it."

"Okay," the younger woman agreed. She turned back to Jane. "Can I—"

"Borrow whatever you want. You know where everything is," Jane answered, distracted trying to untangle herself from Tinkle's leash. Finally managing, she started out the door—only to halt abruptly as her head was suddenly jerked backward. Glancing around with a start, she saw Edie grinning at her, a damp towel dangling from the woman's hand.

"Damn," Jane growled. She'd forgotten all about it. Reaching up, she slicked the tangled mass of her wet hair back with her fingers, hoping that made it at least a touch less disreputable. "Go on in. I'll be back as quick as I can. If you have to leave before I return, borrow what you need and go. But I expect to hear all the details of the date tomorrow."

"You will." Edie grinned and closed the door behind her.

"Come on, Tinkle," Jane said glumly, heading for the elevator. She wasn't at all surprised when the beast decided it didn't want to walk and sat down in the hall to whine. Sighing, Jane picked up the Yorkie and carried her to the elevator. This was a sure sign that Jane wasn't going to get back before Edie had to leave. She suspected she'd be lucky to get back before the lasagna burned.

As she'd expected, Edie had already left when Jane returned. The lasagna had been in the oven longer than the recommended fifteen minutes, but it was still edible. Jane and her gran ate, then watched an old James Bond flick. It was eleven before the show ended and Jane saw to settling Gran and Tinkle in bed.

Quite ready for bed herself by then, Jane made her way to her bathroom, pausing at the sight of her briefcase sitting on the counter with its contents replaced neatly inside. Hadn't she knocked it to the floor and left it to clean up later.

Stepping forward, Jane peered inside. Edie had obviously taken the time to put everything back for her. Which was very nice, but Jane had to wonder why Edie had even been in the bathroom. Her neighbor was a good friend, but generally she borrowed clothes or jewelry rather than anything out of the bathroom. Well, really she tended to borrow mostly jewelry. Jane didn't have that great a wardrobe; it was made up mostly of a combo of business clothes and sweatsuits, and it was sadly lacking in the sexy slinky-type clothes one might want for a date. In any case, whatever clothes and jewelry Edie may have been interested in, they certainly wouldn't have been found in the bathroom.

Jane scanned the contents of her briefcase again. Everything seemed to be there; the BMML, the launched BMML, the shrink wrap condoms. Jane counted those, terrified for a brief moment that the girl might have borrowed one. Wouldn't that have made for an interesting date? she thought ruefully. However, all of the little foil packets were present and accounted for. Even the knockout lipstick remained. She breathed another grateful sigh.

Shrugging, Jane started to close the briefcase, then paused as she realized what was missing. There was only one silver case of personal trackers—the lubricated ones, she saw upon snapping open the container. Setting it on the counter, she quickly shifted through the contents of her briefcase just to be sure.

No, the pack of absorbent tampon trackers wasn't there.

Jane raised her head to peer at herself in the mirror, only then noticing the Post-it stuck to the glass. It was orange and obviously from the pad in her briefcase.

> *Dear Jane,*
> *Borrowed some tampons. Hope you don't mind, but took the case. Knew you wouldn't need them since you borrowed my last ones last week. Will return the case and spares tomorrow when I fill you in on my date!*
> *Toodles, Edie*

Jane groaned, then started to laugh. This was her own fault, of course. She'd left the contents of her briefcase lying around rather than putting them in her workroom. She *had* also told Edie she could borrow anything.

She tried to cheer herself. At least with the trackers there wouldn't be any of the calamities that might have occurred had Edie borrowed the lipstick or the condoms. But damn those had been some expensive tampons, and her friend would never even know.

Jane briefly considered tracking Edie and getting a free test-run out of the deal, but she pushed the thought aside. She couldn't take advantage of her friend that way. She would just have to call them a loss.

Shaking her head, Jane picked up her briefcase and took it to her workroom. She would have to be more careful in the future. She knew better than to leave things lying around! Wasn't that one of the first things they taught you at B.L.I.S.S?

"At least she took the absorbent ones," Jane muttered as she closed the door of her workroom.

Chapter Three

"Here you go, buddy." The cabbie shifted into park, then turned in his seat to add, "That'll be twenty-two twenty-five."

Abel Andretti glanced sharply at the fare listed on the digital monitor on the dashboard. The guy wasn't kidding. The fare from the airport to his sister's apartment *was* $22.25. Amazing. Horrifying. What a rip-off! Shaking his head, he handed the cabbie two twenties.

"You want change?" the cabbie asked as he snatched the bills.

"Yes," Abel said through his teeth. He wasn't in the best of moods at the moment. Not that he'd have dropped the cabbie an almost eighteen-dollar tip anyway. The man had been grouching all the way from the airport about traffic and taxes and whatnot while Abel had sat fretting over his sister, Edie.

His gaze slid to the pleasant Victorian-style building. It was just the sort of place Edie would pick. But it wasn't like her not to meet him at the airport as arranged. Concern drew his eyebrows together. Why hadn't she shown up? Edie wasn't the sort just to blow off a responsibility like that.

His stomach growled and he glanced at his watch. It read 8:44 P.M.—but that was London time. He hadn't changed it yet. By his estimation, it was 12:44 in the afternoon here in British Columbia. Lunchtime. But it was well past dinner in Britain, and he hadn't eaten the food provided on the plane. He'd expected he and Edie to stop for lunch after she picked him up. He hoped she was home, or arrived soon so they could eat.

"Here ya go." The cabbie's grin was evil as he dumped seventeen loonies and three quarters into Abel's hand. "Have a nice day."

Abel's answer was a grunt. He pushed the door open and dragged himself and his overnight bag and small suitcase out of the backseat. He had barely gained his feet when the taxi roared off, its door closing from momentum alone.

Shifting the strap of his overnight bag on his shoulder, Abel hefted his suitcase and started toward the building. A young couple exited as he stepped into the entry. They kindly held the inner door for him, so Abel bypassed the buzzer with a murmured thanks.

It was possible that Edie wasn't home, was either running late and on her way to the airport, or was on her way back after not finding him there. Abel had waited an hour and a half and made three phone calls before giving up and hailing a taxi, but it was possible his sister had mixed up the arrival time of his flight or been held up by traffic. If that was the case, he was going to find himself waiting a bit for her return.

He headed for her apartment. After sitting in airports and airplanes for more than fourteen hours, the last thing he wanted was to sit around a public lobby. But what could he do if she wasn't home? He'd wait in her hallway where he could set his cases by her door and pace off some of the stiffness in his back, legs, and butt.

Abel grimaced at the thought of more waiting, then told himself perhaps he wouldn't have to. Maybe she'd already returned. Or maybe she'd just slept in and hadn't heard the phone—though it was after lunch and Edie was an early bird. It seemed unlikely she'd be here.

With that thought in mind, he paused in front of her door and knocked. No response. He knocked again, but his heart had already sunk. There was absolutely no sound from inside the apartment. Edie wasn't here. She must be somewhere between here and the airport. Car trouble or something had undoubtedly delayed her. He was going to have to wait.

Heaving a sigh, Abel set his bags beside her door, straightened, stretched a bit, then crossed his arms and began to pace, subconsciously listening to the muffled sounds coming through the doors he passed: the garble of people talking at this one, the tinny music of a telly behind that. A scratching at the next door caught his attention and made Abel pause. The noise was followed by the whine of a dog.

"No, Tinkle!" a woman's irritated voice said, its

volume and clarity suggesting she stood directly inside the door, no doubt trying to drag the dog back. "You've been out three times today already and done nothing the last two. I'm not taking you out again right now. I have work to do."

Abel felt his lips quirk at the woman's obvious annoyance. Tinkle? What a horrendous name for a dog! It brought to mind images of a furry little beast with a collar that was always jingling.

There came more scratching and another soft whine.

"No, Tinkle. You'll just have to wait. Come away from the door." The voice began to sound more pleading than stern. It also grew fainter as the speaker moved away from the door, so Abel only caught part of what she said next: "Please . . . Tinkle! I need . . . B.L.I.S.S . . . vibrator!"

Shocked, Abel spun and headed back to his sister's door. He couldn't have been more embarrassed had he been caught in his eavesdropping. Really, that the woman wouldn't take her dog for a walk because she wanted some bliss with her vibrator was more information than he wished to know about his sister's neighbors. More than he wanted to know about anyone! Now his mind was taking paths he'd really rather have avoided.

Shaking his head to rid it of the image of some faceless woman indulging herself while her poor mournful puppy sat nearby, yearning to go outside and lift a leg, Abel paused before his sister's door and tried it again.

It was still locked, of course. He stood before it, slowly becoming aware of a need to "lift a leg" himself.

"It's the power of suggestion," he assured himself

in a mutter. "That dog just started you thinking about it. You don't really have to go."

He wasn't convincing himself. If anything, the more Abel tried to convince himself otherwise, the more he had to relieve himself. His gaze dropped to his luggage sitting by his sister's door. It caused something of a difficulty. He couldn't just leave it there in the hallway for someone to take while he went in search of the nearest restaurant or gas station. And he really didn't want to lug it all with him on his search.

He scowled at his baggage, intensely aware of a building pressure in his bladder. His gaze went to the door again; then he reached for his wallet. Edie would forgive him, he assured himself. He pulled out a credit card.

Breaking and entering looked easy in the movies: The thief produced a credit card, did a little wiggling and jiggling, and voilà! Mission accomplished. It wasn't so easy in reality. After several minutes of wiggling and jiggling and just plain sawing the plastic through the narrow slot between Edie's door and the frame, Abel decided his sister must have a credit-card-proof door.

Wholly intent on the attempt to break into Edie's apartment, he didn't hear the door open down the hall. In fact, he didn't become aware of anyone's presence until a spreading warmth drew his attention to the back of his right pant leg. Twisting to glance down, Abel noted the dog at his back. It took his brain a moment more to process what the little white fur-ball was doing. With a shout of dismay, Abel leaped away from the little monster.

"Tinkle! Get back here! Bad doggie."

Abel wheeled around to stare. A woman stood half in the hall and half in her apartment, a dog leash dangling from her hand. It was the apartment door he'd stopped at just moments before. Apparently the dog's pitiful whining had convinced the woman to forgo her . . . plans, to take the mutt for its obviously much needed walk. However, most of Abel's sympathy for the dog had been washed away. He now suspected he knew why the little beast was called Tinkle, and it had nothing to do with bells.

Abel craned his neck, trying to get a look at the stain on the back of his pant leg, then glared at the woman belatedly kneeling to put a leash on her dog. She seemed unaffected by his ire, and not the least apologetic. In fact, she was watching him with a wariness that both gave him pause and made him wonder how long she'd stood in the doorway. Had she seen him trying to break into his sister's apartment? Abel nervously palmed his credit card and tried not to look like a criminal.

"Hi." He tried for a cheerful tone, but his heart sank when the woman eyed him narrowly.

"Can I help you?" she asked. Her tone was strong and cold. It didn't at all fit the slim young woman in jeans and pink T-shirt. With her long red-brown hair in a ponytail, and no makeup on her piquant face, she looked like a teenager. She wasn't at all what he'd imagined when he'd pictured . . .

Producing a smile tinged with chagrin, he stepped forward. "I was just . . ." He waved vaguely toward his sister's door, only to pause when the young woman took a cautious step backward, pulling her dog with her. He supposed it was smart of her to keep her distance when she'd just caught him trying to break into an apartment.

"I'm Abel Andretti," he said in what he hoped were soothing tones. "My sister, Edie, lives here."

The woman didn't relax at all. She didn't look as if she believed him either. Abel wondered if she knew Edie and therefore knew that he lived in England and wouldn't normally be at his sister's door. But then, if she knew Edie well, surely she'd know that he was coming to visit; she wouldn't now be looking at him as if he were Jack the Ripper returned.

"Edie's not home," the woman announced, her eyes still suspicious.

"Are you sure?" Abel took an excited step forward, pausing again when Edie's neighbor's hand raised to the doorknob beside her. She looked ready to flee inside at any moment, and no doubt her first act—after locking the door—would be to call the police.

"Look," Abel tried again, "I've just flown all the way from England to visit Edie. She was supposed to pick me up at the airport a couple of hours ago. I waited there for an hour and a half before deciding she wasn't coming and then I hailed a taxi. I've waited here for another half an hour and she still hasn't arrived. I'm starting to worry that maybe she's sick, or fell and hit her head or something. So, I . . ." He gestured with the credit card he still held. "I'm really starting to worry."

The young woman didn't exactly relax, but she did appear a little less likely to flee as she considered his words. Her eyes took in his dark wavy hair—a trait he and Edie had both inherited from their Italian grandfather, who was also the source of the Andretti name. As she examined his face, Abel found himself wishing he'd stopped in the airport washroom to shave. He'd inherited a five o'clock shadow from his grandfather as well as his name, and since it had been a good sixteen hours since he'd shaved, he knew he would have a doozy of one right now. It no doubt gave him a roguish air rather than his usual trustworthy, accountant-type look. There was little he could do about it though.

He examined her, as she did him. She was a delicate little thing. Abel had followed in his father's footsteps and become an accountant, but he was built like a linebacker: Six feet two with wide shoulders and a muscular frame he could only assume he'd also inherited from his stonemason grandfather. At five feet eleven, Edie had also inherited that tall, strong frame. In comparison, Edie's neighbor was tiny and delicate. Abel's immediate impression was that of a bird, an exotic bird with a button nose rather than a beak, large green eyes, and deep red streaks through her luscious hair. Yes, a bird, because she appeared ready to take flight at any moment.

His gaze dropped down her tense figure, over the full ripe breasts pressing against the clingy cotton of her T-shirt. He could swear she wasn't wearing a bra. He ogled her breasts briefly, then let his gaze continue down over her slightly rounded tummy— why did he find that so sexy?—to her rounded hips encased in the tightest, oldest, most faded pair of ragtag jeans that it had ever been his pleasure to see. Abel had never before found a rip in the knee of a pair of jeans quite so stimulating.

"You have Edie's hair and eyes," the woman admitted.

Abel's eyes jerked from her knee back up to her face. Much to his relief, the woman had relaxed somewhat. It appeared he looked sufficiently like his sister to convince her. Thank goodness. That problem out of the way, he returned to her earlier claim. "You said Edie isn't home. Are you sure about that?"

She nodded apologetically. "Yes. Gran mentioned that she had taken today off, so I was going to invite her to lunch—but there was no answer when I knocked." She hesitated, then added with some reluctance, "I don't think she's returned from her date yet."

Abel felt a shock at that comment. "Date? Edie didn't mention that when I talked to her. In fact, she said something about her love life being as dry and barren as a desert."

His sister's neighbor shrugged. "Well, she dropped by my place to borrow some . . . things before it. I didn't get a chance to talk to her, because I had to let out Tinkle." She gestured at the dog who was now sitting at her feet, looking cute and fluffy and harmless, as if he wouldn't for the world consider taking a leak on someone's pant leg. Abel's mouth stretched into a scowl as he glared at the beast.

"It is odd though," the woman continued. "This date did seem to come out of the blue. I mean, she didn't mention being interested in anyone or anything before, and it's not like Edie to forget something like picking her brother up from the airport." Her gaze went to the door behind him, and Abel turned to look at it too, wishing he could see through. Edie might be in there, hurt or ill.

"Wait here. I'll be right back," Edie's neighbor said. She scooped up her small dog and then disappeared into the apartment from which she'd come.

Abel stared at the closed door for several seconds, wondering if perhaps she hadn't believed him after all and was even now calling the police.

He didn't mind that so much; he wanted the police called. Something was definitely wrong. But he also didn't think he had the patience to wait for them to arrive. It wasn't just that he was now in desperate need of facilities, but he wanted into his sister's apartment. *Now.* He didn't want to have to wait for police procedure: knocking, asking questions, and then finally making their way to the apartment superintendent to have him or her open the door. He wanted inside *now*.

Making up his mind, Abel left his luggage where it was and walked down the hall. He'd have to return to the entry to find the super's number and buzz him. He'd get him to open the door and—

He paused abruptly as the door behind him opened again. Edie's neighbor stepped out of her apartment, sans mutt, and held up a key on a bunny keychain.

"Your sister and I swapped spares some time ago," she told him. "She has a key to my place in case there's a problem with Gran while I'm walking the dog or something, and I have a set of hers in case . . ." She let the sentence trail off, but he could fill in the blanks: In case something bad happened to Edie.

"Oh." He forced a smile. "That's handy."

"Yes." She held out her hand. "Jane Spyrus. Friend and neighbor of your sis."

Abel smiled at the belated introduction, and took the woman's hand. He found himself surprised at both the softness of her skin and the strength of her handshake. These details were lost, however, as her soft feminine scent reached him. He stared down into her solemn face, breathed deeply, and found his voice dropped so low in tone that it might have

41

been coming from the zipper of his pants. "Hello," he said.

Fortunately, Jane didn't appear to notice. Her eyes had drifted down to his luggage where it was still stacked beside his sister's door. Following her gaze, Abel knew she was reading the tags with his name and address in London, England. Still, he was surprised when a stiffness he hadn't noticed before left Jane, and she beamed a smile at him. If the touch and smell of her had taken him by surprise, the sunny spreading of those full luscious lips and the way her eyes suddenly shot sincere pleasure at meeting him nearly bowled him over. Abel found himself forgetting his worries for his sister and smiling back.

"Gran said that Edie mentioned your coming when she dropped in last night," Jane announced as she reclaimed her hand and turned to Abel's sister's door.

"Gran?" Abel's gaze went to Jane's rear end of its own accord. He'd heard all the jokes about Italian men liking female behinds—looking, pinching, and fondling them were what they supposedly liked best—but Abel had never before seen the attraction. He'd always been a breast man, though he rarely admitted such even to himself. He preferred to claim that he liked a woman for her mind.

Of course, while the mind *was* important to him, when it came to fondling and groping . . . well, you couldn't fondle a mind. He tended to go for the breasts. Jane Spyrus, however, as fine as her breasts appeared to be, might have been able to convert him. She had as fine a behind as—

"Edie?"

Abel's eyes jerked up as Jane pushed his sister's

door open and stepped inside her apartment. He picked up his luggage and followed.

"Edie?" Jane walked hesitantly to the living room and paused to look about.

Abel scanned the empty room over her head as he let the door close behind them; then he set his luggage to the side and stepped forward for a better look. The apartment was silent and still.

"Oh."

Abel glanced down at Jane, who was suddenly bent. She scooped up an orange tabby doing its very best to wind itself around her ankles.

"Hello, Mr. Tibbs." Jane scratched the furry animal behind the ears and straightened. "Where's your mommy? Hmm? Is she home?"

Crooning to the cat, she moved farther into the apartment. Abel followed, glancing into the kitchen through a doorway on his right. He noted the used cup, plate, and silverware on the counter beside the sink, and the empty cat-food dish on the floor beside the fridge. He and Jane walked through the dining room, neat and clean, to the less tidy living room where an open newspaper had been left on the couch. A pair of slippers lay by the chair.

Jane paused to set Mr. Tibbs on the floor, then turned into a small hall on the right. Abel followed again, feeling like an interloper in the silent apartment. There was a door on their right, a door on their left, and one straight ahead. The one on their left opened to reveal a bedroom. Abel's gaze took in the chamber with the same attention to detail as he'd given the other rooms. The bedroom definitely appeared lived-in. A pile of clothes lay in one corner, awaiting laundry day. The bed was unmade, with several outfits tossed on it, obviously discarded as unsuitable for his sister's date. He was pleased to see it didn't look as if Edie had planned on bringing the guy back here.

The door on his right was closed. Abel turned the knob and opened it even as Jane said, "Closet."

It *was* a small closet, the shelves all neatly stacked with towels, washcloths, and linen. Closing it, he turned his attention to the room ahead. This door was open too, and the room was also most definitely lived-in, he saw, peering over Jane's head. It looked as if a cyclone had hit. Makeup was strewn everywhere on the bathroom's counter by a hair drier that was still plugged in but off. An unplugged curling iron lay nearby. A used towel had been left in a heap on the floor, along with what he presumed were the clothes Edie had worn to work.

Abel gave all this some attention before his gaze fell on the apparatus between the sink and tub. The toilet! Despite his worry for his sister, Abel was suddenly, most definitely, recalled to his need to relieve himself.

Jane glanced over, mouth open to say something. She paused at the sight of his face. "Oh. I suppose it was a long trip. Do you need to—"

"Yes. I'm afraid I do," he interrupted, slightly embarrassed. The two of them maneuvered around each other in the tight hallway so that he could get into the bathroom; then he closed the door and took care of business with a sigh of relief.

When he exited the room moments later he could hear Jane talking to someone, and he felt his heart jump with relief. Edie was back! He returned to the kitchen, only to pause in the doorway with disappointment. It wasn't Edie whom Jane was talking to, but the damned cat. She was chatting away to Mr. Tibbs as if the beast might actually understand and answer her while she searched.

"Where's your mama, boy?" she asked, opening all the cupboard doors one by one, pausing only when she found the box of dry food for which she'd apparently been looking.

"Here you go, baby." She filled the cat's dish, then picked up his empty water bowl.

"When was the last time *you* saw my sister?" Abel asked her as she straightened and noticed him.

Jane moved to the sink to rinse out and refill Mr. Tibbs's water bowl. "I told you. Last night, after work. She stopped in to borrow . . . a couple of things."

Abel noticed the hesitation over what had been borrowed and realized that Jane had hesitated much the same way when she'd mentioned it earlier. But before he could think of a way to ask her about it without seeming rude, she added, "She was getting ready for her date."

"Her date," Abel echoed with a frown. He'd talked to Edie only last night. Well, early evening for him. It had been lunchtime here in Vancouver. Abel had called to verify his arrival time. He'd made sure to call on her work lunch hour to ensure that she wouldn't get in trouble for personal calls. That talk was also why he'd waited so long at the airport before hailing a cab and coming here: Edie had assured him she would be there. She'd also said then that her social life resembled a desert, dry and barren. Which meant this date had come up between his call and when she'd got home from work: four or five hours she would have spent mostly in the office.

"It *was* a date?" Abel asked. "Not something to do with work?"

Jane looked surprised. "No. I mean, yes. It was a

45

date, and it had nothing to do with work as far as I know." She peered at him curiously. "Why?"

"Oh." He shook his head. "It's just that she mentioned some strange goings-on at work."

"What kind of strange goings-on?" Jane asked.

Abel hesitated then admitted, "Well, she didn't elaborate. She said only, *'There's something strange going on at work. I'll tell you about it when you get here, but if anything should happen to me . . .'* But then she laughed it off as if she were being silly." He shrugged as if it might mean nothing, but he was truly worried. Edie wasn't prone to exaggeration. Strange happenings at work and cryptic comments like "*should anything happen to me*" were easily shrugged off when things were well, but now that his sister was missing . . .

"Is there anyone we could call?" he asked. "Who was her date with?"

"I don't know, but—" Jane turned out of the kitchen and walked quickly into the living room area. Abel watched with bewilderment as she walked to an end table, opened its drawer, and pulled out a small flower-covered tome.

"This is her personal phone book." Jane moved back toward him. "We'll go through this and call everyone in here if we have to, until we either find her or find someone who knows who she went out with. Come on, we'll have to do it at my place."

"Your place?" Abel asked as she moved past him to the exit. "Shouldn't we stay here in case she returns?"

"Gran is . . . She can't be left alone," Jane answered evasively. Abel thought she sounded slightly embarrassed or perhaps just terribly uncomfortable, but he couldn't see her face as he stepped out into the hall behind her.

"We'll just have to keep checking to see if she comes back." Jane pulled the door closed, started to lock it with her key, then paused and arched a questioning eyebrow at him. "Unless you want to stay here and go through the book yourself?"

"No. I don't know who her friends are here in Vancouver. I could use your help."

Chapter Four

There was a movie blaring on the television when Abel followed Jane into her apartment: some horror flick from the '70s with lots of gore. There was no one watching it. The living room and dining area were as empty as Edie's had been, which seemed to alarm Jane. Abel was sure he heard a soft curse slip from her lips as she turned into the kitchen.

He followed, peering curiously over her head. His gaze fell upon an older woman in a wheelchair. No doubt this was the "gran" Jane had mentioned couldn't be left alone. The woman's hair was short and white, her face still lovely despite its age. She looked very much like her granddaughter. Abel could imagine Jane looking just as lovely in her twilight years. But he had no idea what was alarming her. Maybe it was that her gran had wheeled herself up to a table where a collection of ingredients was set out for use. It appeared the old woman was preparing to bake something.

"Gran? Whatever are you doing?" Jane asked, her voice sounding thin and strained.

Abel watched, curious.

"I thought I'd make some tea and scones," the woman answered cheerfully.

Jane seemed to relax a bit, but not completely. Abel didn't have long to wonder what still bothered her, because Jane's gran had noticed his presence.

"Oh, hello," she chirped. Then her mouth became a sad moue as she looked behind them into the empty hall. "I take it Edie wasn't there, then?"

"Edie? No." Jane sounded distracted. "This is her brother, Abel Andretti. Abel, this is my gran, Maggie."

"Ma'am." Abel nodded solemnly.

"We're going to make a couple of calls and see if we can track Edie down," Jane explained as her grandmother smiled at Abel in greeting.

"That's a good idea, dear." Maggie Spyrus nodded solemnly. "I'm sure you'll track her down. Then we can all have tea and scones together."

"That sounds lovely," Abel agreed, then grunted as he was elbowed in the side. He looked at Jane in surprise.

"We wouldn't want you to go to all that trouble, Gran," she contradicted quickly. "We—"

"Oh, it's no trouble, Janie dear. You know how I love to bake."

Abel thought he heard a groan from Jane; then she said, "Perhaps I should stay and help."

"Nonsense! I'm sixty years old. Surely I know my way around a kitchen by now," the old woman claimed.

"Seventy," Jane muttered, though Abel guessed he wasn't supposed to hear. He contained an amused smile.

"You run along now and track down our Edie," Maggie suggested. "Go on. Shoo!"

Her granddaughter hesitated a moment longer, then said, "All right. But if you need any help—"

"Shoo!" her grandmother repeated.

Impatient with the interruption of their search, Abel took Jane's arm. He urged her out into the hall. "I'm sure she'll be fine."

"Yes," Jane agreed, but she didn't sound happy. She kept glancing back at the kitchen as he urged her into the living room.

"You can check on her regularly," Abel pointed out. He was trying to be understanding though all he really wanted to do was make those phone calls and find his sister. "She'll be fine."

"Yes," Edie's neighbor agreed doubtfully. "Of course she will."

Jane hung up the phone after yet another useless call and ran her finger over the next number. They'd been calling all the numbers in Abel's sister's book for nearly an hour now and were at the letter T. There were very few listings left. So far they'd learned exactly nothing, and Jane very much feared that this was a wasted effort. Picking up the receiver, she started to punch in the next number . . . only to pause when her glance went to Abel. His nose was working as he sniffed the air. He looked like a dog tracking a scent.

"What is it?" She asked.

"I'm not sure," Abel answered. "Do you smell something burning?"

Jane's eyes widened in horror. A smell of char

filled the air. She leaped to her feet at once. "Gran!"

Flying into the kitchen, Jane felt alarm pulse through her. But Gran was still at the kitchen table, happily rolling out gray dough and using a water glass to cut inch-thick circles out of it. All around, the kitchen was beginning to fill with a nasty black smoke that billowed from the oven behind her.

"Gran!"

"Yes, dear?" Maggie Spyrus gave her granddaughter a distracted smile that turned surprised as Jane grabbed up a dish towel and rushed to the stove. Turning her wheelchair, she watched Jane drag the door open, wave at the smoke, and grab up a tray of very black scones to dump them in the sink.

"Oh, my! I guess I lost track of time and left them in too long." Gran scowled as Jane rushed to open the window.

"That's okay, Gran. I wasn't hungry anyway." Jane sighed as she used her dish towel to try to sweep the smoke away before it set off the fire alarm. She gave up the attempt as the alarm blared to life.

Muttering under her breath, Jane hurried to the kitchen closet in search of a broom to reach up and press the reset button on the alarm. It was only when she saw that it wasn't in its usual spot that she recalled having used it in her workroom the night before last. She'd forgotten to return it!

"I'll be right back," she shouted, although it was doubtful Gran could hear her above the alarm.

Rushing past Abel as he entered the kitchen, Jane raced down the hall to her workroom.

The broom was exactly where she'd left it, leaning against the wall by the door so that she'd remember to return it. Jane grabbed it, then froze as her eyes caught the laptop computer on her desk. There was a tiny satellite dish next to it. She stood still for several minutes, a stupid look on her face as she recalled the tracking tampons Edie had borrowed. Then the alarm from the kitchen went silent. Abel must have found a way to silence it on his own.

Letting go of the broom, Jane moved to her desk. Unraveling the cord attached to the satellite dish, she plugged it into the special socket she'd installed in the computer, then lifted the computer's lid and switched the laptop on. The machine finished booting, and Jane clicked on the voice program. "Sam, open BTT," she ordered.

The voice program had needed a call word, something to tell the computer it was being addressed, so Jane had chosen Sam. She was a big fan of *Casablanca*, and the "Play it again, Sam" line had run through her head when she addressed the computer the first time—so Sam it had been.

The screen turned red, then filled with several options. Jane took a deep breath. "Sam, initiate agent tracking," she continued. A small box promptly appeared with the words *enter tracker ID*. Jane hesitated. Each tracker had a different ID number. This was to ensure that Operations could tell whom they were tracking at any given time. However, Jane had no desire to go search out the numbers of the twelve trackers she'd created, then enter the six numbers for the BTTs that Edie had borrowed. After a hesitation she decided, "Sam, select all and click enter."

The screen immediately changed again, this time becoming a large gridded map of the Vancouver area. A yellow beacon representing one of her trackers lit up downtown just before the screen shifted once more: The streets of Vancouver disappeared, replaced by a map made up of main highways as it zoomed out to encompass a larger area that included part of Washington state.

"Oh, God," Jane breathed. But the screen wasn't done yet. It blinked a third time, zooming out even farther. The names of towns and cities became smaller as it struggled to include more than half of Washington. Much to Jane's horror, a red beacon lit up between Seattle and Olympia. And it was moving south.

"Abel!" Jane ran for the door.

"I don't know how I could have burned them." Despite her words, Maggie Spyrus didn't sound all that upset.

"It's easily done, I'm sure," Abel assured the old woman as he stepped down from the chair he'd used to reach the reset button. He assumed that this was what Jane had worried about: Apparently her grandmother, for all her sixty or seventy years, was not much of a cook.

"Jane went to look for a broom to hit that button," Maggie was saying. "She isn't as tall as you and can't reach it even standing on that chair."

Abel managed a smile despite his impatience. None of the calls they'd made so far had gained any results, and he wanted to get back to his search for his sister. Worry was growing inside him and lodging itself in his throat, choking him with its expanding presence.

"I'll go tell her it isn't necessary," he said. He left Maggie rolling out fresh dough for another try at scones. He knew he didn't really have to tell Jane that he'd turned the fire alarm off—surely she would hear that—but he wanted to speed her up, get her back to their task. He had a bad feeling about Edie's absence. They had to find her.

Abel had no idea where Jane had gone to find a broom, but she couldn't be hard to locate. The living room was empty, which left a hall he presumed led to the bedrooms. Edie's apartment was a single-bedroom style; this one had at least two, possibly three. Still, it wasn't that large. Abel passed the first closed door. He moved instinctively toward the open door farther on and nearly found himself bowled over as Jane came rushing through.

"Abel!" she gasped and clutched the lapels of his suit jacket in a panicky grasp.

"What is it?" He caught her elbows with concern. She looked frantic, and that made him frantic too. "What—"

"Edie!" Grabbing his hand, she hurried back into the room she'd just come out of, dragging him along behind her. "She's in Washington state almost to Olympia."

"What?" Abel stumbled to a stop at a desk, staring with incomprehension at the laptop Jane turned toward him. There appeared to be some sort of gridded map on the screen, but he didn't have a clue what it represented. "What are those blinking things?"

"They're . . . The red one is Edie."

"What? How—?"

"Edie borrowed a . . ."

"A what?" Abel prompted as Jane trailed off. A flush had risen to cover the young woman's cheeks, and she looked embarrassed.

"She borrowed a . . . a necklace," Jane got out at last, but the way she couldn't quite meet his eyes made Abel think she was lying.

"A necklace?"

"Yes." Jane flushed even deeper and said, "She stopped in last night before her date and borrowed a necklace that I had brought home from work. It has a tracker in it."

"It has a what?" he asked with bewilderment.

"A tracker. A transmitter."

"A tracker," he echoed blankly. "Why?"

"Why?" She appeared amazed that he would ask.

"Why would she borrow a necklace with a tracking device in it?" he asked impatiently. "Did she suspect something was going to happen? Did you know she might be in trouble all this time? And if you knew we could track her, why didn't you check this"—he waved vaguely at the screen—"sooner?" He straightened and added suspiciously, "And just where the hell do you work, anyway?"

"Tots Toy Development?" Jane answered the last question first, but it came out as more of a question than an answer.

"Are you sure?" he asked.

He wasn't surprised to see irritation flash across her face. "Look," she said, rubbing her forehead as if the beginning of a headache was making itself known. "I work for Tots Toy Development. Most of what we create are toys. However, I came up with the idea of a tracking necklace that little girls could wear allowing parents to find them should they get lost or what-have-you. My boss thought it was a good idea and told me to run with it."

Abel felt absolutely positive that every word that had just come out of this young woman's mouth was a lie. She even appeared to be making it up as she went along. Then it occurred to him that he didn't know this woman. He didn't know anything about her except for what she'd told him—and he was beginning to wonder how much of that was true.

"And you brought one home and Edie borrowed it."

He didn't bother trying to hide his doubt. She ignored it though, and nodded. It seemed they were going to pretend he believed her.

"Yes. Edie came in just as I was taking Tinkle out for a walk, and I said to borrow whatever she wanted. But I never thought she'd borrow tho— that."

"But she did. And you were able to call her up on this thing." He turned to peer at the screen again where the red blip was moving closer to Olympia. Olympia, Washington, he realized and shook his head in denial. "That can't be her. What would she be doing in the United States when I'm here? She must have given the necklace to someone else."

"She would hardly just give away a necklace of mine," Jane pointed out impatiently.

"Well, then, maybe she was mugged and someone stole it," he guessed.

Jane began to rub her forehead again. It was obvious she was upset and anxious, and was searching for a way to convince him. Abel didn't want to be convinced. Edie was just late, not halfway across Washington State.

"She must have been mugged," he repeated. "Edie simply wouldn't take off on a road trip. She knew I was coming."

"That's right," Jane agreed as if he were a slow child. "She wouldn't *willingly* go on a road trip. But the tracker is in Washington and heading south, and it shuts off and turns yellow if taken out—off the wearer. So that is definitely Edie. Besides," she added when he would have interrupted, "if that isn't her heading south, where is she? Why didn't she pick you up?"

Abel had no answer to that. But he definitely didn't like Jane's explanation.

"It's her, Abel. And the tracker is only good for two—"

"You think she's been kidnapped," he said, wanting to be sure that he wasn't misunderstanding. The very idea was horrible. It brought images to mind of his little sister bound and gagged and crying in some dark hole that could only be the trunk of a vehicle. That vehicle was taking her miles away from him for God knew what reason.

Jane blew out a breath of exasperation. "I don't know what to think. However, the Edie I know—if at all possible—would have been at that airport fifteen minutes early to pick you up."

"Yes," Abel agreed unhappily. Edie was the sort to show up early rather than risk being late.

"Only she wasn't there at all," Jane said, as if he might have forgotten. "And she isn't here now. Which suggests to me that she's not *able* to be here. Now, she left wearing that tracker and I *know* she's still wearing it. Which means she's currently . . ." Her gaze dropped to the screen to read the data being spewed. Her eyes widened in dismay. "One hundred and seventy-one miles away. Dear Lord," she exclaimed. "We have to get moving."

"Just a minute." Abel caught her arm when she started around the desk. "Why would someone take my sister to Washington? Why—?"

"California is south of Oregon, which is south of Washington, and they're heading south," Jane pointed out—incomprehensibly to Abel. "And didn't you say she said there were strange things going on at work? Something about if anything were to happen to her . . . ?"

"So?" Abel felt as if Jane were talking a foreign

language. None of this was making any sense. Edie couldn't be kidnapped. She couldn't be in Washington. And what did California's location have to do with his sister's workplace?

"So, it seems to me that Edie once mentioned that the head offices of Ensecksi Satellites were in California."

Abel felt a shock jolt through him. He was silent, absorbing this news, then became aware that Jane was closing her laptop and rolling up all its plugs and connections. What on earth was she bothering with that for when his sister was kidnapped and being dragged to California? "We have to call the police."

"The police won't do anything for twenty-four hours," Jane pointed out, shoving the laptop, the mini satellite, and all its plugs and wires at him. Abel accepted them automatically. "Besides, we don't have time. The trackers are only good for two hundred miles. Another half hour and she'll be out of tracking distance. You couldn't even fill out a missing persons report in that time."

"What?" Abel's hands tightened on the equipment he held, and he gaped at her as she began opening and closing desk drawers and throwing their contents willy-nilly on the desktop. Lipsticks, eyeliners, and perfume vials were rolling every which way. "It's only good for two hundred miles? Why didn't you say so earlier?"

"I tried. You were too busy arguing that it wasn't her." She finished at the desk and rushed around it to survey the room at large as if trying to decide what she needed. Abel glanced about for the first time since entering the room, his eyes widening as he saw that he was in some sort of workshop. The walls were padded with a strange material, work benches ran along each wall, and tools and makeup items were everywhere. There wasn't a toy to be seen. It looked more like a Revlon laboratory than a toy factory . . . except for the tools.

"We have to grab anything we might need and get on the road."

Abel turned his attention back to Jane. She seemed to have decided what she needed and now rushed to the closet beside the door to retrieve a black nylon bag.

"If we lose her . . ." She let the sentence fade away, and Abel felt panic grasp him at the very thought. He started for the door. "I'll go get some things from Edie's apartment."

"There's no time! Just grab the essentials and let's go," she said firmly.

She was now flitting around the room, grabbing up lipsticks and makeup and throwing them in the bag as she went. Abel goggled. Did the woman consider all this makeup as essential, he wondered— then his jaw dropped when she gathered not one, but six neon-pink vibrators from one of her work benches. She threw those into her bag as well.

Dear God, Abel thought with dismay. *I'm depending on some sex-crazed madwoman to help me find my sister.*

"Go tell Gran we're going on a road trip, and to get ready," she ordered.

Abel hurried out of the room and rushed back up the hall to the kitchen. She may be a sex-crazed madwoman, but if what she said was true and that red beacon on the screen was Edie, then Jane was his only link to her.

Actually, he realized, stopping halfway across the living room, *she* wasn't the connection. His gaze dropped to the laptop and mini satellite dish he still held. *This* was the connection. He glanced toward the entry and the door. He could grab his luggage, borrow the laptop, and . . .

And what? He'd have to rent a car. How much time would that take? How much time did he have? And could he figure out how to run this tracking thing Jane had shown him?

Before he could decide, something bumped him in the behind and Jane's voice lashed out: "What are you doing standing around? We have to get moving! Have you even warned Gran to get ready?"

Abel peered over his shoulder to see that she had two black bags in hand, one of them what had hit him. She was frowning at him as if he was proving to be a disappointment. It seemed she was something of a bossy bit of baggage. "I—"

"Never mind. Here, put that laptop in here for now."

Abel reluctantly placed the computer in the nylon bag she opened, setting it on top of half a dozen small foil-wrapped squares. It was only as he released it and retrieved his hand that his brain registered the writing on the little square packets: B.L.I.S.S. Special SW Condoms.

Dear Lord, the woman *was* a sex addict. How could she think condoms were necessities at a time like this?

"Come on." Closing her bag, Jane moved past him and led the way to the kitchen. Abel followed, glaring the whole way. He wasn't at all sure he shouldn't just snatch the laptop and run for the nearest car rental agent. Hell, he could hire a taxi to trail his sister if necessary. Edie was certainly worth the expense.

"Gran, we'll have to forget about scones for now,"

Jane announced as they entered the kitchen. "We're going on a road trip."

"Oh?" Maggie Spyrus blinked, then shrugged and smiled. "All right, dear."

That was it. She didn't ask what sort of road trip or where to, she just rolled her wheelchair back from the table, turned it toward the door to the living room, and rolled out calling gaily, "Tinkle! Come, darling, we're going on a road trip."

Both women were mad, Abel decided. Then, in a somewhat panicky voice he asked, "We aren't taking that mutt, are we?" He hadn't yet forgiven the beast for tinkling on the back of his pant leg.

To give Jane her due, she didn't look at all happy at the prospect either. But she said, "I'm afraid so."

He was about to argue when she pointed out, "Right now we're almost three hours' driving time behind Edie and whoever has her. We might not catch up to her until they stop in California—if that is indeed where they're heading. That's got to be a good fifteen- or sixteen-hour drive. Sixteen there, sixteen back, and who knows how long to actually save her?" She shook her head. "Tinkle can't be left alone for that long. And we don't have time to take her to a boardinghouse."

"No, I guess not," he agreed reluctantly.

Jane set her bags on the counter and began pulling dog food out of the cupboard. Canned of course. Abel wasn't surprised. Tinkle seemed the spoiled sort.

"Could you get a grocery bag out of that cupboard behind you?" Jane asked.

Abel moved automatically to do as she requested. When he turned back with the bag, she'd added bottled water to the stack of dog food. The sight of the bottled water reminded Abel of Jane refilling the water bowl earlier for Edie's cat. He paused and smacked himself in the forehead. "Mr. Tibbs!"

Jane turned in dismay then closed her eyes. For a moment, he thought she'd suggest they leave the cat behind, but instead she dug into her pocket and pulled out Edie's apartment key. She handed it to him, took the bag he'd retrieved for her, then turned back to start filling it with what she'd collected. "Edie keeps Mr. Tibbs's carrier in the hall closet."

Abel went to the door, but he was brought up short by the return of Jane's gran. The old woman wheeled herself into the kitchen, face and clothes still sporting flour, but now she had a huge hat perched on her head at a jaunty angle. Tinkle, leashed, sat in her lap on top of an enormous, bulging purse.

"We're all set," Maggie Spyrus announced cheerfully. "Are *you* ready?"

"Almost," Jane answered, but Abel noticed the suspicious way she was eyeing the bulky bag on her grandmother's lap. Then she seemed to let the matter go. Turning to him again, she said, "Don't forget cat food. And litter. And the litter box."

Nodding, Abel hurried for the door, his heart sinking with each item she added to the list. He could hardly carry all that and his luggage too. And he suspected there wouldn't be time for two trips. Or to change. It appeared he would be riding to his sister's rescue in stained pants.

Chapter Five

"How are we doing?"

Jane was silent for a moment, debating how to answer Abel. They'd whizzed through the border without a problem thanks to two things: 1) Jane had kept her mouth shut about the dog and cat sleeping in the back of the van; and 2) she'd slipped her government-issued high-clearance card into her passport when she handed it over to the border guard. He'd hardly even glanced at Gran's and Abel's passports after that. One eyebrow had gone up, he'd glanced at her speculatively; then he'd handed the IDs back, given a slow nod, and waved them on.

Once through customs, Jane had pulled over and switched seats with Abel, allowing him to drive so she could check on Edie's position. The news wasn't good. While the border guard had waved them through quickly, the line to get to him had held them up for better than half an hour. Edie's tracker had moved out of range. They'd lost her.

"Jane?"

She closed the laptop and prepared for the explosion. "She's out of range."

As expected, Abel jerked in the driver's seat and cursed.

"We'll catch up," she assured him soothingly. "They'll have to stop for gas or something eventually. The important thing is not to do anything that might get us pulled over or slow us down further. Like speed," she added pointedly. Abel eased up on the gas at once.

"You're right." He didn't sound happy to admit it. They were both silent for a moment; then he asked, "So, how long have you known Edie?"

Jane knew he was just trying to distract himself from worrying, but she decided to indulge him. "We met the day she transferred to Vancouver and moved into the building. We got along from the start. She's fun."

He nodded, a small smile pushing the gloom from his face. "She *is* fun. The best sister a guy could ask for. I've missed her."

"She's missed you, too. She keeps hoping you'll fall for one of her friends, marry her, then move back to Canada."

"Yes." He gave a laugh. "She told me. In fact, you must be the Janie she was positive would bowl me over. She had high hopes for us, I think."

Jane choked and felt her face flush. Edie hadn't said anything to her. She peered shyly at Abel, the idea of them matched up now planted in her head. He *was* handsome and seemed intelligent and nice.

"Silly, huh?" He glanced at her briefly, then back to the road.

Jane cleared her throat. "Yes. Silly." Her gaze moved to the window and the passing scenery. Of course, it was silly. Why would he be interested in her—some techie geek with no makeup and wearing an old T-shirt and disreputable jeans? Jane began to pick unconsciously at the frayed hole at her knee. She wasn't at her best and knew it. But what the heck, she thought, forcing herself to sit up straight. She wasn't looking for a man, anyway. Her work was very satisfying, and she had both friends and Gran for company. Who cared about the conclusion she'd come to during the D & C meeting just the day before, that she needed to get laid? Thinking it and actually doing it would be two different things.

Jane wasn't the sort to just have sex without a relationship and, frankly, she worked long hours and didn't really have time for one. Or, at least, she had. If this debacle ever got back to B.L.I.S.S., long hours might not be such a problem anymore.

Jane wrinkled her nose at her reflection in the van window. The trouble she would be in should anyone find out that she had allowed Edie to take the tampon trackers—highly secret, expensive trackers, still in the development stage—well, she was pretty sure she'd lose her job. Not that she'd exactly let Edie take those trackers. But that wouldn't matter to the higher-ups in the agency.

Her fear wouldn't have stopped Jane from calling into the office and seeing if B.L.I.S.S. couldn't help with all their high-tech gadgets and specialized agents, except that the organization was an international unit concerned with world issues. They frowned on using company time and resources for personal matters. And Jane didn't have proof that Edie was in trouble. As Jane herself had pointed out, Ensecksi Satellites was based in California; Edie might just be on an unexpected business trip. She might have left a message to that effect that had been misdirected. She may even have sent someone to the airport to pick up Abel, but the two never connected. Jane didn't think any of this was the case, but she didn't want to bring her bosses in until there was no other option.

Trying to distract herself and Abel from worry about Edie, Jane decided to draw him into conversation. "So, Edie mentioned that you work in the accounting department of some firm in England?"

"Yes." Abel frowned at the road ahead. "Ellis and Smith Construction. I started at the home office in Ontario but got transferred to head up the accounting department in the London branch last year. I didn't really want to move, but it was a step up the ladder."

"How do you like England?"

He shrugged. "The people are nice. More polite."

"Such enthusiasm," she noted with amusement.

"I miss Edie and the rest of the family," he admitted. "And some things there seem strange to me and are hard to get used to."

"Like?"

"Driving on the wrong side of the road."

"Ah." She chuckled, then, having reached the end of her bag of small talk, allowed the silence to drop over them again. A glance into the backseat showed Gran sleeping upright. The woman could nap anywhere. Jane knew she woke easily, however.

Apparently, Abel had reached his limit of small talk as well because he suggested, "Maybe you should rest so you can take over driving later."

"Okay. Wake me when you start to get tired, and we'll switch again." Jane eased her seat back and closed her eyes. She wasn't really tired, but she knew that the ride would lull her to sleep if she allowed. And she suspected she'd need the rest. Jane didn't really expect that Abel would last more than a couple of hours driving. She was pretty sure that it was already late night in England. After a day spent in and out of airports and planes, she suspected, he'd soon tire and then the rest of the driving would fall to her. Resting now was a smart idea.

Much to Jane's surprise, Abel lasted a good seven hours behind the wheel. She saw by the dashboard clock that it was almost midnight when he nudged her awake. Sitting up, she wiped the sleep from her eyes, then glanced around. A double line of red car lights shone from the darkness, curving along the bend in the highway ahead.

"I'm sorry," Abel said. "I was starting to nod off, so thought I should wake you."

"No. That's all right," Jane assured him. "I'm surprised you lasted this long. Just pull into the next rest stop and we can switch." She glanced around the floor for her laptop, frowned when she didn't see it. "Where—"

"Your gran has it. She checked to see if Edie was back in range a couple of times while you were sleeping."

"Was she?" Jane twisted in her seat to see her laptop resting next to Gran's slumbering form. She stretched to grab it then set it on her lap.

"No," Abel admitted unhappily. "We talked it over, and I just stayed on the highway heading south. If they really are going to California, we'll catch up."

His words were more confident than his tone of voice, and Jane felt a moment of sympathy. She knew that his apparent calm hid a wealth of alarm and anxiety over his sister's well-being. He was trying to be strong, but his fear for Edie showed in the strain on his pale face as it was illuminated by the lights of oncoming traffic.

"Sam, open the BT tracking system," she instructed as Abel maneuvered into the right-hand lane, preparing to take the off-ramp to the next rest stop. She almost winced at the sharp look she felt Abel cast her way. Jane had resisted using the voice program while checking for Edie's tracker in his presence until now, but it was so dark she feared mistyping. She ignored Abel and went through the other necessary orders until the map appeared. She recognized the state of Oregon and realized they'd left Washington behind. Then the map switched to encompass both Oregon and California. An excited breath slipped from her lips when a red blip appeared.

"What is it? Is she on there again?" Abel asked anxiously as they reached the rest stop parking lot. He slowed the van and parked.

Jane turned the laptop in his direction and beamed. "You made great time. They're only 150 miles ahead of us." Her eyes narrowed as he turned off the engine and turned to see for himself. "Were you speeding?" she asked.

He shook his head, looking bewildered. "No. I shouldn't have made up *that much* time."

Jane turned the laptop back and peered at the screen. "Hm. They must have stopped."

"Have we made up enough time that we can visit the facilities?" Gran's voice floated from the back.

68

"And Tinkle is awake and whining. She could probably use a walk."

Jane glanced around to see her grandmother straightening on the backseat. Her gaze slid back to Abel just in time to see his unhappy look at the idea of stopping and perhaps losing ground, but he nodded.

"We'll make it quick," she assured him.

Abel nodded again as he undid his seat belt. "I'll pick up some coffee and sandwiches while we're stopped. Any preferences?"

"Surprise us," Jane suggested.

As she'd promised, Jane and Gran were quick about their business in the ladies' room. Still, Abel was faster. He'd purchased the sandwiches and coffee, set them in the van, and was walking Tinkle when they returned.

Jane got Gran back into the van, stowed the wheelchair, then walked out to the edge of the parking lot where Abel and Tinkle were indulging in a silent stare-down.

"Everything okay?" she asked as she approached.

"He tried to bite me when I got him out of the cage!" Abel was obviously affronted by the attack.

"Ah, yes. I should have warned you about that." Jane bit her lip to hide her amusement at his sulky expression. "Tinkle tries to bite everyone."

"Then he nearly took my wrist off trying to chase a police car."

Jane had to bite hard at the image that appeared in her head: a fifteen-pound fur-ball yanking insanely at its leash. Hardly a threat to Abel's wrist! However, all she said was: "*She*. Tinkle is a bitch."

"She certainly is," Abel snapped. Jane couldn't restrain a laugh. Her amusement drew Abel's glare, and he announced, "She hasn't even done anything." He sounded both impatient and frustrated.

Taking pity on him, Jane took the leash from his hand and turned toward the van. "Time to go," she announced.

Tinkle immediately pulled on the leash and whined. Jane paused, not surprised when the dog promptly did its duty. The dog liked to annoy everyone, but not at the risk of her own comfort. Jane waited until the task was done, then she used a bag she'd brought with her from the van for collection and disposal. The three of them then returned to the van.

"Oh, leave her out, Janie," Gran said when Jane started to put the dog back in its cage. "She'll be good."

Deciding it was easier than struggling with the nipping creature, Jane let the beast go. The dog promptly hopped onto the bench seat beside Gran.

"Should we let Mr. Tibbs out too?" Abel asked with obvious reluctance as Jane closed the van door.

"He's sleeping," Jane answered. And she was fairly sure she didn't imagine his relief at not being delayed further.

They got back in the van, Jane taking the driver's seat. After a brief stop for gas they were off, and Abel busied himself distributing the sandwiches and drinks.

"Meatball," Jane said with surprise after swallowing her first bite.

"I'm sorry. I—"

"No, I *like* meatball sandwiches," Jane rushed to reassure him. She laughed. "They're my favorite."

"Mine too."

With her attention on the highway ahead, Jane sensed rather than saw Abel relax. Then he added,

"Actually, I got two meatball sandwiches for myself and chicken salad for you ladies. I guess I handed the wrong one to you."

"Oh." Jane took her eyes off the road to glance at him uncertainly. She held out the sandwich with its missing bite. "Do you want it back?"

"No." He laughed now. "I like chicken salad too. I just didn't think—I mean it didn't occur to me that you might like meatball sandwiches, too. In my experience, most people don't."

Jane shrugged and glanced back to the road. She took another bite. "I have strange taste."

"I'll say," Gran spoke up. "She's the only person I know who likes dill pickles slathered with peanut butter."

"Gran!" Jane glared at her relative in the rearview mirror even as Abel started to laugh. She tossed an irritated glance his way. "What's so funny?"

"Does Edie know you like peanut butter and dill pickles?"

"Yes." A smile curved her lips. "She thought it was a great joke."

"She would. That explains why she thought we'd get along."

"Why?" She cast a curious glance his way, her eyebrows rising at his expression of mirth. "*You* like dill pickles and peanut butter?"

"Ever since I was ten years old and she dared me to eat it. I thought it would be disgusting, but—"

"The peanut butter cuts the tart of the dill, and the juice of the pickle eases the dry stickiness of the peanut butter," Jane finished for him. She nodded. "I tried it for the first time the same way. My cousin Ariel dared me to eat it. That was the most disgusting thing she could come up with at the time."

They smiled at each other; then Jane divided her

concentration between eating and driving and left Gran to carry the burden of conversation with Abel. Maggie Spyrus was good at conversation. It was her spy training, Jane supposed. The older woman managed to pull all sorts of information from Abel while they ate.

Jane listened with interest, learning that the reason for his visit was to interview for a job opening at the Ellis & Smith offices in Vancouver. He was hoping to transfer back to Canada, and Vancouver was just fine with him since Edie was there and his parents were making noises about moving to be closer to Edie when his father retired next year. Abel hadn't told Edie yet, though; he didn't want to get her hopes up in case he didn't get the position. Still, he thought his chances were good. He worked hard for his company, and they wanted to keep him and keep him happy—something he managed to say with a complete lack of ego that impressed Jane.

Gran and Abel talked and Jane listened long after the sandwiches and coffee were gone, but eventually the pair fell silent and dozed off. Even Tinkle settled to sleep with her head on Gran's lap, leaving Jane alone with the road and her thoughts. Her thoughts, of course, drifted immediately to Edie. Concern quickly followed. Despite her confidence when she spoke to Abel on the subject, Jane wasn't at all sure that they'd catch up to whoever had kidnapped her friend and neighbor—or what they should or could do if they did. Abel was an accountant and Jane was a design engineer, for heaven's sake! And not a very respectable one either, she thought dismally as she considered her latest inventions. Shrink-wrap condoms and missile-launching vibrators? Dear Lord, she didn't know what she'd been thinking.

It didn't matter that Ira Manetrue and Y thought they held promise; Jane always doubted the usefulness of her inventions until they proved themselves. For instance, at that moment she was berating herself for not making the trackers capable of longer distance. True, these were just prototypes and she'd kept them short-range for testing, but . . .

She thought of Edie as she'd last seen her: excited to be going on her first date in a while, glowing practically. Where was she now? And why had she used only one of the trackers so far? It was well past midnight on Friday. Saturday morning now. Edie had borrowed the six-pack at around five-thirty the day before. That was well over twenty-four hours. There should be other yellow beacons for neutralized trackers that had been used and discarded.

And why, Jane asked herself, hadn't she thought to design something that could tell the state of the person being tracked? They didn't even know if they were following a live Edie or not.

"Do you think she's okay?"

Jane gave a start at Abel's question. She'd thought he was sleeping. Apparently he wasn't, and his mind traveled a similar path to her own.

"Yes. Otherwise they probably would have dumped her body." Jane came up with that insensitive answer out of desperation, but even as she said it she saw the logic. As long as the beacon was moving, there was a good chance Edie was still alive.

Abel fell silent again, and when she glanced at him moments later his eyes were closed.

Night crept by in a slow haze of glaring lights and

endless highway. Jane slipped an Enrique Iglesias CD into the player and turned it on low. The action roused Abel enough for him to mutter, "Good tape." Then he shifted and seemed to drop off to sleep again.

When she pulled over to get gas at the next station, Gran woke up but he didn't. Jane took Tinkle for another walk, bought a chocolate bar for energy, then pulled out the laptop to check Edie's position. She was a bit surprised to find that the beacon hadn't moved since she'd last checked. They were now only fifty miles behind the red blip. Jane was grateful that Abel was asleep at that point. It was possible that Edie's captors had merely stopped for a nap, but it was equally possible his sister's body was dumped along the roadside. Jane found herself once again wishing she'd thought to include something that would inform her of the state of the trackee.

She toyed with possibilities as she drove for the next little while, then glanced down to see that the beacon was moving again. Jane nearly cried out with relief, but remembering her sleeping companions at the last moment she swallowed the sound. Edie lived! She hadn't been dumped. She had to be alive, Jane assured herself. It was then she decided that a little speeding wouldn't go amiss. There would be very little police activity on the highway at night, she was sure. And even if there was . . .

She spared a quick glance in Abel's direction, smiling when she saw that he was definitely asleep. No man's face looked that unguarded while awake. He looked younger, the lines of worry smoothed away. She peered at him for a moment longer than she really should have, and had the oddest urge to brush her fingers through his thick hair.

Reining in her thoughts, she kept her fingers to herself and turned back to the road, then pushed a button on the dashboard. A small screen opened above the speedometer. This was one of her earlier inventions. It had been inspired by her frequent speeding, but had turned out to be quite handy to agents over the last couple of years as well. It would be useful to her right now. It was a cop finder. Not a speed trap finder, a cop finder. It zeroed in on police-band radios rather than radar and was handy in helping to avoid the law anywhere. The screen was fuzzy for a moment, then cleared to show that while there appeared to be a police unit some distance behind them, the road ahead was clear.

Leaving the machine open, Jane eased her foot down on the gas pedal. It was time to close some distance between. If at all possible she'd rather try to free Edie while on the highway, maybe while the woman's captors were at a rest stop getting food or something. Jane knew the chances of getting that lucky were slim, but it seemed important that they get an opportunity for a rescue attempt before Edie and her captors reached their final destination.

Jane had considered using the cop finder earlier, but she hadn't been able to come up with a way to explain the contraption to Abel. She sighed now. Things would be so much easier if she could just be straight with the guy about where she worked and what she did. However, B.L.I.S.S. was very strict with their confidentiality clauses, and a friend's life wasn't important enough to them to have that confidentiality broken. Compared to world security, a friend meant nothing.

Jane understood that, but she didn't have to like it.

*　　*　　*

Abel was having an erotic dream. Jane was lying on top of him, planting wet little kisses on his face. Murmuring softly in his sleep, he placed an arm around her to cuddle her close, then stiffened in surprise as she growled at him.

"Jane?" he muttered uncertainly.

"Tinkle," her voice hissed, but from the side rather than from where she lay on his chest. Abel's confusion was enough to force him from sleep. He opened his eyes to find himself nose-to-nose with his furry nemesis. Tinkle growled, and Abel jerked upright in surprise, sending the fur-ball tumbling to the floor. The dog took a moment to growl at him threateningly, then scampered back to leap up on the bench seat beside its sleeping mistress.

"I'm sorry."

Jane's voice drew his attention as she pushed a button on the dashboard. A whirring sound reached his ears as his seat slowly returned to an upright position. Obviously, she'd put his seat down while he'd slept to make him more comfortable.

"I tried to keep Tinkle off of you, but I couldn't drive and grab her at the same time." She shrugged.

Abel grunted and wiped the sleep from his eyes. He glanced around. It was still dim in the van, but the sky was brightening outside. He turned toward the back at another growl from Tinkle, and noted that Jane's grandmother was upright in her seat but sound asleep and snoring like a foghorn. The mutt was baring its teeth at him, looking like a ferocious rat with a bad wig.

Damned mutt, he thought and glanced back at Jane. Though he couldn't see her very well in the gloom, he thought she looked exhausted and had to wonder how long he'd slept. Had they closed any more of the distance between Edie and themselves?

Edie. Fear welled up within him for her and he began to fret over her predicament. Had whoever it was hurt her? Knocked her out? Threatened her somehow to make her go with them? He tried to tell himself they couldn't have hurt her badly. They must have used threats; otherwise they couldn't have got her across the border.

The border. He stiffened. How *had* they managed to get her across the border? Surely his sister would have tried to signal to the customs guard that she was an unwilling captive.

"How do you think they got her through customs?" he asked. It was out of his mouth before he realized he was going to ask.

Jane glanced at the man next to her. He'd been sleeping for a solid eight hours—much longer than she'd expected, but probably good for him.

It was just past seven in the morning. Thanks to Jane's lead foot, and another stop their quarry had taken, they'd caught up with Edie's captors a little better than an hour ago. The tracker had helped Jane zero in on the exact vehicle and she'd been following it, hoping yet fearing that it might pull over at any time and give them the opportunity to try to free Abel's sister.

Jane had kept her distance, not wanting to draw attention to the fact that they were following the other car as they'd trailed it south onto Route 99 then east on Route 12. It had also been dark then, so she hadn't been able to see it at first as anything more than a dark shape. But the sky lightened as the sun made its appearance, and she'd gotten close enough as they'd turned south onto Route 49 that she'd finally been able to make out what sort of vehicle they followed. Now Tinkle was making a nuisance of herself.

Jane peered at Abel again, wondering whether she dared tell him the truth. She doubted he'd take it well. She wasn't taking it well herself.

"I'm sorry I fell asleep on you," Abel said, then repeated the question he'd asked a moment before. The one she'd hoped he'd forget. "How do you think they got her across the border? She would have said or done something to get help had she been awake," he reasoned. "But she *had* to be awake. Surely the customs people wouldn't have allowed them to transport an unconscious woman across the border?"

Deciding that nothing would be gained by keeping the information to herself, Jane announced bluntly, "They brought Edie through customs in a hearse."

Chapter Six

As she had feared, Abel didn't take the news well. His indrawn breath and the horror on his face were pretty telling. Still, Jane was startled when he bellowed, "She's dead?"

Gran stirred on the seat behind them but managed to sleep through the explosion.

"No. I'm sure she isn't," Jane soothed. "If she were dead, I don't think they'd bother transporting her all the way down here. They'd have dumped the body. I think they must want her alive for something." She allowed that to sink in, then added, "I suspect she's drugged in the back of the hearse and was brought across the border as a supposed corpse."

She gestured to the dark vehicle on the road ahead and Abel stared at it unhappily.

"You mean, she's probably lying unconscious in a coffin in the back of that hearse?"

"Yes," Jane admitted reluctantly. It was something she'd rather not think of: Edie trapped in a coffin. The fact that she was most likely drugged, didn't make it any better, although it would explain why she hadn't used more of her borrowed trackers during the past thirty-eight hours. It might also explain why Edie and her captors had only made it as far as Washington before Jane had thought to check the tracking program. She pointed that out to Abel: "They probably brought her through customs as a dead family member. That would explain why they hadn't got very far when I found them on the tracker. If they took her any time Thursday night, they should have been out of range by the time I looked Friday afternoon," she went on. "But I think perhaps they had to manufacture paperwork and such to get her across the border as a supposed corpse."

"Corpse." Abel winced at the word, then leaned forward in his seat anxiously as the hearse they followed rounded a curve in the road and briefly disappeared from sight. "Speed up. You could lose them," he ordered.

"If I stay too close, they might realize that we're following. I'd rather not get their guard up. Surprise could be very useful in getting your sister back."

When Abel sat, hands fisted, anxiously scanning the way ahead, Jane suggested, "Why don't you get the laptop out? I closed it and set it on the floor once I was sure which vehicle we were following."

He immediately snatched up the laptop and satellite dish.

Jane ran through the instructions to open the tracking program, hoping that being able to see the blinking beacon would make it easier for him when the vehicle was out of sight, but it didn't. Abel stared at the screen for several moments, glanced at the road ahead to see that the hearse still wasn't in sight, and said, "You've been awake an awfully long time. Maybe I should drive for a little bit."

"Just watch the laptop," Jane suggested wearily. She *was* tired, and she *had* been driving a long time, but she wasn't willing to give him the wheel. She didn't trust him not to ram the vehicle ahead or something else in a mad attempt to retrieve his sister. In her estimation, the man wasn't thinking very clearly at the moment, and she hadn't trailed Edie all the way to California to let him get them all killed.

"Sonora," Maggie Spyrus said sleepily.

"Sonora?" Jane glanced in the rearview mirror to find her grandmother peering around and straightening in her seat.

"That's what the sign said. Welcome to Sonora," Gran explained. She began digging in her purse. Soon she was poking a comb at her hair and taking out her compact to powder her nose. Gran never looked anything less than presentable.

She wouldn't have been caught dead in ripped jeans and with no makeup.

Jane turned her attention back to the road ahead, surprised to find that the red dirt hills and trees they'd been driving past for the last little while had given way to actual buildings. They'd reached habitation. She very much suspected that meant the vehicle they were following would be stopping soon, but she didn't have a clue what to do about it. She'd thought earlier that if they pulled into a rest stop, she and Abel might manage to spirit Edie away while the kidnappers were using the facilities.

But if they'd reached the area of their final destination, Edie's captors probably wouldn't stop; they'd most likely go directly to wherever they were taking her. Someplace that would probably have a lot more people to deal with than one or two fellows who may or may not be armed.

Jane found herself tensing more with every mile that passed, considering all the possibilities of what was to come. She very much feared that Abel wouldn't care how many kidnappers there were or whether they were armed. He seemed wound up tight enough to try something foolish that would get him and his sister killed. She began searching her mind for a way to prevent such an occurrence.

Busy thinking up and discarding possible scenarios, Jane was taken by surprise when the hearse she followed suddenly turned to the right and stopped. She nearly drove straight up behind it. Fortunately, at the last moment she regained her wits and continued past down the road.

"A gated community." Abel craned around in his seat to glare at the vehicle she'd passed. It sat before a white metal gate. "Turn around, turn around! They're there!"

Jane ground her teeth and continued on, taking a curve in the road that put them out of sight of the hearse. Only then did she pull into a driveway to turn around.

"Hurry up, hurry up!" Abel cried, craning his neck to look back, though the bend in the road meant he could see nothing.

Jane deliberately took her time backing up. She was hoping that the hearse would be through the gate and beyond their reach by the time they returned. What if Abel tried lunging out of the vehicle and attacking his sister's abductors? The last thing she wanted was to see him killed on a California street.

"Damn it!" Abel cursed as they drove back to find the hearse gone and the gate swinging closed.

"Abel." Jane tried a soothing tone as she pulled up to the gate and stopped, but he wasn't listening. He opened his door.

"I'll have to climb this fence and—"

"You'd better take this," Gran said. Jane glanced back at the same time Abel did. Recognizing the compact her grandmother held and noting the way the woman's lips were rounded in preparation of blowing, Jane instinctively pulled back behind her seat. A puff of powder blew straight into Abel's face.

"Wha—' " He began in confused tones, then slumped forward in his seat. He was turned sideways, held in place thanks only to his seat belt.

Jane caught her laptop before it slid off his limp knees, and turned to glance sharply at her grandmother. "Gran!"

"My, my, my. Your knockout compact works very nicely, doesn't it?" Gran crowed as she closed the container and replaced it in her purse. "And so quickly. You're a brilliant inventor, dear. I could have used that a time or two back in my day."

"Gran," Jane growled, eyeing her grandmother's close-held bag and wondering once again what it contained. Maggie Spyrus was trouble on wheels, and there was no doubting it. Her propensity to steal Jane's inventions from the workroom and "test them out for her"—usually on neighbors—was the reason Jane had hired Jill. It was purely to keep the woman out of trouble. Coming home to find nice old Mrs. Jakobowski asleep on the floor, or old Mr. Flynn dancing around in a tutu singing bawdy sailor tunes, had been disconcerting for Jane to say the least. It had also put her position at risk.

"Well," Jane's gran said mildly in response to her growl, "he was starting to get on my nerves, dear. I understand that he's terribly worried about his sister, but really, he's more likely to get the poor dear killed than to save her the way he was going off half-cocked."

Since that had been her own concern, Jane could hardly argue. Sighing, she peered at the body in the passenger seat.

"How long is he going to be unconscious?" Gran asked with interest.

"It depends on how much powder you blew his way and how much he inhaled," Jane answered. "It looked to me like a good bit."

"Yes, I blew pretty hard," Gran agreed.

Jane pondered. "Okay. He could be out anywhere from thirty minutes to a couple of hours," she decided.

"Hmmm. That will do, I suppose," her gran said. "So what are you planning?"

"With him?" Jane glanced at her unconscious passenger.

"No. About the gate."

"Oh." Jane glanced at the gate, then at the number pad outside her window, and shifted into park. "I guess I'm going to have to use the calculator."

"Oh, my, yes, that's a good idea," Gran said brightly as Jane climbed out of her seat and slunk toward the back of the van. "I'd forgotten about that. Another very clever invention, my dear. Your genes were proving themselves when you came up with that."

"Thanks, Gran," Jane muttered. She grabbed her briefcase and moved quickly back to her seat.

"Perhaps you should switch on the restraints,

Janie dear. Just in case Abel wakes up. He may not have inhaled as much as we hope and could be trouble."

Jane debated briefly, then sighed and flipped a switch on the console. Padded metal bands immediately closed over Abel's legs, waist, and shoulders. They were another invention of hers, ones she'd tested in this van but had never really thought to use herself.

She opened her case and retrieved her day planner/wallet. From that she retrieved the calculator that rested in the small front pocket. A handy little deal, Jane often used it while shopping and such, but this would be the first time she'd used the calculator for its original purpose.

Sliding open a panel on the back, she withdrew two clips attached by wires, then unrolled her window so that she could reach the gate's number pad. People who lived inside this gated community likely used this panel to punch in the code to open the gate; visitors buzzed to be let in. Everyone else was supposed to be kept out by it. Jane hooked her B.L.I.S.S. code-breaking calculator up, pushed the clear and division buttons at one time, then waited. The code she needed would soon be shown on the small screen.

She'd come up with this idea after one of her grandmother's stories. Gran's tales of her days in the spy business had led to a lot of Jane's inventions. Maggie would mention a problem she'd encountered, and Jane would find herself trying to come up with ways to overcome such a problem.

"You'd better hurry, dear."

Jane glanced around in question, and her grandmother gestured toward a middle aged woman wearing the most god-awful yellow day dress she'd ever seen. The woman was walking down the road toward a small set of mailboxes next to the gate. It seemed even the postman wasn't allowed inside this elite community.

Her calculator gave a soft beep, drawing Jane's gaze back. Four numbers appeared on the screen. Jane quickly unhooked the two clips and set the calculator out of sight on the floor. She punched in the necessary numbers, and was relieved when the gate swung open. Positive the approaching woman hadn't seen her gizmo or its wires, Jane managed a smile and nod when she raised a hand in greeting. She then pushed the button to raise her black-tinted windows, and drove forward.

"What are we going to do?" Gran asked, leaning forward so that her face was next to Jane's.

"I'm not sure. Find out which house Edie's kidnappers went to and then . . . er, come up with a plan, I guess."

A glance in the rearview mirror showed Gran nodding. "Good thinking," she said. "Plans are important. Good agents never rush in without a plan. Well . . . rarely."

Jane felt relief flit through her. She could handle planning. Might even come up with a good one. Also her relief was because Gran thought there was time for a plan, which meant she didn't think Edie was in immediate danger.

"There it is."

Jane slowed the van. She hadn't been driving fast to begin with as she followed this curving lane past the gate, but she slowed almost to a stop as they passed the driveway where the hearse they'd followed was parked. It sat before a huge house, one of the largest Jane had ever seen. But she paid little attention to the mansion, her attention fixed on the six men standing out front. As she watched, one of them got into the hearse and started the engine, while another walked into a side door of a huge garage. A moment later one of the garage's two main doors opened and the hearse pulled inside. The men all followed. One opened the back door of the vehicle, revealing a dark wooden coffin.

Jane had no doubt that Edie was inside that coffin, and she had the almost overwhelming urge to slam on the brakes and rush out to rescue her. She knew darned well that, if Abel was awake, he'd have already been halfway up the driveway. But even as she pondered, the garage door began to close.

"You'd better speed up, dear. No one appears to have noticed us yet, but I don't think we want them to."

Jane hesitated. "But shouldn't I . . . ?"

"An agent never rushes in, dear. I know you want to help Edie, but you could do more harm than good if you try engaging the enemy now. An agent investigates her situation, learns all there is to know, and determines the best way to handle things."

"I'm not an agent, Gran," Jane said wearily. "I haven't the first clue how to investigate or handle this."

"We'll stake it out, of course."

"How? It's a gated community. There's almost no traffic here. Certainly no vehicles on the road. A van sitting around would draw notice." Even that was an understatement. The van would stand out like a sore thumb. In fact, they were already lucky the men gathered around the hearse had been too distracted to notice them. No doubt their very presence made them stand out on this road, for it led nowhere but circled back to the gate. "It's a shame there isn't a hotel or something nearby."

"Hmm. Yes." Gran was silent, her gaze moving over the houses along this select road; then she pulled a cell phone out of her bag. Jane eyed the purse anxiously, wishing she could look through it. What Maggie Spyrus might have in there was scary.

"Who are you calling?" Jane asked when her grandmother started to punch in a number.

"I'm calling in a favor." Maggie put the phone to her ear, then met Jane's gaze in the rearview mirror as she waited for someone to pick up on the other end. "You really should get moving, dear."

Jane pressed down on the gas pedal. When she returned to the gate she asked, "Where to now?"

She knew where she wanted to go: around the circle again. Jane was reluctant to leave Edie behind like this. But, abandoning her friend or not, it was risky to drive around again.

"Head for town," Gran instructed. "We'll have something to eat."

Jane passed through the gate when it opened and turned the van back toward the town they'd seen earlier.

As it happened, they didn't go all the way back. Gran—who hadn't been able to reach her friend, but had left a brief message with the particulars of their situation—spotted a little café called Perko's. Hanging up, she suggested they stop for breakfast.

Exhausted, and knowing she could do with the energy boost that food would offer, Jane pulled into the parking lot.

"What about Abel?" Gran asked as they parked. Turning off the engine, Jane glanced at the man and undid her seat belt. He was still sound asleep and likely to remain so for another half hour or so. Perhaps it would even be an hour if he'd inhaled most of the powder her gran had used.

"We'll leave him be for now," she decided. "He should sleep for a while yet, and if he wakes before we return . . ." She shrugged. "This van is sound-proof, and he won't get out of these restraints."

"Yes," Gran agreed. "This will also give us time to decide what to do with him."

The comment sounded ominous to Jane, but she let it go and opened her door. She got Gran's wheel-chair out and had the woman in it relatively quickly, despite Tinkle's repeated attempts to slip past out of the van. After being sure she had her phone and wallet, Jane locked the van and pushed Gran into the restaurant. Not that she really needed to push the wheelchair: As well as being full of gadgets and gizmos, the chair was self-propelled.

Once seated in one of the café's vinyl booths, with Gran's wheelchair pulled up to the end of the table, Jane took the time to look around. The café was decorated in teal and maroon, with country wallpaper and dried wreaths. The waitress who approached was young, all smiles, and had a perky ponytail that bobbed and swung as she talked. Her good cheer and energy made Jane feel about a hundred years old. But then she'd been up for almost twenty-four hours now, Jane reminded herself, refusing to tuck up the hairs that had come free from her own ponytail.

The waitress gave a cheerful greeting and might have mentioned specials or some such thing as she handed Jane and Maggie each a huge menu; Jane couldn't be sure. Now that she was out from behind the steering wheel, her brain had shut down. The waitress's words all sounded like a cheerful "blah blah blah," and Jane found her mind drifting and her eyes crossing. She stared at the lemon-yellow uniform the girl wore, relieved when she went away and left them to their menus.

"I'm starved," Gran said as she glanced over the selections available. Jane wasn't terribly surprised. A sandwich and a bunch of snack items were all they'd eaten since embarking on this journey. She was starved herself. And jumpy too, she realized when Gran's cell phone gave a sharp ring.

"That will be . . . my friend," Gran said.

As her relative answered the phone, Jane forced herself to relax. She listened as Gran said "yes" over and over. Maggie Spyrus had only left the bare bones of the situation in her message; Edie's name, her situation, the name of the company she worked for, and Sonora, the town they'd arrived in. Apparently, however, that was enough to generate a great deal of information.

"Really?" Gran said, her gaze moving to Jane as if to say, "You see?" But Jane didn't see. She didn't have a clue what was being said on the other end of the phone.

Losing interest in the one-sided conversation, she let her eyes drift around the restaurant again, this time paying more attention to the other diners. It took a minute or so for her weary mind to process what she was seeing as her glance drifted from person to person, but then she stiffened in her seat, her weariness forced aside by panic.

"What is it?" Gran asked, noting her alarm.

Leaning across the table Jane hissed, "This place is crawling with cops."

Maggie Spyrus relaxed at once. She glanced around at the different uniforms worn by those around them. There had to be at least three different types; federal, state, and Sonoran policemen made up three-quarters of the café's clientele. It was like a police convention.

"So? We haven't done anything wrong," Gran said with disinterest.

"I don't think Abel would agree with that. Knocking him out and restraining him are—" She sat up abruptly. "That isn't kidnapping, is it? Using those restraints and parking him there? No," she answered her own hisses with a frown. "He wanted to come to Sonora."

"Relax," Gran instructed, then paused to listen to her phone. A moment later she said, "Madge says the main offices for the state and county police are here in Sonora. It has three branches of law enforcement plus forest rangers. The town has very little crime."

"Tell Edie that," Jane muttered, but she did relax a bit. Abel was in the van. Restrained. It wasn't like he was going to jump out any minute screaming.

"Well!"

The word drew Jane from her thoughts to see Gran close her cell phone and set it on the table. She raised an eyebrow in question and waited for an explanation of the older woman's good cheer.

"Madge says that you're brilliant."

"Why is that?" Jane asked doubtfully.

"Because B.L.I.S.S., as well as the Feds and several other agencies, have been eyeballing Edie's employer Ensecksi Satellites, for some time. Now it seems you've managed to catch them at something illegal. You might even end up with an inside contact. It's enough to start a full-scale investigation."

"Hmm," Jane said. "Yes. It *was* brilliant of me to spill my stuff all over the bathroom floor and be too lazy to clean it up so that Edie would borrow a tampon tracker and be traceable when her evil boss kidnapped her."

Gran chuckled at her dry tone. "Darling, don't belittle yourself. You know the saying that some of the best inventions are accidents? Well, it's true of the spy business too. Some of the biggest take downs have started with an agent stumbling into something unexpectedly. Why, I remember the time I—"

"Gran."

"Yes, dear?"

"What's your friend going to do?"

"Hmm." She pursed her lips and eyed Jane speculatively as if trying to decide how much to say.

"Gran," Jane growled in a warning tone. The older woman sighed.

"Oh, very well. B.L.I.S.S. is buying the house next door to the one Edie is in, and we're—"

"Buying the house?" Jane interrupted. "I didn't notice a house for sale over there."

"It isn't, dear."

"Well, then, how are they going to—"

"Please, Jane. This is B.L.I.S.S. They have their ways. In truth, they probably won't actually buy it. They'll bounce the family who lives there out and take it over for the duration of the operation, then let them back in when it's over. They'll just make it look like it was sold and—"

"Bounce them out?"

"Lower your voice, dear. You're drawing the attention of those hunky policemen over there. My . . . they do grow them handsome here, don't they?" Maggie wondered.

Jane rubbed her forehead and tried for some patience as her grandmother smiled and winked at one of the "hunks."

"Gran."

"Hmm?" The woman glanced at her distractedly.

"Are you saying that B.L.I.S.S. is now aware that Edie borrowed my trackers—highly secret B.L.I.S.S. paraphernalia that no one is supposed to know about? And that they know we tracked her all the way to California with her brother Abel, who is currently locked up in the van?" Jane asked with extreme calm. She very much feared she would be bounced down to the basement when she returned to work on Monday. *If* she returned to work on Monday.

"Of course not, dear," Gran said. Jane was just beginning to relax when she added, "I led Madge to believe that Edie had come to you with suspicions that something was going on at work, that you deliberately had her wear the tracker for her 'meeting,' and that Abel is with us because Edie had already made him aware of the situation and he was in on it from the first."

Jane groaned and lowered her head toward the table, stopping abruptly when a cup of coffee was suddenly set beneath it.

"Here you are, ladies! Have you decided on what you'd like for breakfast?"

Jane turned baleful eyes on the perky waitress and found herself nearly blinded again by the woman's yellow uniform. "That's quite some outfit," she commented.

"Isn't it?" The girl beamed as she glanced down at herself. "It's so new and bright. We use to wear maroon chinos, but the boss thought these were more cheerful."

"Yes. They are that," Jane agreed politely, then cleared her throat and glanced down at the menu she'd opened but not really looked at. Her eyes were exhausted and watery and didn't want to focus. She closed the menu. "I'll have the special."

"Over easy or sunny-side up?"

"Excuse me?" Jane stared at her blankly.

"Your eggs. In the special?" the girl explained. "Over easy or sunny-side up?"

"Oh. Over easy."

"The same for me," Gran announced, handing over her menu. "Thank you."

The girl left them alone again, and Jane glanced around toward an older couple entering the restaurant. The man was wearing a rather loud Hawaiian top in purples and oranges that clashed horribly, both with each other and with the jaundiced yellow sundress his wife wore.

"Dear Lord, what is it with the women in this town and the color yellow?" Jane asked with despair as she turned her beleaguered eyes away.

"Hmmm?" Gran glanced at her in question.

"Well, look around," Jane suggested, peering over the customers in the restaurant. The number of police here wasn't the only oddity. Aside from the waitresses, there were four female customers, and every one of them was wearing a yellow dress. Different shades, different styles, but all yellow dresses. And every male not in a police uniform appeared to be wearing a Hawaiian shirt.

"That could be it . . ." Gran admitted with a thoughtful frown.

"What?" Jane asked.

"Well, there's some suspicion at B.L.I.S.S. that Ensecksi Satellites is using microwaves, along with some new unknown technology, for mind control. They'd have to test it somehow."

"And you think they're testing it by making every-

one wear yellow dresses and loud Hawaiian shirts?"
Jane asked doubtfully.

"Why not? It would be a perfectly harmless test
and wouldn't raise any suspicion in the authorities.
That woman at the gate was wearing yellow too,"
Maggie added, then beamed at her granddaughter.
"It was clever of you to notice, dear. Especially
since you aren't into fashion yourself."

"Hmm." Jane ignored the insult and peered at the
yellow uniforms and dresses with new eyes. "Maybe
this is the 'something strange' Edie stumbled on to
at work. Maybe she overheard or read something
about this."

"That could very well be."

"But, why would they drag her all the way down
here over that?"

"Perhaps they want to know how much she
knows and just who she's told about it."

"Maybe," Jane agreed, then fell silent as their
waitress returned with two plates of eggs and bacon. Jane's stomach growled the moment the scent
hit her nose. Letting go of the conversation, she began to eat.

But moments later she pushed her plate away.
"So, they're going to buy the house next door to the
place where Edie is," she asked. She was completely stuffed. Which wasn't a bad feeling except
that now that she'd eaten, rather than being lifted
her exhaustion seemed to be settling about her
more firmly. Too many carbs, Jane thought, reaching for coffee to try to shake off her lassitude. "Then
what?"

"Then we're to move in and stake it out."

"What?" Jane woke up a bit at that announcement. "But we're—"

"The only agents in the vicinity at the moment,"

Gran finished with satisfaction. "They want to get on this right away, and most of the top agents are on other assignments."

"Gran, I'm not an agent. Neither is Abel."

"But I was."

" '*Was*' being the important word there."

Maggie Spyrus waved the comment away. "I know the business. I can teach you. You'll do fine."

"Gran, Edie's life is at stake. I can't—"

"Do you think you'll be able to convince Abel just to leave it to some unknown and possibly sloppy second string agent and go home?" her relative asked pointedly. When Jane remained silent, Gran continued, "And what do you think he'll do?"

"There isn't much he *can* do. He doesn't know which house she's in."

"But he does know which community, and he knows the Ensecksi name. He'd harass the police and insist they search and ask questions. He'll probably do so himself as well, and stir up all sorts of trouble. The Ensecksis will know at once that there is a problem. They'll get rid of any damning evidence and take down shop for a while."

"I suppose Edie would be some of the damning evidence?"

"I would guess so."

"Maybe we could convince him to—"

"Jane, darling. You saw him back at the gate. He won't be reasonable when it comes to Edie. My goodness, you're just a friend, yet I know you were considering charging out of the van after that hearse when it pulled into that garage. And you're one of the most cautious members of our family. No. He won't let this go and return home. But if he's informed as to what's going on and allowed to participate, he may be controllable."

"Controllable," Jane echoed. Abel didn't really seem the controllable type to her.

"Come. You're exhausted. We'll go shopping, then rent a room and get some sleep."

"Shopping?" Jane asked with disbelief.

"Yes. Shopping. I've been wearing this dress for twenty-four hours now and am quite ready for a change. Besides, it'll kill time while we wait to hear back from . . . Madge."

Groaning, Jane pulled money out of her day planner/wallet to cover their bill and a tip, then wheeled Gran out of the restaurant.

Exhausted and distracted, she stopped the wheelchair by the side door of the van and opened it. The enraged roar that immediately issued from inside made her promptly slam it shut again.

Chapter Seven

Jane glanced around the empty parking lot, relieved to see that no one else had been privy to Abel's rage.

"Good Tinkle. Good doggie. Yes, you're a clever girl, aren't you?"

Jane glanced down at the Yorkie yipping and hopping around Gran's wheelchair. The beast had apparently slid out of the van in the few short seconds the door had been open. Gran was acting as if it were a major achievement.

"Abel seems upset," Jane pointed out, just in case her gran had missed the fact.

"Yes. It would appear so," Maggie Spyrus agreed. She chuckled. "He has a fine set of lungs, doesn't he?"

"This isn't funny, Gran," Jane said. Her stern tones

merely brought forth a louder laugh from the older woman.

"Of course it is, Janie, dear. Where's your sense of humor?"

Jane rolled her eyes and turned to peer into the van. Of course, with its blacked-out windows she could no more see in than anyone else could. But she could imagine Abel straining and struggling beneath the restraints as he bellowed and roared. Her gaze returned to her grandmother. "Now what?"

Maggie Spyrus considered. "I think you should hop back in and knock him out again, dear."

"Knock him out?" Jane's eyes widened incredulously.

"Yes, dear," her gran acknowledged, as if it were the most reasonable suggestion in the world.

Jane supposed it was reasonable to Maggie Spyrus, field operative extraordinaire. Which just proved to Jane that she'd made the right career decision by going into the technical side of the espionage business. She would never manage to be blasé about knocking someone unconscious.

"I'll be right back." Leaving her grandmother and Tinkle, she walked around the van. She peered quickly about to be sure there was still no one about, then opened the driver-side door. As before, shouting immediately issued from within, but this time Jane was prepared. She jumped into the driver's seat, pulled the door closed, and waited for Abel's bellowing to cease. Waited. And waited.

Her presence didn't make him stop, but his yelling did become more intelligible and Jane winced at some of the words pouring forth. He seemed pretty annoyed. Understandably, she supposed.

Jane waited another moment for his rage to wind

down, but when it showed no signs she decided she'd best intervene. After all, Gran and Tinkle couldn't wait in the parking lot forever. Jane considered yelling to get Abel's attention, but she doubted he'd hear her over his own bellows. She considered knocking him out again after all, but the only thing in the van to do the trick was the knockout lipstick that Lipschitz had designed—and Jane didn't think Abel would close his mouth long enough to be kissed. She might have jumped out and retrieved the compact from Gran, but she didn't want to risk some policeman leaving the restaurant at the wrong moment and hearing Abel's wrath.

Finally she grabbed her briefcase and found a piece of paper. She scribbled *Must I knock you out again to shut you up?* on it, hoping the threat would silence him since she wasn't at all sure she was capable of actually carrying it out.

Fortunately, holding up the sign had the effect of shutting him up. For a moment. Then another stream of fury poured forth, this time about his being knocked out. Apparently, he hadn't realized that was the case. Interesting. She should have expected that, of course. Jane recalled that the test subjects for the knockout dust had shown disorientation upon awakening as well. The drug tended to scramble some memories; she hadn't realized just how much. The tests they'd performed on the compact so far were to find out how long the subject would be out and whether he suffered any telling physical discomfort afterward. They hadn't finished everything. She'd have to make a note to learn how much pre-knockout memory was affected, she thought, then realized that Abel's anger had wound down and he'd at last fallen silent. He was glaring. It was obvious she wasn't his favorite person.

"I'm sorry," she began sincerely. "Gran only knocked you out to prevent your getting yourself or Edie killed by doing something wild."

"Wild?" He looked at her as if she were insane. "I'm an accountant! We aren't wild! We're cautious and meticulous and boring!"

"Really?" she asked with interest. "Is that how you see yourself? You don't seem boring to me."

He didn't look pleased by her compliment.

Jane sighed. "Well, your standing as an accountant aside, you were quite wound up and obviously prepared to try to save Edie right there. Which would have been foolish. Her abductors were probably armed."

"I see," he said stiffly. "And this?" He jerked against the padded metal bars holding his legs and arms.

"Oh, well . . . that was . . . so you wouldn't fall out of your seat?" Jane suggested, knowing it was a lame explanation even as she said it. He didn't appear to be buying it either, so she hurried on, "Look, just relax. I'll get Gran in the van, and then remove the restraints."

"Remove the restraints and then get your gran into the van," he countered.

"I can't. She has my purse with the keys." Jane lied calmly. The keys were nestled in her front right pocket, but she didn't trust Abel not to hop out of the van and cause trouble the moment he was free. She intended to only remove the restraints while the van was moving—there was then less likelihood of his leaping out. She hoped.

"I—"

"We're wasting time," Jane interrupted. "Time

that could be better spent figuring out how to get Edie back."

Abel snapped his mouth closed, and Jane felt relief seep through her.

"I'll be right back." She opened the door and slid out, relieved when he remained quiet.

Closing the door, Jane walked back around the van . . . to stop dead when she saw a police officer being attacked by Tinkle. Well, "attacked" was an ambitious description. The little fur-ball *did* have the man's boot in her mouth and *was* snarling and trying to jerk from side to side, but the cop was a bit more than she could manage. His boot wasn't moving. As for the officer, he was staring down at the Yorkie with a rather amused look on his face.

Gran berated the dog ineffectively. "Tinkle! Bad doggie! Let go of the nice policeman! Bad Tinkle. Bad!"

Jane closed her eyes, rubbed her forehead, and wondered how everything had gotten so out of control. Normally, she led the most serene life. Well, aside from nearly blowing off coworker's heads with her inventions.

"Oh, Janie, dear! Thank goodness! Make Tinkle let go of the nice policeman."

Jane opened her eyes and started forward again. Managing to produce an apologetic smile from somewhere deep inside, she bent to scoop up the dog, who promptly tried to bite her. Jane deposited the hellion in her grandmother's lap, then turned to face the officer. Like Abel, he was tall and well put together. Very well put together, Jane noted. And movie-star handsome with sandy brown hair, blue eyes, and strong features.

"You must be Janie."

He offered his hand and a dazzling smile that

Jane couldn't resist. She found herself grinning like an idiot as she placed her hand in his and said, "And you must be . . . that 'nice policeman.'"

"This is Officer Alkars, Jane," Gran announced. "He saw me sitting here alone and stopped to be sure I didn't need any help. I was just explaining that you'd gone to put our purses inside when Tinkle attacked him for no reason." She scowled down at her Yorkie. "Bad dog."

"I'm terribly sorry about that," Jane said as Officer Alkars's eyebrows rose at the lack of heat behind Gran's reprimand. "But thank you for stopping."

"Any time. It's my job," he pointed out, his smile widening. Then he nodded and turned to walk toward the restaurant.

Jane watched him go, thinking that Gran had been right: They did "grow them handsome" here.

"Is everything all right, dear?" Gran asked, drawing her attention away from Officer Alkars as he disappeared into the restaurant.

"Yes," Jane answered. "For now."

Much to her relief, Abel remained silent as Jane got Gran back into the van and stowed the wheelchair. But she could feel his furious eyes drilling holes into her as she worked.

"Dear, why don't you get Abel a breakfast to go? He must be starved," Gran suggested as Jane finished with the wheelchair and crawled out of the van. Prepared to close the side door, Jane paused and glanced between them. "I don't think—"

"I do," Gran said firmly. "Go. We'll be fine."

"No, wait!" Abel protested. "Remove the restraints first, and—"

Jane closed the door on the rest of Abel's protest and headed back into the restaurant. If Gran thought she could manage the man, let her try. It was more than Jane herself felt up to doing.

Jane approached the girl at the cash register with a forced smile. She wanted to wince. The bright yellow uniforms were still painful, but she knew that was only because her eyes were sore and tired from driving all night. She ordered a breakfast special and coffee to go, paid for it, then turned away, ostensibly to survey the other patrons, but really to avoid the glare of the yellow uniform as she waited for her order.

Her gaze drifted to the parked van in the lot and she worried over what Gran might be doing to poor Abel. Hopefully, she was convincing him to cooperate and not doing anything to increase his anger.

Jane sighed. If she thought for one minute that contacting the police would get Edie out safe and sound, she'd have a much easier time of it. But she didn't believe that. Instead Jane feared police intervention would lead to an armed standoff or Edie disappearing altogether. If the Ensecksis were under the eye of B.L.I.S.S., as well as the Feds, they were no small-time organization. The very fact that B.L.I.S.S. was unable to get information about them was enough to prove they had a pretty savvy setup. Calling in the local police would be like calling in the Keystone Cops. Not because the local police weren't likely perfectly competent, but because they simply wouldn't be prepared for this sort of mess. Mind control, she thought with a frisson of fear.

The door to the restaurant opened and Jane glanced nervously toward it. A young couple entered. Starting to turn back to the counter, relaxing, Jane paused, her gaze catching on their clothing. It was the same as everyone else's; the pretty blonde wore a gold sundress of simple design and the fellow wore a Hawaiian shirt.

Jane scowled. This had to be proof of the mind control Gran had suggested earlier. And it was the perfect test, she admitted to herself. A harmless yet telling fashion test.

"Can I get another cream there, Jennie?"

Jane glanced around to find Officer Alkars at her side. He smiled at her as he waited for the waitress to fetch his cream. "The food's so good you had to get some to go, hmm?" he asked conversationally.

Jane managed a smile and a nod.

"Your grandmother will be fine," the policeman assured her; then he explained, "You keep looking out at your van like you fear it is going to be stolen at any moment with her in it. She'll be fine. This is a pretty good town. Not much crime here. Sonora is the county seat, so we have the State Highway Patrol and the County Sheriff as well as the local police. Not much goes on." He grinned again. "Having all these police around scares criminals away."

"I know," Jane said, then could have kicked herself when his gaze sharpened. "That was a selling point in our coming here. No crime," she lied quickly.

"Have you moved here, or are you on vacation?" he asked.

Jane felt panic swamp her. She didn't know how to answer. If B.L.I.S.S. succeeded in buying the house next door to the one where Edie was being held, then she was going to be moving in. But what if they didn't?

"Here you go, ma'am."

Jane turned back to the counter with relief and didn't even mind being called ma'am. She knew she probably looked every one of her almost thirty years thanks to the long drive and lack of sleep. Forcing a smile, she took her coffee and the Styrofoam container of food, muttered a thanks, and then hurried out of the restaurant before Officer Alkars could ask another question she didn't want to answer.

Jane was moving at a quick clip as she left the restaurant, but her steps slowed when she spotted a car pulling into the parking lot. Distinctly recalling Abel's bellowing the first time she opened the van door—and the second time—and unsure what to expect when she opened it this time, Jane slowed, allowing the car to park and its passengers to spill out and make their way toward the restaurant. She wasn't terribly surprised to see yet another middle-aged woman in yellow with a laughing husband in a Hawaiian shirt, but the sight of the two preteen girls with them, both wearing equally yellow dresses, convinced Jane beyond all doubt there was something amiss in Sonora.

Returning the group's friendly smiles as she passed, Jane reached the van and began digging in her pocket as if in search of keys. She waited until the restaurant door had closed behind the family, then quickly opened the driver's door, leaped inside, and slammed it shut.

Much to her relief there was no bellowing this time. Still, she peered at the man in the passenger seat warily. Jane was so exhausted that it took a moment for her to notice that he was no longer in restraints. He also wasn't looking quite as angry, although he didn't exactly look friendly. Abel was eyeing her as if she were some dangerous exotic creature.

"It's time to book a motel room and get some rest," Maggie Spyrus announced firmly as Jane handed the coffee and Styrofoam container of food to Abel.

"I thought you wanted to shop for clothes," Jane said with surprise.

"Madge called. She said we were to check into a motel and sit tight. B.L.I.S.S. is arranging something."

"Did you tell her about all the yellow dresses?" Jane asked as she started the van.

"Yes. They thought it was terribly interesting. Now, let's find a motel before you fall asleep at the wheel."

Jane shrugged, unsure. She *was* exhausted and a nap sounded great, but she didn't trust Abel. While she was doing her napping, she might have to leave him in the restraints in the van. Or cuff him to a bed.

They didn't have to drive far to find a motel. Jane wasn't fussy, she pulled in at the first sign she saw: THE SONORA SUNSET INN. With one long row of rose-colored doors on a pink adobe building it looked terribly gawdy, but Jane didn't care as long as it wasn't yellow.

She parked in front of the door to the main office, left Gran and Abel in the van while she rented two rooms, managing to get them side by side. Then she parked the vehicle halfway between the two.

"Perhaps you should see me into my room first, Janie, dear. Then you can release Abel's leg restraints and cuff him to your wrists. You did bring handcuffs, didn't you?"

"Yes." Jane glanced with surprise at the metal band still around Abel's legs. It seemed Gran had only released the upper restraints, not the ones around his lower legs.

"I told you I wouldn't do anything to jeopardize

107

Edie," Abel said wearily, speaking for the first time since the restaurant.

"I know, dear boy. But love rarely has reason, and you might come up with what you think is a brilliant plan to rescue your sister and do something foolish. I like Edie too much to see you do something foolish."

Too tired to argue, Jane got out, slammed the door, and walked around the van. It took very little time to get Gran in her wheelchair, and Jane wheeled her into the first motel room with Tinkle following.

"I'll just settle Abel in the next room, then bring in Tinkle's food and the rest of the stuff and get you ready for bed," she suggested as she headed toward the door.

"No, dear. You'd better get me ready first, then bring Tinkle's food. Then you can settle in next door with Abel without worrying about me."

Jane paused in the doorway and turned slowly. "What?"

Gran grimaced. "We can't trust him yet, Janie. He will realize soon enough that the smartest route is to follow our lead, but in the meantime you can't leave him alone. You'll have to sleep with him handcuffed to you."

"But . . . Can't I just handcuff him to the bed in the next room and . . ." Her question died as Gran shook her head.

"He isn't a stupid boy. He might be able to unlock the cuffs."

"He isn't exactly Houdini, Gran. He—"

"Trust me, dear. You'll have to keep him close."

Slumping in defeat, Jane moved back toward her. "What if you need me?"

"I can call if I need anything. Trust me, you need to be with him more than me."

Abel stared at the door into which Jane and Maggie Spyrus had disappeared. He had no idea what was taking so long, but he suspected the two women were plotting what to do with him next. It was all right with him, though; it gave him the opportunity to berate himself. He couldn't believe he'd been such an idiot. Hell, he wasn't even sure yet the extent of his idiocy.

According to Maggie Spyrus, she and her granddaughter were agents working for some secret company named B.L.I.S.S. He'd laughed at that claim until she'd pointed out that he was sitting restrained in the passenger seat of a van. How many vans did he think were made with padded restraints? Which had killed his laughter and caught his attention long enough for her to point out more corroborative evidence: Edie was wearing a tracker. Jane, who supposedly worked for a toy company, had a mini satellite computer and a program to follow her. The old woman herself had knocked him out with powder from a face compact.

Abel had promptly bombarded Jane's gran with questions. Had Edie come to them with suspicions about her work? Had the Spyruses been planted as his sister's neighbors to watch over her and failed? Just what were they going to do about Edie's being kidnapped? Maggie hadn't answered any of his questions, however. She'd said she couldn't give him any more information until she had the okay from her superiors.

It all had convinced Abel to quit his shouting and struggling, but he wasn't sure how much to believe. If Jane and her grandmother were spies and had

been asked to keep his sister safe, why wasn't Edie
safe? And why had it taken so long for Jane to
check the tracker? Were they really just incompe-
tent spies? Or were they working with the Ensecksis? They seemed to want to keep him busy and out
of the way for some reason. He didn't know if he
was in the hands of the enemy or the good guys,
but he intended to find—.

Abel's thoughts came to a crashing halt when the
side door suddenly opened behind him. Shifting in
his seat, he craned his neck to see Jane leaning in
to collect Tinkle's empty dog cage.

"I'll only be a couple more minutes," she told
him, catching the cage under one arm and grabbing a bag of dog food.

Abel didn't comment. Not that she'd have heard
anyway; the words were barely out of her mouth
before she straightened, slid the door closed with
one elbow, then disappeared into the motel again.

She didn't take nearly as long this time, but when
she came back out, Abel was annoyed to see Jane
had Tinkle on a leash. She started walking along
the building with the animal, but the evil fur-ball
stopped and sat down, refusing to move. Jane
picked up the spoiled dog and carried it to the
patch of grass at the end of the motel.

Abel watched for several minutes before he realized that he wasn't being productive; his eyes
hadn't left Jane's butt in those tight frayed jeans for
the whole time! He immediately forced himself to
drop his gaze. It fell on the Styrofoam container on
his lap and he considered having something to eat.
He was hungry, but he knew that the moment he
started to eat, Jane would no doubt finish walking
her dog and come to fetch him.

He was right. His gaze raised to the woman and

dog again to see that Jane was carrying it back to the motel room. This time she was inside an even shorter amount of time than before, and when she came out and started toward the van, Abel had the vague hope that he was finally going to be released. But she bypassed his door. Opening the back, she began to drag out bags.

"I could help with that," he offered, his mind running over possible ways to get the upper hand and force her to tell him the truth about everything.

"No, thanks. I'll be right back." The hatch closed and he was left to watch Jane carry her bags into the second motel room. She made two trips. On the last she carried in Mr. Tibbs and all his paraphernalia. That time she was gone longer than the others, and Abel was beginning to think she planned to leave him in the van while she slept, but then the door opened and she slid out again. He felt himself tense as she moved to his door. Free at last!

It opened.

She smiled.

Click.

Abel stared down at the handcuff on his right wrist. It was attached to one on her left.

"It's electrified," she announced apologetically. Pushing a button, she removed his leg restraints. "Programmed so that if you struggle too much you get a zap. So we're going to have to be careful."

"I see." He raised his gaze to hers and challenged, "So I can't struggle. But what if I shout?"

"Then I press this." She held up her unencumbered right hand to reveal a small black box and pushed a button. Abel jerked in his seat as a shock ran up his arm from his wrist. It hurt! "It's set to low right now, Jane added. "I can set it higher."

Abel didn't miss the threat. He didn't appreciate

it much either. It was hard to believe these were the good guys. He'd barely had that thought when Jane explained, "I'm sorry, but like my gran I'm very fond of Edie. We've become good friends. I won't risk her brother doing something foolish to get her killed."

"I'm an accountant," Abel reiterated wearily. "Foolish isn't in my vocabulary." When Jane didn't appear convinced, he heaved a sigh. "Can I at least get out now?"

"Sure." She stepped back so he could.

Abel shifted and stepped down from the van, unable to restrain a groan as his muscles stretched. It had been hours since he'd gotten out of that seat. He noted the sympathetic glance Jane sent his way, but chose not to acknowledge it; ignored her as she closed the van door and locked it. She then led him to the second motel room.

It was the smallest he'd ever seen. It held one double bed, a small table, and a chair. There was a television on the dresser, and a door he presumed led into a bathroom. All of it was crowded together, leaving a very narrow walking space around the bed. He was glad he wasn't claustrophobic.

"I let Mr. Tibbs out, set up his cat litter and fed him," Jane announced as she locked the motel room door. "But I think he's hiding under the bed. He doesn't seem to have taken well to travel. Do you need to use the washroom or anything?"

Abel, who'd been standing at her side thanks to the electrified handcuffs, turned on her sharply.

Jane glanced up from the door, noted his expression, then followed his gaze to the handcuffs and flushed. "Well, it will be tricky but . . ." Her eyes slid away unhappily and he could see her trying to work out a solution.

"I suppose you used the facilities before collect-ing me," he said dryly and was surprised to see the flush on her face deepen. Taking that to mean no, he found himself grinning for the first time in hours. She didn't appreciate it.

"Come on," she muttered and led him to the bathroom door.

He didn't really expect her to join him in the washroom, so he wasn't surprised when she paused in the door, then pulled a key out of her pocket and gestured him inside. Like the main room the bath was incredibly small; it had a tiny sink, a toilet, and a tub. They were all standard white and crowded into the minimum necessary space. Jane cuffed him to the towel rack inside.

Abel wasted a moment examining the rack, but it seemed to be well affixed to the wall. There was no way he could get free without making a lot of noise. Deciding not to try it, he attended quickly to his needs and even managed a sloppy hand wash-ing in the sink before calling for her.

Returning, Jane handcuffed him to the metal frame of the bed while she used the facilities.

When she was done she returned, but she left him chained to the bed. Turning on the TV, she handed him the remote. Then she collected his cof-fee and breakfast from the table where she'd set them earlier, and placed them on the bedside table within easy reach. That done, she took out her com-puter and mini satellite dish, set them up on the table, then sat down and called up her tracking pro-gram.

Ignoring the TV and his breakfast, Abel craned his head to see what was coming up on her screen.

"What is it saying?" he asked, finally. Jane was silent so long he'd started to get nervous.

"She's disappeared," she admitted. The computer closed with a snap.

"What? What does that mean? Is she . . . ?" He broke off, unable to voice his deepest fear.

"It means they've probably moved her into some sort of insulated room."

"Probably? How do you know she isn't dead?"

"I don't, but . . ." Jane straightened and walked wearily to the bed. "Look, Abel, I don't know what they've done. I do know that the signal has disappeared. Your sister being dead wouldn't make it disappear. It would still show on the screen. It isn't, so they've probably moved her into an insulated room that denies radio waves of any kind."

"You think they know she has a tracker on her? Why wouldn't they just take it away? Why—"

"I don't know," Jane interrupted, "and I'm too tired to sort it out right now." She bent to unhook him from the bed and cuffed him to herself again. "What I do know is that B.L.I.S.S. is looking into the matter, and that we'll do everything we can to sort it out."

Ah. Here was an opening. "What *is* B.L.I.S.S?"

"I am way too tired for this," Jane answered.

She gestured for him to shift over on the bed. He moved automatically and she joined him on it, stretching out to lie on her back, her arm at an angle to prevent pulling on the cuffs and shocking him again.

"You can't just go to sleep on me! I need to know what's going on! I need to . . ." He paused as her eyes opened.

"I don't know what's going on, Abel," she admitted in a soft voice. "We won't know until B.L.I.S.S. calls us back. We just have to wait. They'll get Edie back to you. I promise."

Her eyes closed again and this time Abel let her go to sleep. He believed her when she said she didn't have the answers. He believed she was waiting to hear back from her people, and he believed that her faith in B.L.I.S.S. was sincere. He just wished he could share some of it.

Abel shifted on the bed, using his free hand to rearrange the pillows so that he could lean back against the headboard with some comfort; then he grabbed up his breakfast. Opening it, he found a congealed mess. Still, he was hungry. He tried a bite, chewing cautiously at first, then relaxing. It was cold, but still quite tasty.

At that moment, Mr. Tibbs chose to give up his hiding spot. He leaped on top of the bed and ignored Abel to settle himself against Jane's side. She murmured sleepily and gave the cat a clumsy pet, then settled back again.

Abel scowled at his sister's tabby. "Traitor," he muttered, then turned on the television for distraction.

He was in for a long wait, he knew. He wasn't sure how long it would be before B.L.I.S.S. called back, but he knew exactly how he was going to spend the time till then. Worrying. He worried about Edie, he worried about himself. He spent a good while trying to decide the best way to get his freedom and even played it out in his head: He could tell her he needed to go to the washroom again, then this time, lock the bathroom door, rip the rack she cuffed him to out of the wall, and use it to break out the window over the bathtub.

Jane would no doubt start shocking him, but he didn't think she'd really hurt him. He could withstand the shocks long enough to climb out and make his way to the police station. Then he'd tell them—

That was where his plan fell apart. What could he say? That his sister had been kidnapped and brought to Sonora? But he hadn't seen her. He didn't even have any knowledge that had been given to him by anyone except Jane or her grandmother. And he hadn't really been paying attention to the roads they took to get to that gated community where the hearse had stopped.

Also, even if he stole the computer, he couldn't use it to find her; Jane had said Edie was no longer on the tracking system. There was a small possibility that with a little luck Abel might be able to find the gated community again, but then what? He'd been unconscious and hadn't seen the house she was in, so what could the police do? Start a door-to-door search? That, he feared, could very well see Edie dead. At the very least, it would get her moved to another spot where they couldn't find her. Which might happen as soon as the police made *any* misstep.

Much to his horror, Abel was beginning to see why Jane and Maggie didn't want to involve the law. Perhaps, if Jane and Maggie were really part of some secret agency, they really were his best hope to save Edie. If they could—

His thoughts were rudely interrupted by the ringing of a phone.

Chapter Eight

Jane was so groggy that she couldn't at first identify what was dragging her from sleep. When she realized it was the staccato ring of a telephone, she reached out to slap blindly around in search of the nasty device. Her hand hit empty bedside table, empty bedside table, then what felt like a lamp base. Relenting enough to open one eye, Jane found herself staring not at her own bedside table but a strange, cheap little beat-up one with a really tacky lamp.

The motel room, she realized and closed her eye with a groan.

The phone rang again. Jane gave a sigh and rolled to the left. If it wasn't on the right bedside table, the phone must be on the left her weary brain reasoned, then went dumb as she rolled atop something. Abel. Her eyes popped open, and she found herself staring down at the lap of a pair of gray linen suit pants. Edie's brother was still sitting up in bed as he'd been when she went to sleep. Jane had rolled right up on top of his legs, her face landing in his lap. She lifted her head to peer up at him.

He *would* be awake, of course, she thought on a sigh, then took a moment to wonder at the way his lips and one eyebrow were quirked with something that might be amusement. He really shouldn't be in such a good humor. He was handcuffed and held against his will.

"Good morning," Abel said cheerfully. "Looking for this?"

Jane flushed and turned her head to see he'd lifted the phone receiver and was now handing it to her. Even as Jane took it, another ring sounded. It wasn't the room phone ringing. Confusion covering her face, she glanced toward the floor, startled to see the edge of a purse sticking out from under the bed.

Gran's, she recognized, and shifted farther across Abel's legs to reach for it. *I must have brought it in here with the rest of the bags.*

She caught the edge of the purse and struggled upright atop Abel to search through the bag for her gran's cell phone. The elusive object rang twice more and Jane was becoming a bit frantic, afraid it was Gran's B.L.I.S.S. contact and that whoever it was would hang up before she could answer, when her hand closed on the little black device. Relief flooding her, she pulled it out and hit the answer button.

"Yes?"

"Jane?"

Jane recognized Y's voice and straightened in horror. Abel immediately gave a pained grunt and jerked forward in response, nearly getting popped in the eye by one breast when Jane unconsciously thrust her chest out in attention.

"Ma'am!" Jane winced at the alarm evident in her voice. So much for playing it cool.

"This is Y."

"Yes, ma'am. I, er, recognized your voice, ma'am. Is there . . . ?" Jane floundered briefly.

"I understand that you're watching the Ensecksis."

"Er, yes. Yes, ma'am. They kidnapped a friend of mine and—"

"Yes, yes. Bassmuth explained everything."

"Bassmuth?" Jane echoed, losing her military posture. She presumed Bassmuth was her grandmother's friend. And Bassmuth had explained everything? Great, Jane thought, her heart sinking. She was dead. Or at least jobless.

"It was very clever of you, getting this 'in' with the Ensecksis."

"It was?" Jane asked, straightening a little.

"Yes. Edie was one of ours."

"Er, Edie was one of our what, ma'am?" Jane asked uncertainly.

"Informants. She contacted C.I.S.I.S. about her suspicions about Ensecksi Satellites two weeks ago. They started to look into it, then decided this was a job for us. Unfortunately, they only passed the information along on Thursday. We planned to set up a meeting with Edie Andretti next week, but . . ." Jane could almost see her boss shrug. Next week had been too late. Thursday had probably been too late. The Ensecksis had been aware of the fact that Edie knew something, which was why she'd been kidnapped. "Anyway, it was clever of you to crack this case, Jane."

"Er, well, I'm not sure what Bassmuth told you, ma'am. But the case isn't cracked yet."

"Certainly it is. You've confirmed that the Ensecksis are testing microwave mind-control technology by convincing the populace to wear yellow dresses and Hawaiian shirts."

"Well, that's just supposition. I mean, it appears an odd fashion choice for a town, but—"

"Yes, yes. Always the good scientist. Proof and all that. But we happen to think you're right, Jane. Besides, you've also discovered their lair. No one else here managed to do that."

"Was there anyone looking?" Jane asked doubtfully.

"Yes," Y said firmly. "Ensecksi Satellites has been under suspicion for some time. We've been trying to locate their test site and covert-operations headquarters for some time. Every piece of land they own has been thoroughly investigated. This one slipped through the cracks because it was purchased by the Ensecksi daughter using her mother's maiden name."

"I see," Jane said.

"It was always believed that the daughter wasn't involved in any of this, but it appears she has been the focal point all along."

"I see," Jane repeated.

"We need you to get on the case."

"Ma'am?" Jane's horror was reflected in her voice, she knew.

"I know you aren't trained for this, but we have great faith in you."

"Shouldn't whoever was assigned to this from the beginning—?"

"No. They were made."

"Made?"

"Two of our best operatives were set on the senior Ensecksi in Bulgaria. He must have 'made' them—recognized them for agents—because he gave them the slip. We believe he's on his way home to Sonora now, if he's not already there. We believe that Ms. Andretti's discovery has made them move up their plans. They may be preparing for a global attempt at mind-control."

"You think they may be intending to make the whole world wear yellow sundresses?" Jane asked doubtfully.

"Jane."

"Yes, ma'am?"

"How much sleep have you had?"

"Um . . . not much."

"I didn't think so." Y cleared her throat and said patiently, "Jane, the yellow sundresses are just a test. Messing with a woman's fashion sense is pretty tough to do, and yellow makes most people look jaundiced. It is hardly a common choice. The Ensecksis are just testing to be sure the technology they've developed works. It's rather doubtful they intend to use their microwave mind-control technology to make the world wear yellow sundresses."

"Yes. Of course, ma'am," Jane said miserably, wishing she could kick herself for her stupid comment. She wiped one hand over her face, then gave her head a shake, trying to wake up.

"We aren't sure what they intend to do with it. They may plan to use it on politicians: the president of America, the prime ministers of England and Canada. Who knows? They may simply plan to make everyone go out and buy a satellite dish from their corporation. It doesn't matter. What matters is that what they *can* do is damned frightening. And illegal."

121

"Yes, ma'am. It is," Jane agreed.

"We have to stop them."

"I understand, ma'am."

"And you and Maggie are our best bet. You're there on the spot. We'll try to send in some backup, but most of our agents are on other assignments right now. Unfortunately, the Ensecksis aren't the only ones with aspirations of world domination at the moment."

"I see." Jane tried to sound strong, but her heart was plummeting. The world was counting on her and Gran to save them. A techno-geek and a half-paralyzed ex-spy. Oh, this was just great.

"We're putting you in the house next door. It's all set up."

"It is?" Jane asked, surprised at her boss's speed. Dismay filled her. There didn't appear any way out of this mess.

"Yes. A team is out there now, moving the old owners out. It should be all clear within the hour. Fortunately, the Goodinovs weren't very neighborly. Mr. Goodinov has Alzheimer's and Mrs. Goodinov stays with him most of the time. He can't be left alone. They aren't well known by anyone. The cover story will be that he has taken a turn for the worse, they're going to Europe for a few months to try an innovative new treatment, and they've asked his sister—Maggie Goodinov, and her granddaughter Jane—to watch over the house while they're gone."

"I see." Jane cleared her throat, her gaze going to Abel then skittering away when she saw him watching her closely. "Ma'am, Edie's brother—"

"Yes. Abel." Y was silent for a minute. "Is he going to be trouble?"

Jane's gaze captured Abel's and escaped again

before she said honestly, "I'm not sure. He may be if we don't include him."

Another moment of silence passed. Then Y said, "We can include him. Talk to him, explain the situation, and get a feel for him, Jane. If you think he'll be a problem . . . "

She left the rest unsaid and Jane nodded reluctantly, then cleared her throat and said, "Yes, ma'am."

"Good. You'll have to figure it out quickly. You're expected at the Goodinov house within the hour. Once you get there, I want you to watch and listen and find out whatever you can. I'm hoping to get some help up there in a couple of days, but in the meantime, you're on your own." Y was silent for a minute, then added; "Jane, under no circumstances are you to try to retrieve your friend."

"What if—"

"Under no circumstances," Y repeated firmly. "I know you're worried about her, but Edie is probably safe enough for now. According to the probability tests we've run, the Ensecksis are more likely to use her as a test subject for their mind-control technology than kill her. So we just want you to watch and listen for now."

"Yes, ma'am," Jane said miserably. How was she going to convince Abel to do that?

"Talk to Maggie and find out what she thinks. Once you've decided whether to include Abel or not, call me back and I'll arrange . . . whatever needs arranging."

"Yes, ma'am."

"You'll do fine, Jane. Ira has faith in you and so do I." Then the line clicked as the head of B.L.I.S.S. hung up.

Jane immediately slumped where she sat as if the

strings holding her up had just been snipped.

"Bad news?"

Jane stirred at that question, her gaze going to Abel's face. His voice had come out oddly husky and tense. She knew it had to be his worry over his sister, and struggled to find something in her weary mind to reassure him; then she noted the pained expression on his face. He really wasn't taking this well. She could sympathize completely. Now, not only was Edie's life in her hands, but the burden of the world as well.

World domination? Mind control? Dear God, what had Edie got her into?

"It seems your sister stumbled into a hornets' nest," she admitted reluctantly. "My bosses think the yellow sundresses are just a test, that Ensecksi plans on world domination with mind control."

"I see."

"That's good news for Edie, however."

"It is?"

"Yes. They won't want to kill her. They'll try brainwashing instead. She'll be a test subject."

Abel stared at her with horror. "That's good news?"

"She can be deprogrammed," Jane pointed out. "She couldn't be brought back from the dead."

"Oh." Abel was silent as he accepted that. Then he cleared his throat. "Do you think you could . . . ?"

Jane followed his gesture to where she sat on him and felt humiliation overcome her. Dear God! She was straddling him like . . .

She leaped off his lap and tried to move away, wincing when the handcuffs jerked and jolted Abel as she tried to rise from the bed.

Falling back, she wearily closed her eyes. She

really hadn't been made for this end of the business. She wasn't sneaky and graceful like the rest of her family. What had she got herself into?

"What are we going to do now?"

Jane stiffened. She dearly wished that Abel would just be quiet and let her suffer her humiliation while pretending she was alone, but she supposed that was too much to hope for. Besides, she didn't really have time for self-pity; she had to contact Y soon with the decision as to whether Abel was in or needed to be removed.

"We have to talk," she announced firmly, forcing herself to sit up.

"Okay." He sounded wary. She wasn't surprised, but ignored her own apprehension as she turned to face him on the bed.

"Edie stumbled on to some information at Ensecksi Satellites a while back. Apparently the corporation has some technology that combines with microwaves and allows mind control. She learned something about it and went to C.I.S.I.S. They started looking into it, but then decided that B.L.I.S.S. should be brought in. They passed the information to B.L.I.S.S. on Thursday, but our agency didn't get the chance to arrange a meeting before Edie was taken."

"Thursday?" Abel appeared confused. "But you've been her neighbor for months. How—?"

"I've lived in that apartment for several years," Jane interrupted. "Long before Edie ever even moved to Vancouver. It was just dumb luck that we're friends and neighbors."

"But she had that tracking necklace you gave her. Did she mention—?"

"No." Jane cut him off, taking a moment to order her thoughts. Y had said to explain. That gave her some freedom. "Edie didn't mention anything to me about her workplace, or at least not what she suspected was going on there. Why would she? She thought I worked for a toy company."

"Edie doesn't know that you work for this B.L.I.S.S.?"

"No. No one does except Gran and the people I work with. And now you," she admitted quietly. "We're not allowed to release the information as a rule. You're only learning it now out of necessity."

"So, how did Edie end up with your necklace?"

Jane pursed her lips then admitted, "The tracker isn't a necklace."

Abel's eyes narrowed at her embarrassed expression. "No? What is it?"

Jane took a deep breath. "A tampon."

Abel blinked. Once. "Excuse me?"

"I developed these B.L.I.S.S. tampon trackers—a tracker placed in the center of a tampon. It was for women agents, not children. It was to bypass the problem of agents being forced to strip and lose the trackers that are generally put in watches, earrings, or necklaces. We lost a couple of agents when they were forced to do that, and the usual trackers became useless. These trackers were supposed to remove that problem."

"And Edie—?"

"Edie came over just as I was taking Tinkle for a walk. I told her to borrow what she wanted. I didn't realize she needed tampons."

"I see." Abel considered that briefly, then he shook his head. "So it was pure dumb luck that we were able to track her."

"Yes," Jane admitted. "It wasn't until I went to the workroom for the broom and saw the computer that I even thought to look for her that way."

"Well, thank God you did."

"Yes." Jane was silent, wondering how she was to sort out whether Abel should be allowed to stay or leave.

"That was a brilliant idea."

Jane glanced up, uncertain. "What was?"

"The tampon trackers. And you learned this time they work. You should maybe put a longer tracking range on them, though."

"Yes," Jane agreed, oddly pleased at his compliment. "These are just prototypes. I had already decided that more powerful transmitters would be needed for the real thing."

Abel nodded. "So, what do we do now?"

Jane eyed him. "B.L.I.S.S. has arranged to move us into the house next door to where Edie was taken. They're sure that this is the headquarters for the Ensecksi mind-control project. They want us to watch and listen and learn what we can until backup can arrive. Then we'll decide what approach to take."

Abel nodded slowly. "That makes sense. We can't just charge in. We might get Edie killed."

Jane felt relief course through her at his attitude. It was quickly followed by suspicion at his sudden about-face.

Abel apparently spotted her suspicion. He sighed and said, "Look, I'm not saying I wouldn't like to storm the place and drag Edie out, but I thought about it while you were sleeping and realized that could get her killed. Besides, as you pointed out earlier, if they do have mind-control abilities, they're more likely to use them on her than violence. I trust your people to know what they're doing. I just want my sister back alive."

Jane nodded and relaxed. She believed him.

"Well, then. I guess we'd best clean up and go get Gran. Do you want the bathroom first?"

"That depends."

"On?"

"Are we going to have to be handcuffed?" After a moment he added, "Not that I mind the idea of showering with you, but . . ."

Jane flushed and peered down at the cuffs still binding them. She debated the matter for a moment, then finally decided she'd have to trust him sometime. They could hardly move in to the Goodinov house handcuffed together: she might as well test him out now. Reaching into her pocket, she retrieved the key to the cuffs.

"I'm going to go get Gran while you shower," she said as she set the handcuffs aside.

Abel merely nodded and crossed to the washroom.

Jane was at the door when she heard the shower start. She took some pleasure in the sound as she stepped outside.

Jane woke Gran and explained about both Y's call and her talk with Abel as she helped Maggie dress. Then she set Tinkle in her gran's lap and wheeled the pair out of the room.

Abel was out of the bathroom when Jane returned to their room. He was dripping wet, dressed only in a small towel that was draped around his waist, and he was going through one of her bags. Glancing up in surprise he flushed guiltily at the sight of them, but before he could do more than open his mouth all hell broke loose. Mr. Tibbs was sleeping on the end of the bed. Tinkle spied him and went wild. The room erupted in barking and hissing and flying fur as Mr. Tibbs leaped off the bed, streaked across the floor, and climbed Abel in search of safety.

Jane winced as Edie's brother yowled in pain. Releasing the towel he'd been holding in place with one hand while searching her bag with the other, he grabbed instinctively for the cat. He ripped Mr. Tibbs off his chest, then held the terrified creature at arm's length away from the leaping, barking, and yipping Tinkle.

"Oh, my," Gran murmured. "They may make the policemen here in California handsome, but I swear Canada makes the finest accountants."

Abel stared at Jane's gran blankly, obviously confused by her comment until Jane managed to tear her gaze away from his body and gesture. Looking down, seeing that he'd lost his towel and understanding what Gran was ogling, Edie's brother promptly dropped his arms so that the cat hid his nakedness. Tinkle promptly leaped, snapping at the cat, so Abel instinctively raised the poor creature back out of the dog's reach. Again and again he lifted then dropped the cat in a desperate effort to hide himself and yet protect the beast from the barking Tinkle. For Jane it was like watching a rather bizarre peekaboo yo-yo act. Up and down and up and down went the cat, and now you see it, now you don't went Abel's family jewels. Jane was completely enthralled.

"Um, dear? As delightful as this is, perhaps you should grab Tinkle before she decides to snap at something other than the cat," Gran suggested.

"Oh." Jane gave herself a shake and rushed forward to scoop up her gran's dog, then quickly retreated back to Maggie's side with the animal. Abel once more positioned Mr. Tibbs where he was the most effective. Fortunately, he had the cat by the scruff of the neck, so there was no danger of Mr. Tibbs swatting or biting.

"I, er, was hoping you might have a razor in one of those bags of yours," he said apologetically. Backing toward the bathroom door he added, "I should have waited for you, but hoped to finish up before you returned."

"Oh." Jane said, believing him. "I'm not sure if I have one or not. I'll look though," she offered. Her gaze slipped from his face to the cat in front of his groin and back. "Do you want me to take Mr. Tibbs?"

"No! No, we'll be fine." He backed into the bathroom and gave a pained smile. Saying "Thanks," he kicked the door closed.

"Do you want me to take Mr. Tibbs?" Gran repeated with amusement.

Jane flushed. "I meant once he was covered up."

"Of course you did, Janie, dear," Maggie said with amusement, then, "There should be a razor in my purse. I'll fetch it for Abel if you bring it to me. Then I suggest we call Y back and tell her Abel is in for now."

Nodding, Jane moved to collect her gran's purse, mentally kicking herself for not having earlier taken the opportunity to check its contents. Too late now, she decided as she handed the bag over. She waited as her grandmother searched out a pink and white women's razor, then she took the razor to the bathroom door and knocked lightly.

A moment passed; then the door opened a crack. Enough for Abel to peer out, but not enough for Tinkle to get in or Mr. Tibbs to get out.

"Gran found a razor." Jane held it up.

"Thank you." Abel took the item. "I'm sorry about looking through your bags."

130

"That's okay," Jane said with a shrug. "There's nothing personal in them anyway. She noted his curious expression, but didn't respond to it and turned away.

Gran was already talking on the phone when Jane returned to her side. "No, no. That won't do," she was saying. "We simply must stop and shop first. We haven't any clothes with us."

Jane winced at her gran's peremptory tone of voice and worried about how it would effect her own job. With Gran's help she might yet lose it.

"That *would* work," Gran said suddenly. "But we really should pick up a few things ourselves." Gran listened again, then glanced at Jane. "Ask Abel what size he is, dear. I'm guessing a thirty-two waist and forty inseam, but we want to be sure."

Nodding, Jane moved back to the bathroom door. Knocking once she asked loudly, "Abel, what size—Oh!" She smiled uncertainly as the door opened and he appeared, topless but again wearing pants. His face was covered with soapy foam, but Jane noted that absently as her gaze took in his wide, muscular chest.

"My size?"

"Er . . ." Jane tore her eyes away with some effort. It was a very nice chest. "Yes. Gran wants to know what size you are. I think B.L.I.S.S. is sending clothes for us."

"A thirty-four waist, forty leg and sixteen neck," he announced. "My shoulders are a bit wide though and I like roomy casual tops."

"Wide," Jane echoed, her gaze dropping back to his chest.

"Jane?" Gran called.

"Oh, yes." She passed along the information as Abel re-closed the bathroom door.

Gran relayed the information as well, then spoke for a few more minutes before handing the phone to Jane. "Ira wants to talk to you."

Jane took the phone, a touch relieved to know that it was Ira Manetrue that Gran had been talking to and not Y; but only a touch.

"Hello?" she said into the phone.

"Jane, this is Mr. Manetrue. I wanted to tell you how proud I am of you."

"Oh, well . . . Thank you, sir."

"We're sending the three of you in as Maggie, Jane, and Abel Goodinov. You and Abel are brother and sister. Maggie is your grandmother."

"All right."

Mr. Manetrue continued without prompting, "We considered making you and Abel husband and wife, but Y pointed out—and I agreed—that doing so might interfere with your investigations. According to our information, Dirk Ensecksi is quite the ladies' man."

"What?" Jane blinked.

"I'm sorry?" Ira asked. "What what?"

"What did you say his name was?"

"Dirk. Dirk Ensecksi."

"Oh." She gave a nervous laugh. "It's just when you said the name fast it sounded like—"

"Dirk Ensecksi," Ira repeated, then gave a bark of laughter. "Dark and sexy. Yes, well, it may fit. Anyway, that's why we decided on the brother-and-sister deal. That way, neither of you will be hampered if you need to get close to either Dirk or Lydia Ensecksi."

"Lydia Ensecksi," Jane echoed. "Well, at least *she* sounds normal."

"She's a man-eater from all accounts. But she may have useful information. Still, Mr. Andretti isn't a pro, so I want you to keep an eye on him."

"Yes, sir," Jane agreed. But at the same time she had the panicky thought that neither was she a professional spy. Why was no one worried about her? Why did they all assume that this cloak-and-dagger nonsense had somehow been poured into her along with her mother's milk? She was a geek! A scientist! And an absentminded scientist at that.

"Good," Ira Manetrue said, completely oblivious of the panic coursing through his protégée's body. "I also want you to keep an eye on your grandmother, Jane. Maggie was the best in the business, but she has been out for a while now."

"Yes, sir." Jane avoided looking at her gran.

"Very good. Do you have any questions?"

Why are you people doing this to me? But she cleared her throat and said, "No, sir."

"All right. You'll do fine, Jane. I know you're probably nervous right now, but you're a natural. I have faith in you."

"Thank you, sir." *I think.*

"We're working on getting you some backup, but call me if there are any problems or you have any questions."

"All right. Thank you, Mr. Manetrue," Jane said again.

She'd barely hung up the phone when there was a knock at the motel door.

"That's probably our ID," Gran said.

Jane shook her head, not believing that even B.L.I.S.S. could be so quick. But when she opened the door a courier was waiting there. He wore a brown uniform with BQD emblazoned on it.

"Jane Spyrus?" he asked, then held out a clipboard when she nodded.

"BQD?" Jane asked as she took it.

"B.L.I.S.S. Quick Delivery," he said, grinning.

"Quick is right," Jane muttered as she scribbled her name in the appropriate square.

"Actually, I've been here for fifteen minutes, but I had to wait for the call to tell me which envelope to deliver," he explained. Jane shook her head. If it was ID as Gran suggested, then they must have sent out two different packets when she got off the phone earlier: one that included Abel, one that didn't. Her superiors must have flown them in from some branch of B.L.I.S.S. in California to get them here so swiftly. Maybe San Jose. Still, this was extremely fast. Unless the ID had been prepared directly after Gran's first call.

Jane handed back the clipboard and accepted the envelope held out in exchange. Murmuring a thanks, she closed the door on the delivery man.

"What's that?" Abel asked, coming out of the bathroom. Jane lifted the envelope.

"It's our ID," Gran announced as Jane ripped open the resealable package.

Jane upended the envelope over the bed and three card holders fell out. She picked one up, opened it, and found herself staring at a row of cards: driver's license, Social Security card, Visa, American Express; there was even a Sonora Library card. The name on all the cards read Margaret L. Goodinov, and they listed a Sonora address.

"It seems we're American now," Jane said faintly. She handed the card holder to Gran.

The next she picked up was for Abel N. Goodinov. She handed it to Edie's brother, then picked up the last. It was hers.

"All right. Give me your real IDs," Gran ordered, drawing their attention.

"Why?" Abel asked.

134

"Well, you can't get caught with both, can you? It will raise eyebrows. You'll have to use these only."

Jane and Abel exchanged a glance; then both did as she asked. Gran took their IDs, put them in the resealable envelope with her own, then rolled her chair over to the door. Opening it, she handed the envelope to the courier, who was still patiently waiting.

"Thanks." He offered another grin, then walked away as Gran closed the door. "Close your mouth, Janie dear. This is standard procedure. To be safe."

Jane closed her mouth.

"If you wanted a shower before we go, Jane, you'd best hurry," her gran suggested. "We're supposed to meet the Realtor at the house in—"

"The Realtor?" Jane interrupted with surprise. "I thought B.L.I.S.S. didn't buy the house after all. I thought we were just taking over for a little while."

"Yes, dear. But the first thing they did was move the Goodinovs out. Someone had to hear the story of Mr. Goodinov's sudden turn for the worse, their need to leave right away, and our house-sitting for them," she said, "so that the story could circulate. I would guess this Realtor was chosen because she is the local gossip. Now, get to it if you want a shower. Our meeting is at ten-thirty."

Jane glanced at her wristwatch. It was 9:36. She couldn't have slept more than twenty minutes before Y had called the first time, she realized suddenly. No wonder she was still so exhausted and felt slow and stupid. She definitely needed a shower to help shake away some of the sleep. She hurried into the bathroom.

Chapter Nine

"I don't know how you managed all of this so quickly!"

The Realtor, Trixie Leto, sailed gaily ahead of them toward the garage door of the Goodinov house. It was only 10:30 in the morning, but the odor of wine about the woman was staggering. It seemed Trixie liked juice with her breakfast, fermented grape juice and lots of it, judging by the way she was stumbling along in her high heels. She looked to be sixty, but was dressed like a twenty-year-old in a short straw-yellow sundress showing off legs with spiderweb veins. There was also a lot of makeup on her wrinkled face. Her hair was dyed to match her dress—a most unfortunate choice with her nicotine-stained skin and teeth.

She looked like an over-the-hill bimbo, Jane thought, then berated herself for being uncharitable. Some people just aged better than others. But most seemed to do it better and more gracefully than this woman.

"Beatrice Goodinov rousted me out of a dead sleep," the woman said with a laugh. "I nearly fell out of bed when she said she and Arthur were leaving for a clinic in Europe and needed someone to hang on to the keys to this house until you arrived."

Beatrice and Arthur. Jane repeated the names silently, trying to fix them in her memory. It wouldn't be good to forget her "aunt's" and "uncle's" first names. If Mr. Manetrue had mentioned them to Gran, Gran had neglected to pass them on. But then the last hour had been a bit rushed. Jane had hopped in and out of the shower in record time, thrown on her clothes, then stepped out into the motel room to find Abel had already reloaded everything into the van except for Gran, Tinkle, and Mr. Tibbs. Edie's cat had actually been cowering in the bathroom while Jane showered.

Jane had carried the traumatized tabby out to the van and returned him to his cage, while Abel had wheeled Gran and Tinkle out after. The spoiled Yorkie had whined enough that Gran had refused to have her put back in her cage, so the beast had sat on Gran's lap. A short trip to pick up toothbrushes and toothpaste was the only other thing they'd had time for before heading here.

"Of course," Trixie Leto continued, "when she said you were supposed to arrive at ten-thirty, I offered to meet you here rather than have you drive all the way out to my office. I live nearby, you know."

"No, I didn't know," Jane murmured, reaching out instinctively when Trixie stumbled over Tinkle. The dog had leapt off Gran's lap and directly into the Realtor's path on the black tarred driveway, but the Realtor caught herself and Jane pulled back without having to help.

"Oh, what a delightful puppy. Aren't you a pretty girl?" the Realtor said.

Jane's eyes widened in alarm as Trixie knelt to pet Tinkle. She opened her mouth in warning, then bit her lip when the Yorkie behaved, rolling onto her back, belly up, to be petted.

"Stupid mutt," Abel said at Jane's side.

She bit back a laugh, then told him, "Yes, but she's a pretty good judge of character. She only likes those who turn out to be slightly shady or completely evil."

Abel shook his head. "That figures. Then I suppose I should be flattered she tried to take a chunk out of me."

Jane chuckled.

"It's a shame about Arthur." Trixie straightened with Tinkle in her arms, and the silly creature went wild cuddling close and trying to lick the Realtor's face. "He hasn't been well for a while, of course. Such a burden for poor Beatrice. And then for her to have to care for this huge house, too." Trixie shook her head. "I expected her to put the house on the market any time now, and I have been checking in with her every once in a while to see if it was time yet. She never mentioned anything about a clinic in Europe."

Jane managed to keep her revulsion hidden. This woman was a vulture! Checking to see if it was "time to put the house on the market yet?" Dear Lord! Jane felt sympathy well up for her supposed aunt.

"The clinic was my idea," Gran announced. She was glaring at the woman holding her precious Tinkle. Maggie Spyrus could be a bit jealous of the dog's affection. "I was reading about it in *Cosmo*. I mentioned it to her some months ago. She wasn't terribly interested then, but when Arthur took this turn ..." She shrugged and held out her arms. "Come, Tinkle."

The Yorkie hesitated, appearing reluctant to leave Trixie Leto. But then, apparently recalling where and how her bread was buttered, she squirmed free of the Realtor's arms and leapt back into Gran's lap.

"Good girl," Maggie crooned, all smiles once more.

"Well, it was good of you to agree to house-sit while they're gone," Trixie commented stiffly, looking put out by the dog's defection. She turned abruptly and led the way into the garage, addressing Jane. "As you can see, the elevator man has already been and installed the elevator needed for your grandmother. They were just finishing up when I arrived. Beatrice must have let them in before she left. Foolish of her to leave them here on their own. I'd have come over sooner to watch them had she mentioned it."

Jane followed Trixie's gesture to the shiny new elevator in the back corner of the garage. The house was built on an incline; its driveway and garage were on ground level but then the front yard swept up steeply to the right. The front yard and two-thirds of the house were perched on a green hill. The other third crouched over the garage. The only ways into the dwelling itself were a set of stairs at the back of the garage next to the new elevator, or a set of some forty steps leading up from the driveway to the front door. Wheelchairs and stairs were not compatible, so the elevator had been a necessity that Jane wasn't surprised the people of B.L.I.S.S. had recognized. They sure were good with details.

"You are so fortunate to have a lovely grand-daughter willing to take care of you in your old age," Trixie shouted at Gran as if Gran might be deaf, doddering, or both. Since she hadn't done so earlier, Jane could only surmise that this was the woman's petty punishment for Tinkle's defection.

Maggie Spyrus was not amused. Jane recognized the fire in her gran's eyes and took a moment to be grateful her bag was in the car. Had she let Gran bring it, Trixie Leto would surely be lying uncon-scious on the paved driveway.

"I suppose we should test the elevator out. Then I can give you a tour of the house," Trixie went on gaily, obviously cheered by the fact that she'd irri-tated Gran. She stumbled toward the corner of the garage.

"That won't be necessary," Abel announced, and Jane threw a grateful glance his way. Apparently, she herself wasn't the only one eager to escape Trixie's company. They could find their way around the house themselves.

The Realtor turned in surprise. "But—"

"We don't need a tour. So, if you'd just give us the keys . . . ?" He held out his hand in uncompro-mising demand, and Trixie Leto seemed to slump with disappointment. Her lips pursed into a pout that might have been sexy some thirty years earlier, but now just emphasized ridiculously the wrinkles around her lips.

"We have visited before," Jane lied gently, sud-denly feeling sorry for the woman. She didn't think Trixie meant to be so irritating; the woman was just sort of pathetic. "We appreciate the trouble you went to, helping Aunt Beatrice out like this, but we also realize how busy you must be."

"Oh, yes." Straightening, the Realtor took her chance to save face and moved back toward them. "I have *ever* so much to do! It's truly a blessing that you don't need a tour." The words came out in a fruity wave of breath as she handed the keys to Jane. "Since you're all set, I can get on with my busy day! Enjoy your stay!" she finished in her ever-gay voice. Then she stumbled past them up the slanted driveway.

"Pathetic," Gran said with disgust as they watched Trixie Leto fall into her little red sports car.

"Yes, well . . ." Jane grasped the handles of Gran's wheelchair and turned her back into the garage. "Not everyone can age as gracefully as you."

"No." Maggie smiled and straightened the lap rug Jane had placed around her legs. "That's true."

Abel followed them onto the elevator, glancing curiously around as Jane pushed the button to close the door, then a second button to set it in motion. "I didn't even think of the trouble we would have with stairs. Your people think of everything."

"Yes, they do," Gran said with pride.

Jane kept her thoughts to herself. She'd had similar feelings; but now that she thought about it she bet Ira Manetrue had ensured the wheelchair access. He had a huge crush on her grandmother. He wouldn't forget something like that.

The elevator doors opened and Jane wheeled Gran out onto an off-white Berber carpet.

"Expensive," Gran commented, then glanced both ways down the hallway. To their left it went for only a short distance before opening into what appeared to be a kitchen. To their right it ran for a good distance with several doors leading off into other rooms.

"Let's have a look around." Gran gestured to their right and Jane turned her in that direction and moved forward. The first room they came to was a laundry room; the second, a bathroom. The rest, four in all, were bedrooms, two with en suite bathrooms and two without. Every room had a bed, a dresser, an end table, and even chairs and entertainment systems that included televisions and DVD players.

They took a few moments looking these rooms over, then headed back up the hall. Jane almost sighed with pleasure as they entered the kitchen. It was huge. A large island stood in the middle with two sinks and a large tiled counter. Glasses, pots, and pans hung from a rack above. The rest of the room was lined with counter space and filled with two of almost everything; two stoves, two dishwashers, two microwaves. The amount of cupboard space was enough to make any woman happy. It had obviously been designed for people who entertained. A lot.

Jane wasn't big on cooking. She'd taken after Gran that way, but even she could appreciate the functionality of this room.

"I love the dining room set."

Jane took Gran's hint and moved on, pushing across the linoleum floor to the dining room. A large light table with eight chairs filled this space. The far wall held a large hutch of the same wood, its upper half made of glass windows to display a healthy amount of Waterford crystal and a charming china set with a cream background, gold rim, and autumn flowers. Everything matched nicely with the large ceramic rooster set in the center of the table and surrounded by colorful squash. Mrs. Goodinov had already started laying out the Thanksgiving decorations!

"Nice."

Hearing that soft murmur from Abel, Jane followed his glance to their left where French doors led out onto a large deck. But it was the view that had caught Abel's attention. The house was on a hill that sloped out of the valley, so the deck looked out over trees taking on fall colors and sloping away up the side of the mountain.

"What a view," Jane breathed, beginning to think she might enjoy this assignment after all.

"Lovely," Gran agreed. "We can look at that later, though. Let's see the rest of the house."

Turning reluctantly away from the panorama, Jane wheeled Gran through the far doorway into the next room—where they all paused abruptly.

Dear Lord, this room was gigantic! Huge! As big as the great hall in medieval castles of old. It had high vaulted ceilings with wooden beams. Glass windows and French doors comprised the wall looking out over the deck, and there was a fireplace large enough for half a dozen people to stand in and a regulation-size pool table as well.

Closer to hand, a small kitchenette bar and huge-screen television had been built into the wall directly beside them. A small group of overstuffed furniture sat before it, leaving acres of space for a piano against the opposite wall.

"It's like a ballroom, only carpeted." Gran sounded impressed.

"Yes, it is. But Mrs. Goodinov did a good job of making it cozy," Jane commented. There came a knocking sound to their right.

This room, like the hallway, was carpeted in Berber, but there were two stairs directly beside where Jane stood. They ran the width of the room and led up to a hardwood floor that covered the first ten or fifteen feet, making something of an open entry. The hardwood stopped at a huge set of double doors that a truck could have driven through. These doors were where the knocking originated.

Before Jane could speak Abel jogged up the two steps and pulled the huge door open. Standing where she was Jane had a clear view of the man in the doorway, and she moved forward as she recognized the courier from the motel.

"Oh, there you are. I have a package for you," the courier said. He stepped back out of sight behind the other door. Reappearing he had a trolley with two boxes stacked on it.

She reached Abel's side and asked warily, "What's that?" She peered at the boxes.

The courier shrugged. "I'm just the delivery guy. I was told to deliver this directly to the head operative"—he checked his clipboard—"Jane Spyrus. Which is you, right?"

"Yes," she said faintly, the title "head operative" making her queasy. How had she ended up as head operative? Gran had the experience.

"It's standard issue, Janie, dear," Gran announced. "Sign for it and have him put it in whichever one of the bedrooms you want."

Jane accepted the clipboard and signed on the line titled *Received By,* then handed the board back and peered curiously at her loot.

"Where should I put them?" the courier asked.

Jane forced herself to think. They hadn't seen the whole house yet. There was another hallway leading off this large ballroom, opposite the doorway into the dining room. That unexplored end of the house was the side that looked toward where Edie was being held captive. Unfortunately, while it seemed a good possibility there were bedrooms on both sides of the house, there were three steps leading up to this wing. Maggie couldn't manage those steps in her wheelchair, and Jane wanted to sleep close to Gran in case she was needed. They would both have to take rooms in the first wing.

"Follow me," she said and headed back.

The courier wheeled the trolley across the hardwood floor, bumped it gently down the two steps, then followed Jane silently through the dining room and kitchen and to the hall with its cluster of bedrooms. Jane chose the first one on the right, had the courier set the boxes on the floor by the bed, then escorted him back through the house.

Abel and Gran were no longer in the great room, but voices off to Jane's right as she closed the front door behind the courier drew her attention to another room she hadn't noticed. An arched doorway off the ballroom led into a library situated in front of the kitchen. Abel and Gran were inside talking.

"There she is." Gran smiled as Jane entered. "You and Abel should go look at the rest of the house."

"Yes. We'll do that right now," Jane agreed.

As she moved to take the handles of Gran's wheelchair, the older woman waved her off. "Don't bother with me. The stairs rather cut me off from that wing of the house anyway."

"It's only two or three steps, Gran," Jane protested. "I can maneuver you up those, at least to see it."

"Too much trouble. You two go along yourselves. I'll wheel myself out onto the deck and look at the view."

Shrugging, Jane followed Abel. He was already

walking out of the room, up the steps Gran mentioned, into another much smaller hallway. There were only three doors. The one on the right led into an office with two computers, the sight of which made Jane curious. She'd assumed the Goodinovs were retired, but this room was definitely set up as a home office.

Leaving it a mystery, Jane turned to peer through the door on the left. It revealed a large bathroom with a skylight. Very large, Jane thought, her gaze taking in the glass shower, the miles of counter, the two sinks, and the plants that had been set out to fill the space.

"I like this house," Abel announced.

Jane laughed. "Bet you wouldn't like cleaning it."

"Yeah. Everything has its drawbacks."

Turning as one, they moved along the hall to the last door. It led into the master suite, a room easily twice the size of any of the other bedrooms. Half the chamber featured a tall king-size bed that looked so comfortable to Jane she almost sighed. The other half was furnished with a couch, chairs, tables, and another big-screen TV. Jane took in the overstuffed couch and chairs with their large contemporary-patterned upholstery meant to make the room look less cavernous, then turned into the en suite bathroom. It was a dream as well, featuring a skylight, a sunken sauna, his and hers sinks each with a mirrored counter, toilet and bidet.

"Well." Abel paused behind her in the bathroom. "Maggie can't stay here, so I guess it's between you and me. Who gets this room?"

"I have to stay close to Gran," Jane said reluctantly. She wished she didn't—not just because she would have liked this room for herself, but because it was the one facing the Ensecksi house. Also a drawback of her not getting it: The room featured a door of its own, which meant Abel could, if he wanted, slip out without Jane knowing and do any number of stupid things in a misguided effort to save his sister.

"I won't do anything to endanger Edie," he said as if reading her mind. "I promise. I won't slip out in the middle of the night to play soldier boy."

Jane relaxed and nodded. "Thank you."

"I guess I'll start bringing in our bags." Moving around her, Abel left the bathroom.

Jane followed more slowly. Back in the bedroom she moved to the door beside the bed. Opening it, she peered through the screen at the grass and trees outside. The hill the house sat on rolled along for a good thirty feet beyond, then dropped off and down. The house next door, the Ensecksi abode, had been built at the hill's base. Its roof was all that showed from where Jane stood, its brown shingles peeking from between the trees no doubt meant to act as a privacy fence.

She would have to trust Abel, she supposed. Or handcuff him to that huge bed at night. The thought made her smile, and she went back inside silently.

"Abel's gone to fetch Mr. Tibbs," Gran announced when Jane appeared on the back deck. Tinkle had given up her position on Gran's lap and was now racing about sniffing the air, the deck, and anything else she could find.

The sight of the hyper dog made Jane ask, "What are we going to do about Tinkle and Mr. Tibbs?"

"Oh, they'll be fine. They'll scrap it out, then settle down like a couple of peas in a pod."

Jane was a bit doubtful, but she decided to wait and see what happened. If it came to a scrap, her money was on Mr. Tibbs. The cat might have been terrified in the motel room, but he was almost twice the size of Tinkle. One swat from his paw ought to give the dog an attitude adjustment. She wouldn't mind seeing that.

"I'm going to take a look at those boxes the courier brought," Jane announced, turning toward the French doors to the dining room. "Which of the bedrooms do you prefer?"

"The first on the left, I think," Gran decided. "I'll take Tinkle along in a moment."

Jane nodded and kept walking.

The boxes were where they'd been left, but Jane had to make a quick trip back to the kitchen for something to open them. She found a paring knife, then stopped to take a quick look through the cupboards, refrigerator, and freezer. The sight made her pause. There was a large variety of foodstuffs, and everything was new and unopened. Jane suspected B.L.I.S.S. had brought in this food and moved out the Goodinovs'—but only Gran would know if that was the usual routine. She'd ask later. Right now, she was too curious to see what was in the boxes in the other room.

Leaving the kitchen, Jane hurried back to the bedroom and sliced open her deliveries. Folding back the flaps of first one box, then the other, Jane gave a murmur of delight as she found a lovely assortment of listening devices, infrared cameras and weapons. Ignoring the guns, she picked up a long microphone. Its holder made it look like a weapon.

"What's that?"

Jane gave a start and nearly dropped the microphone as she glanced about.

"Sorry." Abel gave up his position by the door and walked to her side to peer curiously at the contents of her boxes.

"It's a shotgun microphone," Jane answered, forcing herself not to cover the boxes and hide their contents. This man was going to help. He would need to know what everything was.

He took the apparatus she held to examine it, then glanced into the box and pointed at a microphone set in the middle of what looked like a satellite dish. "What's that?"

"A parabolic microphone," Jane said.

"Stuff to listen to our neighbors, huh?"

"Yes," Jane answered, terribly aware of his nearness. She swallowed as his arm brushed hers, then cleared her throat and asked, "Did Tinkle attack Mr. Tibbs the moment you let him out of his cage?"

"Hm?" He glanced at her distractedly, then said, "Oh. No. I let Mr. Tibbs loose in the end bedroom and closed the door to keep the dog out." He set the shotgun microphone back in its box and added, "Which reminds me why I came to get you. I think you're supposed to sleep in the master bedroom."

Jane's eyebrows rose. "Why?"

"Come see," he suggested and headed off.

Jane followed him back through the house, her curiosity replaced with confusion when he led her inside and directly to the walk-in closet.

"I somehow don't think these were meant for me," he announced as he opened the doors.

Jane stopped and stared at the women's clothing filling the hangers. "Mrs. Goodinov—"

"There's a picture of the Goodinovs on the dresser. Mrs. Goodinov is definitely not a size twelve. More a twenty-two," he added dryly. "Besides, everything still has the tags on it."

He took a slinky black dress out to show her, and Jane realized these must be the clothes B.L.I.S.S. had promised to supply. Although she had no idea

149

how they'd managed to purchase all this and get it here in the hour between the phone call and when they'd arrived. Unless they hadn't needed to shop. She supposed it would be handy to keep warehouses of clothes around for such emergencies.

"There are underclothes in the dressers too," Abel said as he hung the dress back on its rod. "All women's clothes, all new. I think you're expected to sleep in here. There are probably clothes for Maggie and me in other rooms."

"Probably, but I can't leave Gran—"

"I could listen for her," Abel offered, taking Jane completely by surprise.

She shook her head. "No, she might need something you couldn't help her with."

"Then I could fetch you."

Jane rubbed her forehead as she considered the matter. There was a lot to consider. Not just Gran, but what they were expected to do here. Listen to and watch the Ensecksis. Were they supposed to watch them around the clock? Probably, she answered herself.

"Jane!" Gran's voice drew Jane from her thoughts. Leaving her dilemma for later, she hurried out of the room to find Maggie Spyrus in the great room at the foot of the stairs. A lovely brunette who looked to be in her early forties stood at her side. The brunette wore the standard yellow sundress, but Jane had to admit this one was actually attractive. A very pale, almost white yellow and designed along simple lines, the dress was soothing and breezy rather than painful to look at.

"This is Leigh Senchall, our neighbor until Beatrice and Arthur return and kick us out of their paradise," Gran announced lightly. Her comment elicited soft laughter from Leigh.

"It is a lovely house, isn't it?" The woman glanced about, then turned back and held out her hand as Jane walked down the steps to reach them. "Hello, Jane."

"Hello, Leigh." Jane shook the proffered hand, then gestured to Abel, who had followed. "This is my brother, Abel."

The two greeted each other; then Gran announced, "Leigh came to welcome us to the neighborhood. She brought a yummy-looking cinnamon coffee cake."

"Oh, that's sweet," Jane said in surprise, touched by the action. "Well, I suppose tea would be in order."

"Tea sounds lovely," Leigh agreed. "But only if you aren't too busy unpacking."

"Oh. All we have to unpack are our clothes, and most of that is done," Gran lied easily as Jane wheeled her toward the dining room.

Jane waved away Abel's offer of help and busied herself making tea and setting out plates, cups, and silverware as he, Leigh, and Gran settled around the large dining room table. Jane listened to the three talk, marveling over the smooth way her grandmother steered the conversation toward the Ensecksis.

"Oh, you won't have any problem there," Leigh was saying as Jane carried the tray of tea things out to the table moments later. "Lydia is very quiet. We hardly ever see her."

"Lydia?" Gran murmured. "That's a lovely name."

"Yes." Leigh smiled at Jane as she took her tea cup. "Lydia is . . ."

Jane paused and she and Maggie and Abel all waited breathlessly for the brunette's next words.

"Well, she's interesting," Leigh finished, looking

uncomfortable. Then she added with more ease, "She's very pretty."

Recalling that Mr. Manetrue had claimed Lydia was a maneater, Jane suspected Leigh was merely being polite.

"Pretty, hm? Is she single?" Abel asked.

Jane glanced at him with surprise as she handed him his tea. If it weren't for the pulse ticking in his forehead, the mischievous grin on his face would have fooled her into thinking that he truly was on the make. Apparently, Leigh missed the pulse. She laughed good-naturedly and shook her head.

"Men," she said with mild exasperation. "Yes. She's single."

"There you go, Abel. Maybe I'll live long enough to see you married, after all," Gran teased, then smiled at Leigh. "I don't suppose there's a nice eligible bachelor around here for my Janie?"

"Actually . . ." Leigh paused, looking surprised. "Do you know, Lydia's brother is visiting her right now and he's single." She turned to Jane. "He's very handsome, Jane. And *so* sexy. He has dark hair and a killer smile."

"Hmm." She smiled. "He sounds perfect. I hope I get to meet him while we're here."

"Yes, that would be—Oh!" Leigh sat up straight. "You can! Tonight!"

"Tonight?" Jane and Maggie and Abel echoed.

Leigh nodded. "Yes. I'm having a little neighborhood pre-Thanksgiving get together tonight. I wanted to have it next week, but the Johnsons are going away and . . ." She waved her hand vaguely. "Anyway, you three really should come. You could meet everyone. And Lydia and Dirk are both coming."

"That sounds lovely!" Gran beamed at their neighbor, obviously pleased.

"Yes, it should be nice," Leigh agreed. "Cocktails and a buffet dinner. Semidressy." She glanced down at her watch and made a face. "Speaking of which, I still have a couple of things to pick up. I'm having the food catered, but there are loads of other things to do. I suppose I should head home." She got to her feet and moved to the front door. "Come any time after six."

"We'll look forward to it," Gran said as Jane saw her out.

Jane returned to the dining room a moment later to see that Gran had pulled a pad of paper and a pen from her purse and was making a list.

"What's that for?" She asked, dropping back into her seat.

"I'm making a list of what we'll need to be prepared for tonight," Maggie Spyrus announced, then glanced up to survey her granddaughter critically. "The first thing is that you should sleep."

"Sleep?" Jane echoed. It seemed almost a foreign word at this point.

"Yes. You have bags under your eyes, Janie, dear. You'll never catch Dirk Ensecksi's attention that way."

"And I thought *my* name was bad," Abel said.

Jane ignored him. "Why do I want Dirk Ensecksi's attention, again?"

"To milk all the information out of him you can manage," her gran answered. "Which is point number two. After you've taken your nap, I intend to teach you how to be a woman."

"I thought I was born a woman," Jane muttered.

"Anyone can be born one," Gran sniffed. "I intend to teach you how to be a Spyrus woman. To-night you will be a femme fatale."

Jane choked back the snort that wanted to es-cape her nose. A femme fatale? The closest she *had* ever come or *would* ever get to being a femme fa-tale was nearly blowing Dick's head off with her Mini-Missile-Launching Vibrator. She just wasn't the type.

Chapter Ten

"Shopping?" Jane gaped at her grandmother. She'd just woken from her "nap." Actually, she hadn't woken on her own. Gran had come in and nudged her, saying something about shopping. "We don't need to go shopping, Gran. B.L.I.S.S. sent clothes."

"Yes. I know, dear," Maggie Spyrus said patiently. "That's what I just said. I thought I'd have to wake you up to go shopping, but Abel found the clothes B.L.I.S.S. left so we were able to let you sleep longer. But it's almost five o'clock now. You have to get up and get ready for tonight."

"Five o'clock," Jane echoed. She'd lain down at a little after eleven, got almost six hours of sleep. She almost felt human again.

"Come on. Up and at 'em. We have to get you ready."

Nodding, Jane pushed the sheets and comforter

aside, then sat up on the side of the bed. She'd slept in the room she'd first chosen, wearing only a T-shirt and underwear. She could have searched the master suite for a nightgown, but it had seemed too much effort.

"Abel and I picked out a dress for you to wear," Gran announced, petting Tinkle as the dog stirred in her lap. "It's hanging on the back of the bathroom door, so you can just shower and dress. I'll fix your hair after."

"How did you and Abel pick out a dress?" Jane asked as she grabbed for the jeans she'd been wearing earlier. She started to pull them on. "All the clothes are in the master suite."

"Abel helped."

"Oh," Jane said, then paused to eye her gran sharply. "You didn't pick the underwear I should wear, too, did you?" She found herself flushing at the idea of Edie's brother carrying handfuls of lacy underthings to examine and choose from.

"No." Gran frowned. "I didn't think of that."

"Thank God!" Jane finished doing up her jeans, then moved off to the master suite. "I'll go get some before I take that shower."

The door was closed when Jane reached it. She pushed it open and stepped inside, then paused at the sight that met her eyes. Abel had moved the boxes of equipment here before Jane had lain down. She'd known he would nose through them, but she wasn't prepared to find him knee-deep in spying paraphernalia. The entire contents of her boxes appeared to be spread out on the floor around him, and he stood by the open door facing the Ensecksis' house, headphones on and a shotgun microphone in hand. He scowled impatiently and fiddled with the knobs on the side. The sight was terribly adorable to Jane.

She stood there, just looking at him, until she spotted Tinkle slipping past her into the room. Startled out of her in action, Jane immediately bent to grab for the dog but was too late; the Yorkie had spotted Mr. Tibbs sleeping on the bed and rushed forward out of reach.

Edie's cat had a finely honed survival instinct. His eyes opened, zeroed in on the approaching Yorkie, and he was immediately up and running.

Releasing a growl, Tinkle was after him at once, but Mr. Tibbs led her a merry chase. The two pets raced across the bed, leaped one after the other to the couch, streaked to one chair, then the other. Circling the room, they rushed past Jane in a blur, then reached Abel. That's when the real excitement started.

Tinkle's and Mr. Tibbs's sudden mad rush around his feet was what made Abel finally aware of the trouble erupting. He gave a startled gasp and jerked his microphone up in an attempt to get its long wire out of the way. It was a good try, but a little late. Tinkle was already traipsing through the cord, getting it tangled around her little paws. Abel began to dance around in a circle, attempting to avoid being snared too, but couldn't move as quickly as the cat or dog circling him. He was well and truly entangled by the time Mr. Tibbs gave up his evasive tactic and broke away.

Tinkle, who had stayed right on the cat's tail the whole time, now snapped her teeth closed on that tail. The pair disappeared under the bed, trailing the disengaged microphone cord behind them.

"Argh!"

Abel's cry drew Jane's attention as she approached the opposite side of the bed, prepared to put an end to the circus act. She glanced back just in time to see him tumble onto his butt on the floor.

Wincing, Jane turned back to the bed, but neither Mr. Tibbs nor Tinkle reappeared. There was a brief spate of growling and hissing; then came a yelp. Seconds later, Tinkle charged out and flew from the room. It seemed Mr. Tibbs had handled the matter.

"Well," Abel said, "I guess that takes care of that problem."

Jane glanced up, amusement twisting her lips. Edie's brother sat on the floor, tangled in wire, the bent microphone in hand and his headphones askew.

"Sorry," she apologized. "I didn't know Tinkle followed me. I thought she was still with Gran."

Abel shrugged and got to his feet, began untangling wires.

"So . . . did you hear anything interesting?" she asked brightly.

Abel grimaced. "Birds chirping, squirrels chattering, and deer stomping about."

"Deer? Really?"

"Yeah." He grinned. "A whole herd of them came up the hill," he said with an enthusiasm that quickly faded. "But I didn't hear a peep from our neighbors. I don't think this stupid thing works," he added, glaring at the shotgun mike.

"No. It wouldn't," Jane agreed. "We need the parabolic microphone and definitely the wall-contact microphone for this job."

"Parabolic? That's the one that looks like a satellite dish," Abel said with interest. He gave up on the tangled wire to sort through the mess on the floor.

"Yes." Jane took it from him when he found it. "We'll set this up on the hill once it turns dark." She frowned. "We'll have to think of some way to camouflage it."

Abel nodded. "What's the wall-contact microphone?"

"Exactly what it sounds like," Jane said easily. "A highly sensitive amplifier. You can hear conversations through thirty centimeters of solid concrete with it."

"But you have to attach it to the wall?"

"Everything has its drawbacks." Jane shrugged. "That's why we'll have to wait for night to set it up. We'll do it after the party."

"Ah, yes, the party," he murmured, not sounding very eager.

Reminded of her purpose in coming into this room, Jane moved toward the dresser on the other side of the bed. "I was just going to fetch some clothes."

"Your gran and I already picked out—"

"Yes, I know." Jane cut him off, a blush rising on her face. "But I need some other stuff."

"Ah." Jane could hear the amusement in his voice as she opened the top drawer to reveal rows of neatly stacked underthings. Then he said, "I was going to pick some for you and put them with the dress, but I didn't think you'd appreciate it."

"Ah, no. But thanks," she said. She heard him chuckle. Jane was too embarrassed to examine the contents of this drawer too closely with Abel there, so she grabbed up the first thing to hand, glanced to see that it was the right size, and started to close the drawer.

"Er . . . you might want to wear black," Abel commented, letting her know that he was indeed watching. "The dress we picked is black."

"Oh." Jane tossed back the lavender set of underwear she'd grabbed and snatched up a black set instead. She avoided his eyes as she left the room.

Jane was in and out of the shower quickly. She dried off, tossed her used towel aside, and picked up her underwear. It was lacy and sexy, not her usual style. She generally preferred comfy plain cotton underthings. But Jane doubted there would be any comfy plain cotton anything supplied by B.L.I.S.S. That wasn't *their* style.

She put on the bra and panties, then paused to examine herself in the mirror. If she just looked at her body, it was like looking at someone else. The bra was one of those push-up ones. But Jane didn't need pushing up to make her look full-breasted. She grimaced at the sight of all that rounded flesh spilling out of the black lace and poked at first one cup, then the other with discomfort, but it didn't deflate or make her look any smaller.

Jane had been self-conscious about her breasts since she turned twelve and the boys started to notice and tease her. It had all been downhill from there. Boys had tried to grope her, middle-aged men had started hitting on her, and every male she met had started talking to her chest rather than her face. In grade eight, while Jane was giving a speech in class, Tommy Simpson had shot a spitball at her, right down her top. That had been the end of Jane's public-speaking career.

Each such encounter had made her more self-conscious, more introverted. She might have grown out of it, but then she'd hit the dating age. Her first boyfriend had been Jerry Jordan. He'd asked her to a school dance. Jane had been excited and eager, happily overlooking his unfortunate freckles until his best friend had informed her Jerry was only taking her because she had a big chest and was therefore easy.

Jane had stormed up to Jerry, punched him right in the nose, then bawled him out. But once she'd reached home and the safety of her room, she'd cried. After that, she'd become even more withdrawn, turning her attention to books and her schoolwork and ignoring any boys who showed interest in her. Or trying to. There had been the occasional male persistent enough to ignore her turndowns, who continued asking her out until she gave up refusing them out of sheer exasperation. But those relationships hadn't had much of a chance.

"Janie?"

Jane pulled the selected dress off its hanger on the back of the door, dragged it over her head, then tugged it into place. Then she opened the door.

"Abel said you forgot stockings."

Jane stared at the black silk her grandmother held out. Yes, she'd forgotten them. Abel hadn't. She took the bits of wispy material, noting as she did that there was a black garter belt included. He thought of everything, it seemed.

"That dress is perfect." Gran rolled into the bathroom as Jane sat on the side of the tub to don the stockings.

"Where's Tinkle?" Jane asked. The beastly dog liked to nip and scratch at her legs when she put on nylons, causing huge runs before she'd even got any use of them.

"I don't know. She followed you to the other end of the house when you went to fetch your under things, but she didn't come back. She must be exploring."

The dog was more likely hiding from Mr. Tibbs, Jane thought. That cheered her.

"You should really put the garter on first, dear."

Jane paused with one stocking halfway up and stood up to pull on the garter belt. Then she sat again and returned to the stockings.

"There." She finished and stood to brush the skirt of the black dress back into place.

"Perfect," Gran pronounced.

Jane glanced at herself in the mirror. She wasn't sure if perfect was the word, but she sure was something in this dress. See-through black lace made up the long sleeves and most of the back of the dress, and dipped all the way down to the top of her bra before the solid back underslip started. Now she understood why Abel had suggested the black lace underthings. If she bent over, reached up, or generally moved in this dress, her bra would show in the front. As would the top of her panties in the back, she realized as she turned to check. The see-through lace dipped quite low back there.

Lavender peeking out would have looked ridiculous. The black looked rather sexy, she thought— until she saw her face and damp hair. The dress was B.L.I.S.S., but from the neck up she was the same old Jane. Her shoulders slumped. She looked like techno-geek Jane Spyrus in a sexy dress. Definitely not femme-fatale material.

"I had Abel find a curling iron and a hair dryer while you were sleeping," Gran spoke up. "Fortunately, Beatrice Goodinov had both, plus some heavy-duty hair spray. Abel put it all in the dining room with what makeup we could find. Come on out and I'll fix you up."

Jane followed obediently to the dining room. She seated herself on a small one-step stool they found in the kitchen so that she would be at the right height for Gran to work on her, then sat patiently as Maggie Spyrus fussed over her hair.

It seemed to take forever—not to mention an awful lot of hair spray—before Gran decided her hair was finished. She then set to work on Jane's face. She'd been working on that for several minutes before Jane recognized the compact she was using.

"That's the knockout powder!" she said with alarm.

"Yes, but I'm using the compressed stuff," Gran assured her. The compact had two levels. It opened naturally to a section with a powder puff and real compressed face powder, then had the secret compartment with the lose knockout dust.

Jane relaxed a little until her grandmother picked up some lipstick. Her eyes widened in horror. "That's Lipschitz's knockout lipstick!"

"Is it?" Gran paused and pursed her lips. "Is it safe to wear?"

"There's a clear base coat in the other end. You put that on first. I guess it acts as a barrier or an antidote."

"Good. It's the perfect color." Gran handed the stick and a small mirror to Jane.

"Can't I just wear my own?"

"Yours is dull, Janie, dear. This is hot. Every man's wet dream. Put it on."

Grumbling under her breath, Jane did as she was told.

"Tuck it into your bra," Gran said when Jane had finished applying both layers of the lipstick and started to return it to the makeup pile.

"What?" Jane asked with bewilderment.

"Tuck it into your bra, dear. You might need to reapply it later, and I know you won't take a purse." She waited until Jane had reluctantly done so, then set to work on her eyes, applying a light layer of eye shadow and eyeliner that Jane recognized with relief was Gran's own. But when the older woman picked up a silver bottle of perfume next, Jane pulled back. "That's my truth serum perfume!"

"Yes, I know. It may come in handy tonight. Don't you think?"

Jane nodded after a moment. "Yes. If Dirk gets close enough to inhale it."

"You'll just have to *make sure* he gets close enough." Her grandmother poured some scent out onto a cotton ball and dabbed liberal amounts of it around Jane's ears, neck, and wrists. Jane grimaced as some was dabbed in the hollow between her breasts.

"Try to get him close enough to inhale the perfume, but don't let him kiss you. We may have trouble explaining how a kiss could knock him out."

"As if anyone would want to kiss me," Jane muttered.

Gran paused in putting the makeup away and arched an eyebrow. "Janie, dear, I think you'd best go take a look in the mirror. I have no doubt he'll want to kiss you."

Jane stood and made her way back to the bathroom. She nearly fainted when she saw her reflection. Dear Lord, it was a miracle! She was gorgeous. Sexy. Hot.

"I look . . . good," she said faintly as Gran rolled up.

"You look better than good, darling. You look like a Spyrus." The woman considered Jane with pursed lips then said, "Now we just have to work on your posture and walk."

"What's wrong with my posture?" Jane asked.

"Nothing—if you're a bookworm techno-geek trying to hide a pair of magnificent breasts by hunching your shoulders and trying to disappear into them."

"Don't hold anything back, Gran," Jane retorted wryly.

"And as for your walk, you don't really walk— you scamper like a mouse trying to avoid detection."

Jane heaved a sigh, knowing her gran's descriptions were apt. She did often try to avoid detection. She would be happy to always blend into the woodwork. And yes, she did walk around with her shoulders hunched in an effort to make her breasts smaller. Which was ridiculous, of course. Nothing would make them smaller short of a reduction, which she had seriously considered on several occasions. She simply hadn't found the courage to go through with it yet.

"Stand up straight," Gran ordered. "Shoulders back, chest out."

Jane hesitated, then straightened her back and thrust her chest forward . . . only to immediately slump back to her usual posture. She wasn't ready for this.

"Shoulders back and chest out," Gran repeated firmly.

Jane straightened again, grimacing. Why couldn't she have had a delicate little body with perky breasts instead of this rounded, too-voluptuous carcass? She pondered, watching her back bend and her shoulders slump in the mirror.

"Jane, stop trying to hide what God gave you! The

165

only one you're fooling is yourself," Maggie Spyrus snapped. "Now straighten up, stick that chest out, and sashay—do not scamper—across the floor. I want to see swaying hips."

"Gran!" Jane flushed. "I can't—"

"You need shoes," Gran interrupted. "I'm sure Abel put them in here with the dress."

Spotting them by the door, Jane moved to pick them up. Her eyes widened with disbelief as she looked them over. She always wore flat shoes. Always. These were not flat. They were high-heeled, strappy black sandals. She would surely kill herself.

"No. I can't." Jane shook her head.

"Maybe Jane Spyrus can't," Gran said grimly. "But Jane Goodinov can . . . for Edie."

Jane met her grandmother's gaze and felt her spine stiffen. She *could* do this for Edie. She'd just think of it as playacting. If she thought of herself as someone else, Jane Goodinov, maybe, just maybe she could pull it off.

Determination coursing through her, she slipped the sandals on then straightened, forcing herself to stand straight, chest out.

"Good." Gran nodded in approval. "Now, show me some sashay, Jane Goodinov."

Jane spun away on the toe of one foot and did her damnedest to sashay across the large bathroom, remembering to keep her back straight and chest out.

"That's it!" Gran crowed. "Look at yourself. You're beautiful. You're sexy. You're brilliant. You're all those things. They're your heritage. You should be a field operative. You have been hiding out as a techno-geek, but *this* is the real you!"

Jane could feel confidence pouring into her. She could feel it swelling within her.

"You can do this."

"I can do this," Jane echoed.

"You *are* doing it."

"I *am* doing it," Jane agreed with surprise.

"A little more sway," Gran instructed. Jane forced her hips to obey.

"Now I want you to relax," Gran said as Jane reached the far end of the room and turned back. "You're a little stiff. Think of a slinky. Slink back across the room," she instructed. "Better yet, think ooze. You are a collection of sensual lotion, oozing sex appeal."

"Which is it?" Jane asked with exasperation. "Slinky or oozing?"

"Both!" Gran said firmly, so Jane did her best to move as she thought an oozing slinky would.

"You're thinking too hard. Don't work at it. Let it happen."

"Easy for you to say," Jane muttered. She turned away and started back across the room. *Oozing slinkies*, she thought. *Oozing slinkies. Oozing*—She paused to kick aside the towel she'd used after her shower and the sight of it made her think of Abel. She had a sudden sharp image in her mind of him standing in the motel room, naked but for a small linen around his waist. He'd looked really good in that. *Really* good. She'd wanted to run her hands all over his naked chest and—

"That's it!" Gran cackled, clapping her hands.

Jane swung back in surprise.

"That was perfect. You have it now," Gran told her.

"Great!" Jane said with exasperation. "I wasn't even thinking oozing slinky."

"Well, whatever it was, think of it all night long. It was perfect." Gran rolled over to her. "Now, you have to try to get close to Dirk tonight. Find out what you can. If you can finagle an invitation to his house out of him, even better."

"But—"

"Agents take advantage of every opportunity," Gran lectured firmly. "Take advantage. Exploit your figure and flash a come-hither smile. You've got it; use it. Use everything you've got."

"But what if I mess up?" Jane asked, uncertainty eating her.

"You won't," Gran answered. "But if something goes wrong, I'll be there to back you up."

Jane considered and nodded reluctantly. She could do this. For Edie.

"You're ready," Gran decided. "Now I have to get ready."

Jane helped her change her clothes; then Gran shooed her from the room and took over fixing her own hair and makeup. Jane stepped out into the hall, considered its long length, and decided to practice being an oozing slinky. Lifting her chin, she straightened her posture, thrust out her chest, and followed her breasts down the hall, a picture of Abel in his towel firmly in mind. Then she recalled Abel without the towel, then Abel with the cat over himself, then Abel with the cat up, then Abel with the cat down. It brought a wicked smile to her lips as she entered the kitchen.

"Dear God, I almost didn't believe it."

Jane stopped dead and glanced at Abel. The real Abel. Fully dressed in a suit and tie, looking almost as sexy as he had in just his towel, he stood by the French doors in the dining room. Apparently he'd been enjoying the view.

"Um . . ." Jane started to return to her usual posture, then caught herself and straightened. She asked, "You almost didn't believe what?"

"That you really are a spy," he admitted, moving around the half counter that separated them. "You seemed too sweet, too nice. Even a little inept. But . . ." He paused to let his eyes trail down over her and Jane could feel them caress her body. "Just now, when you walked into the kitchen and didn't know I was looking—I definitely see that you can do it."

Jane felt herself smile, but before she could say anything Gran rolled into the kitchen. "Are we all ready to go?" she asked.

"Yes." Abel took control of Gran's wheelchair and steered her to the elevator.

The trio rode down in silence, passed through the garage, and started up the driveway. Abel was still pushing Gran, which had seemed nice to Jane at first, but she now wondered if she might not do better to push her herself. It would give her something to hold. She really wasn't used to high heels and felt a bit shaky.

"You know, it occurs to me that we may have a problem," Gran said suddenly.

Jane and Abel exchanged a glance, then peered down at her.

"What?" Abel asked.

"Your name."

"Oh." Jane clucked her tongue impatiently. She really hadn't thought of it.

"What's wrong with my name?" Abel asked.

"It's not very common," Jane pointed out. "I think Gran's worried that Edie may have mentioned you."

"Yes." Gran made a clucking sound, too. "I should have thought of it sooner."

"I can just go by my middle name," Abel suggested.

"What is that?" Jane asked.

"Nathaniel."

"Nathaniel," Jane repeated. "Nathan. Nat. Nat Goodinov." She chuckled.

"It's too late for that," Gran pointed out. "We introduced you to Leigh as Abel."

"Hm," Jane murmured. They all fell silent as they crested the drive and started onto the road. Then she said, "I guess we'll just have to hope Edie hasn't mentioned her brother. Or that they don't think anything of your having the same name," she added. Edie probably had mentioned him, since she'd taken a day off to pick him up from the airport.

"And that they'll overlook the fact that you look a lot like Edie," Gran added.

Abel *did* look a lot like Edie. He was a male version of her. Alarm coursing through her, Jane stopped. "Maybe you should stay home."

"That might be a good idea," Gran agreed.

Abel drew himself up, obviously ready to do battle over the issue, but the sound of footsteps on the road behind them made them all glance back. A couple stepped off the driveway where the Enseck-sis lived and started toward them.

"Too late," Abel announced with satisfaction. He began to push Gran forward again. "We'll just have to hope for the best."

Jane reluctantly followed. She remained silent as they started up Leigh Senchall's driveway.

She, Maggie, and Abel all paused uncertainly when they came to a set of stairs almost as intrepid as the ones leading up to their own front door. Jane had never considered the possibility of Leigh Senchall's having stairs. Her gaze went to Gran's wheelchair in dismay.

"I can carry Maggie," Abel said at last. "Can you

bring the wheelchair, or is it too heavy? Maybe you should just leave it and I can come back."

"No. I think I can manage," Jane said quickly. After all, she was forever moving it to the back of the van and stowing it.

Nodding, Abel scooped Gran's slender body out of her chair, then started up the stairs. Jane watched them for a couple of steps, but when Edie's brother didn't falter and seemed fine, she turned her attention back to the chair. She was terribly aware of the approaching couple as she picked it up. These people were all quite possibly evil villains bent on world domination. At the very least they were kidnappers. In other words, they were the bad guys.

That thought running around and around in her mind, Jane started up the stairs with the wheelchair. It only proved that she was not the most coordinated of people. She wasn't holding the wheelchair high enough. It caught on the lip of a step, pulled her off balance, and sent her tumbling backward.

Chapter Eleven

"Whoa!" A pair of warm strong hands caught her upper arms, preventing Jane from breaking her neck at the base of Leigh Senchall's stairway.

Jane—who'd been sure she was about to die—felt her heart start up again, sending blood thundering into her head. She sagged briefly against her savior's chest, overcome with relief that she would live to get herself killed another day.

"A pretty little girl like you shouldn't be trying to cart around that wheelchair." The voice was as smooth as silk, and Jane felt a shudder run through her as a puff of warm breath caressed her ear. She tilted and turned her head to see the speaker . . . and felt her stomach drop right down into her toes. The man holding her was quite the most beautiful creature she'd ever laid eyes on. He had dark hair, dark eyes, long lashes, a straight European nose, high cheekbones, and full luscious lips that were lowering toward hers.

"Oh, let the poor girl go. She's hardly in your league, Dirk."

Jane stiffened at that caustic comment and forced herself to find her feet. Poor girl? Hardly in his league? Her mouth flattened grimly as she straightened away from her rescuer. They'd just see about that!

Oozing slinky, oozing slinky, she thought quickly as she set her gran's wheelchair on the steps. She brought up the picture of a towelless, catless Abel in her mind and held the wheelchair in place with one hand, then turned with what she hoped was a smoldering look on her face. "Dirk? You must be Dirk Ensecksi."

"So women tell me," he murmured with a wicked grin. Jane caught her breath. To distract herself, she turned her gaze to the woman with Dirk. Shorter. Slender. A beautiful ice maiden with blond hair and blue eyes.

Contacts and a dye job, Jane decided cattily. She'd have to keep an eye on Abel. This woman screamed man-eater. "Which would make you Lydia."

Jane didn't bother to hide her lack of enthusiasm, but oddly enough her antipathy brought a smile from the woman.

"Yes." She reached out. "I didn't mean to ruffle your feathers with that crack. I hadn't got a good look at you yet. Lydia Ensecksi."

"Jane Goodinov," Jane responded, taking the offered hand. She wasn't surprised to find it cold and hard.

"We'll see," Lydia said with amusement, obviously playing on her name. Before Jane could respond she added, "You must be the Goodinovs' niece, here to baby-sit the house."

"News travels fast," Jane said.

"Trixie told me this afternoon."

"Trixie the Grapevine," Jane quipped.

"In more ways than one," Lydia agreed with a sharp laugh. Then the woman added, "I think we'll be friends, Jane Goodinov."

Lord save me, Jane thought.

Dirk moved to place his hand over hers on the wheelchair. "Can I take this for you?"

A frisson of awareness shot up her arm and Jane—who had loads of experience with men who didn't attract her, but very little with men who did— felt her mind turn to mush. She smiled at him stupidly, then realized what she was doing. She stopped. Hoping her mind would glue itself back together if she just gave it some distance, Jane shifted the wheelchair between them and nearly knocked him off the stairs. Lydia and she both grabbed his arms at the same time to save him.

"You'd *better* give me that," Dirk said with a laugh as he regained his balance. "You're obviously dangerous with wheelchairs."

Oozing slinky, oozing slinky. Naked Abel. Jane let her lips curve the slightest bit and responded with a husky, "I'm dangerous with a lot of things."

It was a bad line; she knew even before the perplexed expression covered Dirk's face. Apparently the oozing-slinky, naked-Abel thing didn't always work. Sighing inwardly, Jane gave Ensecksi the wheelchair and a wink, then turned to sashay up the stairs.

She didn't look back to see if the Ensecksis followed. Jane was too busy berating herself. How could she be attracted to a criminal mastermind?

How could she have done something as stupid as trip herself up on the stairs, then nearly knock Dirk off them? And what was that crack about Trixie the Grapevine? It had been cruel. She wasn't a cruel person.

"Oh, Jane!"

She gave up her self-flagellation and glanced up at the sound of that apologetic voice. Leigh Senchall was standing in her open front door wearing another lovely creamy yellow dress and looking as if she'd been berating herself as well.

"I'm so sorry," the woman groaned. She looked mortified. "I never even thought of the stairs when I invited you over."

A true smile curved Jane's lips, and she laughed slightly. "Well, better stairs than not being invited at all."

"Oh, yes! But . . . Well, I could have arranged something to make it easier than Abel's having to carry your grandmother up and you having to cart the wheelchair." She paused. "Where *is* the wheelchair? Abel said you were bringing it."

"Right here."

Jane sighed as those words sounded at her back. How the hell did the man manage to make two puny, insignificant words sound so damn sexy?

"Oh, Dirk." Judging by the breathiness of her voice, Leigh Senchall wasn't immune to the man either. "How sweet of you."

"That's my brother. Sweet, sweet, sweet," Lydia commented, continuing up the stairs past Jane and Leigh as well. "I need a drink."

Exchanging a glance with her hostess, Jane continued up the stairs, afraid that if she didn't, Dirk would just continue to stand behind her, breathing on her and sending shivers down her back. Leigh led them into her house and a living room almost as big as the great room in the Goodinov mansion. There were more than twenty people here and every single one of the dozen or so females were wearing yellow evening dresses. The men, however, had bypassed their Hawaiian shirts—in favor of yellow dress shirts. Their ties were loud and almost Hawaiian, though, Jane noted as her gaze slid over the small groups sipping drinks and quietly talking.

She turned away from the crowd as Leigh stopped. They'd reached Gran and Abel. Maggie Spyrus sat in a straight-backed chair with Abel at her side.

"Here we are," Leigh said brightly. Dirk set the wheelchair down. He did so with an easy grace that belied the weight of the thing.

"Thank you for helping with it," Jane murmured.

"That's what neighbors are for," the man said smoothly, opening the wheelchair.

Abel bent and gently relocated Maggie.

"There," Leigh said, seeming relieved. "Everything's all right now."

A murmur of agreement went around, then Leigh turned to Dirk. "I should introduce you. Dirk, this is Abel and Maggie Goodinov. And of course you've met Jane."

"Yes." He gave her another megawatt smile.

Introductions done, Leigh asked Dirk, "Where's your father? I thought Lydia said he might be coming."

"He didn't make it back as expected," Dirk answered. "There was a delay at work. He should show up soon, though."

Jane and Gran exchanged a glance. Y had said that the senior Ensecksi had slipped the agents set on him and was probably on his way to Sonora. They would have to let her know she'd been right.

"Oh, good. He'll be here in time for Thanksgiving then," Leigh was saying. "You'll like Robert Ensecksi," she added.

Jane glanced over to see the woman smiling at her. Then Leigh looked as if a thought had struck her and she turned to Dirk to ask, "Did Jane tell you she's a writer?"

"No, she didn't," Dirk said with interest.

Jane barely noticed as she turned in shock on her grandmother.

"I know you don't like me bragging, Janie, dear. But we were talking and Leigh asked what we all did," Gran explained with a shrug. "Well, I just had to tell her about your writing crime novels. You know how proud I am."

"Yes," Jane murmured, realizing that it was as good a cover as any. It would explain how she could drop everything to house-sit with Gran.

"Crime novels?" Dirk's sexy smile widened. "That sounds exciting."

He was as warm as a sunbaked stone where his arm brushed hers, and Jane had to physically control her reaction. She turned a slightly confused gaze to Abel, wondering why he didn't have this effect on her. She liked him, and there was no doubt in her mind she was attracted to him, but she didn't experience this confusing rush that left her feeling vulnerable.

"Yes, it does sound exciting," Leigh enthused. "You know we have another writer here in the community. Melanie Johnson. She's a sweetie. You two should get on famously." She turned to glance over the people in the room. "She and Brian arrived just ahead of you. Now where is she? Brian works in

Silicon Valley," she added, then smiled brightly. "Ah. There she is. Come on, I'll introduce you two. I know you're going to love her."

Jane cast one helpless glance Gran's way, then found herself led off to meet the Johnsons. She knew Leigh thought she was doing a good deed, but Jane had been right where she needed to be. Unfortunately, she could hardly tell Leigh that.

Across the room, Melanie and Brian Johnson stood talking with an older couple—the Wares, Jane learned when Leigh made introductions. The older couple moved off shortly thereafter, then Leigh excused herself to return to her hostess duties.

"Well, thank you for saving us," Brian Johnson said.

Jane turned back from watching Leigh urge Gran and Abel into some group she presumably felt they would fit. "For saving you?"

"From the Wares," he explained, a twinkle in his eyes. "They were inviting us to dinner and we were trying to politely decline."

Jane raised an eyebrow. "You don't like the Wares?"

"Oh, I like them fine," he assured her. "At a distance. And clothed."

Jane was blinking in confusion over this announcement when Melanie elbowed her husband. With a laugh she explained, "They're swingers. Brian and I don't swing."

"Oh," Jane said blankly. Her gaze moved over the author. Melanie Johnson was a delicate-looking woman. A good foot shorter than her husband, she was slender with fine strawberry-blond hair and wide beautiful eyes. She was also wearing a dress that was white—though it had gold trim. It made

Jane wonder if this was a sign of resistance to the microwave mind control. Perhaps it didn't work on everyone. Leigh and Melanie seemed to be fighting it with their cream colors rather than going full yellow.

"No. We don't swing," Brian agreed. Then he asked straight-faced, "Do you?"

"Brian!" Melanie elbowed him in the stomach again, laughing despite herself.

Jane decided she liked this couple. "Only if I don't wear a bra," she answered equally straight-faced.

The Johnsons gaped at her briefly; then both burst out laughing. His was a deep, rich, full-bodied laugh, while hers was a higher tinkling. Both sounds bespoke real, unself-conscious amusement, and Jane decided that yes, she definitely liked this couple.

That liking helped her decide she was probably better to stay and talk to them than to manufacture an excuse to return to Dirk. Mr. Manetrue had said Dirk was a ladies man. Which suggested he liked the chase. Thus, she reasoned, she really shouldn't be chasing him. It was probably better to let him come to her.

Of course, if he didn't do so, she'd eventually have to make her way to his side. However, it wouldn't hurt to have him think he wasn't the center of the universe.

Jane learned a lot in the half hour she spent with the Johnsons. The three of them were somewhat separate from the rest of the room, so when Jane showed a real curiosity about the people at the party, the twosome was happy to help. A painfully honest rundown filled with dry wit had them all bursting into repeated gales of laughter. There were the usual she-cat out looking for amusement while her dentist husband was busy drilling his patients; a brilliant researcher wife with her bought-and-paid-for beach-bum, boy-toy hubby. There were the Ensecksis, whom Melanie liked to call the Toosexys and—

"And that's Daniel and Luellen..." Melanie peered up at her husband. "What is their last name again?"

"Brownstone," Brian said.

Jane's gaze moved curiously to the couple. A strong, solid blond man and a pretty redhead: she caught both staring at her. The pair smiled and nodded, then turned casually away. And that's when Jane realized that they too weren't under the "yellow" spell. The wife wore red; the husband a normal tie and white shirt.

"Braunstein," Melanie corrected, apparently remembering better. "I don't know much about them. They're new. They just moved in today, too. But they bought a house here," Melanie added. "So I guess they're permanent. Or at least semipermanent."

"Unlike us who are quite temporary," Jane commented.

"Yes. Which is a shame. I think I like you."

Jane smiled, then stilled as her eyes landed on a male guest just entering the house.

"How do you like Sonora so far?" Brian asked.

"Oh, it seems lovely," she answered, her gaze still on the newcomer. "It's very picturesque."

"Yes, it has quite a history," Melanie began, then asked, "Do you know Colin?"

"Colin?" Jane repeated the name, but it didn't ring any bells.

"Yes. Colin Alkars. He's—"

"Oh!" Jane gave a laugh as she recognized the last name. "Officer Alkars. I *thought* he looked familiar. Does he live here, too?"

"Not in the community," Melanie answered. "But he's Leigh's brother and the local sheriff so he gets invited. How on earth did you already meet him? I thought Leigh said you've only been here since this morning?"

"Yes. We arrived this morning. I met him when . . . Well, Tinkle attacked him," Jane admitted, then told the tale, managing to make it sound funnier than it had really been. The three of them ended up laughing again.

"This seems to be the fun group. Mind if I join? Your laughter is irresistible."

Jane's laughter died in her throat as she turned to find herself staring into Dirk's deep dark eyes. They were hypnotizing.

"Everyone!" Leigh's voice saved Jane from drowning in those eyes, and she turned with relief to where their hostess stood by the door. "Everyone seems to be here and the meal is ready, so I guess we can eat. It's buffet style and set up in the next room. Feel free to make as many trips as you want. I'd appreciate not having any food left."

It seemed everyone was hungry. A good number of the twenty or so guests headed into the next room in almost a stampede. Jane noticed Abel, Lydia, and Gran moving that way in a trio, and watched them closely. Abel was smiling and nodding at something Dirk's sister was saying, but there was that telltale pulse. She was oddly relieved to see it. He hadn't fallen under the woman's spell and forgotten that she had his sister.

"Let's go."

Jane turned back at Brian Johnson's eager suggestion. His wife was wrinkling her nose.

"Let's wait for the worst of the rush to end," Melanie suggested, but her husband stared at her as if she were speaking Dutch.

"But you were complaining on the way here that you were hungry," he said.

"I am. But I hate crowds."

"Ah, yes. Well, never fear, my lady. I shall brave the madding throng and fetch ye back some vittles." He quit hamming long enough to add to Jane, "My wife writes romance novels."

"I don't *do* medieval," Melanie said with a disdainful sniff, but her eyes were twinkling.

"Was that medieval?" Brian asked.

"Mostly. But I think 'vittles' is more Hatfield and McCoy than medieval," she said. Then she gave him a nudge. "Go find me some food. And take Dirk with you."

"Okay," Brian agreed. "Come on, Dirk. Methinks the women want to yammer about us."

Dirk turned to Jane, eyebrows raised. "Should I fix you a plate?"

"Yes, please," Jane answered. She was rather hungry; she hadn't had anything since that slice of cinnamon coffee cake with Leigh.

"What do you like?"

"Oh. Ah . . ." Jane shrugged. "Anything. I'm easy."

Dirk's eyebrows shot up, and Jane felt herself flush. *Oozing slinky,* she thought in a panic as she felt herself begin to flounder. The maneuver had an immediate calming effect on her, and she managed a slow wink before turning back to Melanie.

"Dirk's very handsome," the author said as soon as the men were out of earshot.

"Yes," Jane agreed with a frown. Melanie opened

182

her mouth to say something else, but paused and smiled at someone behind Jane instead.

"Hi, Colin."

"Hello, Melanie," a friendly voice said. The sheriff glanced at Jane as she turned to face him, then did a double take and grinned. "And hello, 'Janie, dear,'" he teased. "Fancy meeting you here."

"I was just thinking the same thing, 'nice police-man.'" She laughed, knowing she needn't explain to Melanie. She had already told the tale.

"Call me Colin," he suggested. Smiling at her, he shifted his gaze back to Melanie. "Where's Brian?"

"Fetching food," she answered.

The author's eyes held real liking. It was only then that Jane realized Melanie's smiles had dimmed some when Dirk joined their group. It seemed she disliked Dirk. She seemed to have good instincts.

"I guess I have my answer."

Jane glanced at Colin blankly. "About what?"

"When we were in the restaurant, I asked if you'd moved here or were just vacationing. Your food arrived and you left. I never got the answer."

"I'm—"

"The Goodinovs' niece," Colin finished. "Leigh pointed you out when I arrived. I just didn't realize it was you. You were indulging in the natural and wholesome look this morning."

"He means weary and haggard," Jane told Melanie with a laugh. "I was wearing faded jeans and a T-shirt."

"No," Colin said firmly. "I mean wholesome and naturally pretty."

"Here we are!" Brian announced jovially as he returned bearing two plates. "For you, my love." He handed one to his wife, then smiled easily at Colin.

"Hey there. The line is finally dwindling, but so is the food. You might want to grab some before it's gone."

"There'll be more in the kitchen. Leigh always has more in the kitchen." Colin laughed; then his gaze settled on Dirk, who had moved to Jane's side to offer her a heavily laden plate. The sheriff's gaze cooled as it fell on the man, and he seemed to grow a touch stiff. Then he said, "But perhaps I should hit the buffet just in case. Ladies." He nodded and turned away.

Jane watched him go, then turned her attention to the food Dirk had brought. He had chosen a nice variety—stuffed mushrooms, dill potatoes, turkey, cranberries, stuffing, and several other things. Jane took the fork on the plate and started to scoop up some of the dill potatoes, then suddenly recalled her knockout lipstick. If the clear base coat was an antidote, she shouldn't have a problem. But what if it was just a protective barrier? She couldn't eat without getting lipstick on her fork, possibly on the food. Then, if she swallowed it . . .

She had a brief vision of falling to the ground unconscious, cranberries and stuffing landing all over her pretty dress. That was enough to make her put the fork down. Relieved to see the others busy examining their plates, she quickly wiped her lips with the napkin Dirk had provided.

Glancing around as she picked up her plate again, Jane noticed Abel and Lydia were sitting on the couch. Gran's wheelchair was pulled up close. The icy blonde was ignoring Gran completely and chattering away as she busily pawed Abel's arm and chest. He was just trying to eat.

Slut, Jane thought with irritation. Next she'd be crawling into his lap right in front of everyone. It was a good thing Abel knew she was an evil villain, or Jane might have felt moved to go over and save him. Purely for his own good, she assured herself.

"Dirk." Leigh Senchall approached them, a worried expression on her face. "There's a man here. He says he needs to speak to you, and that it's urgent. About your father."

"Ah." Dirk set his plate on an end table, and took Leigh's hand reassuringly. "Don't worry. It's probably just an update on his travel plans. Is he at the door?"

"No. I put him in Will's office," Leigh explained as they moved away.

"Will?" Jane asked, turning curiously to the Johnsons.

"Leigh's husband," Melanie said. "He's around here somewhere. He's a computer geek too."

"Isn't everybody?" Brian asked lightly, then added, "And it's 'computer guru,' my dear wife. We are computer gurus."

Melanie rolled her eyes with a laugh. Glancing around, she frowned with frustration. "I don't see him, or I'd point Will out to you."

"He's manning the turkey tray," Brian said. "He's directing the caterers and slicing up meat. Like a manly man should."

"Will's nice," Melanie added. "He and Brian are good friends."

"Ah," Jane answered with distraction, busy watching the door to the hall. When she saw Leigh return, she turned back to the Johnsons and managed a smile. She set her plate down next to Dirk's. "Excuse me, I think I have to go to the bathroom."

"You *think?*" Brian raised one eyebrow and smiled.

185

Flushing, Jane merely shrugged and hurried away.

Stepping into the entry, she glanced around. The front door was on her right, but she'd seen Leigh and Dirk turn left and recalled their hostess saying she'd left the man in Will's office. Jane turned left and eyed the long hallway, trying to decide which of the doors might be to an office. They were all closed and all looked the same to her. After a hesitation, she started listening at each door. She was halfway along when the sound of high-heeled shoes on the hardwood hall made her glance back. It was the redhead, Luellen Braunstein. Jane straightened and managed an embarrassed smile as the woman approached.

She was just trying to think of an excuse to give for getting caught listening at doors, when one opened behind her and men's voices drifted out:

"Tell him we shouldn't be too late. It's the usual lame crowd, though there is one interesting newcomer."

Jane recognized Dirk's voice and grimaced. She was about to be caught loitering in the hallway like a lost puppy.

Luellen Braunstein wasn't. The redhead slipped through the nearest door and out of sight. She did, however, leave the door open a crack. Jane noted that and suspected the woman was peering through as she herself turned back to brave the situation out.

Her gaze fell first on the blond with Dirk. He was shorter and had a barrel-shaped body and a pock-marked face. The blond was the first to spot her and his eyes narrowed. Fortunately, Dirk didn't look at her in the same way. He beamed instead.

"Jane, were you looking for me?" Stopping at her side, he waved the other man on.

"No. I was hot and thought I'd step out for some air," she lied with a singular lack of credibility. Even she wouldn't have believed herself—and as Lizzy liked to tell her, she was terribly gullible.

"What a good idea." His smile was wolfish as he took her arm and led her down the hall.

"Where are we going?" she asked nervously. Glancing over her shoulder, she almost hoped that Luellen Braunstein would make her presence known and rescue her. The door the redhead had slid through stayed mostly closed, however, and the man Dirk had spoken to, while still lingering there in the hall despite being dismissed, didn't look likely to offer any aid. In fact, he was eyeing her rather suspiciously.

"Out for some air," Dirk answered. That drew her gaze back around as he walked her into the office he'd just left. "Because you're *hot*."

That double entendre singed her, and Jane began to think perhaps her oozing slinky act had worked too well.

Chapter Twelve

"Jane's gone," Abel said suddenly with alarm. He'd been busy trying to keep Lydia Ensecksi from diving down his pants right there in the middle of Leigh Senchall's living room. The woman had finally excused herself to "visit the ladies' room," and he'd immediately looked around, intent on finding Jane to see how she was doing with Dirk Juan. But Jane wasn't in the room.

"Leigh and Dirk left several minutes ago, and Janie followed," Maggie explained. She didn't seem concerned.

"Maybe I should make sure she's all right," Abel suggested.

"Down, boy." Jane's grandmother added with amusement, "We're the professionals, remember? Janie will be fine. She has several weapons at her disposal."

Abel glanced over. "Weapons? I didn't see any weapons. That dress couldn't hide any weapons, Maggie. You're just trying to keep me from looking for her."

"Call me Gran," the woman ordered, reminding him that he was supposed to be her grandson. Then she finished, "And trust me. She has weapons."

He persisted. "What weapons?"

Maggie Spyrus scowled impatiently, then sighed. "Twenty years of martial arts and knockout lipstick, among other things."

"Twenty years?" Abel asked with disbelief.

"All the Spyrus children are put into martial-arts classes before they turn five. Jane was too. She's taken Tae Kwon Do, jujitsu, karate, kung fu, Go Shin Jitsu, and Jeet Kune Do." Maggie shrugged. "She only gave it up a couple of years ago when her schedule got too hectic. She still spars once in a while, though."

Abel shook his head. He was starting to feel a bit inferior. He'd taken karate for five years as a teenager, but Jane had taken twenty? Someone sat down beside him. Abel felt the hand moving up his leg and didn't have to turn to see who it was. Lydia was back. Great.

"You have the most incredible eyes."

Dirk had led Jane through Will's office and out onto the patio. They'd spent several moments just looking out at the star-filled sky before he'd turned to her and made that announcement in an incredibly deep and sexy voice. Who wouldn't be flattered? Jane certainly was. She was especially impressed by the fact that he'd actually been looking into her eyes rather than talking to her breasts.

189

He went up a little in her estimation right there. The man couldn't be all bad.

Realizing that he was probably waiting for some response, Jane searched for something to say. Unfortunately, the only thing that came to mind was the line from *Little Red Riding Hood*, and she didn't think saying, "The better to see you with" quite fit the moment. Although it was true enough. The man was a pleasure to look at. She could hardly believe that he was showing an interest in her. In truth, Jane was at a loss. She wasn't the most experienced of women. Men like Dirk Ensecksi simply hadn't paid much attention to her through the years. Instead she'd found herself pursued by persistent pests who seemed to feel it was their duty to show her favor, or techies who thought sex on a computer was cool, and "God, I love your mind!" was foreplay.

"And you have lovely, luscious lips," Dirk continued.

Jane started and took a nervous step back, finding herself against the rail of the deck. Dirk raised a hand to brush one finger lightly over her bottom lip. Her skittish reaction was as much from surprise as from the jolt of awareness that shot through her at his touch. For a woman like Jane, the attention of a handsome sexy man like Dirk was heady stuff. So heady that when his head started to lower toward hers, she just stood there wondering what his kiss would be like. It wasn't until his lips were a mere breath away that she suddenly remembered the knockout lipstick and turned her head away so that his lips landed on her ear.

Dear Lord! What had she been thinking? Wouldn't it have been fun to explain why Dirk Ensecksi was unconscious on the deck!

"And you smell good too," Dirk murmured, his

breath causing a tingling along the sensitive skin below her ear.

Then again, she *had* wiped the lipstick off to eat. Perhaps she'd got it all and it was safe to let him kiss her.

Bad Jane! she reprimanded herself in the next breath. *This is the man who kidnapped Edie and plans to control the world. Shame on you for wanting him to kiss you!*

"Mmmm. I wish I could just inhale you into my body." His arms closed around her, and he pulled her close and nuzzled her throat.

On the other hand, Jane thought vaguely as she slid her hands around his neck and tipped her head back, Mr. Manetrue did say that they hadn't been able to find anything while investigating Dirk and his father. And testing mind control via fashion was really a feminine thing to do. Perhaps Lydia was behind all the evil doings at Ensecksi. Maybe Dirk was just an unwitting accomplice. She gave a sigh and allowed herself to sink into his body.

"I've wanted to do this since I first set eyes on you," Dirk murmured, pulling back and eyeing her lips again.

"Really?" Jane asked, hardly able to believe any of this. She was in a handsome man's arms and he was saying such sweet things to her. What had she been missing all these years by burying herself in books?

"Well, no, not really. Actually my first thought when you fell backward on the steps with that wheelchair was, 'Jeez, what a ditz.' But my second thought was: 'No brain, but I'd like to get into that body.' "

Jane was so shocked by his words that she just gaped at him. He tried again to plant a kiss on her

191

lips. It was bad timing. And a bad kiss. Jane had the almost overwhelming urge to knee him in the groin, then throw him over her shoulder to the hardwood deck as his mouth closed wet and sloppy over hers.

Fortunately, just as her leg started to rise, she recalled her truth serum perfume. Dirk had been nuzzling her neck and inhaling it for several minutes. Which somehow made everything worse, since she realized it was the complete truth he'd just spoken to her, but it also recalled her to the reason she was here with this man. Kneeing him in the groin and tossing him on his back might be terribly satisfying in the short term, but it wouldn't get her the information she was seeking.

But, then, neither would suffering his tongue being shoved down her throat like a slippery eel. He could hardly talk like that, she decided grimly, and broke away.

"Um, Dirk?" she said, trying to decide what would be safe to ask him. He'd tell the truth to anything she asked, but he'd also remember everything. She had to be careful.

"You have the tastiest-looking breasts I have ever seen," he announced, his hands moving to grope her. "And this dress is *hot!*"

"Thank you," she said dryly, trying to catch his hands. "Speaking of dresses, have you noticed everyone seems to wear yellow ones here in Sonora?"

"Yeah. I am *so* sick of yellow."

"Yes, but . . ." She hesitated, wondering how to get him to tell her the yellow dresses were a result of mind control without coming right out and asking. She forced his hands away from her chest and he let her, then planted them firmly on her behind.

"You have a great butt too," he announced. "I

couldn't take my eyes off it when you were walking up the stairs in front of me. I wanted to drop that wheelchair and just grab both cheeks."

"Oh!" Jane gasped in surprise when he did just that, squeezing her firmly and pulling her up against him. His words were getting a bit slurred and Jane began to wonder if he hadn't had a lot more to drink tonight than she'd realized. Or if mixing alcohol and the truth serum wasn't having a bad effect. Whatever it was, he'd pulled her firmly against him so that her feet dangled off the ground and he and she were almost on a level. He took advantage of the position to dip his head between her breasts and inhale. "God, I love this perfume."

"Dirk, I think . . ." She reached behind to try to force his hands off her butt so that she could stand on the ground again. Had she ever imagined the spy business was glamorous or fun?

"Don't think. Feel," he said, completely oblivious of her attempts to escape. "I know you want the bone."

"The bone?" Jane gave up on trying to make him release her and gaped in horror.

"Yeah, you women love the bone. And I've got a big one, let me tell you. I could satisfy you like you've never been satisfied before."

"Oh, I . . ." She paused. "Really?"

"Yeah. Not that I would though," he added with scrupulous honesty. "I'll do what I have to to get you into bed, but once there I just want to get my rocks o—"

"Of course," she interrupted with a sigh. It just figured, didn't it? Mr. Gorgeous here could get anyone he wanted, why put any effort into it? He was popping all her delusional balloons. She suddenly didn't have any trouble at all seeing him as a villain. What a selfish, ignorant jerk.

"How long have you lived in Sonora?" she asked, just wanting to get what information she could and get away.

"I don't live here." Dirk pressed his nose against her throat and breathed deeply. He seemed to be trying to snort the serum off her skin. Perhaps she'd put too much pheromone in it. She'd have to cut back on that. Though, she hadn't noticed this strong a reaction in the test trials. Could it be that he was just especially responsive?

"I really love this perfume. I could just eat it up." He licked her throat, and Jane stiffened. This could not be a reaction to too much pheromone. This was just too much—

He swayed slightly and Jane felt alarm course through her. "Dirk?"

"Hmm?" He lifted his head, and Jane stared into his eyes. They were dilated, she realized; then she noted the smudge of red by his lips. Lipschitz's hot-red knockout lipstick. It seemed she hadn't wiped all of it away. But she apparently hadn't left enough to knock him out either. She suspected that it, combined with the truth serum, was what caused this odd, almost drunken behavior. Suddenly she wished she'd paid attention to Lipschitz's presentation so that she'd know what was in the darned lipstick and what to expect. The man might still pass out.

Deciding there wasn't a darned thing she could do about it, except maybe get some answers out of him first, Jane returned to questioning him. "You don't live here in Sonora?"

"No. I live in Canada. I run the Canadian division

of Ensecksi Satellites. Lydia lives here. She commutes to the San Jose office."

"Then you're just visiting?"

"No. Yes."

Jane eyed him closely. "Which is it?"

"Both." He dropped his head, his nose landing in the hollow between her breasts again.

Jane sighed impatiently as he inhaled more of the truth serum. She wasn't finding anything attractive about this man anymore. "How could it be both, Dirk?"

His voice came muffled from her flesh. "I was going to come and stay till after Thanksgiving, but then my assistant Josh and I had to drive E—"

"Here you are!" a voice said brightly. "Gran's getting tired and is ready to go."

Jane glanced sharply over Dirk's bent head as Abel stepped out onto the deck through the office. She could have kicked him for interrupting. Then in the next second, she decided it was probably for the best. If Dirk later remembered what he'd said here, he wouldn't be overly alarmed. Had he continued talking and admitted to kidnapping Edie, however, as Jane thought he'd been about to do . . .

Noting Abel's sudden glare, Jane realized Dirk still had his face buried in her bosom. She'd started to think of him as a rather annoying puppy in the last few minutes, since he'd stopped grabbing and started sniffing and licking her perfume. Abel obviously didn't see it that way, however.

Reaching down with both hands, Jane grabbed Dirk by the ears and lifted his head forcibly away. "I have to go. Gran is tired," she announced.

"Can't *he* take her? I don't want you to go." Jane knew it was the truth, but she'd heard enough truth tonight to know that it wasn't really her he wanted.

It was her hot dress, tasty breasts, and great butt. Actually, she suspected he was now more interested in licking the perfume off her skin. Which might have been fun if she could forget his saying she just wanted the bone. Unfortunately, she couldn't. But she also couldn't alienate the man. He was her link to Edie, not to mention whatever plans Ensecksi Satellites had for the microwave mind-control technology.

She forced a regretful moue and shook her head. "I wish I could stay, but my brother can't change Gran and dress her for bed. I have to go." She smiled sweetly.

"That sucks. I had plans for you," he said with an honesty that almost made Jane laugh. Fortunately, in his disappointment, he lowered her again to stand on her own two feet.

"Yes, well . . . perhaps another time." She tried to move around him in the hope that he'd release the death grip he had on her butt. All she managed was to turn so that Abel had a perfect view.

"Count on it, baby," Dirk said in the husky tone she'd found so attractive earlier. "I know every line there is. I'll have you in bed within forty-eight hours or you aren't worth my time."

"Ah." Jane managed to disengage his hands with a little effort, then moved quickly away before he could grab her again. She said, "I'll, ah . . . look forward to it."

Not!

She passed Abel and moved back into the house. They were through the office and halfway up the hall on their way back to the living room and the party when something fell to the floor with a clatter. Jane glanced down, recognized the lipstick tube, and bent with exasperation to pick it up. No doubt all of Dirk's groping and nosing around had dislodged it from her bra. She supposed she should be grateful she hadn't lost it on the deck without noticing. It was not something it would be good to leave lying around.

"What's that?" Abel asked.

"Lipstick," Jane answered, wondering at his stiffness as he paused at her side. He was acting as if he were peeved with her.

"You'd better put some on." He looked her over critically. "And straighten your hair. You look like you've been necking."

Definitely peeved, Jane realized. She felt the heat of a guilty blush cover her face.

"The washroom is that door there. I used it earlier," Abel added when she appeared surprised by his knowledge.

Jane moved to the door and stepped inside. Her eyes widened in horror as she saw herself in the mirror. Thank heavens he hadn't let her return to the party as she was, peeved or not. She looked like she'd done more than neck on the deck. Was that a hickey? Jeez! She'd known Dirk was 'nosing around her neck, had even felt him lick her once or twice, but how could she have not noticed such sucking?

Jane leaned toward the mirror to examine the angry red mark and shook her head. She'd never had a hickey before. They were really unattractive. Straightening, she did her best to put her mussed hair into something resembling the style her grandmother had created, then reapplied both layers of Lipschitz's lipstick. Deciding she looked a little better and less like a hooker, Jane straightened her shoulders and rejoined Abel.

They were silent as they returned to the main

room. Collecting Gran, they made their excuses to Leigh, then were again silent on the short walk back to their house. It wasn't until they were in the elevator at the Goodinov house that anyone spoke, and then it was Maggie Spyrus. "Did you learn anything interesting from Dirk, dear?"

"Not much," Jane said, pausing when Abel gave a snort.

"It looked to me like you were learning a lot."

She stiffened at his gibe, but merely said, "All I found out was that Lydia runs the San Jose office, while Dirk runs the Vancouver division."

Abel harrumphed. "Fancy that. I learned the same thing from Lydia and didn't have to let her grope me to do so. Not bad for an accountant. Maybe *I* should try out this spy business."

The elevator doors opened then, and he stalked off in the direction of the master suite.

"Actually, she did grope at him quite a bit," Gran announced after a moment.

Jane simply stood glaring after Abel. "Yes. I noticed," she snapped and wheeled her grandmother out of the elevator.

"You were going to say more. What else did you learn?" Gran asked as she was wheeled into the room she'd chosen.

"Just that Dirk and his assistant Josh are the ones who drove Edie here."

"He said that?" Maggie asked with alarm.

"He started to, but Abel interrupted before he could get Edie's full name out." Jane stopped beside the bed.

"Hmm," Maggie Spyrus murmured as Jane moved to the dresser to find her a nightgown. "It's probably best that Abel interrupted, then."

"Yes." Jane agreed. She fetched a housecoat and

slippers as well, and set all three items on her grandmother's lap before taking her into the washroom.

"He's jealous, you know."

Jane paused and met her gran's gaze in the bathroom mirror.

"He is. He's attracted to you, and he's jealous. But he'll get over it," she added.

Jane thought about that possibility as she helped Gran through her ablutions and then into bed. Leaving the door open, she moved into the room across the hall where she'd napped that afternoon, intending to sleep herself. The sight of Tinkle made her pause. The dog was lying in a pool of feathers on the bed. Jane drew a furious breath then caught it and forced herself to relax. Getting upset was exactly what the little beast wanted, no doubt. It was the Yorkie's way of letting her know that while Mr. Tibbs may have got the best of her, Tinkle was still queen over her humans.

"Gran's in her own bed," she announced angrily. It had the desired effect: Tinkle leaped off the bed and scampered out the door.

"There's my little darling!" Jane heard her grandmother say. "Have you been exploring, Tinkle baby? Did you miss your mama? What a good doggie."

Rolling her eyes, Jane turned toward the closet in her room only to pause. Her clothes weren't in here. She didn't have any clothes here but for jeans and a T-shirt. However, the clothes that B.L.I.S.S. had supplied weren't here either. They were at the other end of the house in the master suite—where Abel was even now probably stomping angrily about.

Jane was just thinking she'd have to go down there and face him to get something to wear to bed when she remembered she'd told him they would set up the listening devices after the party.

Jane stood in the center of the room considering the matter briefly, then threw up her hands in exasperation. Making a decision not to head for the master bedroom, she began searching the closets in the other rooms until she found the one holding the clothes B.L.I.S.S. had supplied for Abel. As she expected, they included men's pajamas. Jane chose the only black ones supplied—silk, of course—then moved back to her room.

Perhaps she'd shower after planting the cameras and listening devices outside. Still, she had no intention of traipsing around out there in her black lace party dress and high heels. She wanted them off, now—especially the shoes. Also, Jane wanted to feel more herself before she faced Abel. She'd always liked men's pajamas, they were dark enough for nighttime reconnaissance, and they were comfy.

The top was nice and loose—mostly hiding the fact that she'd removed her bra, Jane thought. But, of course the bottoms were too big. She found a safety pin in her bathroom, and with a little work managed to fix them so that they wouldn't fall down. That done, she moved determinedly through the house toward the master suite.

She'd let Abel help her with the cameras and listening devices if he wanted; then she'd ask him to take first watch while she took a shower. After that she'd send him to bed and she herself would watch their neighbors. She'd probably be watching them sleep, but such was a spy's life, she supposed.

Jane was all prepared for a stiff and angry Abel, so she was pleasantly surprised upon entering the room to find him sitting on the end of the bed, pet-

ting Mr. Tibbs and looking as if his temper had
cooled. He even managed a smile and an apology.

"Sorry about what I said. Lydia was driving me
crazy all night and then . . ." He shrugged.

Jane did the same. "That's all right."

He glanced down at the cat again. "I guess that
must happen a lot, huh?"

"What?" Jane asked.

He shrugged again. "I suppose you have to get
close to a lot of guys in your job."

Jane was silent as she debated what to say.
Should she admit she wasn't really a spy, but a
techno geek? No, she decided; she couldn't do that.
He might lose confidence in her and no doubt in
B.L.I.S.S. too—then he might be moved to try to
rescue Edie on his own. She had to continue to let
him believe that she was competent. She had to lie.
Although it wasn't really a lie, she told herself. She
was being a credible spy now. Though she'd never
imagined it would be like this: all these lies, letting
Dirk grope her.

She certainly *had* imagined what being a spy
would be like. The excitement, the glamour. But
then Gran had been paralyzed and Jane decided
that maybe something safer was better.

"Not really," she said finally. "Dirk is about the
worst I've encountered so far."

"Yeah?" He looked surprised.

"Yeah," Jane said.

"Tell me about some of your cases. Have you
ever had one like this before?"

Jane felt panic swamp her. She knew he was
looking for reassurance that she had experience
with this sort of thing, that the kidnap victim was
always brought back alive. But Jane hadn't been on
any other cases.

"Oh, of course," he said suddenly. "B.L.I.S.S. security and all that. I suppose you can't tell me about any of your past work."

"Yes," Jane agreed with relief. Then she corrected, "I mean no, I can't tell you."

Abel nodded. "It must be exciting being a spy."

"Yes, it must be," she agreed. "I mean, yes. It is."

"I figured. The rush, the adrenaline."

"Yes," Jane said, thinking of the hair-raising stories her grandmother had told her.

"My life would be boring in comparison."

"Yes." She sighed. Both of their lives were terribly boring in comparison to the adventures most of her family faced. On the other hand, she and Abel had a longer life expectancy too. Jane had lost both parents and three cousins to the spy business. It was a dangerous profession.

"Well." Abel stood. "Are we going to put out those microphones and stuff?"

"Hmm? Oh, yes." She looked him over. He'd removed his suit jacket and now wore only the dark pants and white dress shirt. "You'll need to change. You need a dark shirt. And I need shoes."

"I'll go change." He left the room.

Jane frowned after him. He sounded rather depressed. Of course, he had a lot to be depressed about with his sister in the hands of the evil Ensecksis.

Chapter Thirteen

"Heads up!"

At that hissed warning in her earpiece, Jane flattened herself against the wall of the Ensecksi house. She glanced back through the darkness, trying to spot Abel, but he blended in too well with the shadowy shapes on the side of the hill. Jane hoped she was equally invisible. She'd been busy attaching the wall-contact microphone so that they could listen to conversations within the house. Abel had been keeping a lookout from the hill.

Jane and Abel had already positioned several listening devices as well as cameras in strategic positions. Two of the cameras were full-color, night-vision capable. The other two were standard issue. All had a waterproof casing and were wireless. They were also motion-sensing and would transmit their photos to a remote monitoring receiver Jane had yet to set up in the house.

The sound of voices drawing nearer made Jane glance nervously toward the driveway. Lydia and Dirk came into view. Lydia was walking at a fast, impatient clip, her brother stumbling along behind, chattering as he walked.

"She has a great butt. I can't wait to get her naked."

Jane made a face at these first words she was able to hear. It was Dirk, and his speech was still slurred.

"Yeah. I get it. You liked Ms. Goodinov," Lydia said with filial disgust. A disgust Jane shared. She hoped Abel wasn't hearing this. It was embarrassing.

"No, I don't especially like her," Dirk answered with painful honesty. "But she smells really good and has a hot body. Curvy and soft. She's not scrawny and sharp-looking like you and those other women who are always starving themselves."

The truth serum and knockout drug combo were definitely still working. Jane didn't think Dirk would have been quite so honest with his opinion of his sister's figure if it wasn't. A smart man never commented on a woman's body unless to compliment it.

"Shut up!" Lydia turned on him. "I have a great figure."

"Nope." Dirk stumbled to a stop and shook his head. "Jane's is better."

"Jane needs to lose twenty or thirty pounds," Lydia snapped.

Jane stood a little straighter where she was. She'd always wished she were thinner, but twenty or thirty pounds?

Bitch, she thought irritably.

Dirk was shaking his head. "Nope. She's perfect. Soft and cuddly. Like a pillow."

Okay, maybe twenty pounds, Jane thought unhappily. *A pillow?*

"Oh, I'm sure she'd like to hear that," Lydia suddenly laughed, her anger slipping away. "Like most men would want a pillow in bed."

"Most men *would*." Dirk nodded several times as he swayed. "Screwing a skinny woman is like screwing a board. The pelvic bones hit. Bang, bang, bang. It can hurt."

Oh, well, that was just too much truth, Jane decided. She leaned against the wall of the house, wishing the Ensecksis would move on, out of her way. She wanted to finish setting this microphone in place and go home.

"You're drunk." Lydia eyed her swaying brother as if he were a particularly unpleasant bug. "I haven't seen you drunk since you were eighteen. How much did you have to drink tonight?"

"Uh . . . a glass of wine," Dirk answered.

"Yeah, right." Lydia turned toward the house with obvious disbelief. "If this is your response to not getting laid for probably the first time in your life, you'd better stay away from Jane Goodinov. She doesn't seem like an easy lay to me."

"She's hot!"

"Maybe. But she also still lives with her grandmother. She's not your speed—as I said when you saved her from breaking her neck on those stairs."

"You said you liked her." Dirk stumbled up the drive after his sister. "You said you two would be friends."

"Yeah, well, she's smart and I like that. But that's just another reason that she's out of your league. Stick to your brainless twits."

"What about Abel? He still lives with his grandmother, too."

"Abel." Lydia paused again, and Jane found herself straining to hear what the woman would say. "Abel is different. He doesn't live with them. He's only visiting to settle them into Bea and Arthur's house."

"You like him." It looked to Jane as if Dirk was smirking.

"Yes, I do," Lydia admitted. Her teeth gleamed white in the darkness. "Abel is tasty. He definitely shows possibility. And I think he's interested." She sighed. "He'd better be. I've been out here in nowhere land too long. I need to get some action."

"So, invite him over and bang him. I'm gonna invite Jane."

"Oh, Dad would love that." Lydia snorted and started to walk again.

"He doesn't have to know. Besides, he's already in the mountain. He won't come up for air until after he revs up the mike-sat, if then."

"Yeah," Lydia agreed. The pair walked in silence for a few steps before she decided, "We'll invite them to dinner. But I don't think you're going to get anywhere with Jane. And you're not going to drink."

They'd walked close enough to the house that they were out of Jane's sight. Jane heard a door open and close, then silence. She finished what she'd been doing before their arrival, then slipped cautiously back up the hill.

Abel joined her halfway and they walked home together, pausing only when they reached the wood-and-metal table and chairs arranged in the small clearing at the top of the hill. A little stone pathway led to the master bedroom some twenty feet away, but Jane and Abel first turned back to be sure they hadn't been spotted.

There were lights on inside the Ensecksi house now, and the occasional shifting shadow as its inhabitants moved around inside.

"Dirk's right. You do smell good."

Jane turned sharply in surprise at that comment by her ear and stumbled. Abel's arms slid around her, catching her close to keep her from tumbling back down the hill. Jane stayed where she was for a minute, enjoying the feel of his embrace. Abel wasn't aggressive or groping like Dirk; this felt warm and safe. Mostly. There was an underlying zing, too. She could feel jolting through her body at every point of contact.

"*Really* good."

Abel's voice was muffled by her hair, and Jane stiffened as she felt and heard him inhale. *Not again.* She didn't think she could handle too much more truth right now. It was probably better that women didn't know what men thought and were forced to make do with their polite lies. Wasn't it?

"Um . . . Abel." Jane pulled reluctantly back, but paused before completely breaking contact. It felt so nice to be in his arms.

"Yes?" He peered down at her.

Jane's eyes had adjusted to the darkness, and Abel seemed clear-eyed as he met her gaze. She hesitated, then tipped her head to the side and back. "Do you really like my perfume?" she asked.

Abel dutifully bent to sniff. "Yes."

"You're sure?" she asked when he straightened. He hesitated, then leaned forward again, inhaling deeply. She heard him release a soft sigh; then he straightened and smiled at her.

"You smell like vanilla ice cream and apple pie. Good enough to eat."

Jane looked at him closely. His eyes were a tad dilated, but not wildly so like Dirk's had been. She nodded slowly, then asked, "Do you think I have tasty breasts?"

He nodded solemnly. "You have a nice behind, too."

Jane bit her lip, knowing this was unfair. She'd feel guilty for it later, she promised herself. "Do you think my breasts are too large or that I should lose twenty pounds?"

"No. I like your body."

Jane smiled. It was nice to know. But . . . "Is that all you like about me?"

"No. I like your nose too."

Jane blinked. "My nose?"

He nodded. "And your lips."

"I see."

"You have a funny face."

"Funny?" She almost choked on the word. She had a "funny" face? Well, she'd asked for this.

"Yes. When you're thinking or angry, you make funny faces. But mostly you're pretty. You have beautiful eyes. I can see the intelligence in them. I like that you're smart."

"Oh." She smiled at him. He liked that she was smart.

"I don't like it so much when you're bossy though."

"Oh." Her smile faded some.

"And I didn't like it when you handcuffed me. Well, I didn't mind being handcuffed to you all that much, but I would have liked it better if we would have had to shower together. Naked."

"Oh." Jane was at a loss for a minute, then

cleared her throat and asked, "And you thought about this when?"

"In the motel room while I was taking my shower," he answered. "I thought it was too bad you had uncuffed us. That I'd like to rub soap all over your wet body and—"

"Er, yes. I think I get the idea," she interrupted, wondering if the night was getting hotter. Tomorrow was going to be a scorcher.

"I want to touch you everywhere."

"Oh." She swallowed, then muttered, "Well, that sounds better than just wanting to get your rocks off."

"That would be fun," Abel admitted. "But I'd want to make you beg first."

Jane flushed with embarrassment at his overhearing her. Then her eyes widened as she realized what he'd said. "Beg?"

He nodded. "Oh, yeah. I want to see you wanting me like I want you. I want to touch and lick every part of your body until you're screaming for me to fill you."

"You do?" Jane's breath came short. That sounded pretty good. Much better than what Dirk had offered.

"Yes. But I wouldn't do it."

"What?" Jane straightened in outrage. "Why not?"

"Because I like you and you're Edie's friend, and you're a good girl who lives with her grandmother in Vancouver. And I respect you and my sister too much to offer you a fling. I live in England, so that's all we could manage . . . unless I get that job in Vancouver." He paused with a frown. "But you're also a spy with this exciting job and life and meeting all these exciting people in these exciting places and I'm just a boring old accountant, although I'm only thirty-four, so I'm not *that* old, but an exciting woman like you would never be interested in a boring old number cruncher like me."

When he finally paused, Jane took a minute to sort through everything he'd said. All she could think was that here was the nicest and sweetest man who'd ever wanted to touch and lick her all over until she screamed. Jane knew part of this attraction was simply hormones, but another part was Edie's fault. Her friend had spoken much of her brother over the past six months, telling Jane tales of their childhood and how smart and good he was. Jane hadn't known of Edie's plan to get them together, but when Abel told her, Jane realized her friend had labored hard at preparing her to like him before he ever arrived. And it had worked.

He wasn't as good-looking as Dirk. Abel was handsome, but his face dimmed next to the sheer perfection of Dirk's. On the other hand, Abel beat Ensecksi's personality by a mile.

"Jane?"

"Hmm?" She glanced at Abel distractedly.

"I really want to kiss you. I know I shouldn't, but I think I'm going to and if you don't want it, you'd better tell me now because . . ." He'd been bending forward as he spoke. His words died as his lips met and closed over hers. This was no sloppy wet kiss. This was warm and firm and commanding. It sent a shiver through Jane as Abel gathered her closer, not groping and grabbing, but cradling and holding her as if she were precious. This man knew how to kiss, she thought fuzzily. Her mouth opened and he deepened the caress.

No slippery eels here. Jane tasted peppermint and wondered what Abel had eaten or drunk to cause that, then gave up thinking as sensation overwhelmed her. She was just releasing a sigh of pleasure and curling her toes in her sneakers when Abel suddenly broke away, pulled back, shook his head groggily, and began to sway.

"What?" he said uncertainly, then started to fall backward. Alarm filled Jane, but she had the presence of mind to quickly turn him so that he fell back into one of the nearby chairs.

"Abel?" Jane bent over him anxiously and touched his slack face. Then she removed the headphones from his ears. They'd each worn two-way radios so that he could keep a watch on the hill and inform her if Dirk and Lydia should return. As they had. She set his radio and headphones and her own on the table, then swung back to tap his face. "Abel?"

He was out cold. Jane turned to run for the master suite and a phone, ready to call 911, then stopped.

"Lipschitz's knockout lipstick again." The words slipped from her lips with horror as she recalled Abel suggesting she reapply her makeup and straighten her hair after he'd rescued her from Dirk. And she hadn't thought to wipe it off upon returning home. He'd got a full dose.

She turned slowly to peer down at him. The lipstick worked pretty well. It hadn't been a long kiss. She would have liked a longer one. And more. But not much chance of that now; the man was dead to the world.

"Well," she breathed, "isn't this the perfect end to a perfect evening?"

Sighing, Jane sank down in the chair across from Abel. She sat there for several minutes just looking at him, then realized she was rubbing her arms to ward off the night chill. Had she thought it was warm moments ago? It must have been Abel's body heat. Shifting her chair next to his, hoping to share some of his warmth, she sat sideways in her wooden seat and took his hand in her own.

How long did this stuff last? she wondered after a while. She really had to pay more attention at the monthly meetings. If she'd been paying attention, she would know. Becoming aware that she was shivering, she glanced toward the house. There was no way she was going to be able to get Abel inside. He was far too big for that. Which meant he was stuck here until he woke up. And she couldn't just leave him unconscious and alone out here, so she was stuck as well.

Jane rubbed her arms again. She should go get a comforter to cover Abel. He might catch a chill. Yes, she'd get a comforter, then cuddle up under it with him and wait for him to wake. That sounded nice.

Jane got to her feet and grabbed up the two-way radios from the table where she'd set them. She'd return them to the house so she didn't forget later.

In the master suite Jane tossed the radios in the nearest black bag. She paused then, considering the spy paraphernalia. She really should set up the remote-viewing receiver. Her gaze went anxiously to the door. She didn't want to leave Abel out there alone and unconscious, but this would only take a few minutes. She hoped.

Moving quickly, she set up the receiver then returned all extra cables to their boxes and stuffed them in the closet. Next, she grabbed the software B.L.I.S.S. had sent, then her portable computer from her bag. She plugged the power cord to her portable into a socket to save the battery, then set the computer on the coffee table in front of the couch at the foot of the bed. Programming the software, she checked to be sure it was working. When four screens opened with four different pictures of the house next door, Jane sighed in relief.

Leaving the portable on the table, she grabbed the comforter and padded back out of the house. It wasn't until her feet hit the cold concrete on the step outside that she realized she'd shucked her running shoes. She'd probably done it while programming the computer: a habit of hers. Jane considered returning inside to put them on, but they were new and not all that comfortable. Besides, she could tuck her feet under the comforter to keep them warm.

Abel was still unconscious where'd she'd left him, but no night birds had nested in his hair or set up house in his lap—which according to the local sheriff was the only worry she might have out here in crime-free Sonora.

Jane settled the comforter over Abel, tucking it gently around his neck. She was just sitting in the seat next to him and pulling the extra material over herself to wait when a shout and the sudden squeal of rubber drew her eyes to the road. All she saw were bushes and trees. This little nook was blocked by the house on one side and trees and bushes on all others. It was lovely yet isolated.

Jane heard a car roar up the road; then there was the screech of tires. A hollow thudding filled the night, followed by silence. Jane started to move away from the chairs, thinking to investigate, but paused at the sound of a car door closing. The slamming of a second followed.

"Where is he?" a woman's voice asked.

"He ran up toward the Goodinov house." Jane hadn't needed the man's answer, she could hear someone stumbling through the woods in front of her. Growing closer. The skin on the nape of her neck prickled.

"Hello?" she called. "Is someone hurt?"

The night suffered a sudden pregnant silence. The rustling in the trees stopped, and so had any sound from the road beyond. Jane held her breath, waiting, then heard car doors close again. An engine revved, then tore off, heading away down the street toward the gate. Once it was gone there was quiet again.

"Hello?" Jane hissed into the darkness. After a moment the rustling started again, but it seemed slower this time, more labored. It was also no longer moving directly toward her, instead seemed to veer off to the side as if heading toward the Ensecksi house. Jane took a step forward, listening carefully and straining to see movement. "Hello?" She repeated.

There was a hopping, dragging sound now, as if a wounded animal were limping along, dragging a useless limb. And it was growing slower and slower with each passing moment. It also sounded as if it had turned back in her direction. Following her voice? she wondered. Or was the person in such desperate shape that he knew he wouldn't make it to the Ensecksi house?

"Hello!" Jane called firmly, refusing to run away as all her instincts were urging. She wouldn't leave Abel alone and helpless. Besides, this other person might need help. And if he didn't, and was a thief playing possum . . . well, she guessed she might get to use some of those martial arts she'd trained in for so long but never used. At least, if she was lucky and the person didn't have a gun or something and shot her before she could move.

"Too much TV," she muttered under her breath with disgust, then called out again.

This time there was an answering shout. But it came from the direction of Leigh Senchall's house. Jane recognized Officer Alkars's voice with relief.

"Over here," she shouted to both whoever was in the woods and to the sheriff. Whether Colin would listen and come over, she didn't know. The person in front of her was coming, though. Jane could hear breathing now, more a panting really: Labored gasps for breath that had an unhealthy wheeze. She couldn't see anything through the surrounding bushes and trees, however.

"Do you need help?" she asked the darkness.

Her only answer was the ragged panting and rustling drawing nearer.

"Ms. Goodinov? Jane?"

Jane turned to her right as Officer Alkars came into sight on the walkway along the front of the house. Relief coursed through her. The rustling in the trees stopped at once.

"What's going on? Is something wrong?" he asked. He was still dressed in a suit and had obviously just come from his sister's party. "I heard you shouting as I got in my car and thought you were saying hello to me."

"No. I think someone's been hurt," she told him. He stepped off the cobblestone walk and started toward her. "I heard a car's brakes squeal and a thud, then . . ." Jane broke off her explanation and swiveled back toward the trees. The rustling had begun again. It had sounded near, but Jane hadn't realized how near. Now she found herself staring at a dark shape that broke through the tall flowered bush in front of her. The figure paused there, staring, mouth open as he gasped for breath; then he fell forward and landed at her feet with an ominous thud.

Jane stood frozen, gaping at the body until Officer Alkars reached her side. He knelt to turn the fellow over.

"He's bleeding. Bad," Officer Alkars reported. He bent over the man, blocking her view. "He's been hit by a car."

"I'll call 911."

"Bring a towel or something too. Maybe a blanket to stave off shock," Colin instructed.

Nodding, Jane whirled away; then she whirled back and moved to where Abel still lay blissfully unconscious. She snatched the comforter off him and returned to throw it over the legs of the wounded man.

"What's wrong with him? Is he hurt too?" Colin asked with a frown. Her action had brought the unconscious Abel to his attention.

"No." She hesitated then lied, "Passed out. I'll make that call now." She hurried off before the sheriff could ask anything else.

She wasn't gone long, just enough time to make the call and run to the other end of the house to make a quick check on a peacefully sleeping Gran. On her return, she flicked on the home-office's lights, hoping they would splash out the windows and stretch to Colin. She nipped into the bathroom next, in search of first-aid-type things. All she found were bandages and Bactine. She grabbed both and snatched a towel off the rack. Jane hit the master bedroom at a run, but slid to a halt by the door to flick on all the light switches there as well. As she'd hoped, they illuminated the nook on the hill.

Colin was bent over the figure as she hurried outside, but over his shoulder Jane could now see the man's face. She froze at the sight. This was the fellow who had come to Leigh's to talk to Dirk! More disturbing than that, however, without the suspicious squint on his face, he looked familiar to Jane. She'd seen him somewhere else besides at Leigh's. Wracking her brain briefly, she found an image popping into her mind: She was in the car with Edie, dropping her neighbor off at work because Edie's car wouldn't start. This man was getting out of a vehicle next to them and smiling in greeting. Edie waved at him, then turned and said, "That's—"

"Joshua Parker."

Jane's attention dropped to Colin as he read the name off the driver's license he'd just pulled out of the man's wallet.

"Yes. Josh Parker," she murmured. Her gaze went back to the man. Edie had introduced them. He worked at Ensecksi Satellites. He was Dirk Ensecksi's assistant. And Jane was quite sure, as she recalled the expression on his face upon coming out of Will's office with his boss, that he'd recognized her. Had he told Dirk? Damn, this wasn't good.

"He's Canadian."

Jane glanced down again, but this time Colin wasn't leaning over him. Her gaze dropped over Josh Parker's chest. She frowned at the blood-soaked front of his shirt. "Is he . . . ?"

"Yeah. He's dead."

Chapter Fourteen

Jane rubbed her arms and watched the ambulance attendants wheel Josh Parker's body away. They were going to have fun taking him down all those stairs, she thought vaguely.

"So, you didn't actually see what happened?" Colin asked again. He'd asked the very same question earlier when Jane had been telling his sister, Leigh, about the incident. Her next-door neighbor had heard the sirens and come out onto her porch with the rest of her guests to see what was happening. When she'd spotted her brother's car still in her driveway, but her brother himself nowhere in sight, she'd followed the EMTs up to the nook on the side of the Goodinov house. Jane had explained what had happened to her and Colin both; then Leigh had left.

"No." Jane shifted to stand on one foot, placing

the other atop it to warm its bottom. The stone path seemed icy. "Can we sit down?"

"Oh, yes, of course." He followed her to the chairs on the hill. She settled in the one next to Abel and pulled her legs up onto the seat, crossing them.

"Maybe we should move inside," Colin suggested, noting the way she was rubbing her arms and shivering.

"I can't leave Abel out here alone. It's the reason I was out here to begin with."

"Yes." Colin's gaze drifted to Abel. "Are you sure he's all right? He hasn't stirred once, not even when the ambulance arrived."

"He's just had a little too much to drink," she lied, hoping Abel would forgive her. Or, even better, never hear about the lie.

"Hmm." Colin rubbed the back of his neck. "Well, maybe we should get him inside then."

"Could we?" Jane asked hopefully. She'd love to be indoors right now. She was freezing. Which was probably a reaction to someone dying at her feet.

"Of course we can." Standing, Officer Alkars moved in front of Abel, pulled him upright, then tucked his shoulder into the unconscious man's waist to heft him.

"Oh!" Jane had stood to help, but now she stepped quickly out of the way. There was nothing to do. Leaving the bloodstained comforter there to collect and dispose of tomorrow, she rushed around Colin and hurried to the house to pull open the door.

"Where to?" the sheriff asked, pausing just inside.

"Just put him on the bed," Jane instructed.

Colin laid Abel down, then straightened to survey him with a shake of the head. "You're sure he's all right?"

"Oh, yes," Jane swore. "He just doesn't handle booze well."

"Then he shouldn't drink," Officer Alkars said.

Jane winced at the reproval in his voice. "He doesn't usually. And he didn't really have much tonight, but he took an allergy tablet when we returned from Leigh's and the combination just . . ." She shrugged. "Knocked him out."

She thought it a good lie. After all, she didn't want Abel to look like some drunken lout just because she was a bad agent and had let him kiss her when she was wearing knockout lipstick. Unfortunately, Colin's sudden alarm told her she'd made a mistake.

"He mixed booze and medication? Maybe we should take him to the hospital to be checked out. He could be—"

"He's fine," Jane insisted. "I plan to keep an eye on him. That's why I was outside instead of already tucked in bed when Parker came."

She hoped he'd take that subtle hint and leave so she could get to work spying on her neighbors. He didn't.

"Oh, yes. Parker." Wiping one hand down his face, Colin glanced around then gestured toward the sofa and chairs at the opposite end of the master bedroom. "Can we sit over there and talk?"

Jane felt her heart sink. She'd already told him what had happened. Twice. It seemed she would tell him again.

"Sure." Jane led the way to the couch and sat down, then spotted the open laptop computer on the table with its four pictures of the Ensecksi house. She slammed it closed and cast a nervous smile at Colin as he reclined next to her.

He peered at the closed computer, curiosity clear

220

in his eyes, but he didn't comment. Instead, he reached into his chest pocket, frowning when he found it empty. "Do you have a pen and some paper?"

Jane glanced around, relieved when she spotted a message pad and pen beside the phone on a nearby table. "Will this do?" She offered them to him.

"Yes. Thanks." He ripped off a page to write on the blank side. "Now, from what you said, you didn't actually *see* anything."

"No." Jane shook her head. "Abel and I were . . . er, talking on the hill. Then he fell asleep. I didn't want to leave him alone out there, but it was cold, so I fetched a comforter and covered him up. I was about to sit down beside him when I heard a car tearing up the road." She paused and closed her eyes, trying to remember. "Actually, I think I might have heard a shout first." She opened her eyes to be sure he was writing it all down this time. He was. She reclosed her eyes. "Yes. I'm positive I heard a yell, then a car hurrying up the road. Then I heard brakes squeal, then a bumping sound. A thud."

"You heard the brakes first, then the thud?" Colin asked.

"Yes," she said firmly.

He wrote something down, then said, "Go on."

"Well, then I heard two doors close. A woman asked 'Where is he?' or 'Where did he go?' Something like that. And a man answered 'Toward the Goodinov house' I . . ." She paused and opened her eyes again to point out, "They obviously knew whose house this was. That means it was likely someone from the community."

"Er, yes. Well, chances are good of that, aren't they? This *is* a gated community."

"Oh. Yes, of course." Jane's shoulders slumped. She'd been impressed by her deduction.

"It's late," he said by way of excuse, then asked, "Did you recognize the voices?"

Jane considered, then shook her head apologetically. "No."

"It's okay. That could be useful too. I know you met the Johnsons. Did either voice sound like one of theirs?"

Jane didn't hesitate. "No."

"What about Dirk or Lydia?"

She shook her head.

"Okay." He paused to make a note, then said, "See, that narrows it down already. There were four couples still at Leigh's when I came out. Seven couples had already left. And you just crossed two of them off the list."

"Oh." Jane smiled brightly. "Good."

"Now, what happened after the man said 'Toward the Goodinov house'?"

Jane closed her eyes again. "I could hear someone moving through the trees and I shouted 'Hello. Is anyone hurt?' Then it went quiet. The car doors slammed again and the car raced off. Then he—Josh—started to move through the trees again. I kept shouting 'Hello' and he kept moving closer. Then, you called out and came over and . . ." She shrugged. He knew the rest. There was no need for her to go any further.

He wrote down a few more things, then folded the papers he'd used to make notes and slipped them into his pocket.

"You don't look happy," Jane observed.

A faint smile touched his lips. "I'm not. We haven't had a suspicious death in Sonora in . . . well, not in my lifetime as far as I know. Like I told you at Perko's, there isn't a lot of crime here."

Jane was silent. There was more crime than the sheriff thought. A kidnapping for instance. "Why do you say suspicious death? You definitely don't think this was an accident?"

Colin shrugged. "Well, the braking before the thud suggests it might have been a hit-and-run," he admitted. "But the rest bothers me." He stood to pace in front of the couch, his expression troubled. "And why did Parker stumble away from the accident? He was hurt. He needed help. Why didn't he stay where he was and wait for help?"

Jane shook her head helplessly. She had no idea what had occurred, but she also found it hard to believe anyone had deliberately run the man down. Not someone from this community, at least. Didn't he work for the Ensecksis? Who would want to run him down?

"I suppose I should go and let you get some sleep." Colin sounded reluctant.

Jane walked him to the side door out into the nook, pausing when he did and smiling at him in question when he hesitated.

He said, "I'm sorry your first night here was like this. This kind of thing really never happens here."

"Oh." She waved his apology away. "It's hardly your fault."

"No." He stood there for another minute, then said, "You and Dirk? Are you . . . ?"

Jane was silent for a minute, then simply answered, "Dirk and I just met tonight. I just got here today—remember?"

"Oh." He smiled. "Yes. You did."

His eyes dropped to her lips, and Jane had the sudden thought he was considering kissing her. Then she decided she must be wrong. Edie wasn't the only one whose love life had been barren, and to go from no one showing an interest in her, to three men trying to kiss Jane in one night was just a bit too much to believe. Unless it was the truth serum perfume, she thought suddenly. Maybe she really should consider reducing the amount of pheromone.

"Jane, I find you very attractive."

She gave a start as his fingers ran lightly over her cheek. Her eyes narrowed and she asked, "Have you been smelling my neck?"

"Excuse me?" He looked bewildered.

Jane bit her tongue. That was stupid. She had to learn to keep her thoughts to herself. All the solitary time she had while working really wasn't good if it meant she was going to blurt out everything she thought the moment she was in company.

"Never mind." She gave a quick embarrassed smile. "It's just that I've had three men . . . well, who seemed attracted to me tonight. I'm not used to it. I thought it might be my perfume or something."

Taking that as an invitation, Colin bent forward and sniffed her neck. Jane stiffened and almost groaned aloud.

"It's nice," he announced, then paused for another sniff. Straightening, he said, "Very sexy, but not as sexy as those silk pajamas on you. Or that dress tonight." He blew a silent whistle.

"Oh, dear," Jane murmured. She really didn't think she could handle another amorous man. *Was* it the perfume? Maybe Abel had only wanted to kiss her because the perfume had—

"I like you, Jane." She glanced up and he added, "I don't trust you, but I like you."

Jane wasn't sure who was more surprised by those words. Colin's eyes widened even as hers did, and he covered his mouth with one hand.

"I didn't mean that," he said quickly. "I meant that I think you're cute and smart and up to something." He looked even more horrified, and she wished he'd got more of a whiff of the perfume. He'd had just enough to tell the truth, but wouldn't be comfortable doing so. Abel and Dirk hadn't thought it at all odd to be spilling what they really thought—but then they'd both inhaled more.

"I have to go," Colin said through his hand.

"I understand," Jane said solemnly, and was sure she heard him mutter, "I wish I did" as he stepped out through the screen door. She watched him walk past the yellow police tape that had been set up around the trees surrounding the crime scene.

When Colin turned the corner of the house and moved out of sight, Jane went back to the couch. Opening her portable, she glanced at each of the four images as they popped up. She was about to sit back for a long night of surveillance when she thought of Gran. Leaving the woman way at the other end of the house by herself was a bad idea. Not that anyone would break in, but Gran couldn't get around by herself and if she needed something Jane would be too far away to hear. Her gaze fell on the bags in front of the couch. Opening the closer one, she pulled out the two-way radios.

Jane left one on the coffee table and carried the other to her grandmother's room. Maggie Spyrus was sound asleep with Tinkle curled against her side. Jane set the radio by the bedside and turned it on. Gran would know instantly what it was for when she woke up.

Feeling better, Jane started to back out of the room, only to pause when Gran murmured her name.

"I'm sorry. I didn't mean to wake you," Jane whispered. "I was just putting a two-way radio on your table so that you could reach me if you need to. I have to watch the Ensecksis."

"All right, dear."

Smiling at the soft words, Jane left and headed back to the master bedroom. She made a quick detour to the kitchen for some instant coffee to help her stay awake.

Settling on the couch again, Jane checked the four camera broadcasts to see that they hadn't changed. She doubted they would tonight. Surely even bad guys had to sleep. Still, she had to watch. Or thought she had to. She'd never done this before. But Gran hadn't said she needn't bother, so . . . The thought of Gran made her turn on the two-way radio on the coffee table. Then she sat back on the couch and stared at the unchanging Ensecksi house. Mr. Tibbs crawled out from under the bed and moved to join her. He settled up against her side, pawed at her hand a couple of times until she petted him, then closed his eyes and went to sleep.

Jane glanced from the cat to where Abel sprawled on the bed.

It was going to be a long night.

Abel opened his eyes with a groan. Bright sunlight was pouring in through the window and into his face. Ugh. Leave it to California to have sunny days in November, he thought with disgust. Sitting up on the bed, brought about another groan.

His head felt as if it were imploding. Nasty. He tried not to move it too much as he shifted to sit on the side of the bed. He was in the master bedroom and still wearing the dark clothes he'd donned to help Jane last night. Not a good sign. Had he conked out on her? It was all rather fuzzy.

He got carefully to his feet, his eyes going to the screen door. The sight of yellow tape caught his eye. Police tape. It was wrapped around the entire little wooded area on the hill. What the hell had happened last night?

Opening the door, he stepped outside for a closer look. A bright splash of color on the ground by the table and chairs drew him forward. He recognized the comforter from the bed when he reached it. The sight of the bloodstains on it caused him some alarm, and Abel reached instinctively to feel his head. A good whack on the head would explain his headache and fuzzy memory this morning, but his skull appeared to be intact. There were no lumps or abrasions he could find.

He peered around again with bewilderment but, other than the police tape, there was nothing to hint at what had occurred. He turned to his own memories in the hopes of solving the mystery, but they were useless. He had a vague recollection of setting up cameras and microphones, then a rather fuzzy image of talking with Jane on the hill. He thought he might have kissed her, but couldn't be sure, and he didn't at all recall how he'd got inside on that bed.

Bewildered, he returned to the bedroom, pausing when he noticed Jane sound asleep on the couch. Mr. Tibbs was cuddled close. He moved toward her, ready to wake her up and find out what had gone on last night, but then he took a good look at her face. There were exhausted bruises under her eyes and she was pale with fatigue. No doubt she'd stayed up all night, staring at the images being transmitted from their surveillance equipment. She'd probably fallen asleep only a little while ago.

He would let her sleep, he decided, his gaze drifting over the faint freckles on her nose. An odd
warmth welled up in him and he found himself
smiling despite his aching head. He liked this girl.
She was smart and funny and sexy as hell. She was
also a good kisser, if the vague memory he had was
true. There had definitely been some zing when
their lips met.

He brushed an auburn curl back from her cheek
as he recalled some of the things Edie had told him
about her over the last six months. His sister had
managed to sneak at least one story of this woman
into every phone call they'd had, and every e-mail
he'd received from her. And with each one, a picture of Jane had grown until she'd become a faceless woman who was helpful, funny, and fiercely
loyal. The reality was even more compelling.

Abel suspected he'd seen Jane at her worst the
last couple of days. First she'd been suspicious,
then panicked, then worried and exhausted. All of
it had surely made her true personality shine
through sooner than it would have under normal
circumstances. Some women would have been
short and snappy; others would have burst into
helpless tears. Jane had taken each new problem
with equanimity, doing what had to be done with
as little fuss as possible.

Actually, he realized, she'd comported herself
better than *he* had with his alternate panic and frustration at Edie's disappearance. Everything had
been so rushed: Edie's going missing, the trip here.
He remembered the few times they'd managed to
forget their worries about Edie and have conversations in the van. Between those and what Edie

had said about her, he already knew that they had a lot in common. Maybe—

No, he thought. There was no maybe here. Perhaps if she really was plain Jane Spyrus, toy designer and neighbor to his sister, there would be a maybe. But she wasn't. She was an undercover agent. A spy with an exciting life and a dangerous career. Which was just Abel's luck. He'd spent the last several years concentrating on his career. Now that was going well and he was ready to settle down and pay some attention to his personal life, who did he find himself attracted to? Someone he was sure wouldn't look at a boring accountant twice.

Abel almost wished that Edie hadn't told him all her stories. He definitely wished she hadn't been kidnapped. He turned to glance across the room to the screen door. Abel couldn't see the Ensecksi house from where he stood, but he didn't have to. Edie was in there somewhere, maybe hurt and frightened, or maybe under some form of mind control and completely oblivious.

He hated the waiting and not knowing, and he wished he had a crystal ball. Edie was . . . well, she was his little sister. He'd always been protective of her, always done what he could to keep her safe and out of trouble. Abel had failed her somehow by not being there to prevent the kidnapping. He knew that was illogical but his heart didn't, and he determined there and then that he was moving to Vancouver whether he got the transfer or not. Family was too important to live far away from. Funny how losing them made it so clear.

Edie would be happy with his decision, he knew. She'd probably push forward with her campaign to get him and Jane together. His gaze went back to the woman on the couch. Jane would be another benefit to moving to Vancouver. He could have a relationship with her, maybe see if they couldn't . . .

His thoughts halted as he realized he was doing it again. It was fine and dandy that he wanted a relationship with her, but that didn't mean she'd want one with him. Edie thought she would and that they'd be perfect together, but then Edie didn't know Jane was a spy.

His thoughts along that line died abruptly as another intruded: the police tape. He wasn't hurt. Jane didn't appear to be either, but Edie . . . Had she somehow escaped her kidnappers and run to the nearest house for help? Had the Ensecksis given chase and—

Despite his earlier intentions to let her sleep, Abel found himself moving Mr. Tibbs to the floor and taking the cat's place on the edge of the couch next to Jane. He nudged her urgently, but her only response was a snuffle. She was half on her side and half on her stomach, her forehead resting on her hand and her nose squished against her wrist. She looked adorable. And he hated to wake her, but he needed to know what had happened.

"Jane?"

"Hmm?" She rolled back and blinked sleepily. "Oh, Abel. I was dreaming about you."

That distracted him briefly. She was dreaming about him? "What were you dreaming?"

"You were naked, and I didn't need to think oozing slinky to feel sexy."

Her words disconcerted him. They also didn't make a whole lot of sense. "Er, Jane? What's an oozing slinky? And why would it make you feel sexy?"

"It's what Gran told me to think of so Dirk would be interested," she explained sleepily. "But I found thinking of you towel-less and catless in the Sonora Sunset Motel worked better."

"Oh." Abel grimaced. That hadn't been one of his best moments. He cleared his throat and got his thoughts back on track. "Jane, what happened last night?"

"You kissed me and I really, really liked it."

"You did?" He was distracted again and cursed his hormones for their power over him.

"Oh, yes. Until you passed out. Then I was sad." She sighed and stretched a little, nearly knocking him off the bit of couch he'd claimed beside her.

"I passed out?" he asked, managing to keep his seat despite the fact that his attention had shifted to the way her breasts rose as she arched her back. The hem of her black pyjama top also rose, revealing a swath of pale flesh. Abel licked his lips.

"Yes," she answered, then added in grumpy tones, "Stupid knockout lipstick."

"Knockout lipstick?" Abel tore his eyes from her naked flesh as those words sank in. "What knockout lipstick?"

"Lipschitz's knockout lipstick," she grunted, as if that should explain everything. Then she raised one hand, moving it clumsily to rest on his arm so that she could fiddle with the cloth of his shirt. Abel forced himself to ignore the distraction of her touch.

"Okay," he said slowly. "You were wearing this lipstick last night. Right?"

"Yes. I forgot about it when you kissed me," she confessed. "I'm not a very good agent. A good agent would have remembered and not been overwhelmed by your sex appeal."

Abel straightened with pleasure. "I have sex appeal?" he asked.

"Oh, yes," she said solemnly.

Abel enjoyed that for a minute; then another thought struck him. "Were you wearing the knock-out lipstick when Dirk kissed you? Why wasn't he knocked out?"

"Because I'd wiped most of it off to eat, and he got just enough that it combined with the B.L.I.S.S. TSP to make him a stupid, sloppy and grabby pig."

"B.L.I.S.S. TSP?" Abel asked, refusing to think of the way Dirk had been grabbing Jane when he'd found them together. He'd wanted to pop the guy. *Pop, goes the weasel*, as a friend of his used to say.

"Truth-serum perfume."

"Truth-serum perfume?" He stiffened as he suddenly had a clear recollection of sniffing her neck last night on the hill. It came with a much vaguer memory of saying—His eyes turned to her sharply. "How long does this B.L.I.S.S. TSP work?"

"About an hour or so. It depends on how much is inhaled," Jane said.

"An hour?" He puzzled over that. "Then I didn't get any. You put it on before we went to the party, and I didn't smell your neck until—"

"Oh. I thought you meant how long does it affect the smeller. That's an hour. It has a life of about twenty hours on the wearer unless he washes it off."

"Twenty hours?" he echoed in shock.

"Certainly. I had to make it long-lasting. What if it took the agent a while to get the target to sniff her?" she asked reasonably.

"Twenty hours," Abel repeated. It was still working, he realized, and peered at her curiously. She herself seemed to be telling the truth rather easily. There was no sign of discomfort or hesitation. And if he wasn't mistaken, her pupils were a tad dilated. "Does it affect the wearer?"

"Not through skin contact. It has to be inhaled."

Aha! She'd been sleeping with her nose pressed to her wrist, inhaling her own TSP for who knew how long? He could ask her anything he wanted, and she'd tell the truth. He felt a moment's guilt at what he was thinking, but it passed quickly. After all, she'd got the truth from him last night. Turnabout was fair play. But first he needed to know what had happened last night. He had to assure himself that Edie wasn't lying hurt in the hospital or dead in a morgue. "Why is there police tape and a bloody comforter outside?"

Jane explained the events of the previous night, answering every question easily, and Abel found himself relaxing. It hadn't been Edie. She still wasn't safe at his side, but at least she wasn't dead or terribly injured . . . that he knew of.

Abel glanced back to Jane. She was watching him and grinning widely. "What are you smiling at?"

"You have the nicest eyes. I like looking at them."

"You do, do you?" Abel grinned, too. "What about Dirk? You don't think he has nicer eyes?"

"Yes."

Abel winced, deflating under her candor. But he'd asked for it, he thought with a sigh.

"Dirk is perfect looking. Very handsome." She continued to turn the screws. "But he's a stupid and selfish jerk."

That gave Abel some hope, and he stayed silent as she continued. "You're very handsome. Not as beautiful as Dirk, but still handsome. You're also nicer than him. And you're smart, too, and I wish you'd kiss me."

Abel groaned. He wanted to. He really did, but he suspected the TSP lowered all inhibitions, allowing its victim to tell the truth and maybe do things they normally wouldn't. He'd feel like he was taking advantage. It was like bedding a woman who'd had too much to drink, and Abel had never done that.

"I'd like to, Jane, but—"

"You don't want me." She gave a forlorn sigh, her lower lip popping out in a cute sulk that made him want to catch it between his teeth and tug. While Abel was trying to restrain himself Jane added, "I'm a failure as a woman and a failure as an agent." Before he could refute either and say something encouraging, she got a confused look on her face. "Well, I'm not really an agent. Or am I now?"

Her honesty was confusing her. It was confusing him, too. "What do you mean you're not really an agent?"

"I work in development and creation. I'm not a spy. But Y made me a spy because I was here and there was no one else here to do it."

Abel stiffened at this news. "And Maggie?"

"Gran?" Jane shrugged. "She use to be a field operative—until she was paralyzed."

"Then why the hell did you agree to do it?" Abel asked, outrage bubbling up within him. They were three amateurs stumbling around trying to save his sister's life!

"Because Edie needed me, and I love her like a sister," Jane said simply.

His gaze softened. "You'd do a lot for those you love, wouldn't you?"

"I'd die for those I love," she agreed solemnly. "But I'd rather not."

Abel felt a quirky smile pull at his lips. "Jane Spyrus, you are something else. I think I'm falling in love with you."

"Oh, that's so nice." She sighed. "I could love you

234

too, Abel." They smiled at each other; then she asked, "Can we have sex now?"

Abel felt laughter bubble up in his chest. She sounded so adorable. As if she were asking for ice cream. His laughter died, however, when she added, "I've never had an orgasm, and think I could with you."

What? That was like issuing a challenge. She'd never had an orgasm? Dear God, he'd like to give her her first. And her second and . . . *Down, boy,* he remonstrated, catching her hand as it drifted over his chest. She wasn't herself. He couldn't take advantage of her. If she still wanted him later, he would—

"I'd really like you to make me scream and beg like you said last night."

Abel closed his eyes as her words brought an image to mind of her naked beneath him, head thrown back, muscles straining as she cried out for him. He blinked his eyes open, eliminating the image. It was too damned exciting. He was already half hard. More than half. Why did she have to be under the influence of . . . ? A thought struck him and he asked, "Jane, if you weren't under the influence of truth serum, would you still want me to make love to you?"

"Am I under the influence of truth serum?" she asked in surprise.

"Yes. I'm afraid you are."

"Oh." She nodded. "That explains why I feel kind of floaty."

"Um, yes. But, Jane—if you weren't under the influence of the truth serum, would you still want me to make love to you right here and now?"

"I think so. I wanted you last night and I wasn't under the influence then. Besides, the truth serum

235

doesn't make you do things you don't want to do. It's designed to low—"

That was enough to salve Abel's conscience. He silenced her by bending over and covering her mouth with his own. It was very handy catching her midword like that. He was able to deepen the kiss at once and slip his tongue inside her mouth.

Abel had lived in various towns in Ontario and England, and hoped to live in Vancouver, but right there on that couch he was sure he'd found home.

Chapter Fifteen

Jane sighed as Abel kissed her. Yes, this was as good as she remembered from last night. The man could kiss, and she had the compulsive urge to tell him so, but couldn't with his tongue in her mouth. Besides, she reasoned a bit muzzily, if Abel was right and she was under the influence of her own truth serum, then that was what was causing the compulsion.

She forgot about wanting to tell him anything. His hands slid to cover her breasts, closing over them through her black silk pyjama tops so that she shuddered and arched into his touch. Oh, this was nice. No groping or grabbing. This was what was meant by a caress. The heat of his hands bled through the cloth separating them, and he began to rub his thumbs back and forth over her nipples that pebbled and pressed against the silk.

"Oh, that's so nice." She sighed as his lips left hers and traveled down her throat. Then she gasped and arched upward again when his hot mouth closed over one nipple. He nibbled through the suddenly damp cloth. "Abel?"

"Hmm?" He lifted his head.

"I like that, but I think I'd like it even better if you were to do that without my top on."

A slow smile spread across his lips. "I think you're brilliant," he announced. He began to work on the buttons. "And I definitely think your truth serum is going to make this an incredible experience."

"It is?" Jane asked curiously.

"Oh, yes. It is. Especially if it makes you tell me exactly what you want." He finished with the buttons and spread the cloth apart to peer down at the naked flesh he'd revealed, he added, "And there won't be any faking it." He raised his head and asked, "What do you want, Jane?"

"I want you to touch me and kiss me and . . ." She shrugged helplessly where she lay. "I want *you.*"

Abel started to lean toward her, his mouth seeking hers, but she caught him with her hands on his chest. "I want you to take your top off, too. I want to feel you."

Abel quickly complied. Not bothering with the buttons, he simply yanked the shirt up over his head and tossed it aside. Jane drank in the sight of his wide muscled shoulders. "Are you sure you're an accountant?"

"Good genes," he explained with a chuckle. Then he bent to reclaim her lips.

Jane kissed him back, moaning at the feel of his hair-roughened chest brushing her erect nipples. She slid her arms around his back and caressed him eagerly, trying to touch every inch of his skin, then clutched at him instead when his hand closed over her breast again, this time without the cloth to separate them. The next time he broke the kiss, it was to sit up. He drew her with him, helping her to shift to her knees on the couch so that they were positioned face-to-face, watching her face as he caressed her breasts. "Do you like that?"

"Oh, yes." She closed her eyes, leaning into his touch and running her hands over his chest as well.

"What else do you want me to do?"

"More," Jane answered simply.

He slid one arm around her and urged her back against it. His head lowered so that he could catch one nipple between his lips. Jane cried out at the pleasure that shot through her and slid forward a little on the couch, the silk of her pyjamas sliding easily on the cloth material until his thigh stopped her. It lodged between her legs, bracing her and adding to the sensations swirling through her. She felt his free hand slide down her back, pushing the pyjama bottoms off one cheek as he cupped and pressed her against him. His erection was hard against her upper thigh, and she pressed her leg tighter against it before reaching around to touch him through his black jeans.

Abel groaned against her breast, then lifted his head to catch her mouth again with a hard hot kiss. He pushed the cloth of her pyjama bottoms off her other hip. The black cloth pooled around her knees, cool and silky, and he pushed her back on the couch again. He came down on top of her, his hand slipping between their bodies, between her legs. Jane gasped and jerked beneath him, her legs instinctively trying to close, then falling wider apart.

"Abel. I want you," she told him, and reached to find the button of his jeans.

"Not yet," he said. He covered her mouth with his own, his tongue thrusting aggressively between her lips as his seeking fingers found the center of her excitement and drove her into a frenzy.

With the last of her sanity left, Jane managed to undo the button and lower the zipper of Abel's jeans. Her hand immediately slid inside to touch him. He moaned into her mouth, his hips thrusting forward. Then he tore his lips away to move them back to her breast, shifting backward so that his lower body was out of reach.

"Unfair," Jane gasped, grabbing at his shoulders desperately as the pressure building within her became unbearable. "Please, I . . . Please. Abel, *please.*"

She was twisting her head frantically back and forth, her hips moving to the rhythm of his caressing hand, her body arching and vibrating like a tuning fork as she strained toward what he offered. Jane had never experienced this much pleasure before. It was wonderful and terrifying and . . . and. . . . She grabbed desperately at his head, wanting his mouth on hers even though her lips seemed as stiff and taut as the rest of her body and unable to kiss properly. She pressed her open mouth to his when he lifted his head obligingly, and Jane felt herself shatter as his tongue thrust into her mouth.

Abel continued to kiss and touch her as her body shuddered and throbbed and pulsed. At last, her heartbeat began to slow.

"Thank you," she murmured when his lips left hers.

"You're welcome." He kissed her forehead and held her close.

They lay still for several moments until Jane recovered enough to notice the hardness against her thigh. She ran her hands down his naked back, smiling. "Abel."

"Hm?" He lifted his head and peered at her.

She pressed a kiss to his lips, then reached for the back of his jeans to push them forcefully over his hips, saying one word: "More."

Chuckling, Abel helped her push the jeans off. He stood briefly to remove them, and Jane noticed that her own bottoms were hanging from one foot. She kicked them off, then glanced at Abel as he rejoined her on the couch, a shiver going through her at her second sight of him completely naked. He looked even better than he had in the hotel.

She shifted restlessly when he stopped halfway down on the couch. "What?" she asked.

"Just a minute." He leaned sideways off the couch and she could hear him rifling through something on the floor.

"What are you doing?" She started to sit up, but he urged her back down with one hand, then took that hand away to fiddle with something that crinkled. She heard a ripping sound, another rustle; then he hesitated and shifted to sit on the edge of the couch.

"What are you doing?" Jane asked curiously, unable to see past his arm and thigh.

"Protecting you," he answered, obviously distracted. It was the movement of his hands and arms that made everything clear.

"Oh," she said, and relaxed as she realized he was donning a condom. Wasn't it just like him to think of her that way? She wouldn't have to worry about getting pregnant or anything else. She herself hadn't even considered that possibility at this point. He was so—

Condom? Where did he get it? "Abel?"

"All done." He turned to smile and started to shift over her, then paused suddenly. His glance at his now-sheathed erection was one of surprise.

"Abel?" Jane asked in horror. Her thoughts seemed terribly clear now, the fog the truth serum had caused disappearing like morning dew. "Where did you get the condom?"

"The bag," he muttered, staring down at himself with growing discomfort. "There seems to be something odd about it, though."

"Oh, no!" Jane scrambled out from beneath him. Kneeling naked at the side of the couch, she began rifling wildly through the bags she'd left sitting out. The bags he'd got the condom from. Her B.L.I.S.S. Shrink-Wrap Condom. "Where is the relaxing cream? I must have brought the relaxing cream."

"Uh, Jane? Something's wrong with this condom."

She paused to glance over her shoulder. Abel had gone pale and was now struggling to remove the prophylactic. It wasn't coming off, of course. In a second he'd be singing soprano. "There's nothing *wrong* with it. That's supposed to happen."

"Supposed to happen?" He gaped at her. Then, obviously thinking she didn't understand what was occurring, he explained, "It's tightening or something, it's—"

"Yes, I know. It's the B.L.I.S.S. Shrink-Wrap Condom, Abel. It's supposed to shrink. You really shouldn't have used it."

"Shrink-wrap condom? Shrink-wrap condom!" He began tearing desperately at the latex, but it wasn't budging.

"It's okay," she soothed, turning back to the bags. "Don't fight it. That won't work. I just have to find the relaxing cream. The condom will relax and everything will be fine."

"What happens if you don't find it?" Abel asked with alarm.

Jane pictured banana mash in her mind and decided it was better not to tell him.

"Ahhhhhh . . ."

She didn't really want to take the time to look at him, but the thud that followed Abel's pained cry could not be ignored. Glancing back Jane saw that Abel had tumbled off the couch and was now rolling on his back on the floor. His legs were drawn up into the fetal position and his hands were clasped over his groin.

"Cream!" Jane cried and went back to her rifling.

"Jane." It was a strangled sound, much higher than Abel's usual voice. Jane ignored it and continued to search.

"Aha!" She felt a tidal wave of relief as her hand closed over the jar of relaxing cream. "I found it, Abel. We're saved."

His answer was a whimper. He rolled back and forth on the floor, eyes squeezed shut and tears leaking out of them.

"Here!" She knelt at his side and quickly undid the lid of the cream, then dipped in her hand to scoop some out. But when she tried to apply it, Abel shrieked, "Don't touch me!"

"I have to, Abel. I have to apply the cream," Jane said patiently. She tried to urge his hands out of the way—not an easy job when he was rolling back and forth. She finally followed him on her knees, so that when he rolled back he came up against her legs. "Let me put this cream on."

"No! Oh, God, don't touch me. Oh, God, it's ripping my dick off!"

Jane paused. Ripping it off? Could it? She hadn't run test trials on the effects of this item. How could she? Who would volunteer to be a test subject?

"Oh, God! I'm going to be dickless. A eunuch! I'll never have children. I—" He rolled toward her, eyes glaring out of a pain-filled face. "I'm singing soprano here, Jane. Put the cream on!"

"You're the one who wouldn't let me—"

"Put it on!" he roared. Well, he sort of roared. His voice was several pitches higher than could be called a roar.

"Sheesh, listen to you carry on. I thought guys were supposed to be stoic and stuff," she muttered, pushing his hands away.

Abel growled, "Cut my arm off and I promise I won't flinch, but this isn't my arm."

"Oh, dear." Jane winced as she saw how far the condom had shrunk.

"What?"

"Don't look," Jane said quickly, but it was too late. He gaped at himself in horror for a moment, then fell back with a whimper.

"Dear God, its a pencil," he said through clenched teeth.

"I'm sure it's only temporary," Jane babbled. She began to slather the cream on. "It will pop right back to normal size. How big was that?" she added worriedly as the condom began to relax. His penis didn't appear to reinflate much. She hadn't really looked when she'd had the opportunity, just noticed he had a condom on and—

"Huge!" Abel snapped, but he didn't seem as clenched as before. His voice was starting to sound normal, so she was sure he was feeling better. It was just a shame his penis wasn't recovering as quickly. It wasn't as thin as it had been, but it appeared to be trying to shrivel up inside him. At least there was no bleeding, Jane thought.

A groan from him made her glance at his face. He'd leaned forward to look at himself, and had a tragic expression on his face. His voice was wistful and singsongy as he said, "Little Abel used to be so big and brave."

"Umm . . ." Jane bit her lip and removed the now baglike condom, then replaced the lid of the cream and sat back to eye Abel uncertainly. He was lying flat on the floor again, arms limp at his sides, eyes closed. He looked miserable.

"Feel any better?" she asked.

He opened his eyes and stared at her as if she were insane.

"Guess not." She cleared her throat, then got to her feet and moved back to the couch. After quickly redonning her pajamas, she found Abel watching her with a mournful expression. "What is it?"

"I had such plans for you, and now I'll never have sex again," he said.

Jane bit her lip. "I'm sure you'll feel better soon. It didn't look like any permanent damage was done."

Abel grunted, then sighed. "The compact and lipstick are knockout drugs. The perfume is a truth serum. The condoms are a torture device. What are the vibrators?"

"Mini-missile launchers."

"Jesus." Abel closed his eyes. "Remind me to stay out of your bags."

"Janie?"

Her gaze slid to the two-way radio on the table

as her grandmother's voice erupted from it. Jane picked it up. "Gran?"

"Are you up yet, dear?" the woman asked hopefully.

"Yes. Coming." Jane set the radio down and eyed Abel apologetically. "I have to . . ." She waved vaguely.

"Go." He closed his eyes and just lay there, naked as the day he was born, on the bedroom carpet.

"Will you be all right?" Jane asked.

"I'll never be all right again."

Not knowing how to respond, Jane merely left him where he was and walked out of the room. She paused in the kitchen to get the coffee started, then continued on to find Gran.

Maggie Spyrus was sitting up in bed when Jane entered. Tinkle was playing possum beside her. Jane knew the dog wasn't really asleep because its eyes were cracked open. The little beast was only trying to fake her out so that she'd get close enough to be nipped. Tinkle just wasn't a morning kind of dog. Jane was careful to avoid the beast as she helped Gran get ready to meet the day.

Abel was leaning against the island in the kitchen drinking coffee when Jane rolled in her grandmother and Tinkle. His hair was wet from a shower, and he was dressed in fresh blue jeans and a red polo shirt. Jane didn't think he was over his trauma yet, however. He was scowling and stood slightly hunched, his free hand near his groin as if he might cover it protectively at any moment.

He responded to Gran's cheery good morning and the sunny smile Jane sent him with a grunt. Definitely not over his trauma, she thought, and decided to leave him alone for a bit.

She would make breakfast. It was a major undertaking for Jane, who was not a good cook. She could throw a casserole in the oven to warm for fifteen minutes, but anything more complicated than that had always seemed too much bother. She intended to give it her best effort this morning, however. After all, they said the way to a man's heart was through his stomach. Maybe her efforts would help cheer Abel and make him smile again. She was feeling a bit vulnerable at the moment. He'd done wonderful things to her before the condom debacle. Intimate-type things. But the fact that he'd almost been eaten alive by her invention in response was . . . well, it was hardly likely to endear her to him.

To bolster her confidence in her cooking ability, Jane started with the easy stuff. She got Gran a cup of coffee and pulled out some food for Tinkle and Mr. Tibbs.

The Yorkie showed only mild interest in what Jane was doing as she poured the cat's dry food into a bowl, but the little beast was off Gran's lap and at Jane's side at the first sound of the can opener. Feedings were the only times the creature treated Jane as anything other than someone to bite or otherwise aggravate. Jane wasn't impressed.

She set both bowls down and straightened to call for Mr. Tibbs. Tinkle scampered back onto Gran's lap the moment Edie's cat sauntered in, then the little fur-ball lay there whining miserably. The tabby had sampled the dog food and settled down to eat it rather than the dry food that was his own fare.

Somehow encouraged by the cat's meanness, Jane smiled sunnily and walked to the refrigerator. "Who's up for bacon and eggs?"

"Oh, that sounds nice," Gran said. "Are you sure you're up to it though, dear?"

"Of course," Jane said cheerfully, pulling out a package of bacon and the carton of eggs. "What about you, Abel? Bacon and eggs?"

Taking the grunt he gave for a yes, Jane set the food on the counter and dug around for a frying pan. She found a nice-sized one, set it on the stove, and cranked the burner to high.

"What are you doing?" Abel was at her side at once.

"Cooking."

Abel opened his mouth, then paused—she suspected to reconsider whatever he'd been about to say. After a moment, he cleared his throat and said, "Why don't I cook the bacon?"

Jane turned a wary eye on him. "What did I do wrong?"

"Nothing. I just like to cook bacon. I'll do it."

"Want to smell my perfume?" Jane asked, and Abel actually managed to crack a smile.

"That pan is Teflon," he said, as if that explained everything.

"So? You can't cook bacon and eggs in a Teflon pan?"

Abel arched an eyebrow. "You don't cook much, do you?"

Jane made a face, then confessed. "I'm not very good at it for some reason."

"Ah. Well, the good news is I am. I also like to do it," he said easily.

Jane felt herself relax. He didn't mind that she couldn't cook. That was good, she thought as she watched him turn down the burner.

Still, it seemed to her that she should learn at least some cooking skills. She was always willing to learn; she'd just never had anyone to teach her. Gran hadn't exactly been the Betty Crocker of the spy world. She could burn water. "Tell me why you turned the heat down," she said.

Abel hesitated then explained, "You never use Teflon above medium. It wrecks the pan. It also lets off a poisonous gas."

"Poisonous gas?" Jane asked with horror.

"Yeah. Enough to kill small birds, apparently."

"Well, if it kills small birds it can't be much better for humans," Jane said with disgust. "Maybe we should find another—"

"It will be fine. You just have to keep it at medium or lower. It's safe then," he soothed. Offering her a smile, he opened the bacon. "Why don't you make toast?"

"I can handle that." Relieved that he appeared to have gotten over his trauma from earlier and was smiling at her again, she found the toaster and set to work.

"Did you tell your gran what happened?" Abel asked as she opened a loaf of bread.

"Of course not." Jane gasped. "I would never tell her what happened between us, that's personal and—"

"About Parker," Abel corrected.

"Oh." Jane flushed and pushed the toaster button down. Of course he'd meant Parker.

"Who is Parker, and what happened to him?" Gran asked from the table.

"He was Dirk's assistant," Jane answered. "He was hit by a car out in front of the house last night. It was a hit-and-run. He stumbled through the trees to the clearing beside our house and died there."

"Really," Gran said thoughtfully. "Who hit him?"

"I don't know. I couldn't see the road through the trees. I heard it all, but didn't see a thing. It was a man and a woman. Officer Alkars thinks it was someone from the party." She shrugged. "He'll sort it out."

"Does he think it was an accident?" Abel asked curiously as he laid strips of bacon out in the pan.

"I don't know. He's kind of suspicious, but I think it was probably an accident."

"Why, Janie?" Gran asked.

The toast popped up. Jane set it on a plate to butter. "Because Parker was from Canada. No one here knows him. Who would want him dead?"

"I don't know," Maggie said.

The way the older woman spoke made Jane look at her curiously. "You don't know what?"

"If it was an accident. It could have been, but . . ."

"But?" Abel prompted.

The old woman looked unhappy. "It could also mean we have more players here than we expected."

"Like who?" Jane asked with interest.

"There could be someone here after the technology the Ensecksis have." Her gaze sharpened on Jane and Abel. "I want you two to watch your step."

Jane nodded and turned back to the toaster to put in fresh bread. Abel worked silently at her side. Both of them stiffened, however, when Gran suddenly said, "I wasn't going to ask, but the curiosity is killing me. What is this 'personal thing' that happened between you?"

"Nothing," Jane said quickly. Too quickly. She sounded guilty as sin and felt herself flush with embarrassment.

"Guess the truth serum has worn off. Thank God," Abel said under his breath.

Jane felt her blush deepen.

"Hmm," Gran murmured. "And would this 'nothing' that happened be the reason you were so relaxed and cheerful when you came to help me this morning?"

"I just slept well," Jane lied. She'd slept maybe two hours.

"Slept well, huh? That's not what the circles under your eyes suggest."

"Gran, this is—" A knock at the door made her pause, and Jane released a sigh.

"Saved by the bell," Maggie Spyrus said dryly.

Jane moved to answer it. To say that she was surprised to find Daniel and Luellen Braunstein on the doorstep was a bit of an understatement. She hadn't even spoken to the couple at the party the night before, and she had no idea what would bring them to their door.

"We thought we'd stop in and welcome you to the neighborhood." Luellen Braunstein smiled brightly and stepped inside, forcing Jane to back up. They'd come to welcome her to the neighborhood? According to Melanie Johnson, this couple had only moved in yesterday too.

"I hope we haven't shown up too early?" Daniel added, his gaze dropping down over the black silk pyjamas Jane still wore.

"Oh!" She flushed. She'd been in such a rush to get to Gran this morning, she hadn't thought to stop and change. "Come in," she said, despite the fact that the pair had already done so. She closed the door and followed them into the kitchen saying, "Gran, Abel—look who's here. I'll be right back, I'm going to change."

Leaving the visitors in Gran's capable hands, Jane moved to the master bedroom to perform the quickest change she'd ever managed. She was eager to get back out there and hear what the Braunsteins had to say for themselves, because she'd recognized Luellen and Daniel's voice the moment each spoke. This was the couple who had hit and killed Josh Parker last night.

Chapter Sixteen

"It was an accident."

Jane decided to reserve judgment until the woman explained. She'd returned to the kitchen in fresh jeans and a short-sleeved blue shirt to find Tinkle in the process of watering Daniel Braunstein's pant leg. Such an action won points for the man—Tinkle only relieved herself on the best of people—but there was still the little matter of a dead Josh Parker to contend with. Thus Jane put her hand in her pocket, ready to pull out her can of highly concentrated nerve spray if the Braunsteins gave any trouble.

Reminding herself to be careful to keep the stream away from Gran and Abel, she asked conversationally why they hadn't stuck around after the crash.

Dead silence followed. It lasted several moments;

then Luellen repeated that it was an accident.

"It *was*," Daniel insisted, noting their doubt. "He escaped from the trunk and—"

"Er . . . excuse me," Abel interrupted. He'd lifted the frying pan off the burner and moved to the table, spatula in hand. "Did you say he escaped from your trunk? As in the trunk of your car?"

The couple exchanged a glance; then Luellen reached into her purse. Jane, wanting to be prepared, withdrew the bottle in her pocket. Luellen winced when she saw it. "That isn't hair spray is it?"

Jane shook her head.

"I didn't think so." She glanced warily from the can to Jane's face, then said, "I'm just getting my ID out." When Jane kept the can pointed at her but nodded, Luellen moved slowly, opening a wallet and removing a card.

Jane glanced at it. "FBI?"

Luellen nodded. "B.L.I.S.S. contacted our boss and explained the situation."

"Just enough to get what they wanted," Daniel put in.

"They asked for some agents to be sent to back you up until other B.L.I.S.S. agents could arrive." Luellen cleared her throat. "We were told to say 'Why' to you."

"Y?" Jane asked.

"That's what we want to know," Daniel announced. "Why would we say why?"

"It doesn't matter," Jane said, deciding not to explain. Relaxing a little, she slid her can of nerve gas back into her pocket.

"So, the FBI bought a house and moved you in as the Braunsteins."

"No. Actually, the Braunsteins bought the house three weeks ago and were supposed to move in this weekend. They were sent on vacation, and we took the house in their place."

"Why was Parker in your trunk?" Abel asked, still sounding suspicious.

"Because he made Jane," Luellen answered.

"Made Jane?" Abel asked.

"He recognized her," Luellen explained. Then she turned to Jane. "I saw it at the house, in the hallway outside the office when Dirk and Parker came out."

Jane nodded, then explained the situation to Gran and Abel. "Luellen had just come into the hall when the office door opened. She slipped into one of the other rooms. I was too slow to do that."

"It was a closet," Luellen elaborated with a grimace. "I followed you out into the hall to tell you who we were. So you'd know to turn to us if you had trouble. But then *they* came into the hall. I kept the door cracked open and watched Dirk greet you, then noticed that Parker was lurking. I knew from his expression that he recognized you from somewhere. I wanted to warn you, but Dirk dragged you back into the office and closed the door."

Jane nodded. "I think you're right. He did recognize me as Edie's friend."

"Edie?" Daniel asked eagerly. Jane realized just how little they'd been told. She wasn't going to tell them more.

"So you grabbed Parker?" she asked Luellen.

"Yes. I slipped out of the closet and, er, encouraged him to go outside with me." She cleared her throat. "I used this truth serum perfume on him and—"

"Truth serum perfume?" Jane asked, surprised.

Gran spoke up. "Yes, dear. It's probably yours.

255

B.L.I.S.S. shares some of its technology with cooperative agencies."

"B.L.I.S.S. TSP is yours?" Luellen asked with surprise.

"Yes. I developed it," Jane admitted.

"Really?" Luellen squealed. "Why, it's brilliant stuff. I can't tell you how many times it's come in handy."

"Thank you," Jane said, flushing pink. "I'm glad it's useful."

"Useful? Honey, you just don't know," she began in confiding tones—only to pause when Daniel cleared his throat. "Oh, yes. Where was I?"

"You took him out and . . ."

"Oh, yes. He said he recognized you as Edie's friend and that he planned to tell Dirk and Lydia, that they'd take care of you. So, what could I do?" She shrugged helplessly. "I knocked his sorry butt unconscious and tossed him in the trunk. Then I headed back and got Daniel. You three were leaving at the time, and I wanted to tell you then, but Leigh was seeing you out. She kept me for a few minutes, talking; then it took me a while to find Daniel." She shrugged again. "We started to drive back to the Braunstein house to figure out what to do with Parker when I spotted him in my rearview window. He was hurrying up the road toward the Ensecksis." She shook her head in disgust. "I should have tied him up. I still can't believe he recovered consciousness and got the trunk open. I was sure he'd be out cold for the whole night."

"Who shouted?" Jane asked.

"Me." Luellen grimaced. "It was pure shock and outrage. I turned the car around and chased after him. I didn't mean to hit him. In fact, I would have slammed to a stop right beside or just past him, but he turned his ankle on something and fell into my path." She grimaced. "He took a good hit. I don't know how he managed to scramble away."

"Shock, I imagine," Jane decided. "He must not have realized how badly he was hurt."

"Hmm." Daniel nodded in agreement.

Luellen continued, "We came after him, but then someone started yelling."

"Me," Jane admitted.

Daniel frowned. "We didn't realize it was you, or we would have come up."

Jane shook her head. "It's good you didn't. Officer Alkars came out and heard me. You'd have been spotted."

Everyone was silent for a minute; then Abel remembered his bacon and returned to the kitchen. "I'll throw some more food on."

"Nothing for me, thanks," Luellen said.

"I'll have some. It smells good." Daniel stood and followed Abel. "Mind if I have some coffee, too?"

"Help yourself," Abel said easily. "What about you, Luellen? Coffee?"

"I won't say no."

Jane stood and moved into the kitchen to serve the coffee and make another pot.

"So," Daniel said as he sipped from a mug. He watched her fill the pot with water. "Are you going to fill us in on what's going on?"

Jane considered as she set the coffee carafe on its burner and started to scoop grounds into the filter. Y had probably told them all she wanted them to know. Jane likely wasn't supposed to reveal more. But how could she refuse politely? The doorbell again came to the rescue. Relieved, Jane moved to answer it.

She was brought up short, however, when she found Lydia and Dirk on her doorstep. So much for spying on her neighbors. She'd forgotten all about them. Well, not them exactly, but she'd forgotten about watching their movements all morning.

"I know it's early yet," Lydia said. "But we wanted to make sure you were all right."

"All right?" Jane asked.

"Well, it must have been distressing to have Josh die at your feet," Dirk pointed out.

"Oh!" Jane gave herself a mental kick. "Yes, of course. I—"

"Who is it, Jane?"

She glanced back to see Abel peering around the corner.

"Oh. Hello, Lydia. Dirk," Abel said. He even managed to infuse some good cheer into the greeting. Jane was sure no one noticed the way he stiffened.

"Abel!" Lydia sailed past Jane and glued herself to his side. "Good morning. You look good enough to eat."

"Oh, er . . . I have bacon," he offered, slipping the plate between them. Her man fleeing the man-eater. It did Jane's heart good.

"You look cute in the morning." Dirk breathed in her ear, and Jane grimaced as she became aware that he was practically lodged in her back. He and his sister were two of a kind, really. Forcing a smile, she glanced over her shoulder.

"I have no makeup on, and my hair is . . ." She didn't bother to finish. She hadn't even run a brush through her hair yet. She'd dressed when Daniel and Luellen arrived, but that was it. She'd been too eager to get back and confront them on killing Josh Parker.

"You look like you just rolled out of bed. All sexy and mussed," Dirk said.

Jane sighed inwardly. The man never turned it off. Fortunately, she was now immune. "We're having breakfast. Do you want some?" When Dirk nodded, she asked "How many eggs would you like?"

"Two would do me just fine." His eyes dropped suggestively to her chest.

Jane turned abruptly and walked back to the kitchen. There she announced, "Dirk wants two eggs. Coffee, Lydia?"

"No. I only drink tea," the blonde said. Abel managed to escape her and moved back to continue cooking.

"Tea it is." Jane grabbed the kettle to fill it with water. "What about you, Dirk?"

"Coffee."

Jane noticed neither Ensecksi said please. Some people just weren't raised right. But, then, what was she to expect from a couple of kidnapping sex addicts bent on world domination? Saying please would be rather hypocritical, she supposed.

"Oh. Hello." Lydia moved to the counter and eyed the couple seated at the table with Gran.

"Lydia and Dirk Ensecksi, Luellen and Daniel Braunstein," Jane introduced, then realized that she was acting snappish. She needed to get more sleep. Jane liked sleep. She didn't do well without it. She tried her best to remain even-tempered and pleasant, but little annoyances could bother her more when she didn't get her rest. Or big annoyances, she thought as Dirk caught her at the sink and pressed himself close to her side again. No manners, no morals, no boundaries. Dirk was just a mass of deficiencies.

"Here you go, Dirk."

Jane glanced over her shoulder to see Abel holding out a coffee. As Dirk took it, Abel suggested, "Why don't you go sit down so Jane and I aren't tripping over you while we cook?" Jane cast him a grateful glance, then felt bad for her amusement at his problem with Lydia earlier.

"Oh, I'm fine right here," Dirk said. He paused and glanced down in dismay.

Jane followed his gaze. Tinkle had leapt off Gran's lap and returned to the kitchen. She hadn't gone to her picked-over food dish, however. The dog was busy licking Dirk's shoe and wiggling her butt in a frenzy of adoration.

"She seems to like you," Jane commented as the dog started trying to climb him, whining and begging for attention.

"Yes." He shook his leg, trying to dislodge the little fur-ball leaving fine white hairs all over his lovely black dress pants. But Tinkle was not easily swayed once her heart was given. She held on like a limpet.

"Tinkle sure does have good taste," Abel announced. Hearing the underlying laughter in his voice, Jane distinctly recalled telling him the Yorkie liked only those who were either evil or slightly shady. She shared a smile with him and bit her lip to keep from laughing as Dirk began to do an odd sort of one-legged hop.

"I think I might sit down after all," Dirk Ensecksi muttered and started across the room in a shaky-stepped effort to dislodge the adoring canine.

"I think I'm starting to like that dog," Abel murmured as they watched him go.

"She has her uses," Jane allowed. Returning to the toaster, she fed more bread into it.

"I need orders here," Abel called loudly. "Who wants what?"

"Nothing for me," Luellen repeated, then, "Well, maybe some toast, please. And a strip of bacon. It smells too good to resist."

"Toast is all I'll have, Abel," Lydia purred.

Everyone else wanted the full meal deal, so Jane and Abel were able to avoid being pressed by the Ensecksis for a while, and to simply listen to the conversation taking place behind them. Gran offered her condolences on the death of Dirk's assistant. Dirk professed himself terribly upset. He had no idea where he was going to find help as obedient as Josh.

What a guy, Jane thought.

The conversation turned to the subject of Sonora then, so Jane concentrated on her toast making. It was an undemanding chore that had her nearly asleep at the counter, starting awake each time the toaster popped.

"All done over here. How's the toast coming, Jane?" Abel asked. His eyes widened when he saw the two towers of bread. Jane hadn't wanted to get any closer to Dirk than she had to, so she had just kept making toast. She'd gone through almost two loaves. Abel seemed to understand; there was definite sympathy in his eyes despite his laughter. "Looks like you have enough there," he said.

Jane merely grunted and picked up her two plates. She carried them out to the table, then returned to help Abel carry out the individual meals.

"Oh, this looks lovely." Lydia was looking at Dirk's plate instead of the piece of toast she'd taken. She scooped one of her brother's eggs and half his bacon.

"Lydia," Dirk protested.

"Well, I have to see if—Oh." She'd bit into the bacon and now moaned as if it were manna. "Oh, Abel. A man who can cook. You're just too, too perfect!"

"The toast is done to perfection," Dirk added, beaming at Jane as if it were a grand accomplishment. "You'll make someone a good wife."

Jane managed not to roll her eyes and took a seat as far away from him as she could manage. There was no doubt in her mind she'd just heard one of the lines Dirk had mentioned last night: A little hint at the possibility that he was open to a long-term relationship. It was probably meant to put stars in her eyes and rush her off her feet into bed.

The talk about Sonora continued as they ate. Jane mentioned she wouldn't mind walking around some. She was hoping that it would cover her if she ever got caught snooping.

"It's a beautiful area," Dirk agreed. He smiled at her then cautioned, "But there are mountain lions and snakes. Watch out for them."

"Which are you?" she asked under her breath.

Luellen overheard and burst out laughing. Jane found a reluctant smile curving her lips, and some of her tension left her.

"It's a lovely day," Jane commented when everyone had finished eating. "Why don't we enjoy our coffee out on the deck?"

"That would be nice," Gran announced and led the way.

Jane watched the whole group move through the French doors, relieved when Dirk was too distracted trying to dislodge the ever-adoring Tinkle to notice that she hadn't joined them. She had no intention of going outside. She was going to start to work on the dishes. Maybe she wasn't any good at cooking, but she was first-rate at washing up. Besides, she could use a few moments to herself.

She was rinsing china at the sink when Dirk wandered back inside, sans Tinkle. Jane held on to her patience and continued to work as he once more took up his customary stance practically on her heels. She wanted to tell him to bug off, but she had to play nice and finagle that invitation to his home he and Lydia had talked about last night. She wanted to get inside and plant bugs. And if she should happen to accidentally trip into a locked room where Edie was being held captive, Y could hardly blame her for freeing her friend. Could she?

"I'm a little fuzzy about last night," Dirk said quietly, toying with her hair. "I think I may have said a few things that were inappropriate. I hope I didn't insult you?"

Jane frowned. Her testiness had shown, of course. She had known it would. Now she had to convince him she just wasn't a morning person, that she was still attracted to him. What a pain. Pasting a smile on her face, she forced herself to relax against him.

"No. You didn't insult me at all, Dirk."

"You're sure?"

Sheesh! She needed to improve her acting skills. He didn't think she was interested. She recalled her oozing slinky. It didn't seem to help. Even the image of Abel towel-less and catless wasn't doing anything for her. Jane took a moment to recall the more heated moments in the bedroom that morning, and knew it was working when a slow wicked smile spread over her lips. She turned and shone it on Dirk. "Oh, yes. I'm sure. You were honest. I find honesty a turn-on."

That was enough to convince Dirk. He beamed at her. "Really?"

She nodded. "I get so tired of men who pretend to want a relationship when all they really want is sex. Especially when that's all I'm interested in," she lied glibly.

"Really?"

Perhaps that had been overdoing it, she thought. The man looked truly shocked. But she'd pledged herself to this now. Leaning against him, she toyed with the top button of Dirk's shirt and continued. "Certainly. Relationships are a pain. Besides, I like my life the way it is. Who needs a man cluttering up things? I just like to cut loose and have some hot, sweaty, dirty sex once in a while." She did her best to look like someone likely to indulge in "dirty sex" and was now grateful that her hair was a mess. Jane was sure she looked dirtier with knotty hair. Makeup might have helped, too.

The thought was lost with a grunt as she found herself suddenly pushed back against the kitchen counter. Dirk was plastered against her like a clingy shirt. The counter at her back pressed into her, hard, and she felt rather like warm soft cheese being squeezed out the sides of a sandwich. It seemed Dirk didn't think she needed makeup.

She wasn't sure if she was glad about that or not. It was good that she didn't have to work too hard to keep his interest; she didn't know if she had it in her to work very hard. She kept hearing his voice say "ditz" in her head. And "all women want my bone."

"Not here," she said as he began to gnaw on her neck. "The others."

"Yes, here. Now. I want you." It seemed he was

264

into the kinky possibility of getting caught. She should have known.

"Oh, sorry! I just thought I'd nip in for some more coffee."

Jane breathed a sigh of relief as Daniel walked into the kitchen. He beamed at them, apparently oblivious of Dirk's scowl. It seemed Dirk liked the possibility of being interrupted, not the actual interrupting. So sad, Jane thought grimly as she went back to rinsing dishes.

Daniel moved to the coffeepot and proved to be in a chatty mood. He stood there sipping his coffee and ignoring Dirk's fulminating glares, yapping away about this and that and sundry. Dirk suffered through it until Tinkle came trotting back into the kitchen, heading straight for his leg. He then muttered he was going outside, circled the island in an effort to confuse and lose the amorous Yorkie, then hurried back out onto the deck. The dog followed in hot pursuit.

"I can't believe she peed on me but seems to love him," Daniel said with disgust as he watched the pair leave.

"Believe it. She tinkles on all the best people. I use her as an initial judge of character. If she likes you, it's a sign for me to look out. If she tinkles on you, I can pretty much count on your being an okay guy."

"Really?" He brightened.

"Really." Jane turned back to the sink and the last few plates.

"I hope I was reading the signals right and you were happy to be rescued." Daniel moved closer so that he could talk softly and not be overheard.

"Oh, yes. I'm happy he's gone. He's a pain."

"Well, he does seem to come on strong—but I

can hardly blame the guy." He ran one finger lightly along her arm. "You're a very attractive woman."

Jane sighed impatiently and turned to eye him. "It's the perfume."

Daniel blinked. "What?"

"You're not really attracted to me, Daniel. You're hitting on me because of the truth serum perfume. It has too much pheromone in it," she explained. Then she muttered under her breath, "I really have to shower soon."

Daniel burst out laughing. He stifled his mirth when Jane turned an unamused look on him. Apparently realizing she was a tad testy, he cleared his throat and said, "It isn't the perfume, Jane. It's you."

"Yeah, right." She turned back to the sink with a snort. "Four men have hit on me in the last twenty-four hours. I haven't had four men hit on me in the last two years."

"You aren't normally a field agent, are you?" he asked with amusement.

"No. I work in development. I make weapons and stuff," she admitted.

"Like the perfume."

"Yes." She scowled at him. "But why do you say I'm not normally a field agent? Is it so obvious?"

"It wasn't until you said it was the perfume making men attracted to you. If you were a field agent, you'd be used to it and know it wasn't the perfume."

"It isn't—"

"I suppose you must work neck deep in gadgets in some stuffy little hole in the basement of a building."

She bristled. "It isn't in the basement. And if you're suggesting I never see men, there *are* some there."

"All of them neck deep in gadgets, as oblivious

of the women around them as you are of the men."

"I . . ." Jane stopped. Okay, so she had been a little oblivious. "So?"

"So. It isn't the perfume," he said gently. Then he got a resigned look." There's something between you and Abel, isn't there?"

Jane's eyes went to his.

Daniel nodded as if she'd answered. "I thought so. Ah, well, he's a lucky man."

Spying movement out of the corner of her eye, Jane turned to see Lydia standing in the doorway.

"Is there any more tea?" she asked.

"In the pot on the table." Jane watched the blonde, wondering how much she'd heard. Then the peal of the doorbell distracted her from that worry. Jane dried her hands on a towel with a sigh. The entire neighborhood seemed determined to visit today.

"Good morning, Jane." Officer Alkars avoided her eyes when she opened the door. He was obviously embarrassed about his runaway tongue last night.

"Good morning, Officer Alkars."

"Colin," he corrected, then glanced down at the papers in his hands. He held them out. "I typed up your statement from last night and brought it over for you to sign—so you wouldn't have to come down to the station."

"Oh. That was nice of you." Jane stepped out of the way for him to enter, closed the door, then followed him into the kitchen. Lydia was just walking back out the French doors.

"You haven't remembered anything else, have you?" Colin asked.

Jane shook her head apologetically. "I don't think there's anything else to remember. I wish there was, but . . ." She shrugged. "I take it you haven't caught the driver of the car?"

"No. I've managed to cross two more couples off the list, though, and added a couple thousand."

"Added a couple thousand?" Jane asked.

"The gate was open last night. Apparently it was stuck."

"Stuck?" Jane echoed, wondering if Luellen and Daniel had done that or if it was just luck.

"Yeah." Colin didn't look happy. "I should have realized when the ambulance didn't have to buzz to get in. It's happened before. Maybe half a dozen times. Still, it's pretty damned inconvenient that it happened last night. I have men going door to door asking people about it. I'm hoping to find out if it was stuck open before the accident, or after."

"Oh."

The sound of voices made the sheriff glance toward the open French doors. "Company?"

"Yes. The Braunsteins and the Ensecksis showed up for breakfast."

"They did, huh? I'd like to talk to them. May I?" He gestured toward the door and Jane nodded. There was little else she could do. She followed him out onto the deck.

A few moments were taken up with greetings; then Gran said, "A terrible thing about poor Mr. Parker. Have you any leads yet as to who hit him?"

"Not really. It seems the gate short-circuited last night and was stuck open for some time. It muddies the water some."

"It was probably just some kids out joyriding, then," Dirk commented.

"Maybe. Except they knew that this was the 'Goodinov house.' " He watched Dirk trying to push Tinkle away with one foot, and smiled. "You don't know of any reason why someone might want to harm your assistant, do you?"

Dirk stiffened. "I thought it was an accident. A hit-and-run. Are you suggesting it wasn't?"

"I'm not suggesting anything. I'm just getting all the facts," the policeman said blandly. "It was probably an accident. This road curves around; the driver might not have seen him until they were on top of him." He shrugged and turned to Daniel and Luellen. "Mr. and Mrs. Braunstein, can you tell me what happened when you left the party last night?"

Jane's gaze shot to the couple, but they looked completely relaxed. Then again, she supposed they had nothing to worry about. Even if Officer Alkars did sort it out, they would hardly get in trouble for doing their job. The death had been an accidental result of Parker's escaping custody.

"We went home to bed," Luellen lied. "Between the move and the party it was a busy day."

Colin nodded, apparently having expected that answer. He glanced at Jane. "I'll be poking around in your trees for the next few minutes."

Jane nodded.

"We should get going." Daniel took Luellen's arm to urge her up.

"I guess we should too." Lydia stood and moved toward the front door. Everyone followed, but the blonde paused in the kitchen, forcing everyone to stop. "Abel, do you and Jane have plans for the day? If not, I was thinking Dirk and I might show you arou—" A knock at the door interrupted her. Everyone glanced curiously toward the sound.

"Excuse me." Jane wove through the crowd to answer it. She found Melanie Johnson on her front step, a plate of brownies in hand.

"Good morning," the woman said with a bright smile.

Jane promptly returned it. "Good morning. Come in." She stepped out of the way and Melanie walked inside, pausing in the kitchen doorway, obviously surprised by the crowd there.

"Oh! I guess everyone beat me here." The author laughed, then turned back to Jane. "Here. This is for you: a little welcome to the neighborhood."

"Oh, thank you." Jane accepted the brownies with a smile. Then her good manners kicked in and she asked, "Would you like some coffee?"

"Oh, no, thanks. Actually, Brian and I were just heading down to the flea market. I only stopped in to see if you wanted to join us."

"The flea market?" Jane echoed with interest.

"Yes. They have them every weekend. I thought it would be fun to poke around and see if there are any bargains. But I guess you have company."

"Oh. They were just leaving; that's why we were all standing in the kitchen. But the flea market sounds . . ." Jane's enthusiastic grin died. It sounded like fun. But she wasn't here to have fun. She'd have to find an excuse. "I'd like to, but Gran . . ."

Gran what? There was no reason Maggie Spyrus couldn't wheel around a flea market. Abel stepped in to rescue her. "Gran mentioned earlier that she was rather tired after traveling and the party yesterday. She wants to spend a nice quiet day at home."

Good one, Jane thought. But he wasn't finished.

"It's okay, though, Jane. You go have fun with Melanie. I can look after Gran." His gaze went to Dirk and Lydia as he spoke, and Jane knew he really meant that he would watch the monitor. Which was really sweet of him, but it was her responsibility. She would feel too guilty to enjoy the market anyway.

"Why doesn't she just come, too?" Lydia said. "We could all go. The flea market was what I was about to suggest when Melanie knocked."

"That sounds delightful," Gran announced, rolling in from the deck. She'd obviously been listening in.

Jane frowned. If Lydia and Dirk were going to the market, someone really should go with them. But that still left the house to be watched. Unfortunately, Jane realized, she hadn't told Gran that Robert Ensecksi had arrived. Before she could think of a way to stall the plans in motion, Lydia was at the front door.

"Great. It'll be fun. Dirk and I will go get his car and come back. We can ride down in a parade. Come on, Dirk." Lydia urged her brother out. Jane stared after them, something about the blonde's expression bothering her.

"It seems silly to take so many vehicles. I know you need the van to transport Maggie," Melanie said to Jane, then turned to Luellen to say, "But why don't you and Daniel ride with us?"

Luellen smiled. "That would be great."

"Come on, then. We're only two houses over. See you in a few minutes, Jane."

The moment the door closed behind the last of their unexpected guests Jane said, "We have to think up an excuse for why I can't go."

"What? Why ever not?" Gran asked with amazement.

"Because someone has to stay and review the tapes from this morning and watch the house this afternoon."

"But Dirk and Lydia won't be there."

271

"But the father may be," Jane explained, then quickly related the bits of conversation she'd caught between Dirk and Parker last night and that between Lydia and Dirk afterward. She could tell from Abel's expression that he'd forgotten that conversation, though he had the excuse of the knockout lipstick to blame. She'd barely finished when the doorbell rang again.

"That was fast," she said with exasperation.

"Just tell them I'm tired and you're staying with me," Gran suggested. "Abel can go and—"

"Abel is staying," Abel interrupted. "Jane was up most of the night watching the monitors. I'll stay and watch them today. She deserves a break."

"You're such a good boy, Abel," Gran said.

Jane was surprised by the fondness in the old woman's voice, but she didn't know why. She herself was growing rather fond of him too.

Jane answered the door. It wasn't Melanie or Luellen. Her uncertain gaze slid over a woman dressed in a white blouse and pants. Not a Sonoran, obviously. "Yes?"

"You're much prettier than your picture, Jane." The woman smiled and held out her hand. "I'm your new nurse, Nancy. Y sent me."

Chapter Seventeen

"Lock the door."

Jane felt herself stiffen at the order from the woman who strode past into the house. It seemed Nurse Nancy thought she was in charge of the show now. The problem was, she might be. Jane locked the door and followed her into the kitchen.

"Gran, Abel, this is . . ."

Jane stopped her introductions when Nurse Nancy held up a hand, for silence. She whipped out what looked like a lighter, but Jane knew it was an RF signal detector to check for bugs. The woman turned in a slow circle. After making a full revolution, she slid the device back in her pocket, reached into her purse, and took out several small acoustic noise generators. She set one on the kitchen counter, one on the hutch, and one on the table. Anyone who might be using listening devices on them would now find it more difficult. She nodded at Jane and said, "Right. It's clean. Talk."

"Okay." She gestured to Gran and tried to perform introductions again. "This is my grandmother, Ma—"

"Maggie Spyrus," Nancy finished dryly. "And this is Abel Andretti. I've read the file, Jane. There's no need for introductions. I want to know what's going on here. How hot is the situation?"

Jane struggled briefly with irritation at the woman's abruptness, then did her best to explain the past few days in a clear and concise manner.

Nurse Nancy didn't appear impressed. She listened with a bland expression, considered everything, then said, "I want you and Abel to go to the market. Maggie will stay here as my cover while I watch the house on the monitors and see what that old guy is up to."

Jane's gaze slid to her grandmother, worry gnawing at the pit of her stomach. She didn't trust this Nancy not to take off into the other end of the house and forget all about the old woman who was her excuse for being there.

"I'll take care of her," the nurse said as if reading Jane's thoughts.

"She doesn't need taking care of," Jane said a little stiffly. "She's mostly independent. She just needs help with . . . some things."

"I wasn't insinuating she's helpless," Nurse Nancy said coolly. "I would never make the mistake of thinking that. Even in a wheelchair she can probably run circles around me. Maggie Spyrus trained me."

"Yes, I did," Gran said in a neutral tone. Then she smiled at Jane. "I'll be fine. You two go ahead."

Jane relaxed somewhat, but not completely. She

was a bit abrupt when she asked, "What is B.L.I.S.S. planning?"

"That's on a need-to-know basis, and you don't need to know."

Jane winced, finding a sudden sympathy for Luellen and Daniel that had been lacking that morning.

"Can you fetch my cell phone, Janie, dear?" Gran asked sweetly. "I think I left it in my room, and it has Y's private number. She'll tell us—"

"All right," Nancy relented with a scowl. "My orders are to verify that Robert Ensecksi is indeed on the premises, to locate the satellite they intend to use, to find out how much security they have and how far along their plans are. B.L.I.S.S. can then decide whether to infiltrate or just go for a full assault," she announced. Then she added, "I'm the head operative, and you've been demoted. You're just the cover now. So go watch the younger Ensecksis."

Jane opened her mouth to snap a reply, but Abel grabbed her arm and urged her toward the garage. "Let's go."

"Just cover?" Jane snarled as they got into the van. "We were here first!"

"I know." Abel held out his hand. "Keys, please."

Jane handed them over, noticing only then that somehow she'd ended up in the passenger seat. Abel was driving. She didn't care. She was annoyed enough that it was probably better she didn't drive anyway. "I don't like her. She's a supercilious witch."

"I don't like her either. But it isn't just because she's demoted us." Abel started the van. "When she stated her objectives, she didn't mention my sister once. I don't trust her to care about Edie's well-being. You know?"

"Yes." Jane bit her lip. As long as she'd headed up this case, she'd been able to control the outcome somewhat. At least, she'd known that Edie's welfare would be taken into account. Nancy didn't seem to have such a concern. What was one life next to stopping world domination?

"It's okay. We're still in the game, whether they think so or not." Abel sounded grim as he pulled out of the garage. Two cars were already waiting on the road at the bottom of the driveway. Lydia and Dirk were in a small red sports car. A black Jeep was the second vehicle, holding the Johnsons and Daniel and Luellen.

Jane was silent as Abel pulled out to follow the Jeep; then she remarked, "Something she said bothered me."

"What?"

"About finding out how much security the Ensecksis have. That hadn't occurred to me. I mean, no one has shown up on the recordings and—"

"We only installed the cameras and microphones yesterday, Jane. More may show up today," he pointed out.

"Yes, but . . ." She paused again to order her thoughts. "Last night I watched the monitor for a while. Nothing was happening. The Ensecksi house was dark and silent except for Dirk's snoring."

"He snores?" Abel seemed pleased to learn the man had a flaw.

"Yes." Jane smiled, and continued. "Then, because I was bored, I decided to see what the microphone had picked up when they entered the house. You know, while we were on the hill, then during the accident and stuff."

He glanced at her curiously. "Was there anything?"

Jane nodded. "Lydia and Dirk were talking. Lydia was saying she was going to go talk to their father. Dirk said he would go with her, but she said he'd better not; that their father wouldn't appreciate the state he was in. She suggested he might want to lie on the couch and rest, that she'd come back and tell him what was said afterward. Dirk agreed. There was a click, I heard her walking and a rustling that was probably Dirk lying down, then a hissing sound followed by silence. Then Dirk started snoring."

"Was it a really loud annoying snore?" Abel asked with glee.

Jane found herself laughing, some of the unhappiness disappearing. She knew that had been his intention. He was trying to ease her anger at Nurse Nancy's high-handed behavior. It was working. "Yes, it was a loud snore. But the thing is, I checked the camera images for that period of time, and the living room lights go out."

"So Lydia probably turned out the lights so her brother could sleep," Abel suggested, his expression serious again.

"That's what I figured, too, but no other lights went on in the rest of the house after that. I checked the images from the cameras on the hill, and those behind, and the house stayed completely dark."

"Hmm." Abel thought. "Maybe the father was already asleep and Lydia just went to bed."

"Maybe. But if so, wouldn't she have turned on a bedroom light? *No* lights came on," she repeated. "Not until an hour later."

"An hour later?" Abel's eyebrows shot up. He glanced over from the road to see her nod.

"The house was dark and the only sound was Dirk's snoring for more than an hour; then that hiss sounded again. I could hear Lydia's high heels on

277

a hard floor, then rustling that faded away to silence as she went to her bedroom. The cameras show her lights coming on for a few minutes, long enough for her to get ready for bed. The lights went out and the house was silent for the rest of the night, except for the snoring. Well, until I fell asleep anyway."

"Hmm."

They were both silent for several minutes, considering. Then Jane said, "That hissing reminded me of something."

"What?" Abel asked.

"I'm not sure." She bit her lip, thinking. "Maybe a pneumatic door."

"A pneumatic door? You mean one of those sliding doors that swish open and closed?"

"That's it! It was a swish, not a hiss. It sounded just like one of those pneumatic doors at the grocery store." She nodded thoughtfully. "That could be it. The darkness and silence while she was supposed to be talking to her father didn't seem right, but what if they have a basement?"

"A basement? I don't know." He looked doubtful. "The Goodinov house doesn't have one. It's planted on rock, built around the existing shape of the land. This is mountain architecture. That's why the garage and driveway are on level ground and the rest of the house is planted on it and the hill. I'd expect it's the same with the Ensecksi house."

"Well, maybe they have a hollow that their house is built on. That would explain Dirk's comment about his father being 'in the mountain.' They could have a basement with walls made of the mountain itself."

Abel shook his head. "I don't know, Jane. I mean, if he was in the basement, I'd think he'd just say he was in the basement."

"Yes. Maybe. But if there is a basement surrounded by mountain rock, that could explain where the rest of the Ensecksi security people must be . . . and Edie. The rock would insulate it on all sides. All they'd have to do was insulate the ceiling to prevent transmitters from transmitting or to keep listening devices from hearing anything."

"You think Edie could be down there?"

"I think it's a possibility. I think it would also explain why Lydia didn't hear the police and ambulance sirens last night and come out to investigate. She told Colin that she'd been sleeping, but we know she was talking to her father at the time. Why didn't they hear the sirens and come investigate?"

He accepted that in silence. "Who are the other people you think might be down there? I mean, you sound pretty sure there are other people. Who?"

"Well, Dirk and Lydia don't seem like the brightest bulbs in the fixture. They're rather average in intelligence. They might make good businesspeople, but they don't seem the sort to be able to develop and run the kind of technology that could convince a whole town of women to wear yellow, while their husbands don Hawaiian shirts. There must be some technicians, a scientist or two, assistants, security even." Jane shrugged.

"It would have to be a *big* basement," Abel said. "And surely these people would come out once in a while. I mean, maybe they can force Edie to stay down there, but if these people are working for them . . ." A moment later he asked, "And why would they even be *in* the basement? Surely they'd be wherever the satellite is."

"Yes. Of course, you're right," Jane said, dispirited. The car ahead was slowing. They'd arrived at the flea market.

279

She and Abel fell silent as he parked, and then he offered her a grim smile. "More fun with the Ensecksis. We should have stopped and picked up some hockey pads to wear under our clothes."

Jane laughed. "Yes, it would be nice to have a barrier between Dirk's groping and my skin. But I doubt they have much hockey gear here in Sonora."

Dirk and Lydia were getting out of their car nearby. Abel followed her gaze to the red vehicle and said, "I wonder how he got that here. I mean, if he and Josh drove Edie down in that hearse."

"Hmm. Maybe he usually leaves it here and flies down."

"Could be," Abel agreed.

They got out. Jane and Abel met at the back of the van and started toward the others as the Johnsons and Luellen and Daniel exited the Jeep and moved to join them.

"All set to experience Sonora's shopping joys?" Brian asked lightly as the group came together.

"All set," Jane agreed. She smiled.

"You're not going to leave your poor grandmother in the van while we walk around, are you?" Lydia asked with a laugh, not moving when the rest of the group started toward the booths and tables set up in the large Mother Lode Fairground.

"Oh." Jane shook her head. "She isn't in the van. She stayed home."

"What? But she wanted to come. She *said* she was coming." Lydia didn't look happy at the news.

Jane would have understood Lydia's displeasure if it was Abel who had stayed behind, but she was a tad surprised at the woman's reaction to Maggie Spyrus's absence. "Her nurse finally arrived and Gran was really too tired to be bothered," she said.

"She only agreed to go so that Abel and I could, but once her nurse showed up she said she'd rather stay home."

The glance Lydia and Dirk exchanged was definitely alarmed, but then Dirk pasted one of his arsenal of sexy grins on his face and took Jane's arm. He turned her toward the market. "Well, I guess that means I don't have to share you with her."

"No. Now I'm free to enjoy your attentions," Jane agreed. She fought off a shudder.

"And ours," Luellen announced, breaking in between them.

"It'll be a day of play." Daniel stepped over to slap Abel on the back, cutting off Lydia's effort to glue herself to his side. "How about those Sharks, huh? What a team!"

Jane almost laughed at the irritation on Lydia's face.

The flea market was fun, though it would have been more fun without Dirk and Lydia. Lydia spent the whole time putting down everything she saw, while Dirk followed Jane around, crowding her horribly. She couldn't seem to move without bumping into him, and she couldn't tell him to give her space either. She had to put up with it and smile happily. Being an agent rather sucked in some respects.

The other two couples were great, however. They also ran interference for her—which made her wonder if, despite her best efforts, some of her impatience and irritation were showing through. She supposed she'd never make a good poker player, but Dirk's attentions could be overwhelming. The man had no concept of personal space. That, combined with his good looks, had rather thrown her last night. She suspected it was how he got all his women, pretty much steamrolling them into bed while they were confused by what they were feeling.

Abel wasn't doing much better. He had his hands full with Lydia. She was forever touching and leaning into him. He seemed to handle it easier than Jane, but was looking a bit frayed when lunchtime finally rolled around and they all headed to the historic section of downtown Sonora. They found parking in an open garage, then walked out in a group.

Jane paused for a minute and wished she'd brought a camera. A little red church at the end of the street caught her eye, and it was so pretty with its single spire and white trim that she found herself smiling.

"It's gorgeous, isn't it?" Luellen commented. "And look at that building."

Jane followed her gesture and found herself looking at what might have been the local tavern/brothel a hundred years before. It looked as if it had come right out of a John Wayne western.

Luellen sighed. "I have to come back and just play tourist after this assignment's done."

Jane glanced wildly about as that wistful comment slipped from the agent's lips, but the others had already started down the street and were out of hearing. Even Dirk had left them behind. It seemed food was enough to distract him from Jane's charms. *Yay, food!* she thought with amusement.

As if feeling her absence, Abel turned back and called, "Come on, you two. We can sightsee later. This man needs food."

They had lunch in a little restaurant called El Jardin. The three couples sat out in the open air on a tiny shady patio between the restaurant and the adjacent building, enjoying the peaceful burbling of a little fountain and people-watching through an iron gate facing the street. Jane wasn't used to Mexican food and looked over the menu with uncertainty. She ended up ordering the fiesta tostada at Melanie's suggestion, politely declining the fish tacos recommended by the woman's husband. It was almost too pretty to eat when it arrived, but it was also too yummy not to.

The food was delicious and most of the company wonderful, though Dirk managed to make a pain of himself. Jane had been relieved at the idea of lunch, thinking he could hardly be as bothersome there because she'd have a chair to herself and wouldn't have him pressing up against her, but she'd been wrong. While he wasn't able to share her seat, Dirk had moved his own directly next to hers and hung over her throughout the entire meal. He managed to taint what would have otherwise been a perfectly lovely lunch.

It was as they were leaving El Jardin that Melanie insisted Jane and Luellen visit a store called the Banyan Tree. Jane wasn't too enthusiastic at first. She expected rows of yellow dresses, and there were those. In every imaginable shade. From the almost-cream of the dress Melanie wore to an almost-black gold. But there were dresses of other colors as well, and Jane, who had glanced in the windows of several dress shops on the way to and from El Jardin, decided the Banyan Tree was the last bastion against yellow fashion fever. It was also a haven of good taste. Jane even found several things she liked in the store.

She would have walked out a completely happy

camper if Luellen hadn't stopped at a rack and said, "Isn't this gorgeous?"

Much to her dismay, the dress the FBI agent was holding was dyed a hideous yellow. Jane very much feared that Luellen was beginning to be affected by the Sonoran mind-control satellite. Even more alarming to Jane, all these yellow dresses that surrounded them everywhere they went no longer seemed so awful. They were beginning to look bright and cheerful. Which couldn't be a good sign.

It was still early afternoon when the party broke up, but Jane was exhausted. She hadn't got much sleep last night and looked forward to lying down for a nap. Her fatigue disappeared under a jolt of adrenaline, however, when they pulled into the Goodinov driveway to find it filled with emergency vehicles. An ambulance was just leaving, but that still left the county coroner and three police cars.

"Gran!" Jane was out of the van before Abel had brought it to a complete halt. She flew up the stairs to the house at a dead run, then nearly tumbled back down them when she crashed into Officer Alkars at the top. Fortunately, Colin caught her arms and saved her.

"Gran!" Jane gasped.

"She's all right," Colin said firmly, still holding her. "She's fine."

"But . . ." Jane waved back at the driveway with its collection of vehicles.

"Someone broke in," he explained as Abel caught up to her.

"Broke in!" she cried. "I thought you had no crime here."

"Well, we have some crime," he snapped. "Not a lot. And certainly not two deaths in two days. At least not until you people moved here."

"What kind of crack is that?" Abel growled.

"Who's dead?" Jane asked, not caring about Colin's accusation. She'd already known he was suspicious. "Is it the nurse?"

"No. She's fine. A little shook-up, but fine. The fellow who broke in is dead."

Jane sagged with relief.

"Someone broke in and was killed?"

Jane glanced over her shoulder to see Dirk and Lydia Ensecksi on the stairs behind them. Apparently, they were investigating the police vehicles. The Johnsons had also stopped, and the foursome who were riding in the Jeep had just started up the stairs.

"How was he killed?" Lydia asked. She didn't sound pleased. Jane had a sudden flash of the blonde's face when she'd heard Gran had stayed home, and instinctively knew the supposed thief was an Ensecksi henchman.

"Ms. Ellison struggled with him on the deck. He fell off and broke his neck," answered Colin.

"Ms. Ellison?" Dirk asked.

Jane was glad he'd beat her to it when Colin explained: "Nancy Ellison. Maggie—Ms. Goodinov's nurse."

Nancy hadn't mentioned a last name, real or otherwise. She hadn't needed an introduction, Jane thought sourly. Ha! Wouldn't they have looked stupid asking who she was!

"Who was the man? Was he from around here?" Lydia asked far too casually.

"He has no ID on him. We're going to run his fingerprints."

"I'd better go see Gran." Jane left Abel to deal with their neighbors and made her way inside.

She found Gran and Nancy in the great room. The nurse/spy was seated on the couch weeping

285

into a Kleenex while Gran patted her back soothingly. Jane just stood there, staring in amazed horror for several minutes before Maggie Spyrus spotted her.

"Did Officer Alkars leave?"

"Yes," Abel said from behind Jane. "He got rid of everyone else, then left himself."

Nancy's sobs died abruptly and she sat back with a sigh. "Thank goodness. I thought he'd never leave. Are the Ensecksis back then?"

"Y-yes," Jane stammered, completely thrown by the woman's sudden change.

Nancy nodded and got to her feet. "I'd best go watch the monitors then. Those two might say something of value."

Jane watched her go with wide eyes, then asked, "What happened?"

Her grandmother explained: Nancy had seen a man come around the side of the Ensecksi house on the monitor. The cameras had shown him walk through the trees and make his way up the hill. He'd passed out of sight of the monitors then, and she'd stood to peer out the window to see him approaching the door of the very bedroom where she stood. The door wasn't locked. He'd opened it, started in, and got the surprise of his life when he found himself confronted. Nancy had a gun pointed right at him, so he'd tried to flee. Wanting to get information, Nancy had given chase. The two had struggled, and the man had broken his neck when she used a martial arts kick that sent him crashing into the railing that surrounded the deck. It had given way under the strain, sending him plummeting to the ground some twenty feet below. He would have survived the fall without difficulty, but he'd landed head-first on one of the large boulders littering the slope. His neck had snapped, killing him instantly. Nancy had climbed down to check on him, then had called the police.

And apparently sobbed her little heart out over the ordeal to convince Colin she was traumatized and horrified by the day's events, Jane realized. "Now I know why Lydia and Dirk were so upset that you didn't come with us. They must be suspicious," she commented wearily.

"Hmm." Gran scowled. "I'd like to know what tipped them off. I thought we'd covered every angle."

Jane was silent for a minute, then told her about Lydia's entering the kitchen that morning while Daniel and she were talking. She tried to edit what it was exactly they'd been talking about, but really couldn't do so. Knowing she was blushing, Jane avoided looking at Abel and recounted the end of the brief conversation.

"That's probably it, then," Gran agreed. "It was foolish of Daniel to talk like that with the Ensecksis here. You should have stopped him, Janie."

"Yes," she agreed miserably.

"Now. Is there?"

Jane glanced up blankly. "Is there what?"

"Something between you and Abel?"

"Yes," Jane admitted, deciding there was little sense in lying. She'd told Abel what she thought of him while under the influence of the truth serum anyway. That didn't stop her face from flaming, though. Clearing her throat, she stood up. "I'm rather tired. I think I'll go lie down until dinner."

Abel wasn't about to stick around for Gran's third degree, either. He stood. "I'll spot Nancy for a while. She could probably use a break."

Jane went to the room she'd used the day before.

She hadn't thought to collect clothes from the master bedroom, so she wore only her panties. She slept deep and hard and it was dark out when she awoke. Jane hadn't expected to sleep so long; she'd expected someone to wake her for supper, so was surprised at the lateness of the hour. She was even more surprised to find she wasn't alone. Mr. Tibbs had curled up on her chest, and was snoozing happily. But Abel was also there, wide awake and seated on the edge of her bed. A soft smile was on his face.

Jane didn't know what to think when his first words were, "Do you trust me?"

Chapter Eighteen

Did she trust him? Jane stared at Abel Andretti and
repeated his question to herself. The answer was
simple. This was Edie's brother, the man who'd hesitated to make love to her because he felt she de-
served more than a fling. This was the man who'd
shown her pleasure like she'd never experienced.
Did she trust him?

"This morning wouldn't have happened if I didn't
trust you," Jane said solemnly.

That seemed to please him. "And do you still
want me to make love to you?"

Jane gave a short laugh. "I think the more perti-
nent question is, after this morning's debacle do
you still want to make love to me?"

Abel shook his head. "That's not what I asked.
Do you still want me to make love to you?"

"Yes, but . . ." She put her hand against his chest

and stopped him when he bent to kiss her. "Not here. Gran might hear." She flushed with embarrassment at the very idea, but Abel only smiled and finished giving her the kiss he'd intended. It wasn't passionate or enflaming, just a warm and sweet brush of lips. He straightened as soon as it ended.

"These are for you." He lifted a bag off the floor and set it on the other side of her on the bed. "Don't use or wear any of your secret weapons. Just wear these. I'll meet you in the van in half an hour."

The moment he was out of the room, Jane sat up. Mr. Tibbs squawked at being so summarily dumped from her lap then took off, presumably for a bed that didn't move as much as she. Jane hardly noticed. She was peering into the bag Abel had left behind. It held several cosmetics, all brand-new, still packaged and lying on red cloth. Jane pushed the makeup out of the way to get to the cloth and tugged it out of the bag. It was a dress, red and slinky.

"Oh, my," Jane murmured, then peered into the bag again. There were underthings and shoes, too—all impressively sexy. Clothes? Makeup? Meet him at the van? He was taking her somewhere. And in half an hour!

Shoving the sheet and blankets aside, Jane leaped out of bed in only her underwear and raced into the bathroom to turn on the shower. Just as quickly, she raced back to snatch her dress and bag.

"Five minutes to shower, five to dress. That leaves ten on hair and ten on makeup," she muttered, tugging her panties off and stepping into the shower. She could do it. She hoped.

She managed it with a minute to spare, flying down the stairs to the garage to find Abel leaning against the van. He looked dashing in a dark suit and tie. A slow sexy smile curved his lips when he saw her, and he straightened to open the passenger door of a low, sporty car parked next to the van. "Your chariot awaits, pretty lady."

"Where did this come from?" Jane asked as she slid into the passenger seat.

"I borrowed it from Dan. I didn't want to take the van and leave Gran stranded," he explained, then closed her door.

Jane watched him walk around the car, a smile tugging at her lips. He hadn't wanted to leave Gran stranded. He was so thoughtful, and there had been affection in his tone when he'd mentioned her grandmother. Jane was glad. Even if her grandmother couldn't drive the van alone.

"So," she said as he slid into the driver's seat. "Where are we going?"

"You'll see," was all he'd say. He started the car.

They were both silent as he backed out of the driveway and started off down the road. But once they'd passed the community gates, Abel took one hand off the steering wheel and reached out to take hers. "So, did you sleep well?"

"Yes, thank you. And long. I can't believe you guys let me sleep until eight o'clock."

"There was method to my madness," he said lightly.

"Was there?" she asked with amusement. "And what was this method?"

He seemed to debate for a minute, then said, "Well, after you went to bed I watched the monitor for Nancy."

"Did anything happen?"

Noticing the way she tensed, Abel squeezed her hand. "No. And we're not going to talk about the

Ensecksis tonight. I want time away from them. Nurse Nancy's on the job, and it's just you and me this evening. Agreed?"

Jane nodded. "Agreed. But I must say it was kind of you to spot her this afternoon."

"Trust me, it wasn't kindness. It was a purely selfish act."

"Oh?"

"She slept while I monitored. That's why you got to sleep so long. It means no one has to spot her tonight and I can spend all my time with you."

"Oh." Jane felt her heart go all mushy. That was so sweet.

He took his hand away to turn the corner, then gave it back. Jane smiled and relaxed as he continued, "So, I spotted for Nancy, and while I was sitting there staring at the silent, unchanging screen, I came up with a plan of how I wanted to spend my time with you. I called the Braunstein house and asked Dan if I could borrow his car; then I asked Luellen if she could pick up a few things for me at the drugstore."

"The makeup!" Jane started to laugh. "And here I thought you were a particularly clever man, picking all the right products and colors for me."

Luellen had got everything she could possibly need: shampoo, cream rinse, hair spray, lipstick, compact, eye shadow and liner, perfume. Abel had really wanted to be sure she had nothing on tonight that might knock him out or otherwise injure him, she realized. Chuckling softly, she saw a WELCOME TO JAMESTOWN sign, and sat up in surprise. "We've left Sonora!"

"Yes. But we haven't gone far," he said soothingly. "You saw how short the ride was. Besides, I can hardly gaze soulfully into your eyes in Sonora where we're supposed to be brother and sister, can I?"

"Oh." Jane relaxed and pondered a good hour at least of soulful gazing. Then she gave a start as she realized that this was a date! Her first date with Abel. She considered what they'd been doing that morning and decided that they'd got the order of things a bit mixed up, but these were unusual circumstances.

"Here we are," Abel announced. He slowed the car.

She wasn't sure where "here" was, other than that it was in Jamestown. He hadn't pulled into the parking lot of a restaurant, but was backing into an open parking spot on the street. He finished the job, shut the engine off, got out, and came around to open Jane's door with a flourish.

"Madame?" He offered his hand and a snooty look she could easily imagine on the face of a French maître d'.

It was a lovely night, making for a pleasant if short walk. Jamestown had wooden sidewalks, and Jane was a bit distracted making sure she didn't break her neck in the high heels Abel had chosen; so when he suddenly turned her toward a building, she stopped to look around. He'd brought her to someplace called the Willow Steakhouse. It was a charming Victorian-style building with wooden shutters on the windows and a white, gingerbread fence. A pair of double wooden doors with beveled glass panels made up the entrance at the corner of the house where the front and side walls met. Charming!

The wooden sidewalk became hardwood floors in the restaurant. Jane glanced around curiously as she followed the hostess. The lighting was low, with candlelight softly filling the air from glass globes on each table. The dining area was quite small, with private booths and tables to seat no more than thirty people. Jane settled in and smiled at Abel.

"Thank you," she said, after the hostess had handed them their menus and slipped away.

Abel looked uncertain. "For what?"

"For thinking of this."

"Oh." He smiled and reached for her hand across the table, drew it to his lips to kiss. "My pleasure."

Jane flushed as electricity shot up her arm, then turned gratefully to her menu to distract herself. They were served a cheese fondue, then salad and soup, then their entrées. Jane ordered chicken Jerusalem, which turned out to be a delicious dish cooked in white wine sauce and artichokes. Abel ordered roasted lamb and seemed equally pleased with his choice. Jane would have liked to linger before returning home and ending their time together, and they did for a little while, but far too soon Abel paid the check and escorted her back to the car.

Jane sighed wistfully as they drove away. It had been a pleasant diversion in this horrible time. And they'd even managed some of that soulful gazing Abel had promised. Conversation had been amusing and interesting, and it hadn't included the Ensecksis even once. Abel had told her amusing tales of trying to adjust to life in England, and she'd spoken of her work at B.L.I.S.S., making him laugh uproariously with her tale of nearly taking off Dick's head with her missile launcher.

Jane was replaying their evening as he drove, so she wasn't paying attention to where they were headed until the car slowed again.

"Where are we?" she asked as Abel stopped the vehicle.

He turned the engine off and turned to face her. "We're at the Jamestown National Hotel Bed-and-Breakfast. I want to make love to you, Jane. I knew you wouldn't want to with Gran in the next room, and we couldn't go to the master bedroom with Nancy in there, so I made reservations here. But if you don't want to—"

Jane covered his lips with her fingertips. "I want to," she said simply, then turned and got out of the car, not waiting for him.

The National Hotel was a two-story Victorian building lifted directly out of a Wild West movie. Square, white, and with a balcony along the upper floor that acted as an awning over the sidewalk and entrance below, it was beautiful with its lights shining a welcome into the night.

Jane, however, wasn't up to appreciating its Old World charm. Her heart was leaping in her chest with a combination of excitement, nervousness, and joy. The evening wasn't over as she'd feared. It would continue. They would make love. And she was both excited and frightened. Abel had given her great pleasure that morning and would have given her more, she was sure, had the little incident with the shrink-wrap not occurred. What if something else messed this time up? What if *she* messed it up?

All these thoughts and many more assailed her as they claimed the key to the room he'd reserved and they made their way upstairs.

Jeez, Jane thought as he unlocked their door. It was so much easier when it just *happened*. The opportunity to worry and fret over sex was almost painful. She felt like a virgin contemplating this for the first time. Then the door was open and Abel was ushering her inside, and her attention was briefly distracted by the room itself. *I've stepped through a doorway in time,* Jane thought with awe. A high overstuffed brass bed, antique pictures and quilts and lamps filled the room giving it a warm and welcoming air.

Champagne and covered dishes waited on a small table at the foot of the bed.

"I thought we'd have dessert here," Abel said, turning from closing the door.

"Oh." She smiled at him in rapture. Aside from being sweet and romantic, his arrangement also allowed them to be more spontaneous. They could relax and drink champagne and eat the dessert under those silver domes, then make love when the mood struck. And now that the pressure was off, Jane was in the mood.

Walking back to where he stood by the door, Jane slid her arms around his neck and pressed her body against his. She drew his head down for a kiss. There was a thud as Abel dropped the bag he'd brought from the car. His arms encircled her waist to pull her tighter against him, and he kissed her back with a passion that was explosive.

"Dessert," he gasped, pulling back after a moment. "Don't you want—?"

"I want *you*." Jane nipped hungrily at his chin.

Groaning, Abel bent to recapture her lips. His hands ran down her body and then back up, then slipped around to the snaps that closed her dress. She'd thought he picked this dress because it was short, tight, and sexy, but now she saw another benefit. The snaps gave way easily with one pull, and Abel reached for the front clasp of her bra. Within seconds there was nothing between them.

Gasping into his mouth, Jane clutched at his shoulders and held on tight as his questing hands played over her naked flesh. Her legs were showing a terrible tendency toward weakness. Seeming to realize the problem, Abel turned and pressed her up against a wall, one hand cupping her behind and pressing her tighter against him. Feeling the large hardness that was proof he'd recovered from that morning's debacle, Jane was torn between touching him and getting him naked. Deciding she wanted to feel all of him, she pushed his hands away and broke the kiss to set to work on his suit jacket.

Abel was at first startled by what seemed an attempt to end the embrace, but when Jane started to push his jacket off his shoulders, he understood and set to work helping her. The coat hit the floor in a whoosh and was quickly followed by his shirt and tie; then Jane pressed her lips to the hot flesh of his chest. Running her hands over him, she sighed with pleasure. "I love your chest."

Abel chuckled. "I love yours, too."

Jane closed her eyes as he caressed her, then let one hand drift down over his stomach to run her fingertips along the waistband of his pants. She felt his stomach muscles contract, and smiled. Opening her eyes, she began to undo his slacks. Abel's hands stilled, his eyes burning. She managed to get them undone and slipped her hand inside before he claimed her lips again. When she caught him with her fingers, he groaned and slid his tongue into her mouth.

His hand dropped down and she felt his fingers brush her thigh, then she moaned as they slid between her legs. He pressed against her through the silky cloth of the panties he'd chosen for her to wear.

Jane shifted her feet farther apart, offering herself to him, but was disappointed when his hands slipped away. He broke the kiss and his mouth drifted downward, trailing over her chin, along her throat, and down to one breast. He paused there briefly, then knelt before her. Leaning forward, he pushed the half-undone dress to the side and pressed a kiss to her stomach, then ran his tongue along the line of her panties. His fingers slid up to draw them downward.

Jane shivered as the silk panties drifted to the floor; then she stepped out of them, startled to realize that she still wore her high-heeled shoes and the thigh-high tights claiming not to need a garter belt. Her gaze went to Abel as he stood.

"We should move to the bed," he murmured, giving her another kiss.

Jane kissed back, her hand slipping between them again to find him still hard and hot. She freed him from his open trousers and closed her hand around him firmly. Abel broke away with a hiss, one hand going to the wall by her head to brace himself.

"Jane," he muttered through clenched teeth as she fondled him. "I've been imagining this all afternoon while you were sleeping. I don't think—"

His words died in another gasp as she slid her hand along the length of him; then seeming to realize she had no intention of stopping, and unwilling to physically stop her himself, he turned his attention to touching, kissing, and caressing her. He shifted away and dropped his head to take one erect nipple in his mouth, then slid his hand between her legs again, finding her bare flesh and slipping into the warm heat.

Groaning against her breast, he straightened. "Jane, you feel so good. I want—"

"So do I," she murmured, moving against his hand. "Now."

"Thank God," he breathed. His hand fell away as he bent to scoop up the bag he'd dropped, then he caught her up in his arms and straightened. Jane's startled yelp died in her throat as he pressed a kiss to her cheek and carried her to the bed.

Jane slid her hands into his hair, enjoying Abel's kiss, then felt the bed brush against her bottom. Abel started to pull away, but she followed, shifting to her knees on the bed rather than break contact. She couldn't have if she'd wanted to; she needed him like oxygen at that point. She wanted his hands on her body, his tongue in her mouth, his—

His erection brushed her leg, and she groaned into his mouth. *That* was what she wanted. She wanted what they'd missed that morning. The pleasure he'd shown her then had been amazing, but at the end she'd burned to feel him inside her. She wanted him there now.

"Abel, please." Her moaned plea ended on a gasp as he moved his hand back between her legs. She rubbed against it taking the pleasure he offered, and gasped. Then a rustling distracted her. Turning her head, she glanced down at the bag he'd set on the bed beside her. Abel was now fishing through it one-handed even as he caressed her with his other. As she looked, he gave a grunt of triumph and pulled out a package of condoms. She turned to peer at him blankly, and he smiled and shrugged.

"Luellen?" she asked with horror.

"No," he assured her quickly. "I picked them up myself."

"Oh, thank God," she breathed. Closing her eyes, she dropped back on the bed. How mortifying it would be to know Luellen had bought condoms for—

Abel cleared his throat and Jane's eyes popped open. He'd removed his pants and was now shifting uncomfortably at the edge of the bed, obviously unsure whether to proceed if the brief fear had spoiled the mood. Her gaze dropped to his impressive erection and she sat up. She shifted to the edge of the bed and took the condom he still held. Tearing it open, she pulled out the bit of latex and blinked. It was neon pink. When her eyes shot up to him, Abel was grinning.

"I noticed you liked the color," he said.

Jane started to laugh and fell back on the bed.

Taking the condom from her, Abel put it on, then knelt on one knee between her thighs. He ran his hands lightly up her legs. Jane shivered, her laughter dying at once. She didn't know why she'd found it so funny to begin with. Perhaps it had been a release for her sexual tension. That tension was back in full force.

She scooted backward on the bed, making more room for him, then caught at his arms and urged him up over her. Abel complied, settling himself between her legs, pressing against her but not into her.

Jane stared into his face, thinking how handsome he was, how kind and funny. And another sort of warmth squeezed in next to her passion. She smiled and pulled him down for a kiss. He thrust into her at the same moment his tongue slid into her mouth, and Jane gasped and arched as he filled her. Her legs wrapped around his hips, and her arms went around his shoulders. He drove into her. She was drowning in a hot liquid pleasure and wanted more. Abel gave that to her until they both cried out with release and collapsed on the bed.

Jane didn't remember falling asleep, but they did. When she woke, Abel pulled a quilt up over them and ran a hand gently up and down her back.

"Mmm," Jane said. She stretched against him, then tilted her head up to offer him a smile. He was wide awake and smiling, and she wondered how long she'd slept. And how long he'd been awake.

"Ready for dessert?" he asked.

Jane chuckled and rolled to lie on her back beside him. "You mean there's more?"

Her eyes closed, but she felt Abel shift beside her; then the quilt was sliding down. She could feel her nipples growing erect as the cloth slipped over them; then cool air brushed them briefly before one was sucked into moist heat. Jane opened her eyes and peered down at Abel's head as he suckled her. Her body stretched and arched of its own accord in response to the caress as heat pooled in her stomach. Then Abel straightened and slid off the bed to walk naked to the tray with the domed dessert dishes.

Jane sighed, but tried to ignore her body's clamoring. He'd awoken an appetite in her, but it wasn't for sweets.

"Oh, look. I asked for a variety and they really came through. Cheesecake, some other cake, and some other cake and some kind of . . . er . . . yellow kind of cake."

Jane chuckled and leaned up on her elbows to peer at the tray. "What's in the pitcher?"

"Chocolate sauce, I think."

"Probably for the cheesecake," Jane explained when he looked confused.

"Maybe." Abel grabbed a slice of cheesecake and the pitcher and moved back to the bed.

"Want some?" He poured some sauce over the slice, used his fork to cut off and scoop up some of the dessert and sauce, then offered it to her.

Jane grimaced as the chocolate dripped off, landing on her breast, but opened her mouth and accepted the offering. "Mmm." She closed her eyes to savor the flavor—but they popped open again when a moment later he licked the spilled sauce away, paying special attention to her nipple.

Excitement quivered through Jane, and she bit her lip as he straightened. He appeared completely unmoved. Cutting off another bite-sized piece of cake, he offered it to her. Another pebble of chocolate syrup dripped onto her chest before she could take the morsel into her mouth, and Abel bent to her breast again to clean up.

Jane was finding it difficult not to arch into his attentions as he laved her breast, and was aware that her breathing was becoming quicker and shallower. But once again, Abel looked unaffected as he straightened back to the dessert.

"Isn't it your turn?" Jane asked a bit breathlessly when he held out another bite.

"Me?" The fork tipped slightly, and this time the entire piece landed on Jane's breast. "Oops. Guess this one's mine."

Jane moaned and dropped slowly back onto the bed. The bit of cake had slid down over her breast to her stomach and Abel was meticulous licking up every last trace. She was quivering uncontrollably by the time he finished.

"More?" he asked in a husky voice.

Jane opened her eyes to see him offering another forkful of the heavenly cheesecake, but she shook her head. This wasn't what she was hungry for now.

"Guess I'll have to eat my dessert alone," he said with an unconcerned shrug.

Jane closed her eyes again, thinking he was a cruel man to tease her this way. Then something cold splashed her skin.

"What?" she gasped, half sitting up in shock. He was pouring chocolate onto her straight from the pitcher. Not a lot, but a trail from one breast to the other, then down the center of her stomach to her belly button.

"My dessert," Abel explained mildly. He set the pitcher on the bedside table and urged her back on the bed. "Cheesecake is a girly dessert. I prefer Jane a la chocolat."

He bent to one breast, then paused and looked up to solemnly say, "Don't worry, I'll eat every last bit."

And he did, concentrating first on one breast, then following the chocolate trail to the other. No other part of him touched her but his tongue, and somehow that made it a more erotic experience. Every nerve in Jane's body concentrated on his movement across her skin.

She was panting lightly and clutching the cloth beneath her hands by the time he began to follow the trail down her stomach. The path ended at her belly button, but he didn't, and Jane cried out, her hips bucking upward as if released from a spring as his head dipped between her thighs. He had barely found her center when Jane's passion overtook her. Stiff as a board she went, crying out and nearly rending the quilt they lay on as wave after wave of pleasure poured through her and she found release.

Chapter Nineteen

Abel was no longer in bed when Jane woke. She rolled onto her back, relaxing when she spotted him standing by the window in a hotel robe, a cup of coffee in hand. His hair was wet; he'd obviously showered, but he wasn't drinking the coffee, just holding it and staring out the window. She suspected he wasn't seeing anything outside, was just worrying over his sister.

Their moment of magic away from the real world was over, she realized, and she could have wept. Jane didn't want it to be over yet. She wanted more, just a little. And she would have it, she decided. Sliding from under the sheets, she walked to Abel naked. He wasn't aware of her presence until she threw her arms around his waist. Abel placed his free hand over hers as she pressed her cheek against the terry cloth of his robe and hugged him.

"Good morning," he said.

She could hear the distraction in his voice and knew he wasn't back with her yet. That wasn't good enough. She let her hands drift down and slid one inside his robe to find and caress him, and knew only then that she had his full attention.

"We have to get back," he protested. His voice was husky.

"Soon," she assured him, surprised at her own breathlessness. Just touching him and anticipating what was to come was exciting her. She continued to fondle him until he was completely hard, then took the forgotten coffee away with one hand and led him back to the bed.

"You forgot," she said as she paused beside the bed. Releasing him, she pushed the robe off his shoulders, allowing her breasts to brush his chest as she did.

"What did I forget?" he asked, trying to catch those breasts.

Jane evaded him and pushed him backward onto the bed.

"You had dessert last night, but I didn't," she announced. Picking up the half-empty pitcher of chocolate sauce still sitting on the bedside table, she smiled.

"Jeeez." Abel's eyes dilated as she dribbled it over him.

Lydia Ensecksi was mounting the stairs to the front door when they pulled into the driveway of the Goodinov house some two hours later.

"Back to the real world," Abel said dryly.

"No rest for the wicked," Jane responded. Sliding out of the car, she felt more than ready to handle Lydia this morning; she felt reenergized, alive, happy, hopeful. She could have handled ten Lydias at the moment.

"I was just coming to look for you," the blonde called as she started back down the stairs toward them.

"We had breakfast out," Abel explained as he walked around the car.

"And dessert," Jane said lightly. She reveled in the quick flicker of desire in Abel's eyes.

"That sounds nice. Where did you go?"

"Jamestown," Abel responded easily, answering without really answering. "I'm surprised to see you at home today, Lydia. It's Monday, a workday. I thought you'd be in San Jose."

"Oh, I took a couple days off," she said as she reached them.

"So, why were you looking for us?" Jane asked, eager to move the conversation along. She had to get rid of the woman before the way she was rubbing her hand up and down Abel's arm could drive Jane to do her bodily injury. "Or was it just Abel you were looking for?"

"No. Both of you. Dirk and I were hoping you'd come over for dinner tonight so we could get to know each other better." Her voice dropped as she added the last part, and her gaze was focused solely on Abel, communicating just how she'd like to get to know him.

Horizontal and naked, was Jane's educated guess. Not in this lifetime, she swore, but she smiled brightly and lied through her teeth. "That sounds great!"

"Yeah," Abel agreed.

"Good," the blonde purred. She closed the last bit of space between herself and Abel so that she was giving him the full-body press.

Abel glanced at Jane and saw something that turned his expression wary. But his voice was bright as he said, "Well, we'd better get that breakfast in to Gran before it gets cold."

"Breakfast? Surely she'll have eaten already. It's nearly noon."

"We all slept in late today." Managing to disengage himself, Abel moved around the car. "Can you get the garage door for me, Jane?"

She knew he was just trying to get her away from Lydia before she committed some violence; there was no breakfast for Gran. Jane moved to do as he asked, though. She pushed the button to open the garage door for him. Abel immediately drove the car inside and parked; then Jane promptly pushed the button to close it.

"So, come over at seven o'clock," Lydia called, bending to look through the closing door.

"Will do." Abel stepped out of the car. "Later."

The moment the door closed, he took Jane's arm to lead her to the elevator.

"It's only one floor, Abel." Jane laughed. "Why don't we take the stairs?"

"Because I want to do this." He pulled her into the elevator and into his arms.

"Oh," Jane breathed when their kiss ended.

Abel smiled into her face. "You looked ready to commit hara-kiri on poor Lydia."

"Hmm."

"You don't have to be jealous," he announced in rather smug tones, obviously enjoying her dance with the green-eyed monster. "I have absolutely no interest in her. You're the girl for me."

"Yes, I am." Jane shifted against him, feeling his semihard state. "Just like you shouldn't be jealous of Dirk."

That killed the smile on his face *and* his budding erection. Abel's expression turned testy and he opened his mouth to speak, but stopped when Jane burst out laughing. She imitated the tone he'd used just moments before to say, "You don't have to be jealous when Dirk is hanging over me. I have absolutely no interest in him. You're the guy for me."

Abel managed a twisted smile and shook his head, then pressed the button to close the elevator doors. Making the contraption take them to the first floor he announced, "You have a cruel heart, woman."

"Yep, and I'm gullible too. It's all part of my charm," she said airily. Abel laughed and followed her out of the elevator.

"My! You two seem happy this morning. Had a good time, did you?"

"Gran!" Jane stopped short, blushed, then rushed forward to hug her relative, only to back off when Tinkle sat up and bared her teeth in greeting. She took the handles of her grandmother's wheelchair.

"We had a *marvelous* time. Abel took me to the Willow Steakhouse in Jamestown. You should have seen it, it was lovely. And the food! I had chicken Jerusalem. It was yummy."

Jane was no fool; she chattered happily away about the restaurant as she pushed Gran and Tinkle through the kitchen and up to the dining room table. She managed to describe the restaurant, Jamestown, and her meal in minute detail, neatly eliminating the possibility for Gran to ask any embarrassing questions. She put on water for tea and puttered about under the amused gazes of both Abel and her grandmother.

"This is how she always avoids embarrassing conversations," Gran told Abel confidentially. "Any time she becomes a chatterbox, she's avoiding something."

"Thanks for the pointer," Abel said solemnly.

"I have a lot more if you'd like them."

"Please." Abel took the chair next to her, settling in to hear all his woman's secrets.

"She hates to ask for help," Maggie Spyrus explained. "Janie's very self-reliant. She'd rather break her back trying to move something than ask anyone else. And while she's sweet and very giving, she hates being forced to give. If the giving becomes an expected thing, it becomes a burden and she resents it, then lets it eat her up inside until she loses her temper and explodes." The old woman nodded as she said that, then added, "And she's stubborn as a mule and testy when she's hungry, so you'll want to keep her fed. But don't feed her too many dairy products. Her system can't handle it, and she gets cranky with—"

"Gran!" Jane had stopped chattering long enough to actually hear what she was saying. She'd been semiaware of the conversation taking place, but too busy feverishly thinking of what to say next herself to pay attention. Now it was all sinking in, however, and she turned to her grandmother in horror.

"Yes, dear?" Maggie innocently petted her beloved Tinkle. "What is it?"

"You—"

"So, you're back."

Jane turned her attention to Nancy, who had just entered the dining room. She looked tired, and Jane felt a moment's guilt that they hadn't returned sooner as Abel wanted. It didn't last long. Nancy's natural charm soon washed it out of her.

"Get me a cup of tea and sit down. I want to talk

to you," the nurse/spy snapped, and Jane felt her temper rise.

"That's another thing," Gran pointed out to Abel. "She doesn't like to be ordered around. It goes with the independence thing, I think. She likes to rule herself. And that look on her face right now? That unattractive, squinty-eyed 'die, bitch' scowl? That's a good indication that you may as well get out the rain gear, 'cause the weather's going to get stormy."

Abel burst out in great guffaws, and even Jane felt her lips tugged reluctantly with amusement. " 'Die, bitch' scowl?" she asked. "I've never heard you curse before, Gran. California is having a bad effect on you."

"Well, Janie, dear, I do try to avoid vulgarities." She shrugged. "But sometimes the description just fits so well, no other word will do."

"If you three are finished?" Nancy asked with weary impatience. Jane decided to give the woman a break; she was obviously exhausted. She'd forgive the snotty attitude. Again.

"Sit down, Nancy. I'll get out some cookies too. You can have some while you talk," she said, doing a little ordering around of her own. Surprisingly, Nancy sat.

Jane brought the tea tray to the table, poured four cups, and set a plate of cookies in the center of the table. "Now, what do you want to talk about?"

"Unless he's a deaf-mute—and none of the information we have on him suggests that—Robert Ensecksi isn't in that house."

"Yes, he is," Jane insisted. "Josh and Dirk were talking about it."

"Did they actually say 'Robert Ensecksi is in the house'?"

"N-o-o-o," she said slowly. "Dirk just said, 'Tell

him we shouldn't be late' or something." She saw the satisfaction on Nancy's face and added quickly, "But Lydia and Dirk were talking about talking to him when they came back from Leigh's party. Weren't they, Abel?"

"But she didn't talk to him, did she? I've listened to your tapes, Jane. There's complete silence after that, other than snoring. And there are no lights on anywhere."

"That just means that she went into the basement or something to talk to him," Jane insisted.

"There is no basement in the blueprints, Jane. She was probably talking to him on a cell phone near the side door. You neglected to put a camera or microphones there."

Jane groaned. Another failure on her part. If she'd set up the cameras better, she could have proved both that the robber had come from the Ensecksi house and that Lydia hadn't been talking to her father on a cell phone.

"Look," Nancy said. "I have listened off and on to silence from that house ever since arriving. There is no sign of anyone else being there, but Lydia and Dirk. When they were gone yesterday, the house was completely silent The father is not there."

"Yes, he is," Jane practically shouted.

Nancy ignored her. "There is also no—"

"What about the man who broke in here yesterday?" Jane interrupted. "He came from the Ensecksi house."

"None of the cameras show him coming out of the Ensecksi house; he just appears coming around the corner of it."

"Well . . . according to the blueprints, there's a door in the master bedroom like there is here. He probably came out that."

"Perhaps. But we don't know for sure. And there is no sound on the audio tapes to indicate that he was ever in the house."

"Perhaps he was at the other end of the house, where they wouldn't pick him up. And why else would he break in here but at the Ensecksi command?"

"To rob the place," Nancy suggested dryly. "This *is* an expensive neighborhood, Jane. With lots to steal. He was maybe just a robber."

"Without a car?" she asked.

"He probably had a car waiting beyond the gate somewhere. The sheriff will find it eventually."

Jane felt frustration well up within her. Nancy had made up her mind. She wasn't even open to the idea there was something suspicious going on. Nancy would explain away anything she brought up. Still, Jane had to try. "What about Edie? They kidnapped her."

"You don't even know *that* for sure," Nancy said wearily.

"Of course I do," Jane snapped. "She took my tracking devices. I followed a transmitter all the way from Vancouver, narrowed it down to that hearse, and followed it to the Ensecksi house."

"Did you ever actually see Edie in that vehicle?"

Jane shut her mouth.

Nancy nodded patronizingly. "For all you know, Edie ran into Lydia while on her date and loaned her your tampon. It could be Lydia you followed all the way here."

"Lydia doesn't work in Vancouver. She lives here and works in San Jose."

"And Dirk works in Vancouver, but he's here right now. She could have been visiting."

"Then *where is Edie?*" Abel growled, suddenly speaking up.

"Who knows? She could be home by now for all we know. Has anyone called to check?"

Abel and Jane exchanged a glance; then he leaped to his feet and moved to the phone. Jane watched him for a minute, then turned back to Nancy. "What about the yellow dresses all these women wear? How do you explain an entire town of women in yellow sundresses?"

"Bad taste," Nancy said.

"And the Hawaiian shirts?"

"*Really* bad taste."

"There's no answer. She's not there," Abel announced, glaring at the nurse/spy.

Nancy shook her head and said, "Look. I know this is all terribly suspicious, yellow dresses everywhere, Edie missing, and all that. But B.L.I.S.S. has done an aerial scan of this whole area and there simply isn't any broadcasting equipment that could accomplish any mind-control scheme. You'd need a huge dish for this, and there isn't one here. There also isn't anything going on inside that house. Hell, they don't even talk to each other. Your microphones are picking up silence except for the occasional sound of footsteps. I've checked them, and they're installed properly. I can't recommend our people do anything on this information. I'll wait and watch and listen for another day or so, but then I'm going to recommend we close up shop and move on." She stood and left the room.

Jane glared at her retreating back, then turned to see dismay and fear on Abel's face. She reached out to cover his hand where it rested on the table. "Don't worry. We'll find out what's going on when we go for dinner there tonight. And even if we don't, we'll take bugs and spy-cams and place them around the house. We have time. We can do this."

"What do you mean, when you go for dinner tonight?" Gran asked sharply.

"Lydia invited us to dinner," Jane explained. Then, since Maggie didn't look pleased at the news, she lifted her chin and added, "And we're going."

"No, no, no. I don't like this at all. They're already suspicious of you. You could be walking into a trap."

Jane's eyes narrowed. "Do you mean to say *you* believe that they're up to something?"

"Of course I do."

"Well, why didn't you say something to Nancy then?"

"Because it's mostly instinct. Nancy always had rotten instincts. But she's also as stubborn as you are. She won't change her mind until she sees something for herself."

"Well, maybe we can show her tonight," Jane said determinedly.

"I don't like it." Gran eyed her granddaughter grimly. "But I know that won't stop you. I want you two to be careful."

"We will, Gran," Jane assured her. Then because Maggie Spyrus looked more worried than Jane had ever seen her, she kissed the old woman's cheek and repeated her promise. "We'll be very careful."

"Where are you going?" Gran asked when she stood up.

"To offer to spell Nancy at the monitor. She's been at it since last night." Ignoring her gran's suspicious glance, she headed for the master bedroom.

Unlike Gran, Nancy wasn't the least bit suspicious of Jane's offer to take over; she was too grateful for the break. Jane waited until the other woman was safely tucked in bed before she set to work. She was deep into it when a mug of coffee was suddenly set on the table beside her.

"Mmm. That smells good." She straightened to offer Abel a smile in return. "Thank you."

"No problem. Are you going through the recordings?" He settled on the couch beside her.

"Yes. How did you guess?"

He shrugged. "Find anything?"

"Yes. And no. That swishing sound is there repeatedly. But Nancy's right: They don't talk much. They say good morning, they say good night, but after Lydia claims she's going to talk to their father, there isn't anything else."

"They don't strike me as the strong silent types," Abel joked.

"No." Jane shook her head. "Yet they don't say anything in the house. Not even after Josh was killed, or when Nancy killed the guy who broke in here."

"Definitely not normal," Abel decided.

Jane nodded. "I just know there's a basement."

Abel peered at her unhappily and asked, "What about the satellite dish, Jane? Nancy's right about that. Everything falls apart because there is no dish. What if we did follow the wrong tracker? Maybe Edie is somewhere else. Dead or—"

"*No.* We didn't follow the wrong tracker. Edie was in that hearse."

"How can you be sure?"

Jane wasn't. Nancy had managed to raise doubt in her, too, but she had to give Abel hope. She needed some of it herself. Then she smiled as realization dawned. "Because it disappeared."

He looked confused. "How does that—?"

"If Lydia or anyone else borrowed one and removed it upon reaching here, they would have thrown it out. It would be blinking yellow for neutralized. But it isn't. It's disappeared. That means it is somehow stopped from transmitting." She turned back to the screen. "Somewhere inside that house is an insulated room or basement."

She stood and, moving to her bags, began to sort out various weapons, choosing those they would take tonight. Then she moved to the closet and the box of equipment B.L.I.S.S. had sent, picking out what she would need. She would definitely place bugs around the inside of the Ensecksi house in case they didn't find the information they needed at dinner. But how was she supposed to sneak in cameras and conceal them?

She glanced toward Abel. "Can you watch the monitors?"

"Yes. Of course."

"Good, I have work to do." Grabbing up the equipment she'd gathered, she walked over, kissed him once passionately, then hurried out.

There was a worktable set up in one corner of the garage. Mr. Goodinov had obviously enjoyed tinkering before the Alzheimer's had kicked in. Jane would work on it now. No one would disturb her there.

"This is a tie-cam," Jane told Abel as she attached the tie clip.

Abel tucked in his chin and peered down at it. "Attractive and functional too. Just like its creator."

"I'm functional, am I?" Jane asked with amusement. She finished fiddling and stepped back to peer at her work.

"You're more than that. You're beautiful, smart,

funny. But, Jane . . ." He caught her hands and drew her back when she started to turn away. "I'm thinking maybe you shouldn't go tonight."

Her eyes widened in surprise. "Don't you want to see if Edie is there?"

"Yes. But not at the risk of losing you. I'd rather go by myself and—"

"Abel," Jane interrupted, "that's so sweet. Now, let's go."

She turned away and picked up a plant she'd brought.

"What's that?" he asked.

"A thanks-for-inviting-us-to-dinner potted plant spy-cam," Jane said cheerfully.

As she tried to step past him, he stopped her again, catching her arms. "Jane, I'm serious."

"So am I, Abel," she said solemnly. "Edie's over there and I intend to find her tonight. It may be our last chance if Nurse Nancy has her way."

He let his hands drop and nodded. "Do you have weapons or something?"

"Right here." Jane patted the purse she was carrying. He frowned at its size.

"Don't you think that's rather large? They're already suspicious. What are they going to think when they see that?"

Jane shrugged. "If they check it, all they'll find is a bunch of makeup, some vibrators and condoms."

"Vibrators and condoms?" He blanched. "You aren't bringing those?"

Jane grinned. "I hope not to have to use them, but you never know. Oh!" Setting her purse and plant down, she reached into her pants pocket to dig around. She hadn't bothered with a dress tonight. She needed the pockets that pants offered, so had settled for a pair of silky black trousers and

318

a low-cut gold top. She tried not to think what the choice of gold might mean. Was she falling under Ensecksi mind-control? Good Lord! They had to resolve this tonight. From amidst the handful of bugs she had in her pocket, Jane pulled out a necklace—a long silver chain with a medallion. It looked rather feminine, but she hadn't had a lot to work with.

"I want you to wear this necklace. Knockout powder is inside. You push this"—she showed him a tiny lever—"and the lid comes off. Pour the powder into Lydia's drink if you get the chance. That will neutralize her."

"I suppose you have that knockout lipstick on again?" he asked as she slipped the chain around his neck and tucked it under his shirt collar.

"Yes. And truth serum perfume, bomb earrings, a laser bracelet, dart-shooting shoes, and my necklace is a spy-cam." She stepped back and smiled at him. "I have a few other tricks too. We're loaded for bear."

"Well." He smiled slightly. "That makes me feel better."

Nodding, Jane slipped her purse over her shoulder and picked up her plant again. Despite her confident attitude, she was extremely nervous. They were walking into danger, after all—she, shy Jane Spyrus from development and creation, and an accountant. "Let's go."

"All ready?" Gran asked as Jane and Abel came upon her in the great room. She used a remote to turn off a TV she'd been watching.

"All set." Jane walked over and bent to kiss her on the cheek.

Gran caught her hand as she straightened. There was worry in her eyes. "You'll be careful?"

"I promise," Jane said softly.

Maggie Spyrus gave a sharp nod. "Well, then, wheel me up those damn steps and into the master bedroom. I want to watch you at work."

Between the two of them, Jane and Abel got Gran up the short flight of stairs with little difficulty. Nancy and Mr. Tibbs looked up as they entered the master bedroom. Neither looked terribly pleased to see them, although with Mr. Tibbs, Jane suspected it was only Tinkle's presence he protested. The cat gave a show of power, a bored hiss, then went back to sleep in the center of the bed. It was enough to make Tinkle cower and whimper in Gran's lap. She'd learned finally not to mess with Edie's cat.

Nancy, on the other hand, was definitely put out by their appearance. "You're still going through with this nonsense?"

Gran had broken the news to her of their dinner invitation next door when she'd gotten up from her nap. She hadn't thought a foray into the Ensecksi home was a good idea, and apparently still didn't.

"Sure. Why not? There's nothing going on, you say. It's perfectly safe." Jane couldn't resist baiting her. She suspected the agent was having second thoughts and feared their discovering something and making her look foolish. Too bad.

"I didn't say there was nothing going on," the woman argued quickly. "I said there was no proof, and—"

"And we'll get you some," Jane finished calmly.

Nancy scowled. "It could be very dangerous if they really are up to something."

"Well, it's a good thing we have you for backup then, isn't it?" Jane turned to Abel. "Ready?"

He nodded. "Ready."

"Let's go, then." She started toward the door to

the hall, calling over her shoulder, "I've programmed the computer. It's all ready and will start
relaying images the minute I turn our cameras on.
The bugs should already be activated. Wish us
luck."

Chapter Twenty

"Don't eat or drink anything while we're there. Pretend to if you must, but don't let anything past your lips." Jane paused at the end of the driveway and turned to hand Abel the potted plant so that she could turn on his tie-clip camera.

"Okay." He watched as she did the same to her necklace camera. "But what if it's something they eat or drink?"

"No. The glasses could be doctored, or the forks."

"So, how can I pretend to drink?"

Jane finished with her necklace and considered. To keep from raising suspicions they might have to pretend to drink. But if the rim of the glass was coated with something . . . Jane supposed she'd be safe enough; she was wearing Lipschitz's knockout lipstick with its base coat—

Smiling suddenly, she dug the lipstick out of her

purse, opened the end with the clear gel and gestured for Abel to bend close.

"Open your mouth and flatten your lips," she instructed. When he did so, she began to smooth it on. "This is a base coat. It should protect you from doctored glasses and such if you have to put them to your lips." She paused a moment. "It *should* protect you. If it is a base coat," she added.

Abel glanced at her sharply. "If? You don't know?"

"I didn't develop it," she admitted with a shrug. "We'll have to hope for the best."

"It feels weird," he complained. Jane glanced up from putting the lipstick in her pocket to see him flattening and unflattening his lips in discomfort. Catching her watching him he asked, "Is there anything else I should know?"

He looked calm enough, but Jane knew he must be as nervous as she herself was. There was nothing more frightening than the unknown, and that's what they were walking into. They had no idea what to expect this evening. If they were right and the Ensecksis were evil plotters bent on world domination, they were walking into a tricky situation. If they were wrong . . . She didn't even want to think about that.

Pushing the unhelpful thoughts away, Jane tried to summon other warnings or advice to give, but nothing came to mind. In truth, her poor brain was blank. She shook her head and confessed, "Nothing I can think of. I don't know what to expect here, Abel. Just be on your toes."

He nodded, then brushed her cheek gently with one finger. "Okay, Jane."

She smiled, took the potted plant back, and switched on its camera.

Abel took her arm, and they turned along the road toward the Ensecksi driveway. It was early evening, not full dark. The night was cool and the air fresh. Jane could almost have forgotten where they were going and why. Almost.

"Here we go," she murmured as they reached the front door.

Abel pushed the doorbell. "Jane?" he said as it sounded inside.

"Hmm?" She turned to glance up at him. How handsome he was. How considerate and smart and sexy, and how she wished they were back in Jamestown in the bed-and-breakfast, making love rather than here.

"If anything should happen, I want you to know—"

Jane covered his mouth with her fingers. She wasn't sure what he'd been about to say, but it had sounded like a last-minute declaration. She wanted no if-I-should-die, I-really-liked-you crap that he might later regret. She was sure such a thing would jinx the whole deal. If, after it was over, he wanted to say something like that, she'd be more than happy to hear it. But for now, she would have none of it.

"Nothing's going to happen," she said firmly. "Nothing bad, anyway. We're going to knock out the grabby twins, find Edie and bring her home, then let B.L.I.S.S. raid the house or whatever. It'll all go according to plan."

"Yes, but—" He was cut off as the door opened.

"There you are!" Lydia greeted them with a welcoming smile like a shark's, posing so they could get the full effect of the slinky silver dress she wore. Reaching for Abel's hand, she drew him forward.

"Come in, come in. I could hardly wait for you to get here."

Jane glanced around curiously as she followed them inside. She wasn't terribly surprised by the interior of the house. While the Goodinov home was warm and welcoming, this one was a showpiece— contemporary everything made up of sharp angles, glossy surfaces, and cold colors. Much like Lydia herself. The ice maiden had an ice palace.

"Jane!" Dirk crossed the living room as if he couldn't wait to get to her side. He took her free hand and bent, obviously intending to kiss her in greeting, but Jane shoved her plant at him in a panic. She hardly wanted him knocked out yet, not with Lydia standing here looking on. The knockout lipstick would have had him down for the count.

"Oh." He jerked back from the greenery suddenly tickling his nose. "What—?"

"A thank-you for inviting us to dinner," Jane said, smiling brightly.

"Oh. Isn't that thoughtful." He didn't sound too sure as he accepted the plant, but he flashed her another of his patented smiles and took her arm. Pulling her close to his side, he walked her to the couch, his leg brushing hers with every step. Jane didn't sit down, however. She had no intention of getting trapped there on the couch with Dirk. Side-stepping along its length, she settled into the chair at the far end. She set her purse on the floor.

"Good Lord, Jane. Is that purse big enough?" Lydia snorted as she drew Abel toward the couch. "What do you have in that thing? A cannon?"

"Oh." Jane laughed and waved her hand vaguely. "Makeup, a brush, my day planner, a notebook and paper, and generally a novel in case of a moment to read. Essentials, really."

"Something for every occasion," Lydia said with amusement.

"You'd be surprised."

"I doubt it." She turned to Dirk and gestured to white wine in an ice bucket on the coffee table. "Will you do the honors, brother?"

"Certainly." He sat forward on the couch and reached for the bottle, uncorking it quickly and easily. He then proceeded to pour it into four waiting glasses.

"Dinner should be ready shortly. I thought we'd have a drink and get to know each other better before we ate, though," Lydia announced. She settled on the arm of the chair Abel had also chosen instead of the couch. "I hope that's all right?"

Jane murmured something that might be taken for a yes, her mind on other matters. Supper. The meal was cooking and should be ready soon. Yet there was no scent of food in the air. Her gaze slid around the living room, and she began to realize that there was more than just the smell of cooking missing. There were no signs of inhabitation here— no newspaper, no magazine, no *TV Guide*, no family photos. She wasn't surprised by the house's cleanliness, just its complete lack of personality. And the longer she looked at this room, the more positive she became that no one lived in it.

"Here you go." Dirk handed Jane a wineglass and she accepted it with a smile. Her gaze found Abel as he, too, took the wine Dirk offered. Their eyes met across the length of the coffee table, and they both set their glasses down.

"This is a California wine. You should try it."

Jane's gaze jerked to Lydia. The blonde was watching her coldly, her own glass in hand but untouched. Jane knew the gloves were off. They'd stepped into a web and the spider was tired of games.

"Drink," Dirk said quietly beside her.

Jane turned her head slowly to look at him. His usual amiability was missing. He looked terribly serious. His face held a cold beauty now, one that sent an unpleasant shiver down her back.

Jane considered the two Ensecksis, her mind racing. Then she lifted the glass to her lips and pretended to sip from it, hoping to God the base coat of Lipschitz's lipstick would protect her from any contact drugs. She smiled as she set the glass down. "It's lovely."

Lydia didn't smile back. "Have some more."

Okay, Jane thought as she raised the glass to her mouth. Here was a pretty good indication her glass was probably drugged, and they would expect some reaction. But which? An immediate faint? A slow drowsy buildup? Oh, this was tough.

"You too, Abel. You've hardly even touched yours. Taste it." Lydia closed her hand over Abel's and urged it to his lips, then glanced at Jane again.

Deciding her best bet was to play innocent, Jane smiled, shrugged, and lifted her glass, tipping it and making her throat move so it appeared she swallowed. Abel did the same. Setting the glass back down, Jane glanced from Dirk's expectant face to Lydia's suspicious one. They were glancing between her and Abel as if watching a tennis match. When Lydia opened her mouth again, probably to urge her to have more, Jane blinked and said, "Oh, my, I don't seem to have a head for drink."

She blinked several more times, pleased to see this was the reaction the Ensecksis expected: Dirk relaxed and a small smile played at Lydia's lips.

"Oh," Jane said. "Maybe I should go splash water

on my face. Where's the washroom?" She stood, swayed, then flopped back in her chair.

She should get an award for her acting.

"Jane!" Abel's voice was alarmed but faint. Jane slitted her eyes open just as he lunged to his feet as if to come to her; then he crashed forward onto the far end of the couch. She closed her eyes again, unsure whether he'd really drunk and was unconscious, or was following her lead and playacting.

Aware that the room was completely silent, Jane felt panic overwhelm her, then Lydia commented, "Well, Father didn't say it would act this quickly, but oh, well. Now, let's see what she has in this suitcase she calls a purse."

Jane heard a rustle, then felt her leather bag shift against her leg. Lydia was presumably opening it.

"Dear God!"

"What is it?" Dirk asked. She felt his pant leg brush against her; then his hand was planted on her knee closest to her purse. Weight was put on it as if he was leaning on her as he bent forward to see what Lydia found.

"Our Jane is some kind of nympho. Look at this, there must be twelve condoms here. You were in for a wild night, Dirk."

She heard him groan. "I told you they weren't feds! Damn it, Lydia! You spoil all my fun."

"Oh, shut up. I told you what I heard in the kitchen. Daniel said Abel was a lucky guy."

"Well, maybe he meant because she was his sister. Although that's gross. Look! All there is in here is makeup and stuff like she said. What's that pink thing under her wallet?"

"Oh, my," Lydia drawled.

"Vibrators?" Dirk sounded shocked. "How many are there? One, two—"

"Six," Lydia answered with a nasty laugh. "Looks like she wasn't sure you were up to the task. Or you were in for some really kinky play."

"Six?" Dirk sounded bewildered. "Where would you put them all?"

Lydia burst out laughing, but her brother didn't join in. He sounded annoyed as he snapped, "You and your bright ideas. *'They're feds or something, Dirk,'*" he said in a high-pitched voice, obviously mimicking her. "*'Just look how Abel hasn't tried to touch me yet. And I overheard Daniel—'*"

"Oh, cheer up. Maybe you'll still get your chance with our surprising Miss Jane," Lydia interrupted testily. The rustling continued and Jane knew she was still looking through her purse. She wasn't sure what Lydia was seeking, but when she heard the sound of a zipper being undone, she recognized the opening of her wallet/day planner. ID, she realized.

"Like she's going to sleep with me after we gave her a knockout drug," Dirk mourned.

"Yeah, well . . . maybe Dad can do some of his mind-control magic and turn her into your sex slave," Lydia said. She sighed. "Speaking of which, I suppose we'd better take them below and report. He'll know how to figure out for sure whether they're feds or not, and what to do with that grandmother."

"Oh, come off it," Dirk snapped. "There isn't a gun or anything in there. And you checked her ID. It all checks out."

Lydia didn't respond. She merely stood and moved away, the click of her feet on the hardwood floor growing fainter then stopping.

The swishing sound Jane had heard repeatedly over the tapes sounded, and she slitted her eyes open to chance a peek. Dirk was still leaning over her, poking through her purse and muttering about the vibrators. Over his bent back she could see Lydia standing by the opposite wall. A panel had slid open to reveal what appeared to be an elevator. Four men were stepping out. All of them wore black hard hats and glossy uniforms that looked like coveralls, but were more fitted and had the word ENSECKSI on the left breast pocket.

Jane let her eyes close again, and managed not to give a start when she found herself lifted out of the chair into someone's arms. She was carried, probably to the elevator.

"Just leave the purse, Dirk," Lydia snapped from nearby.

"No." That word sounded sulky. Jane could only think he was bringing it for the sex paraphernalia.

A grunt made her risk another peek, and she saw that while the largest Ensecksi henchman had scooped her up, the other three had taken Abel. One had his legs and the others had each taken an arm. They carted him to the elevator and set him on the floor. Jane let her eyes close again as Lydia pushed a button. She felt the elevator begin downward, and said a silent nyah-nyah to Nurse Nancy. She was right and the B.L.I.S.S. field operative was wrong.

Nancy. And Gran. They'd have kicked into action by now. No doubt an emergency call was already being placed to headquarters. But what would they do? They might try a full assault, but how long would that take to organize? Jane had no idea. And when they did get a team together, how would they get inside? She wasn't at all sure that any of the cameras she'd brought had caught the wall panel Lydia opened. Abel's tie-clip surely hadn't. He'd been flat on his face on the couch. And her neck-lace camera likely hadn't either, unless it had shot under Dirk's chest as she'd looked over his back. Perhaps the potted plant had caught it. Jane tried to recall how Dirk had set it down on the table.

The elevator stopped moving, disrupting her thoughts, and Jane had to grit her teeth to keep from opening her eyes. She felt the man holding her move forward.

"Put her in this one and him in that." Lydia's voice had a hollow sound, almost an echo. The curiosity was almost killing her, but Jane kept her eyes closed, listening to the surrounding sounds of movement. The sounds stopped, there were several clicks she couldn't identify; then whatever she was in suddenly shot forward. Jane risked peeking un-der her lashes and saw walls of jagged rock flash past. They weren't in a basement; they were in some kind of tunnel, and riding in some kind of topless shuttle at a nauseating speed. The clanking, of rails beneath them told her they were on some sort of track. Now she knew what Dirk had meant about their father being "in the mountain." He'd been speaking literally.

The tunnel suddenly ended and they emerged into a long, narrow curving room with actual walls painted gray. Lydia stepped out of the shuttle. "Bring them."

Jane was picked up and carried for a distance. Her eyes were closed again, but she heard a door open, then was set down.

"Chain them up," Lydia ordered.

"Is that really necessary?" Dirk asked irritably.

"Yes, it's really necessary. They didn't drink much and might not be out long." Lydia sounded impa-tient, her voice moving away.

Jane peeked through her lashes to see the blonde leave the room, pulling her brother with her.

Lydia paused by a table in the middle of the next chamber and snatched Jane's bag from Dirk. "Give me that damned thing! You can play with that chick and her vibrators later—we have things to do right now. Dad wants to move to the next level at midnight. It's almost eight now. He'll want to check all the systems to be sure they're working." Tossing Jane's bag on the table, she urged Dirk back to the shuttles.

Jane glanced around the dim room she was in as the shuttle with Dirk moved out of sight. Abel was lying at its opposite end. Two men were busy chaining his leg to the wall and cuffing his wrists behind his back. Even as she watched, they finished and turned toward her.

Jane closed her eyes and lay still as they approached. As they bound her she considered struggling or fighting, but she hadn't got enough of a look around to know if these were her only foes so she remained still and patient. When they were done, she heard their footsteps move away then the slam of a door. She cautiously looked around. The room was darker, the only light coming from a six-by-six-inch square glass panel in the exit.

She sat up carefully, wincing as the chain attached to her ankle jingled.

"Jane?" Abel hissed.

She felt relief seep through her. He'd apparently been feigning his faint as she had. That was a plus, she decided, and whispered, "Are you okay?"

"Yeah, but I'm handcuffed and my ankle is chained to the wall."

"That's okay. We'll be out of this in a jiffy." *I hope,* she added silently to herself. She began feeling first at the stiff cuffs around her wrists, then the bracelet she wore underneath. It was a laser bracelet and should slice through the cuffs like a hot knife through butter . . . if the laser was pointed in the right direction and she didn't give herself some unwanted surgery by accident. She fiddled with the bracelet, trying to figure where it was pointed.

"What are you doing?" Abel asked softly in the darkness.

"Playing with my bracelet. Let me concentrate," she whispered back.

He fell silent, and Jane adjusted the laser so that she thought it was directed at the cuff on her wrist; then she sent up a silent prayer and activated it. A quiet hiss came as it began burning something. She felt a moment of fear, but then the cuff fell away from her wrist. Jane shut the laser off and pulled her hands around in front of her. She concentrated on the chain holding her to the wall next, quickly using the bracelet to slice through. Jane then scooted across the room to Abel.

"That's my girl," he murmured, and Jane felt pleasure at the pride in his voice.

She pressed a quick kiss to his lips, grateful he was protected from her knockout lipstick, then set to work on his chains. It only took a matter of moments to free him; then they both stood and moved to the door.

"What now?" Abel whispered.

Before them, through a window in the door they saw two men in black coverall uniforms playing cards at a table. Jane could see her purse lying there in plain view and wished she had it. She looked around. The men were in an octagonal room with six other doors, not including the opening to where the shuttle had been. The table was in the center.

Jane turned her attention to the locks on the six other doors: high-tech with a key-card-swiper system, of course.

"Do you think Edie's in one of those rooms?" Abel asked.

"I think it's a good possibility," she whispered, then knelt to examine the inside of the door in front of them. There was nothing on this side, not even a hint of where the lock might be.

"You said you had bomb earrings on. Can you—"

"Too much noise," she interrupted. "We don't want to alert anyone."

"No," he agreed, but didn't sound happy.

"Tell me if they seem to hear anything," she instructed, then took off her bracelet and knelt. She set to work on the door with the laser, slicing out a section where she thought the lock must be.

"You did it!" If there was a whispering version of a whoop, Abel gave it. The part of the door Jane was cutting fell into her hands.

Jane grinned and straightened. Opening the door a couple of inches, she then pressed it silently closed again and braced herself against the wall. She slipped one shoe off.

"What are we going to do?" Abel asked.

"I'm going to shoot them with this shoe."

"Ah." He sounded rather uncertain.

"I wore my dart shoes," she reminded him. Kneeling in front of the door, she eased it open and took aim.

"Are you a good shot?" Abel asked.

Jane didn't answer. She didn't know and didn't want to worry him. They were about to find out, either way. She aimed down the heel of the shoe, pointing it at the chest of the guard on the right, took a deep breath, and fired.

"Uh-oh," Abel muttered. Jane would have echoed it, but there was no time. She'd missed her target. The dart had struck her purse on the table, a good foot to the left of the guard's arm. Both guards gaped at the missile, swiveled to stare at the door, then were on their feet and charging forward.

Jane and Abel leaped out of the way as the door crashed open. Jane rolled, coming up pointing her shoe at the guard rushing her. Not knowing what it was, he continued forward. Jane fired again. This time she hit her target.

The reaction to the drugged dart was almost immediate, and Jane gave a grunt as the man crashed down on top of her. She managed to shove him off herself and sat up to peer wildly across the room, ready to save Abel by shooting the other guard, but Abel didn't need saving. He was thrashing the man with open-hand blows and heel kicks.

He knew some martial arts, she realized and watched with interest as he fought. There was something incredibly sexy about it—the play of his muscles and grace of his movements—and she could have watched forever. Fortunately, though, Abel didn't fight forever. Quickly he put the guard out with a nice flat-fist punch to the side of the neck. Which impressed Jane even more. Such a punch needed a lot of power behind it to knock a target unconscious and not just leave him gasping on the floor.

Abel whirled toward her, looking for the other guard, apparently all wound up and ready to take on another opponent. He relaxed, however, when he saw Jane sitting there, now cross-legged on the floor, grinning at him.

"You were brilliant," she praised.

Abel grinned back. He walked forward to offer her a hand up, and she saw it was an embarrassed grin. "I took a little martial arts for a while when I was younger."

"More than a little," Jane said as he pulled her to her feet. "That's something you forgot to mention the other night."

"It's nothing next to your twenty years of training," he demurred. Glancing at the men on the floor he asked, "What do we do with them?"

Jane snatched the security card off the chest of the nearest guard and walked out of the room. Approaching one of the six available doors, she peered into darkness, then flicked a nearby switch. Light immediately filled the cell. It was empty. She used the guard's card on the swiper. A buzz sounded and the door swung open.

"Let's lock them up in here," she suggested, rejoining Abel.

He nodded.

They dragged the men into the new room, chained them at the ankles as they themselves had been, then locked the door. Next they began checking the other rooms, looking for Edie.

Jane found her in the second cell. "Abel," she called softly and used her card to open the door.

"Jane!" Edie leaped off the bed she'd been seated on and stared with amazement as Jane hurried into the room. She was chained to the wall, but not handcuffed. She also wasn't drugged, or brainwashed, as far as Jane could tell.

"Edie!" Abel rushed in and caught his sister in a hug. "Damn, girl! You scared the loving daylights out of me."

"Oh, Abel!" Edie collapsed against his chest. "I

was so scared. I . . ." She pulled back suddenly. "What are you doing here? How did you find me?"

"Her." Abel beamed and caught Jane's arm, pulling her into a three-way hug.

"Jane?" Edie peered at her, bewildered. "How did *you* find me, then?"

Jane just shook her head. "It's a long story. Let's just get you out of here."

Edie babbled out what had happened as Jane worked on her bonds. It was all pretty much as they'd thought: Edie had overheard Dirk talking on the phone to Lydia about the mind-control plans. She'd contacted the C.I.S.I.S.; then on Thursday, Dirk had asked her out. She'd convinced herself she might learn something useful for C.I.S.I.S. and went. Dirk had picked her up, explained that business had held him up and he needed to change. They'd gone to his place, he'd offered her a drink and bam—the next thing she knew she was waking up chained to a wall in a dark cell. She was more than a little shocked to learn she was in California.

Jane finished with the manacle, then ushered the Andrettis out of the cell. She pulled its door closed, then closed the one to their own former prison. Maybe no one would notice the cut-out lock or missing guards too soon. Jane then stopped at the table to grab her bag and an automatic rifle that the guards had not used on them.

"They can't have had just one gun," she muttered, and started to search for another.

"I think they did," Edie said. "One always stood by the door with his gun while the other brought my food in and stuff. The one who entered never had one."

"Probably so he could never have it taken away.

The last thing the Ensecksis would want is an armed person in here," Abel pointed out.

"I love your logical mind," Jane said with a grin.

"Love?" Edie looked excitedly between them. "Oh, wow! I knew you two were perfect for each other. I just knew it. It was the pickles. Didn't I tell you, Abel? Isn't she perfect?"

"Yes, you did. And yes, she is," he admitted in wry tones.

Jane just laughed. Moving to the entrance of the shuttle tunnel, she peered up the way they'd come, which was now a pit of blackness, then peered the other way. A lit track loomed ahead with doors leading off of it. Digging around in her purse, she found a pen and pulled it out.

"Okay," she said, flicking up the clip. A strong beam of light shot out of the pen tip as she moved back to the others. "You two take the gun and this, and head back the way we came. Be careful, though. Only use the light if absolutely necessary. You might run into guards, and the light will give you away at once."

"Aren't you coming with us?" Edie asked in amazement.

"No." Jane ignored the gathering thundercloud on Abel's brow and concentrated on her friend. "They plan to activate their mike-sat—whatever that is—at midnight. It's going on nine o'clock. I don't know how long it will take for B.L.I.S.S. to get it all together, but we can't risk the Ensecksis succeeding. When you get out, tell them I'm going to try to stop them and how to get in here. They should—"

"Over my dead body," Abel growled.

Jane sighed and turned to him. "Abel, I can't let—"

"Not by yourself," he interrupted again. "I'm coming with you."

"So am I," Edie announced firmly. When Jane glared at her, the young woman lifted her chin. "I'm not sneaking out of here and leaving you two on your own after you came to save my hide. Besides, how far could I really get? I'm not walking up that tunnel alone in the dark—there are probably rats." She gave a shudder. "I hate rats. And if I use a light, I'll be caught before I go ten feet."

Jane glared at both Andrettis but they just glared back. After a moment, she gave up. She didn't have the time or heart to argue with them. She could use their help. "Fine. Edie, you take the gun. Abel . . ." She hesitated, then reached into her bag and pulled out her belt of vibrators. "These are mini-missile launchers. Twist each top and base in opposite directions, then push the on/off button to fire. They're just prototypes, but they still carry enough explosive to do a lot of damage—so make sure you aim carefully." She handed them over.

"What are you going to use?" Edie asked anxiously as Abel slipped the belt over his head so that it hung across his chest like a bandolier. "You need a weapon too."

Jane hesitated, then slid her shoes off and held them up. "These. Let's go."

She turned to lead the way, but froze at the sight of at least a dozen men standing in the mouth of the shuttle bay. All of them had automatic rifles like the one she'd given to Edie.

"Er, should I use one of the vibrators?" Abel asked out of the corner of his mouth.

"No." Jane sighed. "You might bring the mountain down on us."

"What do we do then?" Edie asked.

339

Jane considered their options. There really weren't any that seemed likely to see them walk out alive. Not at the moment. Raising her hands, she stepped forward. "We give."

Four of the men moved forward. They took away the gun Edie held, Abel's belt of vibrators, and Jane's bag and shoes.

"Um, can I wear those?" Jane asked hopefully. She still had her laser bracelet and bomb earrings, but the shoes had six unspent darts in one heel and four in the other. They could come in handy.

Her mouth dropped open when the man shook his head, turned, and shot a dart at the wall. "How did you . . . ?" She paused when he smiled and pointed to a camera in the corner of the guard room.

"Smile. You're on *Candid Camera*," he said dryly. He held out his hand. "Earrings, necklace, and bracelet."

Sighing, Jane slipped off her jewelry and handed it over. She and the Andrettis were then quickly searched. Abel's tie clip was taken away, but then the sound of an approaching shuttle could be heard and they were directed to the platform.

Chapter Twenty-one

"Move."

Jane jerked her arm away from the guard who grabbed her and stepped out of the shuttle of her own volition. She, Abel, and Edie had been separated into three different cars for this trip. They'd traveled farther than she'd expected, passing a good forty doors along the way. She assumed those doors led to housing for the guards and technicians, maybe even for Lydia, Dirk, and their father as well. It would explain the un-lived-in feel of the Ensecksi house.

Now Jane found herself standing in a large shuttle bay, standing before huge double doors at least twenty feet tall. She barely gave them a glance, her interest focused on the two cars that had pulled up behind her own. Edie and Abel were being urged out and led toward her by guards.

Jane wanted to say something reassuring to Edie—her friend was pale and trembling, obviously terrified—but she didn't get the chance. The moment the brother and sister reached her, one of the four guards who'd ridden with Jane took her arm and led her away. The huge double doors parted, and she gaped as bright light and sound exploded out.

Jane wasn't sure what she'd expected, but it hadn't been this large white dome-shaped room that rose a good ten stories overhead and bustled with activity. Men and women—some in the black Ensecksi uniforms and some in lab coats—hustled about. It was as if someone had hollowed out the inside of a mountain and set up shop.

"Here's the satellite dish Nancy couldn't find."

Jane nodded at Abel's words from behind her, her gaze already taking in the monstrous apparatus. She'd never seen one quite so big. It filled most of the huge room, leaving a ten-foot walkway cluttered with computers, desks, chairs, and people.

The guard at her arm urged Jane forward, and she moved into this assault of sound and activity. Her eyes went everywhere. At first sight, their situation seemed even worse than it had been. The number of people to overcome here was staggering, but then she took a second look. There were a lot of people, but most of them were unarmed technicians and scientists. They wouldn't be much of a problem and were likely to stay out of any battle that might take place. Jane hoped. It was the security men she had to be concerned with.

Gazing around, she saw that there were very few of those: Just the ones who had accompanied them into this dome—six in all.

She wondered briefly if the others who had captured them had again dispersed to wherever their guard stations were, or if they stood waiting out in the shuttle bay in case of trouble. She might need to blow up the control panel for the door, locking them out. In any case, she had to stop that satellite dish from doing whatever it was the Ensecksis planned. She wished she had her bag. Her earrings and vibrators would come in handy about now.

"Jane and Abel Goodinov, I presume. I've heard a lot about the two of you." The voice was deep and strong and seemed to come from everywhere. Loudspeakers, Jane thought and turned slowly, trying to find the man behind the voice.

"In the control booth," the voice instructed. "On your left."

Jane turned to the left and peered at several men all seated along a panel comprising at least thirty screens. She didn't see anyone who might be the speaker, but she did see her bag, her jewelry, and the vibrators that had been taken away from Abel. She considered the distance to them, but didn't think she'd get far. Two-to-six weren't good odds. She could count on Abel to aid her, but not Edie. As far as she knew, her friend had not taken martial arts. And what if some of the technicians jumped in to help?

"No, that's the security panel," the voice said. "Up here."

Jane looked above the screens, but all there was to see was smooth curving wall. It was like standing inside an egg. Well, half an egg, anyway.

"No, no." The voice was growing impatient and sounding a little less deep and booming. "Over here. Someone show her where—Never mind, I'm coming down there."

Jane's eyes followed the wall around to the right, and she finally spotted what she thought was the control booth. It was a booth, anyway—all glass on top with a metal bottom. She even spotted a microphone that the speaker might have been using. However, if that was where the speaker had been, he wasn't there now. The booth was empty. She saw a door and glanced along the walkway leading down from it, then at the expanse of walkway between it and where she stood, but she didn't see anyone moving toward her.

Shrugging, she shook her head.

"How much trouble are we in?" Abel asked by her shoulder. Glancing back, she saw he'd sidled closer to her. Edie was nearby, too.

"You don't want to know," Jane answered with a sigh. It looked to her like they were in pretty deep. She just hoped B.L.I.S.S. was on its way.

"Well, you were right about the basement and the technicians and security," Abel admitted. "And about Edie."

"Somehow being right doesn't make me feel better," she said. "Besides, this isn't exactly a basement."

He was silent as his gaze slid over the satellite dish. "So, this is how they've been making everyone in town wear yellow dresses and Hawaiian shirts."

"It looks that way," Jane agreed.

"How could a big satellite dish make anyone do anything?" Edie asked, moving up next to her brother. "I mean, I overheard Dirk talking about something like this, but—I understood just enough to be scared and call C.I.S.I.S., but I don't really get how they could control people. How could a satellite dish control what people do?"

Jane explained, "Some researchers believe that

EMRs can control human impulses as easily as ESB."

"EMRs? ESB?"

"EMRs are electromagnetic waves, like microwaves. And ESB is electrical stimulation of the brain."

"Oh, you mean the electrodes on the brain thing," Edie said. "We touched on that a bit in a psychology course I took at the university—or was it biology?" The woman paused then shrugged. "Whatever. They put the electrode here and the cat licks itself, put it there and it does something else—is that what you mean by electrical stimulation?"

"Yes. I think the Ensecksis are doing the same sort of thing, only using focused microwave beams and intending a more complex reaction than licking."

"Oh." Edie peered at the dish with new respect. "That can't be good."

"No. It isn't," Jane agreed. After a moment she admitted, "I'm sorry, guys. I should have insisted you leave the moment we got out of those rooms."

"We never would have made it out." Edie sighed unhappily. "None of this is your fault, Jane. You guys wouldn't even be here if I hadn't accepted that stupid date. If I'd used my head, I wouldn't have gone. I should have realized something was up. Dirk had never looked at me twice before—"

"Shh. Both of you," Abel said firmly. He slipped an arm around each of their waists. "No one is at fault but the Ensecksis. And I'm glad I'm here. There's nowhere I'd rather be than here with my two favorite ladies."

"Isn't that touching."

Jane jerked out of Abel's embrace and turned. It hadn't come from the loudspeakers this time, had seemed to come from—

"Down here."

Jane lowered her gaze to stare at the prune-faced midget standing next to her. Dear Lord, he couldn't be more than three feet tall. With his shock of white hair, big dark eyes, and sour expression, he could have been Grumpy from *Snow White and the Seven Dwarves*. "Who are you?"

"I am Robert Ensecksi," he announced with the self-importance of a god. Then he waved a stubby little arm. "And this is my empire."

"That's Dirk's father?" Edie gasped. "No way!"

Jane bit her lip to keep from laughing. It didn't help when Abel murmured by her ear, "I think Mrs. Ensecksi may have been friendly with the milkman."

Jane gave both Andrettis a reproving look, then offered a polite smile to a scowling Robert. "Your . . . um . . . empire is quite impressive, Mr. Ensecksi."

"It is, isn't it?" His little chest was puffed with pride.

"Hmm." Jane nodded. "What does this do?"

The dwarf smiled and Jane saw a hint of Dirk in the expression. Mrs. Ensecksi had not been unfaithful. "My people found the way to control the masses with EMRs."

Just as Jane had feared. "To what end, sir? Surely not simply to make everyone wear yellow dresses and tacky Hawaiian shirts?"

"That was just a test," he admitted. "Lydia thought that—people being vain by nature—if we could control the fashion sense of an entire town, then we could control and rule the world." Robert Ensecksi's deep voice was filled with glee.

"You and Napoleon. Why is it short guys always want to rule the world?" Abel muttered.

Jane was pretty sure no one else had heard, but she glared at him anyway. It was difficult enough taking this little fella seriously without Abel's cracks.

"But how can you rule the whole world with one satellite dish?" Edie asked. She looked rather suspicious, as if she thought the man was trying to pull one over on her.

"One satellite *here*," Robert Ensecksi corrected. "We have—" He stopped as the huge doors behind them swished open again.

Jane turned to see Lydia and Dirk. She was in time to catch the surprise on their faces as they spotted her standing with their father.

"Jane." Dirk smiled and moved to her side. "You're awake."

"They broke free, knocked out the guards, and locked them up," Robert Ensecksi accused. Lydia gave her brother an I-told-you-so look.

"So you *are* spies?" Dirk asked. Jane suspected it was loss of a potential sex-fiend partner that had him looking so blue.

"I'm afraid so," she admitted, not seeing any reason to deny it now.

"Oh, Jane." He sounded disappointed.

"I was just going to show them what we've accomplished here," Robert Ensecksi announced. "Why don't we move to the control booth?"

His children started toward the walkway, and Robert took Jane's arm. He led her along at a slightly slower pace, leaving Abel and Edie to follow, and the guards to bring up the rear.

"I've worked very hard over the years at acquiring the finest technology and scientists that money can buy," the little man announced grandly. "We have the finest minds in both microwave technology and

347

neuroscience here—as well as the most up-to-date security, of course."

He waved toward the security video panel with its many screens as they walked past, but Jane's eyes went to the things that had been taken away from her. If she could just get her hands on a weapon . . .

"Oh, look. Your grandmother is going to save us the trouble of going to fetch her."

Jane turned back to the screens. One showed Gran and Nancy entering the living room of the Ensecksi house. Nancy made a quick sweep of the rooms; then the two women moved to the wall where the elevator was hidden. One of Jane's cameras must have transmitted its image after all!

"Send an escort for the ladies," Robert Ensecksi ordered, and several men immediately left to do as he commanded.

Jane remained silent as she watched Nancy and her gran travel down in the elevator on another monitor. Neither woman appeared terribly surprised when the doors opened and they were met by armed men. Gran was wheeled onto a shuttle, Nancy was seated in another, and then everyone disappeared from the screens. They popped up on a new one when their shuttles pulled into the bay outside the doors to this dome.

Jane turned to the doors as they swished open and watched Nancy wheel Gran in under an armed escort. Neither woman looked alarmed. Jane hoped that meant B.L.I.S.S. backup was on the way.

"Oh! There you are, Janie, dear." Gran stopped petting Tinkle long enough to push the button on the arm of her wheelchair. She rolled toward Jane. The men escorting her immediately raised their guns, but Gran continued forward. "Have you been having fun with your friends?"

Jane almost laughed at the question, not to mention Robert Ensecksi's expression. The old man obviously thought her dotty. Shaking his head, he gestured for his guards to lower their guns. That's when Tinkle went into action. The furry beast had spotted the object of her affections, and leaping from Gran's lap the dog hurried to Dirk. She did her butt-wiggling love dance at his feet, then rolled onto her back, legs in the air and tongue lolling. When none of it had the desired response, Tinkle proved herself a shameless tramp and resorted to trying to crawl up the man's leg.

Yessiree, all the gals want your bone. Jane thought with amusement as Dirk began hopping about, shaking his leg to dislodge the Yorkie.

"Will someone shoot this damned dog?" he bellowed finally.

Jane decided it was time to move. She didn't care for Tinkle much herself, but Gran would be heartbroken to lose her. Noting that everyone was concentrating on the dog, Jane jammed her elbow into the stomach of the man beside her and snatched his rifle in one motion. She rammed the butt of the weapon down on his head as he bent forward in pain.

"Stop her!" Robert Ensecksi roared. Jane sent him sailing backward with a well-placed kick. "Watch him!" she ordered Edie.

"Okay." The other woman hesitated, then dropped to sit on the dwarf's chest. When he began to kick and flail at her with his tiny fists, screeching at the top of his lungs, she tweaked his nose and grabbed him by the hair. She gave his head a shake. "Be good, short stuff, or I'll put you over my knee."

349

Deciding Edie had that particular foe under control, Jane glanced toward Gran. The older woman sat calmly in her wheelchair, powdering her nose with a compact. There were four unconscious guards on the ground around her. Not far away, Nancy and Abel were standing back to back, preparing to take on several guards who were closing on them. They were going to kick some butt!

She wished she could watch, but a yelp of pain drew her gaze. Dirk had sent Tinkle flying through the air with a well-placed kick. Mouth flattening, Jane charged him. In her stocking feet, her approach was silent. Still, something made him turn just before she tackled him. Instead of sending him crashing to the ground on his face, he landed on his back with her on top. She expected him to be stunned, or to have the wind knocked out of him, but he recovered quickly and rolled. A moment later, he was on top of her.

To Jane's amazement, he pinned her arms on either side of her head and drew back to smile down at her. "I've wanted to get you in this position since we met. As I expected, the fit is just right." He ground himself against her. "You and I could be so good together."

"Thanks, but I prefer a personality to complement the looks," Jane said sweetly. And with that she slammed her knee into his groin.

Dirk's smile disappeared. He paled, then flushed, then dropped off of her to curl into a fetal position. Jane stood up and stared down at him. He was moaning and rolling around on the floor, clutching himself.

"I seem to have that effect on all the guys," she told him cheerfully.

Glancing around, she checked how things were

going. Gran's pile of unconscious men had grown by two, Abel and Nancy were whaling on several guards as she'd expected, Edie was tormenting Robert, and—

Jane's heart stopped as she spotted Lydia in the control booth. The blonde was flipping switches like crazy. Before Jane could even try to stop her, a loud whirring sound came from above. The top of the mountain opened to reveal a starlit sky. The huge satellite dish started to rise.

Jane looked at the control booth. Inside, Lydia smiled at her triumphantly. The blonde leaned forward to speak into the microphone: "The door to this booth is locked, Jane. You'll never get in. And even if you do, I've locked the program in. You can't stop it without the password. You might as well relax. In exactly two minutes and thirty-two seconds, it's going to be you five against the world. Join us now, or die then. It's up to you."

Jane hesitated. All fighting in the room had stopped. Everyone was waiting to see what would happen. Her gaze slid from Robert Ensecksi to the man's son. Since Dirk was at her feet, she chose him. Lifting her foot onto his neck, she faced down Lydia across the room.

"Shut it off, Lydia, or I'll break his neck, then your father's," she bluffed.

"Jane!" Dirk gasped in wounded tones.

"Go ahead!" Lydia laughed. "Then I'll be queen of the world!"

"Lydia!" Dirk shrieked.

Jane glared at the blonde for a minute, then glanced to the satellite. It was halfway out of the mountain and starting to tilt upward. Nausea began to swell in her at the thought of a world full of brain-dead drones following queen bee Lydia's orders;

then she remembered her vibrators and glanced wildly around. Abel and Nancy were nearest them. "Abel! The vibrators!"

Lydia realized she intended mischief. "Stop them!" She shrieked into the microphone as Abel grabbed the belt of missile launchers.

Several technicians moved toward Abel, but Nancy stepped into their path. Abel didn't even look back. He pulled a vibrator from the belt, glanced from it to the satellite dish, to Jane. Then, apparently realizing there wasn't time to waste, he twisted, aimed, and fired.

There was a hiss of smoke and then the satellite exploded with a deafening boom, bits and pieces of it flying every which way. Jane dropped instinctively, hands going over her head to protect herself from falling objects. What sounded like World War III erupted above. It went on for what seemed forever.

When at last it stopped; Jane lifted her head and blinked her eyes against the dust and smoke filling the air. She made a quick check of those around her. A few of the Ensecksi people had been injured, but most had escaped. As for her friends, Abel had a cut on his cheek, but everyone else seemed fine.

"You *do* care."

Jane glanced down at the man she was lying on. She'd dropped where she stood and landed on Dirk, unintentionally protecting him with her body. Jane didn't even respond to his husky comment. Suddenly aware of the hand sliding toward her butt, she reached down and caught him in a wrist lock that made him squeal like a girl. She kept her hold on him as she got to her feet, forcing him up as well, then stiffened when she heard the doors to the dome room swish open. Forcing Dirk around before her, she faced the doors ready for anything.

Twenty agents rushed in, all wearing red jackets with B.L.I.S.S. emblazoned across the breast. Ira Manetrue and Y brought up the rear. The agents spread through the room, taking people into custody. They'd missed all the fighting, but Jane was glad to leave the cleanup to them.

She watched as a sputtering and shrieking Robert Ensecksi was removed from beneath Edie and cuffed, then watched as Dirk was cuffed as well. She glanced toward the booth to see if the B.L.I.S.S. agents had managed to capture Lydia, but the blonde wasn't there. Jane glanced around with a frown.

"What's wrong?" Abel asked, moving to her side. "You should be happy. You were right about everything, and you saved Edie and the day too!"

"With a little help," she agreed.

Abel smiled. "So, why are you frowning?"

"I don't see Lydia. Who has her?"

Jane had barely finished asking that question when the swish of the pneumatic doors sounded behind her. Whirling, she saw Lydia Ensecksi escape.

"Oh, no, you don't!" Jane charged after her. She heard footsteps following and knew it was Abel. They both slipped through the closing doors with a hair breadth to spare, but they got through. Still in her stocking feet, Jane slid when she tried to stop and nearly tumbled into an empty docked shuttle. Catching herself, she looked up the tunnel and saw the brake lights of Lydia's shuttle swerve out of sight.

"Jump in!" Abel yelled. He leaped behind the docked shuttle's controls.

"Do you know how to drive one of these?" Jane

asked as she scrambled in beside him.

"How hard could it be?" He began throwing switches. Jane nearly got whiplash as they shot off in pursuit. Abel glanced at her, grinning widely. "This is great!"

She'd created a monster, she realized and started to laugh.

Lydia's empty shuttle was waiting at the end of the tunnel. The elevator was already on the lake's way up. Jane spent several moments worrying the blonde would jam it or do something to prevent it from returning for them, but apparently she was in too much of a panic to think of it.

There was no sign of her in the living room when they exited the elevator. Jane and Abel hesitated, then heard an engine roaring to life. They raced for the door. Outside, Lydia was driving away in Dirk's sports car.

"Come on!" Jane charged up the hill and ran for the garage of the Goodinov house.

"Is your van going to be fast enough to catch her?" Abel asked as they got in.

"Oh, yeah," Jane said with a smile. She hit the gas and flew backward down the driveway. "I've added some modifications over the years."

The gate had slowed Lydia down; she was just slipping through it when they pulled onto the road after her. It started to close as they approached, but Jane hit the gas and passed through just in time.

"That was close," Abel noted.

Jane didn't say anything. Lydia had spotted them and really put on speed. Jane followed suit and concentrated on the road ahead, nervous about causing an accident. For that reason she left a small distance between them as they sped along the house-lined roads. This inhabited area, its curved streets with reduced night visibility made this risky. Catching Lydia Ensecksi, evil as she was, wasn't worth killing anyone.

The moment they left the houses behind, however, Jane hit her booster. Her van leaped forward, nearly ramming the red sports car in the rear before Lydia could put on more speed. They were covering ground at a deadly rate, and Jane felt herself tense further as the trees on their left gave way to a sheer mountain wall.

Abel suddenly cursed, and Jane glanced his way. "What?"

"Look." He pointed.

At first Jane wasn't sure what the problem was; then she realized the road ahead clung lovingly to the mountain and curved sharply to the left. Straight ahead was a wide flat surface reflecting the moonlight. Water. A lake.

Jane gritted her teeth and glanced down at the speedometer. They were going too fast for the curve. She glanced to the sports car, but it wasn't slowing. They probably couldn't have slowed in time anyway.

"Do up your seat belt," she ordered.

Abel reached across to do her belt first. Jane would have cursed him for the foolish move if she hadn't been too busy trying to see around his obstructing arm while controlling the steering wheel at the same time. She'd planned to hit the brakes the moment he had his seat belt on, but he was delaying her ability to do that with his concern for her.

We definitely aren't going to make this turn, she realized with horror.

Abel finally finished with her seat belt and grabbed his own. The moment she heard it snap into place, Jane started braking. She knew even as she did so that it was far too late. They were going to crash off the road and straight into the lake. As for Lydia, she never had a chance. Jane didn't know if the blond woman had actually thought she could make the turn at that speed, but she couldn't. She smashed through the barrier with an almost explosive boom and sailed into the air. Jane's van, at least, didn't have any guardrail to smash through, it simply raced right off the road behind her. The best they could hope for was a flat landing instead of a nosedive.

Abel started shouting. As they went airborne, Jane joined him and slammed hard on the brakes. Uselessly. They seemed to sail forever through the air, then landed with a bone-jarring crash. Jane swore her brain was briefly shaken loose from her brain stem. When it started to function again, she was caught between her seat and the air bag that had popped out of the steering wheel.

"Jane? Jane!"

She lifted her head and turned it slowly toward Abel. He was struggling to push his own air bag out of the way. He cursed in frustration, then dug out a pocketknife and popped it. A moment later, he had his seat belt off and was moving to her side to free her. He peered into her face.

"Thank God," he breathed when he saw that her eyes were open. "Don't worry. I'll get us out of here. I won't let you drown."

"Hmm." Jane gave her head a shake, relieved when her thinking seemed to clear a bit. "No need. We're waterproof."

"Waterproof?" He paused in his efforts to undo her seat belt.

"Waterproof, fireproof, soundproof." She

shrugged and set to work on the belt herself. "I'm constantly adding new features."

"Jeez," he said. But she noticed he was looking around the van as if in search of leaks.

"Where's Lydia's car?" Jane asked to distract him.

"I don't know." He moved back into the passenger seat and squinted through the windows. All around them was water; they bobbed on the lake's surface. "I think she sank."

"Surely she wouldn't have sunk that fast." Sitting up, Jane turned on the windshield wipers. It helped a little.

"The top was down on her car," Abel pointed out. But he kept looking anyway.

"Oh. Yes." Now that he mentioned it, Jane recalled that the top *had* been down on the convertible. It would have sunk quickly. Lydia might have been thrown clear and survived, though. Maybe. Jane squinted through the night, searching for any sign of life.

"She crashed into the water nose first," Abel said. "I doubt she made it."

"I suppose," Jane agreed.

"So," Abel asked, "what now? Are you going to power this baby up, push a button to turn it into a boat, and steer us to shore?"

Jane laughed.

"No?" He looked surprised.

"I didn't think of that," she said apologetically. "I only made it waterproof and fireproof because Gran is in a wheelchair and would be helpless in a crash."

"And the soundproof part?" he asked.

"Oh. Well . . . we went on a road trip one weekend and I got tired, and we stopped to take a nap, but the rest stop we stopped at was terribly busy and noisy and I couldn't sleep a wink." She shrugged and leaned forward to switch the CD player on. Enrique Iglesias began crooning about a lost love. "I soundproofed the van so that wouldn't happen again."

"A nap? Does your seat recline then, like you reclined mine on the way here to California?"

"Yes. But I didn't sleep in my seat. I opened the bed."

"The bed?"

Jane flicked a switch on the dashboard, and Abel jerked around as a humming erupted behind them. He watched in amazement as panels opened on either side of the back of the van and two halves of a bed unfolded to meet in the middle. When he turned to look at her again, there was a wide grin on his face.

"You're good," he announced, and Jane felt herself blush. Then he moved out of his seat. Grabbing her hand, he dragged her with him into the back.

Jane laughed as they tumbled onto the bed, but her laughter died on a sigh as he kissed her.

"I love your mind," he said after several heated moments. "You excite me, you amuse me, and you never fail to surprise me." He punctuated each compliment by undoing a button of her shirt. It was half undone when he finished. He spread the cloth and ran his fingers lightly over the pale skin revealed; then Jane sat up and leaned forward to pull his head back down for another kiss.

"Janie? Jane! What's happening? Jane? Did you catch Lydia?"

Abel lifted his head and peered around with a frown. "Is that Gran?"

"Yes." Jane sat up and leaned forward to pull the

lighter out of the dash board, then spoke into it. "Here, Gran. We're fine."

"Did you catch Lydia?" Gran asked.

Behind Jane Abel commented, "You're talking into a car lighter."

"It's an emergency radio. Only Gran has the frequency," Jane explained. Then she said into the lighter, "No. Lydia crashed into the lake."

"Oh." There was a brief silence. "Did she survive?"

"I don't think so. No." Jane stiffened in delight as Abel began to nibble on her neck.

"Which lake? Are you on your way back?"

"I'm not sure what lake. A big one," she answered distractedly. "And, no, we're not on our way back. We, er . . . We're in the lake too."

"Oh, dear! Is the waterproofing holding?"

"Of course," Jane said, a touch indignantly.

"Good. Well, don't worry, dear. We'll zero in on the tracker in the van and find you. Just sit tight."

"Mmm," Jane moaned as Abel slid his hands around to cup her breasts. "Gran?"

"Yes?"

"There's no need to hurry." She sighed as he unsnapped the clasp of her bra and replaced the cloth with his fingers.

"Oh?" Gran radioed back.

Jane didn't answer. She couldn't; she'd turned her head so that Abel could cover her mouth with his own. Replacing the lighter in the dash, Jane fell back on the bed and pulled him with her.

Epilogue

"I can't believe that jerk Dirk got away! What kind of morons are they letting into B.L.I.S.S., anyway?"

Jane grimaced at Edie's outraged words. She hadn't been too pleased herself to hear that Dirk Ensecksi had managed to escape. When she'd heard who it was that lost him, she'd been doubly upset. "It wasn't an agent who let him go, it was Richard Hedde. He isn't an agent. He's in D & C like me."

"Oh, yes," Gran said. "Now I know why the name sounded familiar when Ira mentioned it. It's that Dick fellow who irritates you so much." She turned to Edie to explain. "He's an arrogant little brown-nosing weasel, dear. Not an agent."

Jane laughed as her grandmother echoed her oft-repeated complaint; then she glanced to Edie who asked, "Well, then, what on earth was he doing in California?"

"Apparently he couriered some equipment to Ira from the office in Vancouver, then just"—Jane shrugged helplessly—"stuck around. Y wanted all the bodies she could get, so they let him stay. During the confusion after Abel and I left to chase Lydia, one of the other agents mistook Dick for a field agent and put the responsibility of watching Dirk in his hands."

"And he, as we know, messed up," Gran finished calmly. "But all is not lost. Dirk did take your bag, Janie dear. You have a lot of dangerous items in there disguised as everyday things. If he uses anything, he'll no doubt end up at the hospital. B.L.I.S.S. will get him."

"Hmm." Jane nodded. A slow devilish smile spread over her lips. "I hope he uses the shrink-wrap condoms."

The three women burst into gales of laughter at the very thought. Edie was the first to stop laughing. Blowing out a depressed breath she said, "I guess I'll have to get a new job." She stared gloomily into her teacup.

"Maybe B.L.I.S.S. has a position for you," Maggie Spyrus suggested as she fed a sugar cookie to a whining Tinkle.

Jane rolled her eyes, both at the comment and the way Gran was spoiling the mutt. She'd been treating the Yorkie like a princess ever since they'd returned home, insisting that Tinkle had saved the day. Never mind that it had been an accidental result of the dog's affection for criminals.

"Do you think?" Edie perked up at Gran's suggestion, her expression brightening. "That would be cool. Edie Andretti, secret agent.

"More like Edie Andretti, secretary and general dogsbody," Jane corrected. Seeing the way the other girl deflated, she added more gently, "Edie, honey, you haven't got the training to be a secret agent. They need to be trained martial-arts experts, marksmen, and—"

She paused, and all three women glanced toward the door as the doorbell rang.

"Maybe that's Abel, back from his interview," Edie said hopefully.

Jane didn't comment, just stood and moved into the entry. She was hoping it was Abel. She was also worried that it was. What if he didn't get the job? What if he had to return to England? What would happen to them? Nothing, she assured herself firmly. They'd just have a long-distance relationship until he was able to get a job here, or she might be able to transfer to England. B.L.I.S.S. had an office there. They had offices everywhere. She could transfer. Gran had always claimed to love England. Still, long-distance relationships were hard. She would miss him. Funny how that could be. She hadn't known him long, and yet her life would feel empty with him gone.

Pausing at the door Jane raised her head and softly said, "Please, God." Opening it, she found that it was indeed Abel. He stood in the hall, hands behind his back and a big smile on his face. Jane was almost afraid to hope it meant what she hoped it meant.

"You got the job?" she asked.

His smile widened and he drew one hand out, shoving a bunch of roses at her. The moment Jane took them, his other hand appeared with a small velvet jewel box. "Will you marry me, Jane Spyrus?"

"You got it!" she shrieked, and threw herself at him.

Laughing, he caught her to his chest and swung her around, then kissed her deeply. Jane kissed him back with all the passion inside her. They were both breathless when it ended.

Sighing, she laid her head against his shoulder and closed her eyes. "I knew you'd get it."

"Yes. Well, actually I didn't."

Jane straightened away from him abruptly. "What? You didn't? They didn't give you the job? Why not?" she asked in outrage.

"Because I missed the original interview." He shrugged. "They decided I wasn't serious enough about it. They'd already given the job to someone else and only agreed to another appointment to explain that."

"Well, those—" she began, angry for him.

"It's okay, honey. Really," he added when she looked doubtful.

Jane fell silent for a minute; then her gaze fell on the jeweler's case, and confusion clouded her expression. "Then, how can you propose—"

"Because I love you," Abel interrupted. "I do, Jane. You're smart and funny and passionate and . . . Jane, I've seen you at your best and your worst this last week. You have the courage of ten men. You fight for those you love. I want my children to be like that. I want you to be the mother of my children. I want to spend my life with you. I want to face whatever adversity life has in store with you at my side."

"Oh, Abel." Jane sank against him, her heart melting. "I love you, too."

"Do you?"

"Oh, yes. And for all the same reasons. You make me laugh, you make me burn, you make me like myself, and you make me feel safe. I want to spend my life with you, too."

His chest shook as he chuckled. "And I didn't even need the truth serum perfume to hear it."

"Oh!" She gave him a smack, then kissed him again.

"All right. Enough of that nonsense," a voice said with some asperity. "We've waited long enough. Now let's see the ring."

Abel and Jane broke apart and turned to find Gran and Edie in the entry with them, waiting expectantly.

Laughing, Abel let her go and dutifully opened the jeweler's case, smiling as the women crowded around to ooh and ah. He took the ring out of the box, turned to Jane, and slipped it on her finger. "There, now it's official. You're mine."

Jane leaned against him. He kissed her forehead as she stared at the ring.

"Sorry about the job, Abel," Edie said unhappily. "It's all my fault."

"No it isn't, squirt." He hugged his sister with the arm not around Jane. "No job is worth the life of those I love."

Edie hugged him back, then stepped away and asked, "So, how long until you have to go back to England?"

"Never, I hope." He smiled when Jane pulled back to peer up at him. "I asked for some time off. I'll stay with you, Edie, for the next couple of weeks—if that's okay?" He waited for his sister to nod, then continued, "And I'll spend that time looking for another position. Something will come up. And if it doesn't—"

"If it doesn't, I'll see about a transfer to the London office," Jane said firmly.

"I always liked London," Maggie announced, giving her approval. But neither Abel nor Jane was listening. They were smiling at each other.

"You're amazing, Jane Spyrus." He brushed the hair back from her face.

"So are you, Abel Andretti." They kissed again.

"Ahem."

Jane and Abel broke apart again, turning this time toward the door they'd left open in all the excitement.

"Y! Mr. Manetrue!" Jane blushed, embarrassment and alarm battling for supremacy within her as she gaped at the pair standing in her doorway. "Is something wrong?"

"Something's always wrong, Jane. We're in that kind of business," Y said blandly. "May we come in?"

"Oh, yes, of course." Jane backed up a step, nearly stumbling over Gran's wheelchair. Abel caught her arm and pulled her to his side as the couple entered the apartment and closed the door.

"Hello, Maggie. You look beautiful as usual," Ira said with dignity. Taking the handles of her wheelchair, he turned it around and pushed her into the living room, leaving the others to follow.

"Well," Y said once everyone was seated, "you look like you've come through your ordeal well, Ms. Andretti."

Edie nodded.

"I gather you didn't get the job you'd hoped to?" she said to Abel next.

He shook his head.

"Good. We happen to have an opening in the

accounting department that I think you'd fill nicely."

"B.L.I.S.S. has an accounting department?" Jane asked with surprise.

"*Everyone* has an accounting department," Y said. "Someone has to keep track of expenditures," she pointed out, then turned back to Abel. "We pay well and do what we can to keep employees happy; but of course you can't tell anyone about anything having to do with us and would have to sign a privacy contract. You'll take the job?"

"Yes," Abel said promptly.

"Good. You have the job."

He blinked. "Just like that? Don't you want references or—?"

"Dear boy, we investigated you the moment you got involved in the Ensecksi incident. We know more about you than you know about yourself."

"Oh, yes. Of course," Abel murmured, looking a touch discomfited.

"It's settled then. Now, on to the reason we came."

Jane felt herself stiffen. She couldn't think of a single good reason for Y and Mr. Manetrue to be here.

"We have a problem. A case that needs special agents."

"Special?" Jane asked uncertainly.

"An extended family," Mr. Manetrue explained. "A husband and wife, and the grandparents of one of them."

"Yes." Y nodded. "Of course, we don't have many male agents at B.L.I.S.S., but since you three did so well with the Ensecksi case . . ." She shrugged. "And Ira has offered to play the grandfather."

"Oh." Jane looked at Abel uncertainly. He wasn't looking happy.

"Do we have to take it?" he asked finally.

"Only if you want the position in accounting," she said easily.

Jane bit her lip, but when Abel groaned she knew he'd agree.

"Did you hear that, Tinkle?" Gran asked cheerfully. "We're on another case!"

Abel moaned.

"I could be extended family. Can I come too?" Edie asked.

"Dear God!" her brother said.

NINA BANGS
FROM BOARDWALK WITH LOVE

The world's richest man, Owen Sitall, is a flop at a certain game, but now he's built an enormous board so he can win on his own. His island is a playground for the rich. But he doesn't know that L.O.V.E.R.—the League of Violent Economic Revolutionaries—has come to play in his hotels . . . and the plans to bankrupt him have already passed Go.

Camryn, novice agent #36-DD of B.L.I.S.S.—the international organization that fights crime anywhere from St. Croix to St. James Place—finds her assignment clear: Protect the fanatical Sitall from financial ruin. But being a spy doesn't just mean free parking. Before this is over, she'll be rolling the dice with her heart.

LISA CACH

DR. YES

Dr. Alan Archer doesn't seem evil. But Rachel Calais knows the insidious truth: The doc is down in Nepal searching for the lost city of Yonam—and a plant that, when properly refined, will have every female in the world on her knees . . . or her back.

Rachel's mission: Stop Archer at any cost. B.L.I.S.S.—an international organization fighting such dastardly villains—has given her a kit to help, as well as a dangerously sexy man who knows how to watch a woman's back. With a stun gun, infrared goggles, and other less conventional forms of protection, Rachel is a regular Jane Bond. She doesn't know that playing spy will make her pay the ultimate price: her heart.

Improper English
KATIE MacALISTER

Sassy American Alexandra Freemar isn't about to put up with any flak from the uptight—albeit gorgeous—Scotland Yard inspector who accuses her of breaking and entering. She doesn't have time. She has two months in London to write the perfect romance novel—two months to prove that she can succeed as an author.

Luckily, reserved Englishmen are not her cup of tea. Yet one kiss tells her Alexander Block might not be quite as proper as she thought. Unfortunately, the gentleman isn't interested in a summer fling. And while Alix knows every imaginable euphemism for the male member, she soon realizes she has a lot to learn about love.

Aphrodite's Kiss
Julie Kenner

Crazy as it sounds, on her twenty-fifth birthday Zoe has the chance to become a superhero. But x-ray vision and the ability to fly are only two things to consider. There is also her newfound heightened sensitivity. If she can hardly eat a chocolate bar without convulsing in ecstasy, how is she to give herself the birthday gift she's really set her heart on— George Taylor? The handsome P.I.'s dark exterior hides a truly sweet center, and Zoe feels certain that his mere touch will send her spiraling into oblivion. But the man is looking for an average Jane no matter what he claims. He can never love a superhero-to-be—can he? Zoe has to know. With her super powers, she can only see through his clothing; to strip bare the workings of his heart, she'll have to rely on something a little more potent.

___52438-4 $5.99 US/$6.99 CAN

Dorchester Publishing Co., Inc.
P.O. Box 6640
Wayne, PA 19087-8640

Please add $1.75 for shipping and handling for the first book and $.50 for each book thereafter. NY, NYC, and PA residents, please add appropriate sales tax. No cash, stamps, or C.O.D.s. All orders shipped within 6 weeks via postal service book rate. Canadian orders require $2.00 extra postage and must be paid in U.S. dollars through a U.S. banking facility.

Name_____
Address_____
City_____State_____Zip_____
I have enclosed $_____ in payment for the checked book(s).
Payment <u>must</u> accompany all orders. ❑ Please send a free catalog.
     CHECK OUT OUR WEBSITE! www.dorchesterpub.com

CONTACT
SUSAN GRANT

A BEAUTIFUL CO-PILOT WITH A TERRIBLE CHOICE.

"After only three novels, Susan Grant has proven herself to be the best hope for the survival of the futuristic/fantasy romance genre." —*The Romance Reader*

A DARK STRANGER WHO HAS KNOWN NOTHING BUT DUTY.

"I am in awe of Susan Grant. She's one of the few authors who get it." —*Everything Romantic*

A LATE-NIGHT FLIGHT, HIJACKED OVER THE PACIFIC.